CLIVE CUSSLER'S
HELLBURNER

TITLES BY CLIVE CUSSLER

DIRK PITT ADVENTURES®

Clive Cussler's The Devil's Sea
   (by Dirk Cussler)
Celtic Empire (with Dirk Cussler)
Odessa Sea (with Dirk Cussler)
Havana Storm (with Dirk Cussler)
Poseidon's Arrow (with Dirk Cussler)
Crescent Dawn (with Dirk Cussler)
Arctic Drift (with Dirk Cussler)
Treasure of Khan (with Dirk Cussler)
Black Wind (with Dirk Cussler)
Trojan Odyssey
Valhalla Rising
Atlantis Found
Flood Tide
Shock Wave
Inca Gold
Sahara
Dragon
Treasure
Cyclops
Deep Six
Pacific Vortex!
Night Probe!
Vixen 03
Raise the Titanic!
Iceberg
The Mediterranean Caper

SAM AND REMI FARGO ADVENTURES®

The Wrath of Poseidon
   (with Robin Burcell)
The Oracle (with Robin Burcell)
The Gray Ghost (with Robin Burcell)
The Romanov Ransom
   (with Robin Burcell)
Pirate (with Robin Burcell)
The Solomon Curse
   (with Russell Blake)
The Eye of Heaven (with Russell Blake)
The Mayan Secrets
   (with Thomas Perry)
The Tombs (with Thomas Perry)
The Kingdom (with Grant Blackwood)
Lost Empire (with Grant Blackwood)
Spartan Gold (with Grant Blackwood)

ISAAC BELL ADVENTURES®

The Saboteurs (with Jack Du Brul)
The Titanic Secret (with Jack Du Brul)
The Cutthroat (with Justin Scott)
The Gangster (with Justin Scott)
The Assassin (with Justin Scott)
The Bootlegger (with Justin Scott)
The Striker (with Justin Scott)
The Thief (with Justin Scott)
The Race (with Justin Scott)
The Spy (with Justin Scott)
The Wrecker (with Justin Scott)
The Chase

CLIVE CUSSLER'S
HELLBURNER

A NOVEL OF THE *OREGON* FILES®

MIKE MADEN

G. P. PUTNAM'S SONS

NEW YORK

PUTNAM
— EST. 1838 —

G. P. PUTNAM'S SONS
PUBLISHERS SINCE 1838
An imprint of Penguin Random House LLC
penguinrandomhouse.com

Library of Congress Cataloging-in-Publication Data

Names: Maden, Mike, author. | Cussler, Clive.
Title: Hellburner: a novel of the Oregon files / Mike Maden.
Other titles: Title appears on item as: Clive Cussler's Hellburner
Description: New York: G. P. Putnam's Sons, [2022] | Series: Oregon files
Identifiers: LCCN 2022019007 (print) | LCCN 2022019008 (ebook) |
ISBN 9780593540640 (hardcover) | ISBN 9780593540657 (ebook)
Subjects: LCSH: Cabrillo, Juan (Fictitious character)—Fiction. |
Ship captains—Fiction. | LCGFT: Thrillers (Graphic works) | Novels.
Classification: LCC PS3613.A284327 H45 2022 (print) |
LCC PS3613.A284327 (ebook) | DDC 813/.6—dc23/eng/20220427
LC record available at https://lccn.loc.gov/2022019007
LC ebook record available at https://lccn.loc.gov/2022019008

Printed in the United States of America

1   3   5   7   9   10   8   6   4   2

CJKB

Book design by Pauline Neuwirth

CAST OF CHARACTERS

THE CORPORATION

Juan Cabrillo—Chairman of the Corporation and captain of the *Oregon*.

Max Hanley—President of the Corporation, Juan's second-in-command and the *Oregon*'s chief engineer. U.S. Navy and Vietnam swift boat veteran.

Linda Ross—Vice President, Operations. Retired U.S. Navy intelligence officer.

Eddie Seng—Director, Shore Operations. Former CIA agent.

Franklin "Linc" Lincoln—Operations. Former U.S. Navy SEAL sniper.

Marion MacDougal "MacD" Lawless—Operations. Former U.S. Army Ranger.

Raven Malloy—Operations. Former U.S. Army Military Police investigator.

Tom Reyes—Operations. Former U.S. Army, 82nd Airborne Division.

Eric Stone—Chief helmsman on the *Oregon*. Former U.S. Navy officer, weapons research and development.

Dr. Mark "Murph" Murphy—Chief weapons officer on the *Oregon*. Former civilian weapons designer.

Dr. Eric Littleton—Director of the *Oregon*'s biophysical laboratory.

Mike Lavin—Chief armorer on the *Oregon*. Retired U.S. Army armament/fire control maintenance supervisor.

Bill McDonald—Senior armorer on the *Oregon*. Former CIA paramilitary operator.

George "Gomez" Adams—Helicopter pilot and chief aerial drone operator on the *Oregon*. U.S. Army veteran.

Hali Kasim—Chief communications officer on the *Oregon*.

Dr. Julia Huxley—Chief medical officer on the *Oregon*. U.S. Navy veteran.

Kevin Nixon—Chief of the *Oregon*'s Magic Shop.

Maurice—Chief steward on the *Oregon*. British Royal Navy veteran.

THE PIPELINE

GREECE

Sokratis Katrakis—Founder of Katrakis Maritime, co-founder of the Pipeline.

Alexandros Katrakis—Sokratis' son, CEO of Katrakis Maritime.

Archytas Katrakis—Son, captain of the *Mountain Star*.

Stephanos Katrakis—Son, general manager of Katrakis Maritime's shipyard.

MEXICO

Víctor Herrera—Head of the Herrera Cartel, son of Hugo Herrera, Mexico's "King of Meth."

Lado Zazueta—Assassin employed by the cartel.

REPUBLIC OF ARMENIA

David Hakobyan—Co-founder of the Pipeline. Naturalized American citizen.

REPUBLIC OF TURKEY

Cedvet Bayur—Regional mercenary commander in Libya. Former Turkish Army intelligence officer. Member of the Gray Wolves.

Yusuf Toprak—President of the Republic of Turkey.

Meliha Öztürk—Independent journalist and human rights activist, daughter of Dr. Kemal Öztürk.

UNITED STATES GOVERNMENT
Alyssa Grainger—President of the United States (POTUS).
Langston Overholt IV—The Corporation's CIA liaison.

CLIVE CUSSLER'S
HELLBURNER

1

That's his third course correction, sir," Santos said. "There's no doubt he's chasing us."

Captain Calvera heard the tension in his first officer's voice. They were both hovering over a military-grade electronics suite—something his commercial fishing trawler *El Valiente* shouldn't have but did.

Calvera stood scratching his beard, a nervous habit. It didn't make any sense. According to the automated identification signal, they were being chased by an Indonesian-flagged vessel, the *Sungu Barat*, a 590-foot break-bulk carrier scheduled to arrive in Caracas in two days. Santos had examined its shipping records. The unremarkable cargo ship had been built in 1971 and had exchanged ownership at least thirteen times over the decades, most recently a month ago. Judging by its Vesseltracker photo, it was a floating wreck. Its hull, bridge and cranes were streaked with rust and grime. It was better suited for a trip to the breaker yard than sailing the open water.

The slow-moving vessel hadn't caught anyone's attention over the last few days, but Santos had programmed their search radar to pick up on behavioral anomalies. Three hours ago, the *Sungu Barat* triggered an alarm and Calvera initiated course corrections to see if the radar's warning software had made a mistake.

It hadn't.

Stranger still, the *Sungu Barat* was over twice the length and double the weight of *El Valiente* and yet the broken-down cargo ship not only kept pace but was actually gaining on them. Now it was just a little over two kilometers behind and closing in.

"Who do you think it is?" Santos asked.

"Your guess is as good as mine. If anything, I'd say it might be pirates." But even as he said it, Calvera shook his head in disbelief. "But sailing an old rust bucket like that? I doubt it."

"What do you want to do, sir?"

Calvera frowned, thinking. There were only three choices ever available to a captain in his position: run, hide or fight. *El Valiente* was indeed a commercial fishing vessel, but it had been modified to function as a covert smuggler. He and his crew had spent years perfecting the art of hiding in plain sight, plying the fishing waters and port cities of the Atlantic and Mediterranean for over half a decade. Not being noticed was their first and best defense.

Apparently, the *Sungu Barat* had breached that first defense. Now the options were either to run or fight. His eyes quickly scanned the radar screen again. They were the only two ships within five hundred kilometers, which meant they had this patch of the ocean all to themselves. A gun battle wouldn't be noticed.

Calvera's inclination was to attack, but as his grandfather taught him, it was always better to defeat an enemy without actually fighting him. It was a lesson the old man learned as a young guerrilla alongside Che and Fidel in the Sierra Maestra mountains over sixty years ago. While they may be far out at sea, there was always the chance that if Calvera overplayed his hand, the authorities might be alerted. Better to play it safe.

He turned to the ship's helmsman. "Rico, full speed ahead."

"A la orden, mi capitán."

The helmsman advanced the throttle. The ship's massive diesel engine roared to life. While the trawler normally cruised at eleven knots, its top speed was rated at seventeen. But with the specially modified engine fitted for just such an occasion, *El Valiente* accelerated to an incredible thirty. The entire vessel thrummed with the vibrations of the racing pistons now hammering belowdecks.

The sudden increase in speed brought a smile to everyone on the bridge, including Santos, still hovering over the radarscope. Calvera knew that showing such speed ruined the illusion that *El Valiente* was a mere fishing trawler, but shaking off this biting tick from the back of his neck was worth it.

"Captain, we caught her flat-footed," Santos said. "We're pulling away."

"Excellent."

Calvera crossed over to Rico and clapped a hand on his shoulder. The young helmsman was grinning ear to ear with pride in his vessel and his captain. They would put plenty of distance between themselves and the old junker within minutes.

"Captain. She's closing on us—fast."

Calvera charged back over to the radar station. He couldn't believe his eyes. The *Sungu Barat* was making over sixty knots.

Sixty knots!

"Check your radar, Santos. There must be something wrong with it."

"I ran a complete diagnostic earlier. Everything is in working condition."

"It's not possible." Calvera's face darkened. "And yet, there it is."

The two men exchanged worried glances.

"You know what's at stake."

Santos nodded.

A vein throbbed on Calvera's forehead. He had a young wife and several children. So did Santos and the other officers. It was one of the reasons they had been recruited into the organization. If they were boarded and their cargo seized, not only would they be killed but their entire families would be wiped out.

Failure was not an option.

Santos saw the flashing comms light. He pulled on his earphones and tapped a button. A moment later, he glanced up at Calvera.

"Captain, we're receiving a message from the *Sungu Barat*. Their captain wants to speak with you."

Calvera nodded. "Put him on speaker."

Santos flipped the toggle switch.

"This is Capitan Calvera of *El Valiente*. We are a flagged ship of the sovereign nation of Argentina sailing lawfully in international waters. Who are you and why are you pursuing us with the intention of harm?"

"This is Captain Jorge Soto on the *Sungu Barat*. We have no intention of harming you. But you are ordered to shut down your engines and allow us to board and inspect you for contraband cargo."

"Under color of what authority?"

"International maritime law."

"In other words, you have no authority, Capitan Soto. That means you are a pirate, and piracy is a violation of international law. We will not allow you to board us."

"If you say we are pirates, call the Suriname Coast Guard and report us, Captain Calvera. Go ahead. I'll wait."

That *pendejo* captain called his bluff, Calvera thought. They both knew he couldn't call the Coast Guard. That would be even worse than letting this pirate Soto on board. He signaled to Santos with a finger across his neck to kill the call.

Now what?

"Evasive maneuvers, Captain?"

Calvera stood, tugging at his beard. "No. Keep a steady course."

"Sir?"

"Do it."

"At this rate of speed, they'll overtake us in less than two minutes."

Calvera's eyes narrowed, focused on a bead of sweat glistening on his first officer's forehead. "My math skills are equal to yours, Santos."

"Mis disculpas, mi capitán."

Calvera checked his watch, his father's vintage Rolex Submariner. He called over his shoulder to the weapons officer. "Valentín, ready number one."

Valentín nodded grimly. *"A la orden, mi capitán."*

Calvera's watch hand swept toward thirty seconds. "Distance and location?"

"Five hundred meters, directly astern."

Calvera's eyes remained fixed on his watch. He was doing the calculations in his mind, a more reliable instrument than any computer.

"Valentín . . . ready—now!"

The weapons officer slapped a button. Three mines were released beneath *El Valiente*'s hull, deployed directly in the path of the *Sungu Barat*.

Calvera stepped outside onto the bridgewing and raised a pair of binoculars to his eyes. The frothing white wake from his churning propeller drew a straight line to the bow of the distant freighter like a tracer round to its target.

Santos called out the seconds before impact with the first mine.

"Five . . . four . . . three . . ."

Calvera grinned.

Any moment now.

"Captain!" Santos shouted.

He didn't have to say a word. What Santos saw on his radar screen Calvera witnessed with his own bulging eyes. His jaw dropped.

The *Sungu Barat* suddenly shifted ninety degrees to his port.

Impossible!

Calvera's heart pounded. In all his years at sea, he'd never seen anything like it.

"Fire the mines!"

Valentín hit the remote trigger. Three towering geysers erupted harmlessly to the *Sungu Barat*'s starboard as it veered away.

The violence of the *Sungu Barat*'s sudden shift sent water crashing over its high deck like a rogue wave. The ship rolled steeply with the impact, then righted itself and resumed its forward speed. But now it was running three hundred meters parallel to Calvera's course to avoid future mine attacks and catching up quickly.

Santos appeared in the hatchway, his face ashen. "Your orders, sir?"

Calvera had never seen his number two this shaken up before. Santos was as loyal as an old hunting dog and just as reliable. But Santos had more to lose. He kept several spoiled young wives and fifteen fat children in three separate countries.

"Get that *cabrón* Soto on the horn."

Calvera keyed his radio mic. "Soto, this is Captain Calvera, over. Do you need assistance? We saw three explosions—"

"Cut the crap, Calvera. Those were mines. Your mines. Kill your engines. Now."

"Look, Soto. If this is about money, I'm authorized to pay a small fee—"

"There's no fee you can pay, Calvera. No bribes. No negotiations. Kill your engines now or I'll kill them for you—and maybe your entire crew."

Calvera swore violently. He'd butchered men for lesser insults. But he swallowed his pride—a tactical necessity.

"I will comply, but under protest. However, your inspection team must not be armed."

"You're in no position to dictate terms, Calvera. Kill your engines, come to a halt and be prepared to be boarded. *¿Entiendes?*"

"*Entiendo.*" Calvera spat out the word like a curse and shoved the mic into Santos' hand. He shouted at Rico, "Kill the engines!"

Rico confirmed the order and throttled down. "Full stop, *mi capitán.*"

Calvera turned toward Valentín at the weapons station.

"Ready number two. Wait for my signal."

Valentín smiled.

Moments later, *El Valiente* was dead in the water.

Calvera crossed back out to the bridge's outer wing to get a better view of his pursuer. He pulled his binoculars to his eyes and scanned the wreck. It was even more disgusting and dilapidated than the photos had suggested. How was it possible for such a poorly maintained vessel to have performed so incredibly? he wondered.

The *Sungu Barat* came to a full stop three hundred meters directly to port. Calvera adjusted the focus ring on his binoculars and zoomed in on the bridge. His eyes fixed on the occluded windows, caked with salt and grime. He couldn't see into the bridge, but he knew that *bastardo* Soto was standing up there grinning down at him.

"Valentín—fire!"

Down on *El Valiente*'s deck, a single-barreled Chinese 20mm Gatling gun leaped through the roof of a fake shipping container and opened up. The deafening chain saw roar unleashed a stream of continuous lead, showering the steel deck with brass casings.

Calvera laughed as the *Sungu Barat*'s bridge windows shattered instantly and chunks of the rusted bridge pulverized beneath the hammering shell fire.

But before the laugh had escaped his mouth, the two six-barreled rotary cannons of a Russian-made Kashtan close-in weapons system opened up from the top of the cargo ship's forward mast. The cannons delivered ten thousand rounds per minute, but it only took one brief, earsplitting second for the Kashtan to deliver enough 30mm explosive tungsten-tipped ammo to utterly destroy Calvera's smaller weapon.

In a single beat of Calvera's pounding heart, the gun battle was over.

Calvera dashed back into the bridge, shouting at his helmsman.

"Flank speed—now!"

Rico slammed the throttle. The specialized diesel engine roared to life, groaning belowdecks. The ship reared up like a racehorse exploding out of the starting gate.

Calvera shot a hopeful glance at Santos. The big, turbocharged diesel had saved them before.

But hope fled his first officer's eyes with the dull, metallic thud that rang like a hammerblow beneath their feet. They felt the entire ship fall back onto its haunches.

"*Capitán*, we've lost speed," the helmsman shouted.

"Give it more power."

"Throttle's maxed out, sir."

"Putting Montoya on speakers," Santos said.

The chief engineer's voice called out from the engine compartment.

"Captain. We've been hit!"

Calvera snatched up the comms mic. "Damage report."

"We've lost the prop. The shaft is damaged and torquing badly. I'm shutting the engine down."

Santos pressed a hand against his wireless headphone.

"Lookout reports a fast-moving rubber skiff with armed men heading our way."

"We can fight them," Rico said, his face flushed.

Calvera ran a final calculation in his head. The numbers all pointed in one direction.

He snatched up a satellite phone from his command station, then turned toward Santos as he pulled his pistol from its holster.

"You know what to do."

Santos stood smartly and flashed a smile in the face of fate.

"*A la orden, mi capitán.*" He pulled his pistol, squared his shoulders and headed for the lower decks.

2

The rigid-hull inflatable boat launched out of the *Sungu Barat*'s water-line garage's Teflon-coated ramp and hit the water with its paired outboard engines screaming.

Blue-eyed, sandy-haired Juan Cabrillo—posing as Captain Soto—held on tight. The RHIB bounced beneath him as it raced across the dark blue water. The four-man team was kitted out in body armor, flash-bang grenades and silenced Heckler & Koch MP5 submachine guns strapped to their chests.

Boarding a hostile ship was always a risk and Calvera had already played his hand with two failed direct attacks on the *Oregon*—currently disguised as the cargo ship *Sungu Barat*. The 200-foot-long Argentine fishing trawler raised all kinds of red flags when it first came to Juan's attention, including the unusual ports of call it had made. Captain Calvera's attempts at evasion and kinetic defense only proved he was smuggling something of incredible value—and no doubt illegal. Smuggling was as old as seafaring itself, but Juan's gut told him that the unusually capable fishing trawler was connected to something bigger than simple larceny.

Juan had to find out what *El Valiente* was carrying and the only way to do that was to get boots on its deck and eyes on its cargo. He led the boarding expedition, leaving Linda Ross in charge of the ship and Mark Murphy on overwatch with his vast array of automated guns at his disposal in case things went sideways. He gave orders not to fire unless fired upon because, as Ross reminded him, they had no legal right to board the trawler.

What troubled Juan now was the disappearance of the entire trawler crew, no doubt preparing to repel boarders. He kept his assault team small, to minimize casualties, but they all punched above their weight. No matter what came at them, his people would handle it.

Blond ex-Ranger Marion MacDougal "MacD" Lawless was in back on the wheel driving the RHIB.

Eddie Seng, a lean and wiry Chinese American, sat near the bow. The ex-CIA operative held the pneumatic telescoping boarding pole. It featured a grappling hook and a wireless video camera so that he could see what they were up against before climbing up the rope ladder. He wore augmented-reality goggles synced to the camera.

Buckled in behind him was Raven Malloy, a combat-decorated Native American fluent in Farsi and Arabic who could do more pull-ups in one go than most of the males on the ship.

Juan smiled to himself.

His people would handle it.

"Ten seconds," MacD said into his molar mic as he wound the engines down. His voice echoed clearly in their skulls, masking the roar of the twin Mercurys in back.

"Ready, Eddie?" Juan asked.

"Good to go."

MacD drove the rubber hull right up to the edge of *El Valiente*'s steel skin, then killed the engines. The trawler rocked in the gentle swell but was otherwise dead in the water thanks to the *Oregon*'s surgically targeted wire-guided mini-torpedo that took out the propeller and ruined the shaft.

Eddie leaped to his feet and fired the pneumatic telescoping pole. The grappling hook snagged on the steel railing high above. His head swiveled as the augmented goggles took in the sweeping view of the deck. Juan stood right behind him.

"Clear!" Eddie shouted.

"Go!" Juan shouted back, laying hands on the ladder first and scrambling up.

Whatever surprise waited for them up top, he wanted to be the first to face it.

MacD secured the RHIB to the rope ladder and raced up last. He cleared the railing, pulled his MP5 and charged toward his assigned position, sweeping the main deck.

According to the downloaded schematics, there were two ladders down into the ship—one fore, one aft—and a third up into the bridge. MacD's head was on a swivel. He watched Eric and Raven with his peripheral vision racing toward their respective hatchways, each heading for the lower decks.

MacD spun around in time to see Juan clambering up the bridge ladder, his gun up, his motion fluid and swift, like a raging river running uphill.

But MacD had his own job to do. He raced forward, the MP5 stock welded to his cheek, the Primary Arms micro-prism sight centered in his field of view with both eyes open. He first pointed his weapon down into the empty holds that should have been brimming with fish, then checked behind barrels, covered pallets, stacks of nets—anywhere a threat might be crouching in ambush.

Nothing.

Juan stormed up the bridge ladder, his EOTech holographic sight pointing the way.

"Chairman, the Sniffer just caught an encrypted burst from a sat phone," Hali Kasim said in his comms.

"Copy that," was all Juan said as he reached the bridge's hatchway, his bloodstream supercharged with high-octane adrenaline.

He grabbed the hatch's handle with his left hand but kept the gun sighted and his finger on the trigger with the right.

He flung the hatch open—just in time to see Calvera slap a button on a console. The air stank of burnt gunpowder. Two corpses were sprawled on the deck behind him, bleeding from head wounds. Pieces of a broken sat phone were scattered at his feet.

"Drop your weapon!" Juan shouted as Calvera whipped around, pistol in hand.

Terror blazed in the captain's eyes.

Calvera shoved the pistol beneath his chin and pulled the trigger. The top of his skull erupted, splattering blood and brains onto the steel ceiling.

Before Juan could react, he heard explosions rippling through the lower decks and felt the vibrations running through him, rattling his teeth.

The dead captain was scuttling his ship.

Worse, he was threatening Juan's team.

Juan bolted for the hatch, barking orders to abandon ship.

He prayed he wasn't too late.

Juan and his team scrambled back onto the main deck as the ship began to list.

Raven and Eddie had reported on their comms that they had found eight dead crewmen, each killed by a bullet to the head.

And nobody else.

Juan ordered the others to the RHIB while he ran back to the stern hatch that led belowdecks.

"You're taking on water fast," Linda said in his comms. "You have less than a minute to get off that death trap."

"Copy that."

Juan stood in the hatchway, staring down the steps leading into the abyss. Everything in him wanted to rush below and see what was worth a wrecked ship and a slaughtered crew but knew he'd be dead before he found out anything.

He scanned the rest of the deck for any kind of clue. Then the ship lurched beneath his feet and his lizard brain kicked in. Time to get back to the RHIB before his team came looking for him.

Juan raced back to the ladder, with MacD calling for him over the molar mic. He threw one leg over the side and began the climb down. The others had already reached the RHIB and were staring up at him. Juan knew the RHIB had to get away before the ship plunged beneath the waves; the suction of a seventeen-hundred-ton vessel would pull them under if they were too close.

Halfway down the ladder, Juan glanced below. MacD had already fired up the engines, the others urging him in his mic to hurry as the stern began to rise against the plunging bow diving for the deep.

The rope ladder snapped tight in Juan's grip as the ship rolled over, rolling him higher like Ahab's corpse strapped to Moby Dick. He was sixty feet above the water, too far to jump without injury—and fatal to his crew in the RHIB if he crashed into it.

"Take off!" Juan shouted into his molar mic.

"Chairman—" MacD said.

"That's an order!"

MacD gunned the throttles; the RHIB turned on a dime and sped away just far enough from the sinking ship to avoid its deadly suction. Every eye in the RHIB was fixed on Juan.

Or something else?

Juan glanced up at what sounded like a buzz saw whirring over his head. It was the *Oregon*'s new twelve-bladed xFold Dragon cargo drone—capable of hauling a thousand pounds. A knotted rope dangled just inches from his head.

"Need a lift?" Gomez Adams, the *Oregon*'s chief drone pilot, asked. "Or do you want to wait for the next cab?"

Juan grabbed the rope just as the ship rolled all the way over and plunged away from him in its death spiral to the bottom. The downdraft from the drone's powerful rotor wash ten feet above his head battered him like he was in a wind tunnel.

As the drone lifted higher, Juan began to spin like a top.

"Sorry about the rotation, boss," Gomez said. "No time to set up a ladder."

"No worries. Reminds me of my fraternity rush at Caltech," Juan said.

He glanced down. His vision whirling, he saw the white wake of the RHIB speeding far beneath his feet, racing for the *Oregon*, the same direction he was now heading in.

Home.

3

The camouflaged T-72 tank idled on the road in the narrow mountain pass, the lead unit in a column of ten commanded by a young Armenian Army captain, his uncle's namesake. The oily stench of the diesel exhaust and the sharp tang of his driver's cigarette choked the cold, sweet mountain air he'd come to love these last several weeks. The passing clouds had finally parted and the high morning sun felt warm on his face as he sat on the hard steel turret.

The aggressor Azerbaijani Army stood poised on the far side of the range, preparing to strike deep into Armenian territory inside the mountainous enclave. But the young captain wasn't concerned. With their reactive armor and large cannons, his platoon's Russian-built tanks remained formidable weapons on the modern battlefield, especially in this part of the world. The Azeris had tried to seize Armenian territory before. Poorly led and trained, they had always been pushed back by the heavy armor, technical superiority and relentless valor of the Armenian Army. His commanders assured him victory was certain. And it was.

Until now.

* * *

A Turkish-built TB2 drone circled eleven thousand feet above the captain's position. The slow-cruising aircraft carried a high-tech avionics package but was powered by what amounted to a glorified lawn mower engine fueled with unleaded gasoline. Its unusual triangular box tail provided exceptional stability and control.

Ten miles away, a Turkish drone pilot and his sensor operator sat in a cramped command vehicle parked on an Azerbaijani airfield. Under President Toprak, Turkey had positioned itself as the new head of the Islamic world defending Muslim nations like Azerbaijan against the predations of infidel countries like Christian Armenia.

The entire Turkish drone squadron and its operators were experienced fighters. They had flown dozens of successful combat missions against Russian ground and air defense forces in Libya and Syria over the last several years. Given Armenia's heavy reliance on Russian weapons systems, their drone squadron's deployment in this conflict seemed inevitable to the pilot.

The drone's targeting reticle locked on the lead Armenian tank. The sensor operator then locked onto the next three tanks. With all four of the "fire and forget" laser-guided missiles assigned to their targets, the pilot waited for the squadron commander's signal.

Thirty seconds later, the signal came. The pilot punched the launch button—and unleashed hell.

The TB2's laser-guided missile smashed through the thin roof armor of the first tank. The warhead flayed the Armenian captain's flesh, killing him instantly. It also ignited the two dozen auto-loaded 125mm shells stored in the hull, shattering the T-72 in a ball of flame. Nanoseconds later, the rest of the Armenian column lit up like torches, each vehicle and crew annihilated in the storm of burning steel.

In total, four slow-cruising Turkish drones loitered in the airspace undetected. Armenian air defenses had been destroyed earlier by other Turkish drones fitted with electronic spoofing systems and laser-guided munitions. Hundreds more Armenian tanks, artillery pieces and air defense units were destroyed by similar attacks in the days to follow.

According to military experts, this made Azerbaijan the first nation in history to win a war with drones.

It also made Armenia the first country to lose one.

4.

David Hakobyan stood by his nephew's graveside. Bright sunlight in a cloudless azure sky sparkled on the snows of Mount Ararat in the distance.

The elaborately carved casket remained closed at the wake and the service. It contained the burnt fragments of the boy's corpse recovered after his tank was struck by Turkish bombs.

Hakobyan brushed the dirt from his soft hands as he stood. "Dust to dust," he whispered to himself.

His nephew's death was unfortunate. But it was the passing of his beloved wife, Edit, thirteen months earlier that had robbed him of all joy. She had curbed Hakobyan's most savage instincts. Her death set him adrift.

Now seventy-two years old, Hakobyan was the last of his clan. His younger brother, long since dead, had only one child, who was now buried in the cold ground of the family cemetery. David was the last Hakobyan.

What was to become of the name?

The funeral was an obligation that the old man could have met remotely from his home in California. He was not one to travel. But the funeral in Armenia presented Hakobyan with an opportunity.

And with that opportunity, a new legacy.

* * *

Modestly dressed in a black off-the-rack suit, felt trilby hat and gloves, Hakobyan stared through his large, owlish glasses with unblinking eyes at the freshly turned dirt at his feet.

He was an American now, having moved to Glendale, California, decades ago with his bride. He rarely visited the Armenian family homestead or the vast apricot farms they had tended for generations. But the Hakobyan name still carried weight in the old country as did Hakobyan money.

This morning's church service had been crowded with some of the most powerful and influential people in Armenia. Nearly all of them owed a debt to the Hakobyan family, in one form or another, either now or in the past. Some came out of genuine respect, but most came out of fear of reprisal for the insult of not attending.

One foreign guest came at Hakobyan's personal invitation. Dr. Artem Petrosian was not only a Russian national but also an ethnic Armenian. Neither respect nor fear had brought him the great distance he had secretly traveled. Greed—and a Lufthansa jet—had.

The local bishop himself offered the eulogy, praising the nephew as a valiant warrior in the holy cause of Armenia and the Church against the forces of Satan and Islam.

The mayor even blocked the streets so that the soldier's hearse could be followed by the parade of mourners from the church to the cemetery, now empty.

Hakobyan nodded to the groundskeeper, who knelt down beside the grave. The man twisted the knob that lit an eternal flame in front of the giant headstone. It was engraved with the life-sized image of Captain Davit Hakobyan standing in his combat uniform, a shadow in granite. Passersby a century from now would assume a great war hero was entombed beneath the monument, as was David Hakobyan's intention.

He dismissed the groundskeeper with another nod and the man hurried away, his eyes cast reverently downward.

Hakobyan stared at the flame guttering in the breeze. Well, that is that, he told himself.

Now it was time to move on to the real reason why he came to Armenia.

Hakobyan turned and faced the Mercedes limousine parked on the far side of the tree-lined gravel road.

A towering, uniformed chauffeur opened the rear door. A middle-aged man unfolded out of the backseat, his London-tailored suit unwrinkled by the long journey. His dark hair was lightly salted with gray. He crossed the distance over to Hakobyan, his hand-stitched Italian leather shoes crunching on the gravel with each step.

"It was kind of you to have come such a long way, Alexandros," Hakobyan said as he offered his hand to the younger man, a Greek surnamed Katrakis. The Greek's hard green eyes sparkled with fierce intelligence above a sharp, handsome nose, classic in its proportions.

"Your nephew's death grieves my entire family. Such a terrible waste of a brilliant young life." The Greek's English was excellent, perfected during his university studies abroad.

"You obviously received my message." Hakobyan glanced over the Greek's shoulder. Katrakis' chauffeur was scanning the area, his head executing a slow-moving swivel like a radar dish.

"Obviously."

"And you have good news for me?"

Alexandros Katrakis leaned in close and whispered, "Would you mind stepping into my Mercedes?"

Hakobyan sighed, exhaling through his nose. He'd come a long way for this meeting.

"If you insist."

Hakobyan and Katrakis sat facing each other, swallowed up in the soft leather seats of the big Mercedes. The automatic door locks thunked shut like a dead bolt in a jailhouse door. The rear cabin was sound-proofed and protected from the latest optical and electronic surveillance measures.

The chauffeur, a former German KSK, Kommando Spezialkräfte, stood fixed just beyond the rear bumper. Unknown to Hakobyan, a secret metal detector in the doorframe had scanned him as he entered the cabin. The image was then sent to the German's smartphone. The only metal on the Armenian was a set of keys.

Katrakis pointed to the minibar's bottles and crystal glasses. "Whiskey? Ouzo?"

Hakobyan shook his head. The cabin air was thick with the Greek's expensive cologne, a strongly aromatic mix of cinnamon and tobacco.

"I've asked for a face-to-face meeting with your father. Is there a problem?"

Katrakis shifted uncomfortably in his seat and straightened his tie. He had to tread carefully. The old Armenian was not one to provoke.

"It's been over a year since you last spoke directly with him."

"As has been our arrangement for decades." Hakobyan pointed to the Mercedes' soundproof cabin. "As you well know, what can't be overheard can't be used against us."

"When was the last time you saw him in person?"

"When you were a baby crawling on the floor in a diaper loaded with *skatá*."

The Greek darkened with the insult. He scanned the Armenian's face for any sign of deceit.

Hakobyan read his eyes.

"You're concerned I'm setting some kind of a trap for him."

"It had crossed my mind."

"He and I are old friends. He has nothing to fear."

"Brutus and Caesar were old friends as well," Katrakis said.

"Brutus and Caesar were Romans. Our families come from a more civilized part of the world, do we not?" Hakobyan offered a conciliatory smile.

The younger man softened. "On this we can agree."

"What I'm offering him now is the greatest business opportunity he'll ever hear. But time is short."

"Can you be more specific?"

"No."

"My only concern is for my father. I mean no disrespect."

"Dear boy, you have a decision to make. Either make this meeting happen or report back to your father that I had nothing to offer. A complete waste of time."

Hakobyan leaned closer and locked eyes with the Greek. "But you know he can smell a man lying the way a dog can smell a body buried in the dirt."

Katrakis couldn't look away or stop the rush of blood to his face. The Armenian was right. His father was a human lie detector. He hated all liars and punished them severely.

Worse, his father loved money even more than he hated liars.

Hakobyan had him boxed in.

"My father has new living arrangements that you aren't aware of. No one sees him but me." Katrakis checked his watch.

He had to make a decision.

"We must leave immediately. There are certain security protocols that must be followed."

"Excellent." Hakobyan patted Katrakis on the knee, a patronizing gesture. "A good son makes a father glad."

Katrakis rolled down his window and called to his chauffeur.

"Wolfie, it's time to go."

The crunching tires of the black Mercedes limousine pulled out of the cemetery and onto the paved road, heading for a private airport. Hakobyan and Katrakis shared a glass of fiery Greek ouzo in memory of Davit, completely unaware of the long-range digital cameras recording them from a great distance.

5

Back on board the *Oregon*, Juan and the raiding team hit the showers and grabbed a few minutes of downtime to process what had happened on *El Valiente*.

Thank God, Juan told himself, Eddie and Raven hadn't yet reached the lowest decks. Otherwise, they would have been killed in the explosions that sank the trawler. They were already heading back up the ladders when he called for them to abandon ship.

Now they were all assembled in the conference room, modeled after the White House's Situation Room. High-backed leather chairs lined a long, polished mahogany table, while large digital monitors hung on the walls for displaying information or for live videoconferencing.

Cabrillo's looks, like his ship the *Oregon*, were deceiving. He was a tall, blue-eyed, broad-shouldered model of the classic Southern California surfer, a reflection of his adventurous youth. Even his close-cropped hair was the color of sun-bleached sand. Yet there was nothing of the laid-back beach bum in his manner or intellect.

Similarly, the 590-foot *Oregon* appeared to be a rust bucket tramp steamer. That was merely a disguise. In reality, she was one of the most advanced combat and intelligence-gathering ships in the world and the operational platform for the Corporation, Cabrillo's private security firm. Since Juan ran his ship and crew like a corporation, he called himself the Chairman. And his senior staff had corporate titles as well.

For today's debrief, Juan called in his chief weapons officer, Mark "Murph" Murphy, dressed in his signature skater-punk black ensemble, with a wispy chin beard and mop of uncombed hair.

He also brought in the *Oregon*'s helmsman, Eric Stone. In stark contrast to his best friend Murph, the Annapolis grad wore his hair neat and precise like the ironed creases on his khaki slacks and white button-down shirt.

Juan wanted Max Hanley there, too. He was the *Oregon*'s second-in-command and the President of the Corporation. The Vietnam swift boat combat veteran had a high, hard belly, thick forearms and a halo of graying ginger hair circling the crown of his nearly bald head like a tonsured warrior monk.

Linda Ross was also present. Despite her helium-pitched voice, tall, lean figure and green, almond-shaped eyes—all of which gave her an elfin look—Ross was the Vice President of operations and number three in command on the *Oregon* after Juan and Max.

The *Oregon*'s communications director, Lebanese American Hali Kasim, sat to Linda's right.

"You were all in on our comms, so you know the basics," Juan began. "There are only three reasons why the captain would scuttle his own ship and kill his crew or let them kill themselves. Either something on board was too important to be discovered or the crew was desperately afraid of getting caught. Or the third option: both."

"Agreed," Hanley said. "Scuttling the ship solves the first problem. But murder or suicide seems like an overreaction to an arrest that would most likely result in minimal jail time."

"Unless they weren't afraid of getting arrested," Linda said. "Maybe suicide was a better alternative than what their bosses would do to them for getting caught."

"Their HR department must be hell on wheels," Hanley said. "Could be a terrorist organization, an organized crime outfit—even a government operation."

"The key in figuring out who they are is trying to find out what they were carrying," Juan said. He pointed at the communications director. "Hali, any chance with that encrypted satellite burst the Sniffer grabbed?"

The *Oregon* carried a wide array of NSA-quality electronic intelligence-gathering equipment that the crew referred to collectively as the Sniffer. It was capable of sweeping, recording and decoding any and all electromagnetic data above and below the sea for miles around.

"The Cray supercomputer decoded it just a few minutes ago. It was a simple sequence of numbers. The first three numbers were ones and the second set of numbers were the exact GPS coordinates of *El Valiente* where it sank."

"The coordinates I get. The first three numbers must have been a call for rescue," Murph said.

"Why call for rescue a nanosecond before you paint the ceiling with your brains?" Juan asked.

"I'm guessing it was a salvage call," Max said.

"Not a salvage call," Juan said. "Otherwise, they wouldn't have scuttled the ship along with its cargo—or its potential witnesses."

"Too bad. We could've hung around and seen who showed up," Linda said. She then asked Hali, "Any chance we found out who received the transmission?"

"It was bounced around on three different satellites. Whoever received the call doesn't want to be found."

"Where does that leave us?" Stone asked.

"The wreckage is some fifteen hundred feet down," Max said. The *Oregon*'s deep submersible, the *Nomad*, had an operational depth of just one thousand feet. "I'm afraid it's out of our reach."

"Any sensor indication that cargo was hazardous?" Juan said.

"Not that we picked up. If there were contaminates, they could all be self-contained down there or harmlessly dispersed. There's no way to tell," Murph said.

"Linda, let's drop a pin on our permanent map in case we need to revisit this place."

"Aye, Chairman."

"Do you want me to put in an anonymous call to the Suriname authorities about the trawler? Untraceable to us, of course," Hali said.

Juan shook his head. "It's not a shipping hazard at that depth. Let's hold off until we get some clarity."

"Roger that."

Cabrillo glanced around the table. He couldn't have been more proud of this team—and all the other crew on the *Oregon*. They were all professionals who followed wherever he led. That was an honor and a responsibility he held dear.

"Shall I resume our course for New Orleans?" Linda asked.

"Aye," Juan said. Unlike the fictional *Sungu Barat*, the *Oregon* was scheduled for a food resupply. But not just any food. The *Oregon*'s chefs—worthy of Michelin stars—demanded only the finest ingredients. The incredible menus they prepared were just one of the many perks of serving on the *Oregon*, often gone away from home for months.

He checked his watch. "I have a call to take in just a few minutes. You all are dismissed."

Everyone shuffled out in good spirits while Juan remained impatiently behind. He couldn't wait to find out what was coming their way next.

Five minutes later, Hali's voice came over the intercom.

"Langston Overholt is on the line."

"Patch him through."

Juan knew his old friend and CIA mentor hated videoconferencing so he took the audio call, grabbing a seat and plopping his size-fourteen LA Dodgers canvas boat shoes up on the mahogany table to get comfortable.

"My dear boy, how are you?" Overholt asked. His voice was stronger and more youthful than his advanced age might suggest. Langston

Overholt IV had recruited Juan directly out of college into the CIA's field operations. When Juan quit the CIA, it was Overholt who suggested he start his own private security concern. While the Corporation was free to take on any jobs it wanted, Juan never took on anything that put the United States at risk. He and Overholt were cut from the same cloth: old-school American patriots.

And more often than not, it was Overholt who employed him—and at a very lucrative rate.

"Still vertical, Lang. Yourself?"

"Racquetball and gin rickeys keep me young. What's the latest?"

"Funny you should ask." Juan gave him a rough sketch of what had transpired with the rogue trawler and its ultimate demise.

"Any ideas?" Juan asked.

"Nothing comes to mind immediately. Smugglers, no doubt. It is rather curious. Any chance of salvaging the cargo?"

"Beyond our reach and most likely destroyed. No indication of hazardous materials in the water. Not that that's conclusive."

"If you'll be so kind as to forward the after action report to me with the particulars, I'll have my people take a gander and see what they come up with."

"Of course."

"Still on for a restock in New Orleans?"

"A quick stop unless you have other plans."

"Fill up your larder, then you'll head down to a little assignment I'd like you to carry out."

"Where?"

"Mexico?"

"And how little?"

There was a long pause on the other end of the line.

"Perhaps *little* was a poor word choice. *Limited* is probably more accurate."

Overholt laid out the mission. All Juan could do was let out a long whistle.

It was a doozy.

6

AN ISLAND OFF THE COAST OF GREECE
THE AEGEAN SEA

David Hakobyan sat, ashen-faced, white-knuckling the seat harness. His eyes switched back and forth between the pilot next to him, slick with sweat, and the looming mountain shrouded in fog filling the Eurocopter's windscreen.

"How can you see?" Hakobyan asked, breathing heavily into his mic.

"I'm flying on instruments."

"Why not wait until the fog clears?"

"This peak is covered in fog most of the year. We don't have a choice."

Hakobyan wanted to shout at the pilot to pull away and take him back, but he'd come too far and gone to too much trouble. Worse, the clock was ticking. He'd rather crash into the mountainside and tumble in the sea than give up now.

Minutes later, the helicopter skids touched down on the summit and the turbines switched off.

A large, hooded monk approached the helicopter with an umbrella in one beefy hand. He opened the cabin door. When Hakobyan exited the helicopter, the monk held the umbrella over his head despite the lack of rain.

Hakobyan doubted the pistol-shaped bulge beneath the man's robe was an oversize hymnal.

"I don't need it," he said, pointing at the umbrella.

The monk ignored him.

He led Hakobyan toward an ancient monastery hewn by hand from mountain rock.

The monk approached a heavy wooden door and knocked three times with a thick knuckle. Hakobyan noticed the gold ring on his finger fitted with a large diamond.

The door swung open noiselessly on greased hinges and the man stepped through and Hakobyan followed, passing yet another large, hooded monk, silent and hard as the mountain itself.

The small, primitive chapel was appointed with a few hand-carved chairs and other, ecclesiastical furniture. Icons hung on the walls and the sweet tang of incense filled the dank, moldy room. Windows high up toward the vaulted ceiling reflected light into the flickering, candlelit gloom. On the far end of the chapel was a door leading to the rest of the monastery. It opened.

A dead man stood in the doorway, smiling.

"David," the man said. His bright eyes wrinkled deeply at the edges like rutted roads. He was a decade older than Hakobyan but still tall and ramrod straight. His feet were shod in simple sandals and he wore a monk's robe like the others, only with the hood pulled back away from his face.

A mass of wild frost-white hair and beard couldn't hide the familiar green eyes, dark as the angry sea. His leathered flesh was hard and brown like deck planking, burned by decades on the water.

Years before, the old Greek had faked his death, planting doctored autopsy reports and photographs from the funeral with law enforcement and news organizations he controlled. As far as the authorities knew, Sokratis Katrakis was no longer of this world.

"Sokratis," Hakobyan said.

The two men approached and embraced. The Greek stood back and held Hakobyan by the shoulders and looked him up and down. "You look well, my old friend."

"I want to vomit."

Katrakis pointed a long finger at the monk who had escorted Hakobyan from the helicopter. "Two cups of hot tea. No sugar."

"Yes, sir," the man said. He strode quickly through the doorway Katrakis had entered and disappeared.

"That should settle your airsick belly," Katrakis said. He turned to the other monk, who was guarding the door. "We'll be fine. I'll call for you when I need you."

The monk nodded and exited the chapel, shutting the heavy wooden door behind him.

Katrakis pointed Hakobyan to a pair of the carved, olive wood chairs. They sat.

"You've come a long way," Katrakis said. "I know it's been a difficult journey for you."

Hakobyan was shuttled secretly among three cars, a private jet and finally the helicopter, boarding each under cover of a garage or hangar. At the same time, a body double with fake identification boarded a commercial flight in Yerevan, connecting in Frankfurt, with a final destination of LAX.

Hakobyan's eyes fixed on one of the high windows. "Where is this place?"

"You are in the Monastic Republic of the Holy Island. Like Meteora, though much smaller." Katrakis was referring to the other autonomous, self-governing monastic region of Greece. Meteora was famous for its dozens of monasteries and a favorite of pilgrim tourists. Holy Island contained numerous stone huts and hermit's caves but only two monasteries, the oldest and smallest of which the two men now sat in. No tourists were allowed.

"How long have you been here?" Hakobyan asked.

"Nearly two years now."

Hakobyan looked his friend up and down. His monk's robe was tattered and threadbare. "You used to have a better tailor."

Katrakis laughed. "When in Rome . . ."

The first large, hooded monk returned with two steaming mugs of tea and then departed, to give the men some privacy.

Hakobyan blew on the scalding tea to cool it, then took a thoughtful sip.

"Armed guards dressed as monks fool any cameras, and a remote location legally protects one from extradition. Heavy stone walls and a mountain shrouded in fog prevent unwanted snooping." Hakobyan chuckled. "Even an umbrella to keep any spy satellite from spotting me when I got out of the helicopter. No wonder you can stay dead for so long. Who else knows you're here?"

"The abbot, of course. He oversees the island and granted me sanctuary in exchange for a rapacious annual donation to the republic. He tries to frighten me like a child about God's damnation and the eternal fires of Hell. Besides the money, he requires that I live according to the rules of the order, fast weekly and meet with him privately every Monday afternoon to attend to the care of my soul."

"And no one else knows you're here?"

"No one else on the island knows who I am or why I'm here. Besides the pilot and my guards, only my son Alexandros and you have ever visited me."

"I'm honored."

"We've known each other for over fifty years. We made money together, whored together. We built a business the likes of which has never been seen before. If I can't trust you, who can I?"

Hakobyan searched his old friend's face. They had indeed built a business that was the envy of the criminal world. They called it, simply, the Pipeline.

Katrakis inherited a modest shipbuilding company from his father but developed it into one of the largest shipping and ground transportation companies in Europe. That legitimate business provided both the means and cover for operating a vast network smuggling guns, drugs and human beings all over the Mediterranean and beyond.

While Katrakis provided the transportation infrastructure, Hakobyan arranged suppliers and sellers and handled the complex array of secret finances that shielded them all from police and government scrutiny. In short, the Greek handled the boats and trucks and the Armenian handled the relationships and money.

Katrakis set his mug down. "I understand you have a business proposal."

Hakobyan glanced around the empty chapel just to be sure no one was listening. He leaned in closer, his voice a whisper.

"Kanyon."

7

Kanyon?" Katrakis asked. "What is Kanyon?"

"The Americans call it Kanyon. The Russians call it Poseidon, which a pagan Greek like you would prefer." Hakobyan laughed. "Before, they called it Status-6."

Katrakis sat back, his face hardened. "If I wanted riddles, I'd call that jabbering abbot. Speak plainly, man."

"We know better than most that war is good for business," Hakobyan began. "The Pipeline smuggled weapons, munitions and soldiers into Eurasia, Africa and the Middle East. Of course, it wasn't nearly as profitable as their drug trade."

"There are plenty of wars right now," Katrakis said. "We're making good money from them."

"Big wars, big profits. Little wars, little profits."

"Now you're yammering. Get to the point."

Hakobyan ignored the insult.

"We're on track to double our money with the new meth source I've secured. But with my plan, there's a way to make even more. Far more. Wealth beyond imagination."

"Explain."

"Our greatest threat has always been national governments. If they're fighting for their survival, they won't have the time or resources to contend with us."

"And how does this Kanyon play into your scheme?"

"Istanbul," Hakobyan said. "It's the crown jewel of the Turkish empire." Hakobyan paused for effect. "I intend to destroy it."

"You want to kill sixteen million Turks?"

Hakobyan shrugged. "What do we care about filthy Turks?"

Like most Armenians, Hakobyan loathed the Turkish state. It had never admitted to its role in the twentieth-century holocaust of one and a half million Armenians.

"You and I have done a lot of business with Turks over the years," Katrakis reminded him. "We still do."

"We'd do business with the Devil himself if it turned a profit. It doesn't mean he still shouldn't burn in the lake of fire for eternity."

"My son is building three new LNG tankers for the Turks right now to transport liquid natural gas for a very large sum of money."

"It is all the more poetic," Hakobyan said. "It means the Turk has paid for the rope we'll use to hang him with."

"This Kanyon of yours . . . What is it? A ship? A plane?"

"A torpedo."

Katrakis frowned. "Istanbul is not a boat to be sunk."

"This is no ordinary torpedo. It's nuclear-powered and packed with stealth technology so that even the Americans can't detect it. Most important, it carries a hundred-megaton warhead."

Katrakis crossed his arms, incredulous. "I have never heard of such a thing. A hundred megatons? Are you certain? That's enormous."

"So-called experts in the West say it's a Russian fantasy weapon. But it's real, trust me. There is no other weapon on earth like it."

"But what good is a torpedo against a city?"

"You mean against Istanbul? A sprawling city crowding both sides of the Bosporus Strait like mewling kittens around a bowl of cream?"

A smile crept across the Greek's wrinkled mouth.

"A tidal wave?"

Hakobyan laughed as his hands shot up, his fingers splaying in explosion.

"Exactly! The Kanyon is designed to create a giant tidal wave. We'll drown sixteen million dirty Turks in a flood of their own radioactive bathwater."

"How would you acquire this Kanyon torpedo?"

"I have made arrangements to steal one."

"How?"

"That is my affair. Trust me, it will happen. But we have a very narrow window to commit."

"How narrow?"

Hakobyan checked his watch, a Timex. "Twelve hours." Travel time to the monastery had narrowed the window of opportunity considerably.

"Why?"

"My contact has set that time limit. There are technical considerations."

Katrakis seethed inwardly but hid it behind a knowing smile.

"Another one of your secret relationships."

"The beauty of my plan is that the circle of knowledge remains very small. Only I, my contact and you will have the full details. The fewer people who know, the less likely there is to be a leak."

"And you trust your contact with your life?"

"Completely."

"Which means you plan to kill him."

"Of course."

"Assuming you can steal the Kanyon and detonate it as planned and, further, you manage to destroy Istanbul . . . Tell me, where is the profit in that?"

"It will be made known that the Kanyon was the Russian weapon used to destroy the city. In so doing, Turkey will declare war on Russia."

"Why would Turkey blame Russia? President Ivanov would deny it was an authorized attack."

"I have a source inside the Kremlin. A Turkish fighter recently shot down a Russian jet in Syria. Ivanov made private threats to 'smash the Turks' and the meeting was recorded. Those comments will be publicized at the appropriate moment. There are other measures I have undertaken to ensure the Russians will be blamed. Once Turkey declares war, NATO will be forced to intervene. World War Three will be the result."

"Why will NATO be forced to act? They failed to do anything to stop the Russian theft of Crimea a few years ago."

"Don't you read the papers anymore? The date of the attack will correspond with the upcoming meeting of the thirty NATO defense ministers in Istanbul—a meeting that will include a televised summit between the American and Turkish presidents. It's the perfect setup."

Katrakis tugged his beard, thinking.

"You're right. This will cause World War Three."

Hakobyan smiled. "The bigger the war, the bigger the profits for us."

"What if the war goes nuclear?"

"Turkey has no nuclear weapons and neither Brussels nor Washington will commit atomic suicide to avenge the death of a Muslim city. Best of all, it doesn't matter who wins, though my bet is on NATO. Reconstruction will prove even more lucrative to us as nations rebuild."

Katrakis sat back in his chair. The olive wood creaked under his weight. He still wasn't convinced. His green eyes bored into Hakobyan's.

"The death of your nephew . . . Is this all about profit or revenge?"

"Profit, I assure you. I've been working on this plan for the last year. My nephew's death was unfortunate, but he was a brute and even more dull-witted than my brother. I merely used his funeral as a cover for my trip to Yerevan."

The FBI had tried desperately over the years to connect Hakobyan to various criminal organizations and activities but could never find a shred of evidence against him. He was, however, still a person of interest.

"This plan of yours . . . Millions will die. That's unlike you."

"I've felt the gush of warm blood on my hands before."

"One man's blood. Not an entire city. What has changed you?"

"I'm near the end. And I have no heirs."

Katrakis arched a skeptical eyebrow, appraising his old partner.

"You're only telling half the truth."

"You know me too well." Hakobyan shifted in his chair, his hands fidgeting like a wayward sinner in the confessional booth.

"Edit turned a blind eye to many things in my life but not the slaughter of innocent people. I couldn't bear the thought of what I might see in her eyes if I had done this thing while she was alive."

"She may be watching you now."

"She is food for the worms. Not even that now."

"What about God? Heaven? Don't you fear his judgment for such a crime as you propose?"

"My only religion is money."

"And what will you do with all this vast wealth we shall create from your scheme?"

"The war has left many widows and orphans in Armenia. I will leave them a fortune so vast that they will sing my name long after I have died."

"What role do I have in this plan?"

"Quite small, actually. But we'll split the profits fifty-fifty just like we've always done."

"That's generous of you."

"We're old friends, are we not?"

"So what do you require of me?"

"My contact requires a payment of one hundred twenty-five million euros equivalent in Bitcoin to his dark web account. You and I will split that fee. Second, he has made arrangements for the Kanyon to appear at a specified location. You need to provide a ship capable of retrieving it and a trustworthy crew for transport to its final destination."

Katrakis suspected there was still more.

"Anything else?"

Hakobyan shrugged. "Just the simple part. We must have that money transferred in less than twelve hours or the plan dies forever."

Katrakis sighed through his long nose as he stroked his beard, searching his old friend's face. The Armenian was cautious to a fault. He had never seen him this animated before. It was an insane plot and a dangerous gamble.

And a chance for revenge.

Katrakis grinned, flashing crooked teeth, tangled and stained like old barbed wire.

"Agreed."

The helicopter lifted off from the grassy helipad. Amid the swirling fog of the rotor wash, Sokratis Katrakis, hooded again to avoid detection, raised a leathery hand wishing David Hakobyan a safe journey. The chopper wobbled and yawed as it climbed in the high winds.

Katrakis chuckled. The old Armenian would be puking in his felt hat within minutes.

Back inside the seclusion of the chapel, Katrakis pulled back his hood and headed for his private chambers.

The Greek's mind swam with possibilities.

Before Hakobyan left, the two of them discussed more details of the plan, including the specifications for the retrieval ship. Difficult but not impossible. He owned one of the best shipyards in Europe.

Hakobyan's plan was indeed brilliant. A devastating war between Russia and Turkey would swell the coffers of his criminal and legitimate enterprises.

And the Armenian was right about police and intelligence units all being diverted to the war effort.

His plan to blame the Russians was equally faultless. Ivanov was a nail and NATO owned a lot of expensive hammers. A showdown was inevitable. Destroying Istanbul with a Russian nuclear torpedo would light the fuse that would set Europe on fire.

He understood Hakobyan's hatred for the Turks. The Greeks, too, had suffered under the heel of the Ottoman boot, grinding them down into the dust in a sustained and brutal campaign of rapes, murders and deportations. Greeks, including his own family, had occupied Anatolia for four thousand years. Now they were strangers there.

Yes, Katrakis hated the Turks as much as the Armenian did. In fact, more so. And for other reasons altogether. Killing millions of Turks didn't bother him at all. In fact, the more he thought about it, the more he relished the idea—but only so long as he could act without him or his family being blamed for it.

He and Hakobyan had been partners for a very long time. He'd recognized the genius in the Armenian early on, when they were both much younger men, Hakobyan's mind the sharpest he'd ever encountered. Together, they were able to separate themselves from their respective organizations and form a partnership that made them the equal of, then later superior to, the mafias they had worked for.

But Hakobyan quickly positioned himself to become an equal partner with Katrakis, something the Greek deeply resented. The slimy little Armenian clerk had siphoned off half the fortune that was rightly all his.

Katrakis had always sought the means to get rid of Hakobyan, but year after year he brought new contacts, new product lines, more revenues—and kept all of it out of the reach of their enemies. The wily Armenian's secrecy kept them both out of jail and alive—and made Katrakis rich beyond his wildest dreams.

The key to their entire operation now was the new Mexican meth supplier. The highly addictive drugs were the fuel that ran their machine.

Unknown to Hakobyan, Katrakis had been able to find the Mexican and cut a deal with him. Sokratis was just days away from ordering the assassination of his old friend.

As luck would have it, the Armenian delivered the Kanyon plan at the last possible moment. A fair restitution for all the wealth Hakobyan had stolen from him over the decades.

Since he was going to betray his friend, he would be sure Hakobyan took the fall if somehow the Russian angle failed.

He now saw all the possibilities. His old heart raced as if he were about to take a woman again.

Katrakis marched over to the wall safe embedded in the stone and opened it. It served as a Faraday cage to prevent any electronic break-in. Katrakis removed his encrypted cell phone and called his son Alexandros.

"I need you to come immediately. We have much to discuss."

8

Juan Cabrillo stood at the head of the conference room table once again, the earnest, eager faces of his assembled team awaiting their orders. As Chairman of the Corporation, he ran the show, but he wasn't vain, knowing he couldn't do squat without his handpicked operators and crew, the best in the business.

The mercenary business.

Juan felt the distant thrum of the *Oregon*'s four magnetohydrodynamic engines racing belowdecks, the vessel's beating heart. It was the most technologically advanced maritime propulsion system on the planet. It deployed superconductive coils cooled by liquid helium to strip free electrons from seawater for an inexhaustible supply of free fuel. That electricity powered four pump-jets through two rotating Venturi nozzles, driving the cargo ship along like a racing hydrofoil, seemingly defying the laws of physics. Without the power the engines provided, most of the high-tech command, control, comms and weapons systems above and below its "derelict" decks couldn't function.

Cabrillo wasn't former regular military, but he exuded a commanding presence. He was a master of disguise and undercover work and handled small-arms and close-quarters combat as well as any man or woman aboard.

But it was his incredible confidence that inspired his people—mostly former military—to follow wherever he led them into battle—often against overwhelming odds.

It also drew women to him like hummingbirds to sweet nectar.

Juan's eye caught the golden Roman eagle battle standard hanging on the far wall, a recent gift from the Italian government for services rendered. The *aquila* symbolized the gallantry of his crew and its sacrifice. Next to it hung the plaque inscribed with the names of fallen comrades along with their photos. The wall was a reminder that once again he was about to lead good men and women in harm's way.

The mission they'd accepted from Overholt was simple enough—and equally impossible. They were tasked with capturing alive Hugo Herrera, the boss of the most dangerous cartel in Mexico. Herrera was the self-proclaimed King of Meth, a title he had rightly earned. The filthy chemical, now laced with an even more potent variant of Chinese fentanyl, was addicting and killing tens of thousands of people throughout Mexico and the United States. But the distribution networks he designed had proven unassailable. The United States government wanted Herrera seized and remanded to custody so he could be questioned and his organization dismantled. Unfortunately, he had to be breathing to be able to do that. An assassination, however satisfying or justified that might be, wouldn't solve the larger problem.

Repeated requests to the Mexican government failed to generate any action. Those Mexican officials and law enforcement personnel who hadn't been compromised by Herrera's vast reserves of dirty money were either too scared to act or slaughtered in the attempt.

The American government was neither able nor willing to mount any kind of military or law enforcement incursion into Mexico. Such an action would be viewed as an act of war and would further weaken an already strained relationship with America's most important southern neighbor.

As usual, when there was a job too difficult, too dangerous or in need of plausible deniability for the American government, Juan Cabrillo and his Corporation were enlisted for action. The mercenary organization worked for money—big money. Juan had insisted from the Corporation's inception that each member of the crew receive a share of their profits, making each of them rich over the course of time.

He paid them well because the risks were high, especially on this mission. Just getting to Herrera was nigh impossible.

Round-the-clock surveillance by his ops team on the ground only confirmed Juan's worst fears. Herrera's vast wealth had purchased a world-class security outfit with state-of-the-art electronics, cameras and, most important of all, combat-tested ex-military operators from Europe and Russia—not the typical narco-cowboy hit squad with gold-plated AK-47s.

With armored vehicles, encrypted comms and even shoulder-fired anti-aircraft missiles targeting all his safe houses, it would take a small army to defeat his highly disciplined security team.

The other mission parameter adding another layer of complexity was that "it must all be done quietly, without drawing undue attention," Overholt had said.

One thing Juan knew for sure. Full-on assaults were seldom quiet and usually fatal to at least some of the parties involved.

There was, however, one possibility.

Juan pressed the remote and a live image of a soaring skyscraper appeared. He turned to the rest of the room and reviewed the broad outlines of the plan one last time and reminded them that Herrera's security setup was nearly perfect.

Nearly.

Herrera's arrogance opened a breach in his otherwise airtight defenses. Like clockwork, he arrived every Thursday by helicopter from his armed compound two hundred miles away for his weekly debauch in the city of Monterrey. He owned the entire skyscraper—paid for with laundered cash—and his private penthouse served as half office and half whorehouse. Sitting on top of his own skyscraper, the King of Meth must have felt like the King of the World—and invincible. He kept his security people on the lower levels while he occupied the penthouse so he could enjoy his revelries in private. If Juan's team were ever going to snatch him alive, it would have to be there.

"We're a go tonight."

"Amen," Max Hanley said, his teeth clenched on an unlit pipe.

If anybody loved the *Oregon* more than Juan, it was Max. His seniority and good sense made him the President of the outfit, but his passion was being the chief engineer of the technological marvel. Max was anything but a yes-man. If he saw something amiss, he'd be the first to call Juan out.

Eddie Seng, however, wasn't as enthusiastic about the mission as Hanley. As director of shore operations, he planned all combat missions and was usually the first in with Juan's Gundogs to take the fight to the bad guys.

But tonight Juan would lead this mission and Eddie would remain aboard.

"Are we good to go, Eddie?" Juan asked.

"Aye, Chairman. Good to go."

"We're inserting a three-man team. I'm point," Juan said. "MacD and Tom are the two and three—just like we've drilled. Gomez will get us there in the Tiltrotor."

MacD grinned broadly.

"I just can't wait to try out my new toy," he said in a Louisiana accent as smooth and buttery as a creole praline from Aunt Sally's. The new toy he was referring to was a SUB-1 XR crossbow that shot one-inch groups at one hundred yards. Juan bought him the new unit after Raven lost his old one, "Diana," due to a ship sinking in Melbourne Harbour.

"Tom, any questions?" Juan asked.

Tom Reyes flashed a smile, lighting up his otherwise fearsome face. With his dark hair and eyes, wiry build and sharp nose, he'd earned the nickname Falcon at the U.S. Army Airborne School both for the way he looked and moved—like a swift-flying killer.

"All good, amigo." Tom was one of the old-timers who had retired from the game but recently decided he needed to play one last inning.

Reyes was that classic story of an East LA *cholo* gangster wannabe who got turned around by a good cop and a tough priest. After six combat tours with the Army, he joined the Corporation and served admirably. Several years ago, he retired comfortably on his Corporation share payout and started his own private security service back in Los Angeles. He was with the Corporation again. At least for now.

Juan wasn't looking for any new operators when he was tasked with finding Herrera. He reached out to Reyes, who had contacts with actionable intel in the murky underworld of SoCal drugs.

Reyes was more than happy to oblige so long as he could be in on the snatch and grab himself. His younger brother OD'd on Herrera meth a few years earlier and Reyes wanted to see justice done, preferably by his own hand.

Since Reyes was a proven operator and a Spanish speaker, Juan let him try out on the Herrera mission workups. Reyes didn't miss a beat. He'd stayed in top shape over the years and kept his operator skills sharp by not sitting behind a desk. Juan agreed to bring him on board. Cabrillo understood the need for justice—or at least closure. But because he was the one who brought Reyes in, Juan didn't want Eddie to be responsible for him on this op in case things went sideways.

"Gomez?" Juan asked. Gomez was a veteran of the 160th Night Stalkers Special Operations Aviation Regiment and the Corporation's lead helicopter and drone pilot. His bad boy good looks, horseshoe mustache and pilot's natural self-assurance made him the *Oregon*'s most accomplished Lothario. He earned the moniker Gomez because he once swabbed the tonsils of a drug lord's girlfriend who looked just like Morticia from the old *Addams Family* TV show.

"The weather's clear until seven a.m. tomorrow. A slight wind is picking up on the ground but still within parameters. Other than that, I've got gas in the tank, air in the tires and love in my heart. Should be an easy ride."

"Max, what's the ETA to our launch point?" Juan asked.

"According to the op center, at our current rate of speed we'll be in position in approximately two hours."

Juan stole another glance at the live digital feed from one of *Oregon*'s surveillance drones. Nothing had changed. His operators on the ground in Monterrey, ex–Navy SEAL Franklin "Linc" Lincoln and former Army MP Raven Malloy, knew how to handle themselves and the drone.

"All right, then. We know our mission, our target, our plan, our assignments. Just keep your eyes on the prize and your heads on the swivel." Juan checked his watch. "We'll saddle up down in the hangar in one hour for an equipment check. Questions?"

Nobody had any. Juan dismissed them and they shuffled out, joking and laughing, each heading to their duty stations. Tom Reyes was the last out, stopping briefly by the memorial wall and whispering something that Juan couldn't hear.

Juan didn't need to hear. He'd done the same thing himself more times than he could remember.

9

Junior Lieutenant Yashin was standing his very first watch as the officer of the deck in the submarine's control room. It was the third shift and most of the officers and crew were in their bunks. He, in effect, was the captain of the sleeping sub. They were traveling at thirty knots at a depth of three hundred meters, well below the thermocline and beyond the unblinking gaze of American sonar and satellites.

Not that they need have worried. Departing its Arctic base at Severodvinsk with five other Federation submarines to confuse American tracking efforts, the *Penza* slipped beneath the polar ice cap and disappeared. Their historic mission would soon prove to both NATO and China that Russia's undetectable submarine force gave it a strategic advantage that couldn't be overcome in the event of war. The success of this mission would prevent the loss of tens of millions of Russian lives.

And right now, the success of the mission depended entirely upon Yashin. He bore the pride and the burden of that thought each moment of his watch.

All his life, Yashin dreamed of being an officer on a war-fighting submarine like his famous father, a decorated first captain in the Russian fleet. He followed in his father's footsteps and graduated with highest honors from St. Petersburg Naval Institute, the nation's most prestigious academy. For his efforts, he earned a billet on the *Penza*, Russia's newest and most advanced submarine.

Like most junior officers, he was full of pride and ambition when he first came aboard seven months earlier, but he had no practical experience. He had been what American submariners called a NUB—a non-useful body. The senior enlisted officers and crew, guided by tradition and practice, knocked the sharp edges off the untested young academy graduate so that he could fit into the precise and demanding rhythms of a crowded fighting machine.

Over the course of a grueling regimen of work, study and more work, he moved from department to department, memorizing every circuit, air filter and emergency procedure in all areas of the boat. He was tested and harassed each step of the way by the enlisted grades, who knew much more than he did about communications, navigation, weapons systems, the nuclear reactor—even medical procedures.

This was no longer his father's Navy, with its poor training, faulty equipment and spoiled food. The Russian Federation submarine service was producing officers and crew every bit the equal of their American counterparts.

After several months of grueling work, Junior Lieutenant Yashin had finally proven he had the knowledge to serve anywhere on board in any emergency. He had earned his qualification from his commander and also his submariner's badge. But most important of all, he had earned the trust of his crew.

Humbled by his captain's final approval and confident in his newly acquired knowledge and skills, Yashin felt he had finally begun to measure up to his father's impeccable standard.

Yes, he told himself, someday he would command his own sub.

The junior sonarman sat at his station, headphones perched over his big ears, intently listening for any threat that might be approaching. The sonar computer was programmed to do the same work but the creativity and witchcraft of a human sonar operator at his station still couldn't be matched by electronic circuits and software algorithms.

Suddenly, the sonarman yawned violently.

"Sakarov!" Yashin said.

Red with embarrassment, Sakarov turned in his chair. "Sorry, Lieutenant. I don't know what's wrong with me."

Yashin's instinct was to rebuke the man. He couldn't have any of his crew falling asleep on his first command watch—or ever. What if the captain appeared? Yashin could lose his career right here and now.

But Yashin bit his tongue. "You need a cup of coffee?"

"No, Lieutenant, I'm fine." He turned back around to his station, clearly fighting the need to yawn again.

In truth, Yashin himself was fighting the urge to yawn. He felt tired, his mind clouding like a winter fog.

He caught sight of one of the pilots now yawning, raising his hand from the joystick to cover his mouth.

Of course, Yashin thought, everybody knows that yawning is contagious. His own urge became irresistible. He clenched his teeth so tightly, his jaw muscles flexed. He didn't dare yawn. Not now. Not in front of the men.

His eyes watered. He wiped them with the back of his hand and saw that the sonarman was sound asleep, his head resting on his station.

Panic shot up Yashin's spine. Was something wrong with the air?

He dashed over to the environmental controls station. His sudden movement caught the attention of the diving officer, a senior enlisted man named Grakov.

"Something wrong, Lieutenant?" Grakov said, himself yawning.

Yashin's eyes swept over the digital readouts. The air scrubber was functioning at one hundred percent capacity, oxygen levels were at 20.9 percent. Nitrogen and CO_2 levels were all normal. According to the gauges, the atmosphere was perfectly fine.

A sudden crash turned Yashin around. Sakarov was sprawled out on the deck, the headphones askew on his shaved head, the lips of his open mouth a startling blue. Others began to fall, crashing onto their stations or dropping to the deck.

Yashin felt light-headed, his breathing fast and shallow. He steadied himself on a railing, legs shaking.

He turned and stumbled toward the intercom to report an emergency to the captain.

He reached for the mic but never made it.

Brain damage and loss of consciousness can occur within three minutes of oxygen deprivation. After fifteen minutes, the victim dies.

But given the peak physical condition of the *Penza*'s eighty-six officers and crew, the automated software now controlling the boat was programmed to wait twenty minutes in order to ensure they were all dead and incapable of interfering with the next phase of the operation. The atmospheric readouts at the environmental control station still read normal.

It was a lie.

The *Penza* was Russia's latest and most advanced naval warship above or below the surface of the ocean, carrying a variety of autonomous underwater, surface and air vehicles. The engineers who designed the vessel relied heavily on highly sophisticated software to execute nearly all its functions. This was a nod to the reality of the demographic winter facing the Russian Federation; there simply weren't enough able-bodied men to crew all their subs and women were still banned from serving on them. The dependence on automated technologies also reduced the possibility of human error, the single greatest threat to any submarine.

But as the last twenty minutes had demonstrated, an overreliance on software generated unanticipated vulnerabilities.

The next set of automated instructions dove the submarine and its dead crew to its maximum operating depth of six hundred meters and slowed the boat to a near standstill. The *Penza*'s main computer activated the automated torpedo system and loaded its single Kanyon torpedo into its enormous launch tube.

Minutes later, the outer torpedo door opened and the Kanyon gently swam out.

As soon as the torpedo had safely cleared away, its nuclear-powered engine accelerated, driving the eighty-foot-long weapon to its operational depth of one thousand meters. It then proceeded at its full speed of seventy knots to its first preprogrammed waypoint. At this depth and speed and arrayed with a variety of sonar-defeating technologies—including the hull's next-generation hydrophobic coating—the Kanyon was untouchable.

With the massive torpedo successfully dispatched, the *Penza*'s autonomous algorithms programmed a new course and speed. Like the Kanyon, the submarine relied on uploaded underwater map coordinates along with sonar-driven collision avoidance and navigation systems. Within eighteen hours, the boat would dive to its near-crushing depth of twelve hundred meters to settle on an underwater shelf where it would remain entirely intact and operational should the need arise.

To conserve power, the lights were killed and the heat reduced to just above freezing to protect the electronics.

Lieutenant Yashin would forever stand his first and only command in a cold steel tomb far beneath the sea, his body and the bodies of his shipmates slowly rotting in the dark.

10

MONTERREY, MEXICO

Juan Cabrillo stood in the Tiltrotor's doorway hovering thirteen thousand feet above the city lights of Monterrey, his parachute and weapons secured.

The AgustaWestland 609 was the civilian version of the Marine Corps' Osprey. It was built like an airplane and able to fly like one, with its giant turboshaft prop engines located on the end of its wings. But those thundering engines could also be rotated so that it could fly—or in Juan's case, hover—like a helicopter.

Tonight wasn't the highest jump he ever made nor the first night jump.

But it was going to be a doozy. Like stepping off a cliff.

And falling for miles.

He turned his attention back to the live digital feed on the glass viz screen of his augmented-reality helmet. Three bikini-clad girls splashed around in the shimmering lights of the glass-bottom penthouse pool jutting ten feet beyond the edge of the building. The two men floating in the far end were clearly enjoying the show. One of the men was as big as an elephant seal.

"See one you like, Gomez?" Juan asked.

"I hope you're talking about the girls," Gomez said. "Not that I'm judging or anything."

As good as Gomez was behind the stick, tonight's operation posed its own particular flying challenges. Among them was the fact they were hovering over a megacity and trying not to draw attention to themselves. Local air traffic control was already trying to raise him.

"I figure five minutes tops before air traffic control dispatches a *federale* jet to check us out," Gomez said.

Juan studied the digital feed one last time to confirm. As interesting as the girls were, tonight's snatch and grab target was the corpulent drug lord lounging in the pool, Hugo Herrera. His bookish son, Víctor, wasn't deemed a threat and his role in the organization marginal according to their meager intel sources. It was his old man Hugo that ran the show.

An op like this could go wrong every which way. Doing it in a large foreign city added more complications, a night drop even more so. Juan's orders were to capture Hugo Herrera alive without causing diplomatic harm.

Juan was more concerned with the harm that an RPG, a rocket-propelled grenade, slamming into one of the AW engines would cause. Hence, the altitude.

And the jump.

The drone surveillance conducted by Linc and Raven earlier confirmed that neither Herrera nor his son was armed and only two body-guards were stationed outside near the pool, as they had observed in the past.

The plan was stupidly simple, Juan reminded himself.

Trust the plan.

To meet the mission parameters, the three-man team would neutralize all parties with flash-bangs as they parachuted onto the penthouse deck, then tranquilize anyone still moving, especially Hugo Herrera. Kinetic weapons—suppressed Glock 19s firing subsonic munitions—would only be used as a last resort. Gomez and the AW would arrive moments later. They'd harness the fat drug boss onto the hovering bird and vamoose out of there before the rest of Herrera's security team could react.

Once the fireworks started and the big rotors of the AW came roaring in, the most time Juan could hope for before the security on the lower floors would reach them was sixty seconds.

They rehearsed the entire operation—from helicopter parachute drop to helicopter exfil—until they got it down to just under three minutes if nothing went wrong.

And, of course, something would. Murphy's Law was immutable. So they planned contingencies and backups, doing the best they could to prepare for the unexpected. His team's ace in the hole was their ability to improvise under fire. Juan wasn't concerned.

He glanced back over to MacD. He wore his brand-new "toy" crossbow in a custom leg harness.

"How's it hanging, Mac?" Juan whispered into his molar mic.

"I so do hope you're referring to my crossbow. In that regard, I'm good to go. So is Brother Tom." He and Reyes were doing a last-minute equipment check.

"Chairman, *Oregon* just picked up a Fuerza Aérea Mexicana scramble order," Gomez reported on comms. "Looks like two F-5 interceptors will be heading our way."

The Northrop F-5 was a Vietnam-era relic but still perfectly capable of blowing them out of the sky. Juan glanced at his viz screen one more time. Herrera was still in play. It was now or never.

He glanced at Reyes and MacD, their faces hidden behind their visors. He could tell by their stance they were good to go.

Two war dogs straining on their leashes.

"Gentlemen, on me."

Juan turned, gripped the doorway handles and leaped into the void.

11

Look at that *cabrón*."

Lado Zazueta pointed at the digital image of Hugo Herrera in his rooftop pool. "He's a heart attack waiting to happen."

The Turkish-built Kargu-2 drone provided a live feed to the laptop screen. Its onboard, AI-driven facial recognition software identified Hugo Herrera, Víctor Herrera, the two security men and the three girls and automatically posted their photos on the screen sidebar for targeting.

The beardless technician checked the drone's battery charge on the monitor. "Eighteen minutes left until we have to recall." He was a robotics engineering graduate student at Universidad Nacional Autónoma de México, UNAM, in Mexico City working for Zazueta to pay off his father's gambling debts.

"Relax. We still have plenty of time."

Zazueta's quiet, even voice matched his average height and ordinary features though he was clearly in good shape beneath his loose clothing. He wore the kind of sleepy, uninterested face you see only in profile, sitting behind some small desk, in some unimportant government office.

It was the kind of face one forgets the moment it turns away—if one was even aware of it in the first place.

It had also been the last face that many people had seen before they died, sometimes horribly, with the smell of his mint-sweetened breath filling their nostrils.

It was the face of the most successful assassin in Herrera's organization and formerly his most trusted soldier. Zazueta was, in fact, the reason why *el gordo* had been able to seize power. The assassin had been his instrument of destruction, liquidating rival drug lords at his command.

Zazueta acquired many names and identities over the years but shed them like a molting snake after they had served their purposes. Herrera simply called him Z (which he pronounced "zee" like the Americans would), which was entirely coincidental. Herrera had no idea what Zazueta's true name really was. He called him Z, short for "El Zeta," because Zazueta had been one of their top *sicarios* years ago.

The assassin and his tech occupied one of the penthouse suites of a nearby hotel facing Herrera's building. Zazueta stepped out onto the balcony with his MilSpecs German binoculars and scanned the taller skyscraper. He couldn't see the top, but he caught an eyeful of Herrera's gigantic rear splayed against the glass.

Zazueta headed back into the suite and over to the screen.

He and the technician watched Hugo's son Víctor step out of the water and towel himself off, then make his way toward the penthouse suite, two of the girls padding behind him.

"Are we still ready?"

"Waiting for your order, sir."

He laid a hand on the technician's pencil-thin neck, pulling him close. "And you're certain this will work as planned?"

The technician thought he saw a glimmer of fear in Zazueta's unblinking eyes.

"Yes, sir, I'm certain."

Hugo Herrera ran a well-oiled machine with a top-notch security crew—the best that money could buy. The ex-military operators brought the kind of swagger and panache that tickled the fat man's ego. Over time, Zazueta found himself called to the armed *rancho* less and less, no longer enjoying Hugo's favor.

Well, there were others who appreciated his gifts.

Zazueta's problem was that Herrera's security organization had few flaws. It had proven impossible to get close enough to the gangster to kill him and still be able to get away. The Turkish kamikaze drone gave Zazueta his first legitimate opportunity to take down Herrera and survive.

But the assassin knew his Emerson. *When you strike at a king, you must kill him.* If this attack failed, he was a dead man. And he would die in the most unpleasant manner imaginable. If the drone missed, he would do himself a favor and put the barrel of a shotgun in his mouth.

Zazueta's grip tightened on the technician's neck.

"Do it—now!"

"Yes, sir."

The technician locked Hugo Herrera's enormous body in a target reticle on the screen and clicked the engage button.

Instantly the kamikaze drone plunged toward the penthouse pool.

"How long will it take from this altitude?" Zazueta asked.

"Sixty seconds."

Juan had jumped out of the hovering Tiltrotor and into the dark with his two-man team right behind him.

The digital altimeter on his viz screen spun like a roulette wheel as he plunged through the black. When the altimeter hit a thousand feet, he braced himself.

His chute unfurled, the cords snapped tautly as the straps grabbed at his chest and thighs.

Juan pulled the multi-shot flash-bang grenade launcher from his harness and aimed it at his targets below. Lightning cracked with an ear-splitting scream as each 40mm shell erupted.

The two guards dropped first, knocked out cold by the concussion, their weapons clattering to the terrazzo floor.

Hugo Herrera was climbing out of the pool when he was knocked out, falling backward into the water with an orca-sized splash. The young woman in the pool near him screamed and clutched her bleeding ears.

Víctor Herrera stood just inside the open sliding glass door of the penthouse suite with two of the women draped over his shoulders. The first rounds that took out the guards blinded him. But it was the next round that landed near him that shattered the slider glass into thousands of tiny pebbles and knocked the three of them to the ground, where they grabbed their ears in agony.

Juan's feet hit the penthouse deck first. His viz screen displayed Reyes' and MacD's in-person viewpoints as they touched down just behind him. MacD's targets were the two unconscious guards. Juan gave Hugo to Tom Reyes, who wanted that assignment badly—and it was the safest position of the three.

"Clock's ticking," Juan said. "Sixty seconds to go."

He shed his parachute and pulled out his pistols—his suppressed Glock in one hand, his tranq gun in the other. He charged toward the farthest targets, Víctor Herrera and the two girls. MacD raced over to the two guards, who were beginning to stir. Reyes dashed for the pool and jumped in.

MacD got to his targets first and shot both of them with tranquilizer darts. "Sleep tight, fellas," he said as he whipped out two pairs of plastic flex-cuffs and began zip-tying their limbs like trussed chickens.

Juan dashed into the penthouse with his tranq gun raised. He put one dart each into Víctor Herrera and the two girls. They were down and out seconds later. He holstered both guns as he glanced at his viz window showing Reyes standing in the pool and rolling the fat narco-boss into a harness for transport. The other girl out cold and cuffed.

We might just get away with this, Juan thought.

He knelt down by the young Herrera and reached for his flex cuffs.

The penthouse elevator dinged.

So much for sixty seconds.

"We've got company," Juan barked into his molar mic.

"ETA thirty seconds," Gomez said.

"Make it fifteen." Juan leaped to his feet, drawing his Glock as he rose. He didn't wait for the doors to open. Might as well make them poop their pantaloons, he thought as he fired his pistol, pounding 9mm rounds into the polished steel doors.

"Reyes?"

"Just trying to squeeze a hippo into a tutu," Reyes said.

"Shove an apple into his mouth and let's get out of here," Juan said.

MacD charged up next to Juan, crossbow up, just as the elevator doors slid open. Automatic rifles flashed inside, spraying outside wildly as Juan emptied his first mag into the elevator.

The two Herrera operators inside charged forward in bump helmets and Level IV heavy body armor—impervious to large-caliber rifle fire.

MacD's bolt dropped the first operator. An exposed human throat had no chance against a 435-grain arrow firing at four hundred ten feet per second.

Juan's volley of 9mm hollow-point bullets crashed into the other man's face, turning him into a corpse before he hit the plush carpet.

Juan and MacD turned and ran toward the pool, the thundering beat of the AW's tiltrotors coming on like a storm.

Juan's eyes fixed on Reyes, who was standing in the shallow end of the pool, one hand clenching Herrera's harness by the D-ring he would use to secure the obese drug lord to the rope hook now just a hundred feet above his head. The rotor wash churned the water around his thighs.

"Good job, Tom—"

The pool erupted, throwing rubble and plexiglass around like shrapnel.

The blast concussion knocked Juan sideways, but he somehow kept his balance. He stumbled forward past the debris of broken outdoor furniture toward the pool wreckage, splashing water with every step, the stench of burnt munitions in his nose.

He skidded to a stop at the edge of the remains of the pool. All that was left were the jagged shards jutting out like shark's teeth and the last of the water sloshing over the side. Linc's voice boomed in his comms.

"Chairman—status?"

"We're sideways up here. You and Raven exfil according to plan."

"Need backup?"

"Negative. Get a move on." Juan wouldn't risk any more casualties.

"Aye."

Juan charged over to the glass guardrail spidered by the blast, slipping on water mixed with blood as he ran. Cabrillo peered over the edge just in time to see the last of the torrential fall of water and debris raining down on the pavement far below. Brakes squealed and metal crunched as vehicles crashed into one another or were crushed by the falling wreckage.

His eyes searched frantically.

Reyes was somewhere down there, far below.

Gone.

"Juan!" MacD shouted as he grabbed Cabrillo by the shoulder and pulled him away.

Juan snapped out of his haze as the big Ranger dragged him toward the hovering Tiltrotor. Bullets shattered the remnants of guardrail glass behind them as they hooked their D-rings to the rope. The hurricane-force rotor wash scattered the broken pool furniture.

A minute later, they launched into the sky, twisting on the rope as the AW rose and banked, Gomez slamming the throttles to the stops.

Juan's stomach plunged into the bottom of his boots as they rocketed into the night sky, the flashing automatic rifles firing up at them from the rooftop far below.

He scanned the street as it fell away in a last vain search for Reyes' corpse.

What happened?

12

THE INDIAN OCEAN

O n the electromagnetic spectrum, he was invisible.

Archytas Katrakis stood on the bridge of his blacked-out vessel, the dim glow of red emergency lamps barely lighting the space. All topside incandescent lights were killed and active radar shut down to avoid detection by anyone monitoring. Two hours earlier, he shut down his AIS transceiver to eliminate his ship's identification signal, which also indicated its speed, direction and, most important, location. It was a violation of international law but tonight it was a matter of survival.

So, too, was his sixth-generation Russian electronic intercept system. Able to invade and control an opponent's system, his technician was able to change the radar readings of anyone attempting to find and track him, making his own ship disappear and spoofing phantom objects onto their screens as needed.

A blanket of shimmering stars glittered in the vast expanse above his 120-foot dry-cargo vessel. He would have preferred a new moon, but he hadn't set the calendar. At least the sliver of lunar light was muted by high clouds.

He needed the dark, especially now.

Underwater lights blazed like a sunken star beneath his hull as the dive crew completed its dangerous task. One mistake on their part might prove fatal to them all.

Getting caught certainly would.

At least the Russians only shot their enemies.

The GPS pickup location selected by Dr. Artem Petrosian—the mystery Russian traitor—was excellent. It was far from the busy shipping lanes that hugged the coasts of India and Africa where freighters and tankers streamed back and forth to the Persian Gulf and the Red Sea. The big industrial fishing vessels that crowded these waters didn't come out this far. A welcome respite for the marine life decimated by the ceaseless harvesting.

And yet, there it was. An Indian Navy frigate. Katrakis could barely see the outline of its superstructure in the distance.

"How far?"

"Five kilometers and closing," the first officer said, standing at the passive sonar display. Rather than sending out an active ping, the passive system merely listened for approaching targets. Judging by the vessel's twin-screw sound signature, his sonar technician—a retired NATO submarine officer and also his younger half brother—determined it was a Talwar-class frigate, a Russian-built vessel deployed by India's blue-water Navy.

The only luck Katrakis believed in was bad luck, which was why he expended such great efforts in preparation for any assignment, especially this one. A sharp-eyed Indian lookout with a pair of remarkable night vision lenses must have spotted them.

"Unidentified vessel, this is the Indian naval vessel *Tabar*. Repeat, this is the Indian naval vessel *Tabar*. Are you able to receive my radio transmission? Over." The male voice spoke perfect English but with a decided accent. This was the second time they had transmitted.

Katrakis admired the captain's seamanship. He could have easily avoided the dead boat in international waters, particularly if he was on a military mission of any importance. But the Indian captain likely thought his darkened vessel presented a seaborne hazard to any shipping traffic and was perhaps concerned that the crew aboard was imperiled.

Katrakis picked up his intercom mic and spoke in Greek to his chief engineer belowdecks.

"What's your status?"

"Divers are maneuvering the unit now."

As promised, the Kanyon was located at the exact GPS coordinates Petrosian had provided. It arrived on station at five hundred meters below the surface. After receiving a single coded ping from Katrakis' vessel, it emptied its ballast tanks and rose to thirty feet so that the Greek divers could secure it in a specially designed harness and lift the massive torpedo. Once it cleared the hull's underwater double doors, the torpedo would be locked into place in a customized hold and readied for its next launch. The doors and hold were lead-lined to prevent any possible detection of the Kanyon's nuclear power plant and warhead.

"How long until the Kanyon is secured and we're ready to proceed?"

"Two hours at most."

"You have one."

Katrakis killed the intercom and picked up the ship's radio mic. He switched to his Oxford University–trained English.

"INS *Tabar*, this is the commercial vessel *Mountain Star*. We receive your transmission. Over."

"*Mountain Star*, what is your situation?"

"We are making engine repairs. We should be underway shortly."

"Do you require assistance? We have excellent engineers on board."

"That will not be necessary. But thank you for the offer."

"Why is your AIS not broadcasting? That is a violation of international maritime law."

"We have had electrical issues. They are also being resolved."

Katrakis suddenly realized the Indian would wonder how he was transmitting now. "My radio is on battery power."

"What is the nature of your cargo?"

"Steel pipe. Oil field construction."

"What is your destination?"

Katrakis switched off his mic and swore. Clearly, this captain was suspicious. The Indian Navy had a reputation for killing pirates in international waters when threatened. He wondered if the Indians might even dare attempt to board his vessel if they deemed it to be a security concern.

Katrakis saw his first officer's eyes narrow in the dim red glow. He was concerned as well. The *Tabar* was still heading their way.

"Our destination is Muscat." That was a lie. Part of the fabricated AIS identification Katrakis was using included the fictional name *Mountain Star*. That's what the Indian captain would see when Katrakis powered on his AIS transceiver. As soon as they were out of *Tabar*'s radar range, he would switch to yet another false identity—and his true destination.

"We will approach your position and wait with your vessel until repairs are effected," the Indian captain said. "I would hate to leave you stranded out here."

"The offer is greatly appreciated, but we are well supplied and our mechanical situation is improving by the minute."

"I'll radio you when we are within one thousand meters—" The captain cut the transmission off sharply.

Katrakis swore again.

There was no telling what electronic or optical devices the *Tabar* might activate when closer. The Kanyon wasn't yet stored in its special hold. He had been assured that the Kanyon warhead emitted no nuclear radiation, but the nuclear reactor driving the torpedo's engine was another matter. He couldn't allow the Indian vessel to approach any closer. The only weapons he had on board were small arms along with a half dozen RPGs and two Russian Igla anti-aircraft missiles. Hardly enough to do any damage in a surprise attack against the Indian frigate. But the *Tabar* could sink his transport vessel with a single burst of its automatic deck gun.

Bad luck indeed.

"Where's our last drone?" Katrakis asked his first officer.

"Last known position was approximately two hundred forty kilometers from here."

Katrakis made a quick calculation. It would take the frigate at least five hours to arrive at the drone's location. More than enough time to finish loading the Kanyon, change his AIS profile and get underway.

Katrakis picked up his encrypted satellite phone and punched the preset number.

One hundred fifty miles away, a small drone floating in the ocean like flotsam received a coded satellite signal. The miniature vessel looked like a solar-paneled skateboard and was equipped with both an emergency radio broadcasting unit and an AIS transceiver identifying it as an Indonesian oil tanker.

When the satellite signal from Katrakis was received, the drone immediately responded by sending out an emergency distress call, reporting an explosion, fire and imminent loss of life.

"The Indian's turning," his cousin said, smiling, his hands cupped around his earphones. "At a high rate of speed."

"What happens when his radar doesn't confirm the sinking vessel?" the first officer asked. "He'll be beyond our spoofing range."

Katrakis nodded to the electronic intercept technician sitting at his station next to the sonar operator.

"What do you say to that, Stefanos?"

The operator's keyboard clacked beneath his swift moving fingers. He swiveled around in his chair. With his thick, shoulder-length black curly hair and full beard, he looked every inch the Spartan warrior painted on an ancient amphora. All he lacked was the helmet and spear.

"The Indian already thinks he has a radar problem because we didn't show up on his screen. He'll proceed to the location anyway—it's an emergency distress signal. When he arrives, he won't find a burning hulk, but they'll do a search of the area for survivors just to be sure. I also planted a worm in his mainframe that will shut his radar and comms completely down in"—the operator checked his Apple

Watch—"five hours and thirty-nine minutes. He'll get back to base as fast as he can to get them repaired."

"Satisfied?" Katrakis asked.

The first officer smiled at his boss. "Who needs luck when we have you?"

Katrakis nodded, acknowledging the compliment. He had dropped three such drones at various points along the way for just such a contingency. Unfortunately, he had no tricks to overcome what waited for them at the next crucial juncture. The sooner they got there, the better.

He turned toward the helmsman.

"Plot a course for Istanbul. I want to be underway the minute the Kanyon is secured."

13

THE GULF OF MEXICO

The *Oregon* sailed into the sunrise at twenty knots, less than a third of its maximum speed. There wasn't any point in drawing attention to themselves.

Juan stood on the fantail, lost in thought. The churning wake roiled the green-gray water behind them, leaving a trail that stretched to the far horizon. He took another long pull on his Dominican Cohiba. The heavy wooden tang of cigar smoke lingered in his mouth before he let it escape, wafting away in the breeze like a fleeing ghost. He and Tom had shared one the day he came on board. Smoking one now in his honor seemed the thing to do before the debrief.

Tom Reyes' death shook him. What should have been a moment of personal triumph for the man turned into an inexplicable tragedy. Whoever planted that bomb in or beneath the pool hadn't targeted his team. But Tom Reyes was the one who paid the price for Herrera's assassination.

And that meant whoever killed Tom needed to be paid back. In full.

Juan was angry. But he didn't blame himself. He never second-guessed his decisions—outcomes were never guaranteed in life and especially not in a high-kinetic environment.

They had done their pre-mission surveillance. The penthouse was the only opportunity to snatch the drug lord and poolside was the only option to grab him while there. Locked up tight inside the penthouse suite, they had no chance to get him without blowing the house down and quite likely killing Herrera in the process.

The team had also practiced a variety of scenarios and every member cross-trained for everyone else's role. They had prepared as well as was humanly possible.

The plan was treacherous for sure, but less crazy than a hundred other successful missions he had pulled off in the past. But fate also has a plan.

And fate usually wins.

Still, Juan ordered a debrief. It always paid to go over any op but especially the ones that went toes up. Failure always taught the most important lessons.

At least Tom's remains had been recovered—stolen, actually, when one of Overholt's cleaner teams climbed into the coroner's ambulance and drove away with him. His body was already on its way back to California. He would be buried with honors, according to his family's wishes, as soon as the arrangements Juan would pay for could be made.

Small comfort to Tom's family, he was sure, but at least they would have some kind of closure.

Over the whining roar of the Tiltrotor's turbines in the cabin, Juan reported the mission outcome to Overholt while still en route to the *Oregon*. Everything in Cabrillo wanted revenge for his friend's death. But Overholt made it clear that they needed to evacuate the area immediately. The local officials were already blaming the American government for the attack. It was a diplomatic disaster in the making.

Juan had to choose between finding Tom's killers or fulfilling his contract—which included keeping a low profile and off the Mexican government's radar, literally and figuratively. The cartel gunmen on the roof had seen the Tiltrotor, but at least the cameras had all been fried. The AW690 was such a new model that they likely wouldn't be able to identify it—and certainly it had no markings. The unusual hybrid air-craft was probably the reason why the Americans were being blamed.

Cabrillo finally decided to bug out, in part, because Overholt's advice to stand down and see how things shook out was tactically sound. It was likely Herrera was the victim of a rival cartel and now his organization would be absorbed or destroyed.

"Whoever was behind this will eventually be revealed," Overholt said. "And I promise you, when we find out who was behind it, you'll be the first to know."

That satisfied Cabrillo. Overholt was an old-school fieldman from back in the day when eye for an eye was a code of honor. His seasoned mentor was promising Juan his revenge—delayed for now for the sake of American national interest but not denied for the sake of a fallen comrade.

And Juan was a patient man when he needed to be.

He checked his watch, took a last drag on his cigar and tossed it into the sea.

Time for the debrief.

The sat phone on his hip trilled. It was Overholt.

"Lang, what's up?"

"Juan, my boy. I'm sure it's too much to ask but something's come around the bend if you and your crew are up to it."

Juan felt his pulse quicken. He was worse than a retired police dog when it heard a gunshot in the distance.

"Name it."

"Come see me in Istanbul and we'll talk."

14.

MEXICO

The sprawling hacienda stood in the shadow of Sierra San Miguel looming in the distance some twenty-five miles northwest of Monterrey. A recently constructed concrete-block wall surrounded the residential complex of buildings including the main house. Cattle grazed beyond the wall on a thousand acres of sparse, rolling hills beneath a sweltering sun.

The black armored SUV pulled to a stop at the gate. The driver lowered his window and flashed his ID at the guard. The big Russian mercenary, sheathed in body armor, gripped a full-auto UZI Pro pistol in one gloved hand and a wireless tablet in the other. The two men knew each other well, but this was a necessary precaution—the hacienda was on high alert after the killing of the boss, Hugo Herrera. Security cameras recorded everything. Failure to adhere to standard operating procedures resulted in severe punishment.

The Russian nodded to the blackened window behind the driver. The window lowered. The Russian checked his tablet. The face matched. He waved the SUV through the gate.

The vehicle traversed the circular driveway beneath the unblinking gaze of still more security cameras. It pulled to a stop beneath the brightly tiled porte cochere. Four more security guards, kitted out and gunned up, stood at the doorway.

One of them approached the rear passenger's door, tablet in hand. A second followed behind him with a metal-detecting wand. A third checked the undercarriage of the vehicle for bombs with an inspection mirror.

The rear window lowered again. The first guard confirmed the ID facially and opened the door.

"Señor Herrera is waiting for you," the guard said in German-accented Spanish.

Zazueta the assassin stepped out of the vehicle.

"Thank you."

He held up his arms as the second guard wanded him. The guard holstered his wand and then frisked Zazueta roughly from ankles to collarbone with ungloved hands. Satisfied, the guard reported to his commander in a braying Saxon accent that the passenger was clean.

The first guard looked Zazueta up and down. He thought the older man looked just about as dangerous as a railroad clerk. Still, orders were orders.

"Follow me."

Zazueta nodded deferentially and did.

The guard led Zazueta into the cool inside the hacienda's thick adobe walls and across plush handwoven carpets and blue lace Sevilla tiles to the main study. The violins and organ of Albinoni's Adagio in G Minor mourned faintly behind a pair of heavy wooden doors.

The guard outside the study was an Austrian. His clear gray eyes examined Zazueta, searching for any telltale signs of nervousness or deceit. Finding none, he exchanged a few words with his escort. Zazueta's German was rusty but good enough to glean that he had already been cleared to see the new boss of the Herrera organization. The Austrian opened one of the doors just as the strings swelled in crescendo and the Austrian guard led Zazueta in.

Hand-carved bookshelves lined every wall and heavy antique furniture imported from Europe filled the space, darkened by the closed curtains. Víctor Herrera sat in an overstuffed wingback chair, his tented fingers covering his face, lost in thought. He didn't look up when the door opened.

"Excuse me, sir. Señor Zazueta to see you," the guard reported.

Herrera looked up with dark, sad eyes. He hadn't slept since the events of the previous evening. An open bottle of twenty-three-year-old Pappy Van Winkle stood on the low table in front of him along with a pair of crystal lowball glasses. Herrera nodded and stood with a sigh. He forced a smile for his father's old friend.

"Lado, thank you for coming."

"Don Víctor, I am so terribly sorry," Zazueta said. "He was a great man and a great leader." He stepped toward Herrera, but the guard grabbed him by the shoulder, stopping him.

Herrera waved a dismissive hand. The guard released his grip.

Zazueta approached.

The two men embraced.

"How may I serve you?" Zazueta said. "Anything at all. Just ask."

"My father's murder must have hurt you almost as much as it hurt me."

"Perhaps even more," Zazueta offered. "He was both a brother and a father to me."

That elicited a genuine smile, however small, from Herrera.

"We must find my father's killers," Herrera said. He turned toward the guard. "Do you hear me? Find them!"

The German nodded. "We are on the hunt, sir, but it will take time."

Herrera grunted dismissively. "Leave us."

"Sir?" The guards were under strict orders to protect the new boss at all costs. He eyed the middle-aged man one more time. Despite the pleasant smile, there was something unsettling about Zazueta's insipid gaze.

Herrera laid a heavy hand on Zazueta's shoulder as he spoke. "This man is my father's oldest friend. I value his wisdom and loyalty and consider him my friend as well. *Verstehen Sie?*"

The German nodded. "Sir." He turned and left, closing the door behind him.

Herrera pointed to the six-thousand-dollar bottle of American bourbon on the table.

"Won't you join me?"

"Delighted," Zazueta said.

The first graceful piano notes of the first movement of Beethoven's
Moonlight Sonata stepped tenderly out of the hidden stereo speakers.
Herrera picked up the remote and increased the volume, then poured
Zazueta a glass and refilled his own.

He handed it to the older man and the two of them prepared to toast.

Zazueta glanced around the room.

"I swept for bugs myself not an hour ago. We're quite alone."

"Excellent." Zazueta lifted his glass. "To your father."

Herrera lifted his. "The king is dead." He smiled. "May he burn in a
thousand Hells."

"One is quite enough, I would imagine. Long live the new king."

Their glasses touched.

They sipped their bourbons.

Herrera waved Zazueta to another overstuffed chair as he resumed
his. The two men sat contentedly, sipping the expensive liquor, savoring
the moment. Young Herrera had taken the reins of his father's empire
thanks to Zazueta's handiwork.

Víctor Herrera had long appreciated Zazueta's skill set and noted his
father's foolish neglect not utilizing it. He was happy to nurture the
assassin's growing resentment and secured his loyalty by offering him
the honors due for his long service to the family.

Having put the rook in place, it was only a matter of time before he
would checkmate his father. That time came when Hugo rejected David
Hakobyan's offer to quadruple their drug business by supplying the
Armenian's pipeline into Europe.

As far as Víctor was concerned, if his father was too stupid to see the
brilliance of the move, then he was too stupid to live.

As if reading his mind, Zazueta said, "Hakobyan's drone worked
perfectly. You've made an excellent partnership."

"We must inform the paranoid Armenian his first shipment is ready for transport." Herrera took another sip. "It's ridiculous he doesn't use an encrypted phone. Face-to-face meetings are a waste of valuable time."

"I'm leaving for Glendale tonight. He will be pleased to see me." Zazueta had formed a kind of friendship with the Armenian over the years. Another meeting with good news would only strengthen that bond—and lower his suspicions.

"And remind him that he promised us more drones. I have a number of ideas about how I want to use them."

"I believe they are already in transit."

"What news on last night's attack?" Víctor's bodyguards filled him in on what little they knew after he awoke from the tranquilizer dart hours before. But details were sketchy at best. "Did I hear correctly that one of the guards was killed with an arrow from a crossbow?"

"Yes. It's actually quite an effective weapon in a stealth scenario."

"Sounds medieval. I like it." Herrera laughed into his glass as he took another sip. "What else do we know about these assaulters?"

"Your security team identified the aircraft as a Tiltrotor of unknown design. Eyewitnesses on the ground said they saw and heard a helicopter. Unfortunately, all our digital security cameras failed—most likely jammed by the assaulters. I suspect the same will be true of all other cameras in the area."

"Americans, obviously."

"Most likely. But I'm trying to confirm it with my sources in the American intelligence community. We were fortunate, certainly. The local *policía* don't know who to blame for the attack. They're calling it a bombing because our people inside their organization are telling them that."

Herrera leaned back, smiling with satisfaction. "It's perfect. We killed him but the Americans get all the blame." He searched Zazueta's face. "It worked out so well, I almost think you planned it that way."

Zazueta shook his head. "I wish I were that smart. Trust me, I was as shocked as *el jefe* when the operators suddenly dropped onto the deck with their chutes."

"Let's not wait for confirmation. We need to reach out to our friends in the media and tell them that this was definitely an American attack—no, an invasion of Mexican soil."

Zazueta paused, thinking. "I wonder if it might be better to blame the Cortez syndicate instead."

"Why?"

"If we anger the Americans, they might get more interested in our affairs. If your father was the target and he's now eliminated, perhaps they'll move on to other things—including those *pendejo* Cortez brothers."

"No. I prefer to blame the Americans. We can whip up public opinion against the gringos easily enough. That will get El Presidente involved and he'll keep the Americans at bay."

Zazueta nodded, impressed with the logic.

"When does phase two begin?" Herrera asked. He was referring to the assassination of his benefactor, Hakobyan.

Weeks earlier, Sokratis Katrakis had reached out to Herrera and offered an irresistible opportunity. "Kill Hakobyan, deal directly with me and I'll double your profits."

Herrera cared nothing for the Armenian. As far as he was concerned, Hakobyan was merely the conduit that led him to a greater reward, the way a mother bird might unwittingly reveal the location of her nest of eggs to a hungry snake.

"As soon as the drone shipment arrives, it shall be arranged."

"I leave all the details to you."

"The Greek will make you very rich very fast."

"You mean, he'll make both of us very rich very fast." He lifted his half-empty glass. "You and I are partners, Lado."

Zazueta lifted his glass. "I'm grateful, Don Víctor."

Víctor smiled. Don Víctor. He liked the sound of that.

He drained the rest of his glass and poured another for the two of them.

Long live the king!

15

ISTANBUL

Meliha Öztürk was a modern woman in every sense of the word.

She was a lone female navigating one of the poorest neighborhoods in Istanbul infamous for its roving gangs of jittery teenagers high on glue, flashing their purse-snatching knives. The air stank of fetid garbage, restaurant grease and exhaust fumes. Angry car horns blared on crowded, narrow streets as forlorn horns of boats echoed across the wide Bosporus Strait nearby.

Istanbul was one of the most beautiful cities in the world. Soaring minarets, gleaming skyscrapers, thriving outdoor markets and the best food in the world reflected the melding of millennia of cultures, religions and peoples. It was a place of incredible contrasts—weathered marble mosques and mirror glass buildings, prayer beads and cell phones, spit-roasted lamb and sushi. She loved this city like no other.

Except for this neighborhood. Even the most gorgeous runway models had blemishes they preferred to hide.

She wasn't afraid in this place, merely cautious. She'd crawled through the rubble of the hottest war zones in Syria, Libya and Iraq, dodging bullets cracking overhead, to chase stories while being hunted by killers, both in and out of uniform.

She survived all that and more by being smart—and as invisible as possible. It wasn't easy. She was a beautiful young woman. And, right now, she was walking down narrow streets in a dangerous neighborhood near the harbor. She hid her lustrous brown hair beneath a headscarf and her strong, athletic figure in loose clothes that covered every inch of skin except her face and hands. She avoided looking anyone in the eye, particularly the men leering at her from shadowed doorways, smoking cigarettes and killing time. She kept her shoulders back and her chin up as she searched for the address while keeping a sly, careful watch for any agents from MİT, the Turkish intelligence agency, who might be following her.

She ran a surveillance detection route, just as her father had taught her, all the way from her home and across the city until she reached this sad, sorry enclave of poverty and despair. Her clear green eyes searched the reflections in shop windows and car mirrors for anyone walking and stopping like she was. She cut ninety degrees across busy streets to change her point of view and at times turned around to examine fruit or a pair of shoes just to throw off any potential threat. It was the anomalies she was watching for, the unexpected, awkward moves of strangers like herself in a neighborhood none of them belonged in.

She was reasonably confident that she hadn't been followed. But MİT operatives were experts in surveillance and they knew all those tricks as well as the means to defeat them.

No matter. Her life was not her own but God's.

She made her way down one street in a particular state of ruin and disrepair. Windows were barred and the walls scarred with graffiti. She was surprised the American wanted to meet her here. She began to wonder if he had given her the wrong address by mistake.

After making sure no one was watching her, she stopped inside the portal of a locked doorway and checked her GPS map. She was close.

She turned onto the next narrow street and saw a beggar sitting on the sidewalk, his back against the sooty wall of a three-story building that had seen better days. An old wooden crutch lay next to him on the pavement along with a bundle of rags. Even from a distance she could see he was missing part of his leg.

She tried not to stare as she approached, but he was sitting on the corner where she was about to turn again. His black trousers were stained and his right pant leg was knotted shorter above the partially missing limb. His tattered shirt strained against the enormous gut bulging beneath it. His face was covered in blistering scabs and his monstrous nose was veined and crusted with mucus. Long, greasy black hair tumbled onto his broad shoulders. One of his large hands held up a Styrofoam cup and rattled the few coins inside. He muttered in Arabic for alms and for mercy, his whited, blind eyes upturned to an indifferent sky.

She shuddered at the sight of him as she turned the corner onto a small, crooked alley that led to a dead end. She took three steps and stopped. She reached beneath the folds of her dress as she returned to the street and dropped her last heavy coins into the cup. The man's face broke into a broad smile that flashed stained and missing teeth. He showered blessings on her as she turned and sped away.

Meliha made her way past battered garbage cans buzzing with flies, her feet crunching on the broken glass around them. Up ahead, she saw a rusted steel door spray-painted red with the number seven—the same number as the address given to her. She picked up her pace and approached the door. There wasn't any doorbell or knocker, so she pounded on it with the heel of her fist.

Nothing.

She turned back around. The beggar shook his cup at a man passing by who ignored him.

A heavy lock thunked on the other side of the door and it opened.

But nobody was there.

She stepped inside.

Meliha was shocked at what she saw.

She expected a run-down tenement apartment or a homeless shelter.

Instead, she stood beneath a coffered ceiling in a wood-paneled living room beautifully appointed with furnishings as fine as any banker's home in Istanbul. The air was sweet with cinnamon incense, the floors covered with handwoven rugs of the highest quality.

"My dear girl, you finally made it. I was getting worried."

The American behind the door stood in the shadows so as not to be seen from the alleyway. He ushered her farther in with a wave of his manicured hand and shut the door behind them with a clang.

The man was tall and lean in his perfectly tailored linen suit and polished oxfords. His snow-white hair was trim and precise and his eyes as bright as his welcoming smile. Only the fineness of his parchment-thin skin and the small wrinkles on his clean-shaven face hinted at his advanced age.

"It's good to finally meet you in person, Mr. Overholt."

"In person is so much more civilized. I so do hate Zoom. But I'm old-fashioned that way. Please, come sit."

He steered her toward one of the great tufted-silk couches.

"Tea? Coffee? Something livelier?"

"Coffee, thank you."

"No one followed you, I trust."

"No one. But there was a beggar outside—"

Overholt waved a hand dismissively. "There's always a beggar underfoot in this part of town." Standing next to a large, ornately crafted ceramic samovar he began to prepare two cups of Turkish coffee.

"Mr. Overholt, we have so much to discuss."

"We certainly do."

The steel door thundered beneath the weight of a meaty fist hammering on it. Overholt set his cup down.

"Excuse me for a moment." He crossed over to the door and opened it.

The blind beggar stood in the doorway, wobbling uneasily on his crutch.

Overholt bowed his head slightly and touched his right hand to his chest and then his forehead—the gesture meaning *salaam*—as he stepped aside.

The beggar returned the greeting uneasily, then hobbled past him down a hallway with the bundle of rags strapped to his back. He disappeared behind an interior door as Overholt shut and locked the front door.

Meliha stood, utterly confused.

"That was the beggar I told you about."

Overholt smiled. "Was it?"

16

Zazueta hid his disgust over the small dog in Hakobyan's lap. The Yorkshire terrier stared at him through rheumy eyes glazed with cataracts, its tongue lolling out of its toothless mouth. The tiny diaper it wore crinkled as the dog shifted around, trying to get comfortable.

Zazueta was surprised that the fastidious Armenian would have a dog like this. Hakobyan's modest, three-bedroom rancher was spotless, the white patterned wool carpet throughout pristine and the air thick with the pungent odor of Pine-Sol liberally applied by his Guatemalan cleaning lady. Even the gold brocade couch he sat on was covered with clear plastic. The home office they sat in was as perfectly organized as his polished cherrywood desk.

Hakobyan read his mind.

"JoJo was my wife's dog," he said, rubbing its matted head. "He's older than Methuselah. He's my last living connection to her. I don't know how much longer he'll be with me and I don't know what I'll do without him."

"Dogs are better than most people," Zazueta said. "Fine companions, too."

"I don't trust a man who doesn't like dogs."

"I couldn't agree more." Zazueta's stomach soured as he watched the dog's drool ooze onto Hakobyan's hand.

Zazueta looked past him through the large plate glass window. A half acre of apricot trees stood in neat rows behind the house.

Hakobyan followed his eyeline. He turned around, then faced him again, smiling. "Do you know where apricots came from?"

Zazueta shrugged. "No, sir. No idea at all."

"*Prunus armeniaca* is the scientific name. 'Armenian plum.' We've been cultivating them for three thousand years. Legend has it that Noah brought it down from the Ark after he landed on Mount Ararat. My wife loved them. I bought this place for her just because of the trees."

"She must have been a wonderful woman."

"The light of my life . . ." Hakobyan's voice trailed off.

"Death is not the end."

"Are you a religious man, Lado?"

"Not especially. More like an optimist."

"Well, let us speak of better things. After all, we have much to celebrate today."

"Yes, we do."

Zazueta's eyes fell on the big olive green IBM Selectric typewriter on the shelf behind Hakobyan's desk. It was a model from the seventies, but it looked as if it had just been unboxed fresh from the factory. He knew all about it because his father, a government clerk, slaved for years behind one just like it. He and Hakobyan had even talked about it in the past. It still worked well, Hakobyan said. He used it for typing errand and grocery lists. "In Armenian, of course."

Hakobyan was a true Luddite. But also brilliant.

In the years since he'd gotten to know him, Zazueta developed a healthy respect for the man's computerlike brain. The Armenian ran his lucrative enterprises without computers, cell phones or even paper. Hakobyan had a perfect, eidetic memory. That meant there were never any electronic or paper trails to be followed by FBI or DEA forensic accountants and therefore no arrests. Hakobyan remembered every date, every meeting and every transaction to the last penny, centavo or luma. He forgot nothing, including petty insults. Crimes against his person and his family were unforgivable and always dealt with severely through other parties. He was as ruthless as he was brilliant.

"Dessert is served."

A deep, gravelly voice spoke from the office doorway. It was Hakobyan's driver, Gevorg, who also served as his bodyguard. He'd done so since the eighties. Nearly seventy himself, the big Armenian was built like a mountain, though most of the bulging muscles had run to fat over the years. He wore an apron to protect his tailored shirt and silk tie as he carried a silver tray with hand-painted demitasse cups and pastry on matching dishes and set it on the desk.

Hakobyan smiled. "Here's good Armenian *soorj* and *paklava* for us to enjoy."

Zazueta leaned forward. The cups were filled with dark coffee capped with an earthy foam. It looked just like Turkish coffee, but he knew better than to call it that. Gevorg set up a small TV tray in front of Zazueta and put a napkin and silverware on it.

"I'm not familiar with this dish."

"The Greeks mistakenly call it *baklava*. They also don't make it as good as we do."

"My mouth is already watering."

"We serve *soorj* and *paklava* when we have something to celebrate."

Gevorg set a cup of Armenian coffee and a plate of *paklava* in front of him.

Hakobyan pinched a piece of *paklava* and mashed it between his fingers, then smeared the gooey paste onto JoJo's runny nose.

Zazueta had observed Hakobyan's set routines over the years as they had done business together. He'd also taken note of Gevorg's routines, equally predictable.

The big goon wore a tailored suit every day but took the coat off inside the house. He carried a heavy steel Colt .45 in a well-oiled leather Galco shoulder holster that he wore even now. He also swept the entire house for bugs once a week with a handheld RF, a radio frequency detector, on aching, arthritic knees. He ran errands as needed, mostly to a local Armenian market that carried items from the old country and fresh baked goods that Hakobyan favored.

He also took a thirty-minute nap in the spare bedroom every afternoon at two o'clock.

When Gevorg drove Hakobyan to his doctors' appointments around town, he squeezed his big frame behind the wheel of a 1986 Mercedes 240D with some three hundred thousand miles on the odometer. Gevorg arrived each morning promptly at nine a.m. and left for his own home on the other side of Glendale at five p.m. sharp, taking the Mercedes with him for cleaning, gas and maintenance. For all his brilliance, Hakobyan had never learned to drive.

A blind man could see that the bodyguard had lost his edge over the years. But Zazueta knew a killer when he saw one. If the big man were ever roused to action, he'd be dangerous, arthritic knees and all.

"Come, my boy. Drink the coffee while it's hot."

Zazueta took a sip. It was dark, smoky and sweet.

"This is excellent."

"You like it?"

"I never had better."

The old man grinned, obviously delighted.

Zazueta observed Gevorg in his peripheral vision looming in the far corner of the room, glowering at him, his meaty hands clasped in front of his enormous gut.

Zazueta took a bite of his pastry. The phyllo dough melted in his mouth, soaked with sweet honey and roasted nuts.

He hoped the challenge of killing Hakobyan would prove equally delicious.

17

Fifteen minutes later, Juan Rodriguez Cabrillo emerged from behind the door, no longer a begrimed street beggar covered in sores and hobbling on a crutch. A quick, hot shower with soap and brushes scrubbed away the prostheses and glue. His folded ragged costume, fake hair and props lay on the bathroom bench; the white translucent contact lenses and dental appliances had been returned to their cases.

Once again, Kevin Nixon's special effects wizardry in the *Oregon*'s Magic Shop had transformed him into an unrecognizable creature. But props were only half the battle. In another life, Juan could've been an actor. He committed more deeply to his undercover roles than any thespian because, more often than not, his life and mission depended on it.

He stepped into the living room with an easy, athletic gait where Meliha and Overholt sat sipping hot Turkish coffee. Though in his forties, Juan was still in top condition, with broad shoulders, tapered waist and chiseled legs, swimming daily in the Olympic-length lap pool located in one of the ship's long ballast tanks. A tight-fitting athleisure shirt and slacks complemented his powerful build. Juan's body bore the scars of many battles, but he always wore an incongruous smile no matter the hardship because he loved his life and loved living it to the fullest.

He saw Meliha's eyes widen with surprise. And interest.

The attraction was mutual.

Overholt stood. Meliha remained on the couch.

Juan stepped over and extended his hand to her. She took it firmly.

Juan liked a firm handshake.

"Juan Cabrillo, I'd like you to meet our new friend, Meliha Öztürk."

"It's a pleasure, Ms. Öztürk." Juan dug into his front pocket and pulled out the fistful of coins Meliha had generously dropped into his Styrofoam cup. "I believe these are yours."

She shook her head, smiling. "You keep it. You earned it with that performance. I thought you were the most pitiful man I'd ever seen." She nodded at his legs. "Last time I counted, you had only one."

Juan glanced down at his pant leg and pulled it up, revealing a pros-thetic limb that extended from the knee down, fashioned out of carbon fiber and titanium—just one of several models he used, also designed by Kevin Nixon.

"I kept this thing hidden in the bundle. One of those street kids nearly stole it."

"Were the theatrics really necessary?" Meliha asked.

"Langston and I just wanted to be extra-careful with your security."

"I've been on the MİT watch list for two years now. I know how to take care of myself."

"No doubt." Turkey's infamous national intelligence organization was nobody to fool around with.

Juan snapped his fingers. "Wait . . . Öztürk . . . Are you related to Dr. Kemal Öztürk?"

"My father. You know of him?"

"His arrest made international news. I'm sorry he's still imprisoned."

"So am I."

"That's partly why we're here today," Overholt said. He steered Juan toward the couches as he poured him a coffee. "Have a seat."

Juan sat and took the cup from Overholt. His favorite coffee in the world was the Cuban pour-over his chefs served on the *Oregon*, but stout Turkish coffee over sugar cubes with cardamon came in a close second.

"Have you been to Turkey before, Mr. Cabrillo?" Meliha asked.

"Many times. It's a beautiful country and the people warm and welcoming."

His admiration was genuine. What he didn't tell her was that the last time he was in Istanbul, he and Jerry Pulaski drank themselves stupid in a dive bar not six blocks from there. Jerry had long since died on a mission, gutshot in a remote Argentine jungle.

Juan smiled. "I have good memories of this city."

Overholt poured another coffee for himself and took a seat.

"You're both wondering why I invited the two of you here today, but in a moment I think you'll see the method to my madness."

He turned toward Meliha. "Let me start by introducing Juan more formally. He and I are old colleagues. I first recruited him into the Company out of college. The lad was smart as a whip and the best field agent I ever worked with."

Juan hid his surprise. It wasn't like his old boss to spill family secrets to strangers. Either he'd gone soft in his dotage or he really trusted this woman. Or . . . he was really trying to earn her trust. Juan followed his lead.

"If I had any success, it was because you're the one who trained me, Lang."

"Without getting into details, suffice to say that Mr. Cabrillo is no longer an employee of the American government. He's now an independent contractor who runs an organization known as the Corporation."

Meliha turned toward Juan. "In other words, you're a mercenary." Her voice dripped with cynicism.

"I prefer 'privateer,' but yeah, that works."

"Because of our long-standing relationship, Mr. Cabrillo and I have worked together on a number of projects of mutual interest to himself and the United States over the years. There's no one I trust more than him and his valiant crew."

"You mean, he does the dirty jobs the American government doesn't want to get blamed for," Meliha said.

"Couldn't have said it better myself." Juan chuckled. He liked this woman's moxie. "And the pay's better."

"You'll have to excuse my bluntness, Mr. Cabrillo. It's an occupational hazard."

"Please, call me Juan. And I'm guessing your occupation has something to do with investigations—a journalist, if I had to bet."

"You're quite correct. My father was a career diplomat with postings in Greece, Eastern Europe and Germany—"

"Ms. Öztürk is fluent in five languages," Overholt said, interrupting. "Quite impressive."

Meliha ignored the compliment. "Given my background, I was drawn to journalism. For a time, I worked for *Die Zeit*, but now I'm independent, writing on Substack."

"Quit or fired?" Juan asked.

"I raised too many difficult questions affecting the governments of the NATO alliance. My editors tried to shield me, but in the end it was the paper or me, so they let me go."

"What kinds of questions?"

"Mostly corruption but also criminal enterprises. They're connected, of course."

"And Substack lets you write about anything you want without anybody looking over your shoulder?"

Juan was familiar with the online subscriber platform. Some of the best reporters and editors in the world had found a home there.

"Correct. At least no publisher is looking over my shoulder. I now have others who are doing that."

"You mean MİT," Juan said. "They're brutal."

"As my father has learned every day for the past year." Meliha fought back the tears clouding her eyes.

"I'm sorry," Juan said, "but I don't recall why he was arrested."

She smiled bitterly. "He was arrested for telling the truth. President Toprak's people charged him with the crimes of defaming the Office of the President and libel against the military. He's still awaiting trial while so-called evidence is being gathered."

"And what, exactly, did he say?"

"My father spoke out against the foreign wars that Toprak is waging illegally all over the region. Specifically, he reported on several civilian massacres carried out by ISIS mercenaries under Turkish command. The government denied it all, of course, and arrested him when he spoke out."

Overholt tipped the last of his coffee into his mouth and set the cup down on the burnished walnut table. "Dr. Öztürk is one of the leading lights of the Turkish democracy movement and Ms. Öztürk has followed in his footsteps as both an investigative journalist and human rights activist. The American government is concerned for both of them—and for all the Turkish people."

"And by 'American government,' you mean the CIA?" Juan asked.

"Higher than that. President Grainger herself has taken a deep personal interest in the Turkish situation. She believes that a democratic Turkey would be a less dangerous country. She considers the fate of Dr. Öztürk—and by extension, Turkey—to be a matter of vital national interest."

Juan set his empty cup on the table next to Overholt's. He sat back and crossed his arms against his thick chest. "That explains why POTUS is coming to Istanbul next week to meet with President Toprak."

"At the NATO defense ministers' summit," Meliha added. "It's going to be live-streamed on every major international social media platform. The whole world will be watching."

"President Grainger's meet and greet with Mr. Toprak is partly the reason why I'm in Istanbul," Overholt said. "I'm something of an advance man scouting the situation out. But I'm also here to set up meetings much like this one."

"I've never met the President. They say she's all that and a bag of chips."

"She is indeed one of the most remarkable women I've ever met."

"Is it true she ran a Montana ranch?" Meliha asked. "Or was that just a publicity campaign?"

Overholt grinned. "She launched her Senate campaign by branding a steer on live TV. Her campaign slogan was 'Now imagine what I'll do when I get to Washington.'" Overholt chuckled. "She won by a landslide."

"I should like to meet her."

Overholt nodded. "I'm sure that can be arranged. I'd be delighted to make the introduction."

"Well, we've made our introductions," Juan said. "And we've had our coffee. So what's this meeting really all about?"

18

Ms. Öztürk has been doing yeoman's work investigating a criminal enterprise known as the Pipeline. Have you heard of it?"

Juan shook his head. "No."

"Almost no one has. And the intelligence community knows precious little. But according to Ms. Öztürk—"

"Please, both of you, call me Meliha."

"Yes, of course. If you don't mind, would you share your expertise with Juan?"

"I'd be happy to." She turned to Juan. "In brief, the Pipeline is a smuggling operation that's responsible for the movement of contraband across Europe, Central Asia, the Middle East and more recently Latin America. Mostly by ship but also by other means."

"With shipping, it's easier to avoid inspections and cheaper to haul heavy materials," Juan said. "What kind of contraband?"

"On the one hand, weapons and mercenary fighters are being smuggled into war zones, especially where NATO or UN arms embargoes are in place. The Caucusus, Syria, Iraq, Lebanon—and, most important, Libya."

Juan let out a long sigh. It was an old story. He'd been battling gun-runners for years all over the planet. Too many innocent lives had been lost for the sake of a dirty dollar. He was always happy for the chance to stomp on those blood money cockroaches.

Meliha continued. "My sources also tell me that a very large shipment of the latest Saab laser-guided air defense missiles was stolen. I don't need to tell you that they're the most effective short-range anti-air missiles in production today."

"Thermal imaging, automatic target tracking, five-mile range, three-mile altitude—yeah, a twenty-four/seven headache for any pilot. Where were they headed?"

"The shipment was intended for a NATO ally but was hijacked in transit. Rumor has it that the missiles were heading for Venezuela by ship."

Juan scratched his chin. "I wonder if the trawler we intercepted off the coast of Suriname fits that bill?"

Overholt nodded. "My thoughts exactly."

"May I ask what you're referring to?" Meliha interjected.

"Several days ago, we intercepted a fishing trawler we suspected was up to no good. When we boarded her, the crew killed themselves and sank the ship."

Meliha nodded. "That sounds like a Pipeline operation. They leave no evidence or witnesses behind."

"Besides weapons, what else is this Pipeline into?" Juan asked.

"The worst. Human trafficking. Women mostly. Sometimes children. The sex slave industry is alive and well. And so is indentured servitude," Meliha said. "And drugs are driving all of it, exchanged for guns, for fighters, for slaves and also for money—big money."

"Who runs the Pipeline?"

"Nobody knows. Mafia gangs across the region are loosely connected, but they are just the low-level players. These gangs are operating in countries with massive police and intelligence operations and yet somehow the Pipeline is never discovered or stopped."

"Money buys politicians," Juan said. "And big money buys the biggest ones." Juan started putting two and two together. "Do you think President Toprak is tied into the Pipeline?"

"Right now, I can't find any evidence that he is. However, in my country there is an organization known as the Gray Wolves. They are a group of ultra-nationalists who support Toprak's Neo-Ottoman policies, pressuring him to keep expanding his military reach into places like Libya. Many high-ranking military and political figures in Turkey are secretly members of the Gray Wolves. But there are Gray Wolves who are also big-time criminals."

"And that's where you see the connection between the Pipeline and your government."

"That's my working theory."

Juan put it all together. He turned to Overholt. "If we find the Pipeline, we bring down the Toprak government—or at least the Gray Wolves driving his bus. Then the Turks will start to play nice again and NATO doesn't break up."

Overholt smiled. "You're halfway there."

Meliha frowned. "You see, the Gray Wolves and the militarists backing Toprak are the primary obstacles to democracy for my people."

"So we're talking regime change," Juan said.

Overholt nodded. "The President prefers the term 'reform.' Either way, this entire conversation is off the record. The American government can't be seen interfering with the internal affairs of a NATO ally."

Juan turned to Meliha. "In the eyes of your government, just having this conversation makes you a traitor."

Meliha held his gaze. "'Truth is treason in an empire of lies.'"

Juan nodded and smiled. He was liking Meliha more and more. "Orwell."

"A journalist," Meliha said. "And a prophet."

He turned back to Overholt.

"How can I help?"

"You can see why President Grainger has taken a personal interest in

Meliha and her father," Overholt began. "From where I sit, the future of Turkey is bright."

"Thank you, Mr. Overholt, but that bright future is still a long way off."

"Quite right. I'm confident today's meeting brings us one step closer."

Overholt tented his fingers as he turned his gaze toward Juan.

"By definition, a pipeline has two ends, the input and the output. Find either end and you find the rest of the buried pipe, so to speak. Meliha believes she knows where the input side might be. I need for you and your crew to go and prove it."

"Where?" Juan asked.

"Libya," Meliha said.

"Libya's a big place in the middle of a decade-long civil war," Juan said. A civil war caused when NATO knocked off Muammar Gaddafi ten years ago, he wanted to add. Libya was the wealthiest per capita nation in all of Africa at the time of Gaddafi's demise. His overthrow had only brought ruin and chaos. The most recent cease-fire had collapsed. "Can you be a little more specific?"

"I can't tell you where, but I can tell you what's arriving there. It's a new compound of fentanyl-laced methamphetamine. Its street name is Diamante Azul—'Blue Diamond.' This new meth will kill thousands and ruin the lives of tens of thousands more. The meth problem was already bad before but now it will become exponentially worse."

"We're talking about Mexican meth," Overholt said. He was baiting a hook.

Juan leaned forward.

Overholt yanked hard. "We suspect Víctor Herrera."

Overholt watched the muscle in Juan's jaw bulge. His words landed where he hoped they would.

"Víctor Herrera? Hugo's son? I thought he wasn't a player."

"Rumor has it that he may have had something to do with his father's killing. We think he's now in charge of the entire operation."

"Then Víctor Herrera is responsible for the death of Tom Reyes."

"It would seem so."

Juan sat back, a cold rage welling up in his blue eyes. "When does the shipment arrive?"

"Soon," Meliha said. "Or it might already be there. I'm not sure."

"And if you can prove it's Herrera's meth, we can mobilize more resources to take him down," Overholt said. "Right now, he's untouchable where he is. The Mexican government is in his pocket and President Grainger isn't prepared to act against him—yet. Libya is our best shot at taking him down."

"Then I'm all in," Juan said. "But you already knew that."

Overholt grinned. "And if you find it, I want you to acquire a sample for chemical analysis. The molecular signature of meth compounds are as unique as fingerprints."

"Which means you have Herrera's meth signature on file."

"We do."

"The *Oregon* has a gas chromatograph on board. Forward me your file and I'll get it to my lab techs for comparison."

"Consider it done, my boy. One more thing. If Libya really is one end of the Pipeline, I want you to follow wherever it leads and take out as much of the organization as you can along the way. Where you can't dismantle it, mark its location and players for later . . . disassembly."

"That goes without saying." Juan touched the side of his nose. An unspoken way of telling Overholt that they'd discuss his fees later. Overholt acknowledged the gesture with a single nod of his head.

"Thank you, Mr. Cabrillo," Meliha said. "Mr. Overholt told me that you and your team were the best in the business and I'm inclined to believe it."

"And you'll be coming to Libya as well?" Juan asked.

"Yes."

"I can't wait to introduce you to the *Oregon* and my crew."

"I will be coming to Libya but not with you. I have other plans."

Juan glanced at Overholt, confused. He could have called him with all this information. Why arrange this meeting with her if they weren't going to work together?

"I don't understand."

Meliha explained. "There are rumors of a number of villages recently massacred by mercenaries led by a Gray Wolves commander. I have a Libyan guide who will take me to one of them on the coast, a place called Wahat Albahr. If I can gather enough evidence, I can prove my father's innocence."

"I can escort you there myself."

"I need you to go after the meth," Overholt said. "Meliha knows what she's doing."

Juan started to tell her how dangerous Libya was, but he saw the grit in her eyes and held his tongue.

She read his mind.

"There's nothing I won't do to save my father—or my country."

"You're heading into a kill zone. You're not afraid?" Juan asked.

"Of course I am. But my father taught me there are worse things than dying. Don't you agree?"

Juan nodded. There were indeed.

Overholt shot him a look. His eyes answered Juan's earlier question: now you know why I wanted you to meet her.

She'd make a great addition to the *Oregon*, Juan thought.

Overholt leaned forward. "Should Meliha ever need your assistance, you must give it—whatever it might be."

That was as close as Overholt ever got to issuing Juan an order. Technically, he and his crew didn't work for him or the U.S. government. The Corporation operated independently against bad actors of their choosing—usually based on potential profits—but never to the detriment of innocent people or vital American national interests.

But Juan owed Overholt everything and completely trusted his mentor's judgment. Overholt never called upon the *Oregon* to do anything unless it threatened the United States. Whatever Overholt asked from Juan and his patriotic crew he got.

Juan nodded. "Understood."

Overholt smiled his thanks. He said to Meliha, "If you ever need help, I expect you to contact Juan. He's the best friend you'll ever have."

"I'm grateful to you both. I'm sure we'll see each other again when this is all over. Good hunting, Mr. Cabrillo."

"Same to you, Ms. Öztürk."

She was very brave, Juan thought. And smart.

But so were the friends he'd lost over the years.

Maybe she was lucky, too.

19

LIBYA

The Russians know their business," Cedvet Bayur said. "But so do I."
The forty-one-year-old Turk lowered the binoculars from his eyes and handed them to his second-in-command. The entire left side of his darkly handsome face was marred by a five-pointed burn scar, smooth and waxy like melted plastic.

The small seaside village of Wahat Albahr had fallen victim to Libya's endless civil wars. In better years, it was home to over three hundred villagers settled in a collection of small mud brick and concrete-block buildings straddling the crooked coastal road. But a month ago, the thriving town was abandoned by its civilian inhabitants.

Now it was occupied by Libyan rebels from the eastern half of the country. They were fighting alongside Russian mercenaries to defeat the illegitimate government in Tripoli.

The Tripoli government, in turn, was supported by Turkey, who sent weapons and commanders like Cedvet Bayur to lead ISIS mercenaries in the war against the rebels.

Rebel soldiers armed with automatic rifles and RPGs were stationed on buildings around the T-shaped perimeter and hidden behind defensive barricades. Inside the fortified perimeter stood two GAZ

Tigrs—the Russian version of the American Humvee—mounted with medium machine guns.

Cedvet Bayur knew what lay ahead. As a former Turkish Army intelligence officer, Bayur commanded ISIS fighters in Syria against Russian troops supporting Assad's regime. In addition to battlefield tactics, he had helped pioneer the coordination of drone and conventional operations against Russian and Syrian positions. His work in Libya was much the same, only now he was in charge.

From his survey of the village, Bayur counted over sixty Libyan fighters and three Russian mercenaries. No doubt the Libyans would be organized in three equal platoons, each led by a Russian following the traditional order of battle. One of them would be the lead commander. Bayur's instinct told him it was the Russian with the binoculars standing atop the two-story building fronting the west end of the village.

Bayur's orders were clear. Retake the village. Kill every man in it.

The problem Bayur faced was that he had no air support and, even if he did, the Russians had brought along shoulder-fired anti-aircraft missiles. He was outnumbered two to one. His local commander brought up the area's only T-72 tank, a deadly but ancient relic of the fallen Gaddafi regime. The tank's 125mm gun could pound the mud brick buildings to dust and its steel tracks grind the rebels to mush. But the tank could aim its gun only by firing line of sight, exposing itself. The Russian anti-tank missiles would take the T-72 out after it fired its first shot.

The ISIS fighters under his command—Syrians, Chechens and three British-born Pakistanis—were willing enough to sacrifice themselves for the cause of Allah if Bayur was foolish enough to unleash them on the village.

Given the rebels' excellent defensive position and available weapons, it was seemingly impossible for Bayur to carry out his orders. But as an officer in Turkey's infamous intelligence agency—and as a member of the Gray Wolves organization—he knew that failure to accomplish his mission here and in the rest of Libya would prove as fatal as a direct assault on the village.

In truth, he was less motivated by fear than family honor. His father was a career Army officer who parachuted into Cyprus in the 1974 invasion. His great-grandfather had served under Atatürk in the victorious Gallipoli campaign against the British. No man in his family had ever run from a fight. Innumerable medals, promotions and scars from wounds were proof of that—including a few of his own.

No, he would not be the first man in his family to fail his country. But he harbored no particular desire to die for it in this godforsaken place either.

He had one other option.

Today's mission would be the first operation with the new technology. If it failed, he would lead the charge himself and see how well the Russians had marshaled their Libyan lackeys. Death was preferable to dishonor.

His only prayer was that his remains would be sent home to his father and buried with his ancestors.

Cherenkov lowered his binoculars and lit an American cigarette.

The Russian mercenary commander stood on the flat rooftop terrace of the two-story building, which faced the west. Most of the Turkish-led ISIS killers opposing him were now under the cover of rubble, rocks and sand berms. An hour earlier, one of their dimwitted snipers had climbed a palm tree and taken a poor shot at one of his men. Cherenkov's own Spetsnaz-trained sniper dropped the cross-eyed ISIS shooter like a coconut with a single round. Since then, the opposition had kept its head down.

Cherenkov felt the cool, salty breeze from the nearby Mediterranean wick away his sweat. The weather was relatively mild at this time of year, but the sun was climbing.

What was the Turk waiting for?

Cherenkov had tangled with the swine in Syria. Of course, Russians and Turks had fought against each other for centuries. He imagined a distant battlefield where their martial ancestors once squared off with sabers and muskets. All that had changed over the years were the weapons and the locations. The killing—and the glory—remained the same.

The Turks held their own in Syria but had been no match for Russian forces until they introduced their new drone technology. The Turkish Army scored several embarrassing victories over his countrymen, overwhelming superior Russian weapons and manpower with sophisticated UAV strikes and swarms. But every battlefield loss is a lesson learned, he had taught his men. And they had learned his lesson well by the time they reached Libya. Any high-flying weapons would be taken out by his handheld anti-aircraft assets.

Cherenkov had briefed his Libyan troops through his interpreter. The civil war cease-fire hadn't held, but both sides had used the temporary respite to restock and reposition. Now the war was back on and his mission was to hold this village, a key point in the coastal road and the only freshwater *wadi* for sixty kilometers.

He and his two Russian comrades did their best to train the Libyans, mostly poor, working-class men. But sprinkled among them were shopkeepers, mechanics and even a dentist. What they lacked in battlefield skill they made up for with rage. All they had in common was their suffering. Their women had been raped, their children killed and their homes demolished at the hands of the Turkish-backed government in Tripoli.

Of course, his Libyans had done the same to the other side, Cherenkov reminded himself. It was a brutal war with no end in sight. The Libyan people were suffering pawns in the great game of nations. Both the wars and the truces were cloaked in the language of democracy and human rights. But all anyone really cared about was the vast reserves of Libyan oil and gas they coveted. To the victor go the spoils.

No matter. He didn't concern himself with politics, let alone morality. He was well paid and serving the Rodina the best way he knew how. He sucked one last, long pull on his cigarette and crushed the smoldering butt with the heel of his boot.

What was the Turk waiting for?

* * *

Cherenkov pulled off his ball cap and rubbed his shaved head, thinking. Waiting was always the worst. He had radioed for reinforcements earlier, but there was another Turk advance farther to the south. It would be at least twenty-four hours before any help came.

He spat. No matter. He was well supplied with ammunition, rations and water. Let the swine do their best.

An anxious voice crackled in his headset. It sounded like Gudanov, but the static was terrible. Cherenkov responded, calling his name, but Gudanov clearly didn't hear him. He reached down to the transmitter on his hip and switched channels, still calling Gudanov's name, but the other channels buzzed with electronic noise as well.

The Turks were deploying jamming technology.

Suddenly, a thunderous voice speaking Arabic erupted in his skull like a gunshot. He didn't understand the angry words, but the threatening tone was clear. It was an attempt to frighten children.

He leaned over the rooftop parapet to see how his Libyans were reacting to the noise. To his horror, he saw squads of them leaping to their feet and throwing down their weapons, their numbers growing by the second. Even his most trusted rebel fighters dropped their handheld anti-aircraft launchers in the dust.

"Gudanov! Tarkovsky! Get your men back in line or shoot them down—now!" He screamed his orders over the racket of the Arabic voice booming in his head knowing his men couldn't hear him otherwise.

He shouted down to the Libyans gathering at the foot of his building. "Cowards! Pick up your guns and stand your ground!" The big Russian pulled his pistol and fired near their feet, hoping to scare them and spur them.

They didn't budge.

A burst of light exploded in his eyes. A flash-bang, he told himself. But he felt no concussive force and heard no eardrum-piercing crack.

He raised his gloved hands to his face and rubbed his eyes, still holding his semi-auto pistol. Screams of terror echoed below him.

He pulled his hands away.

He was blind.

Had the same happened to his men?

Gunfire erupted in the distance. Down below, he heard the unmistakable sound of bullets crashing into mud brick walls and thudding into flesh. Cherenkov hit the deck for cover with the cries of his men in his ears and the voice speaking Arabic still booming in his skull. Blind, he couldn't judge the distance to the floor and knocked the air out of himself when he landed, the pistol flying from his grip.

Panic welled up in him as the gunfire rapidly approached, but he choked it back. He scrambled to recover his weapon. When he finally snatched it up in his shaking hand, he lifted it in the direction he thought the doorway might be. He wouldn't go down without a fight.

He then felt the building itself begin to shake, accompanied by the roar of a racing diesel engine and the clanking of speeding tank treads charging toward his position.

His courage fled him like a shadow at dusk.

He cried out, raging against the voice still thundering in his head, knowing that he was a dead man.

20

THE MEDITERRANEAN SEA

Juan stood outside on the faux starboard bridgewing of the *Oregon*, sailing into a cool sea breeze, as dawn brightened with a gray-pink sunrise behind him.

Nothing lifted his spirits like setting out to sea on a new adventure with the wind in his hair and his eyes fixed on the far horizon. The missions were all different, but the excitement remained the same.

He first conceived of the Corporation as a ship-based organization. The high-tech *Oregon*, disguised as a broken-down tramp steamer, was the perfect vehicle for traveling unnoticed around the world, a stroke of tactical brilliance. Cabrillo had designed the vessel himself and he could rightly claim it was one of the most sophisticated covert operations vessels that had ever been built.

But in truth, it was Juan's love of the ocean that willed the legendary ship into being. He had sailed the *Oregon*—or one of its previous versions—on every sea on the planet in fair weather and foul. He never tired of the endless journey. And never would. The boundless ocean called to him like a dangerous woman, each horizon another whispered promise, making his heart race.

It was also a siren call that could end in death. Juan knew all too well that the ocean surging beneath his feet was a bottomless grave.

His own demise gave Juan no pause. It was only a matter of time before he would shuffle off this mortal coil, most likely in a hail of gunfire.

That was the job.

He had no doubt the Libya assignment entailed innumerable and perhaps even insurmountable risks. But shutting down the death and destruction pumped through the Pipeline every day was worth it—and the chance to take down Víctor Herrera even more so.

If Overholt could solve the Pipeline problem with a squadron of Apache helicopters or a regiment of fire-breathing Screaming Eagles paratroopers, he'd do it in a heartbeat. But Juan's mission required a degree of stealth.

After all, the shortest distance between two points was a high-velocity projectile—laser-guided, preferably.

But given the politics of the region, he and his team had to keep a very low profile. That was part of the contract and why Overholt paid them handsomely.

In turn, Overholt promised Juan that he was committed to getting justice for Tom Reyes. Now that Víctor Herrera was identified as Tom's killer, Juan had his target.

But Cabrillo's patience was wearing thin. Justice delayed was justice denied. The impulse to act surged through him like an electric charge.

But he'd play it Overholt's way. For now. This wasn't just about the business of being a mercenary, as far as Juan was concerned. It was personal.

And the clock was ticking.

"I thought I'd find you here."

Juan turned around. He smiled.

"Oh, Hux. Just what the doctor ordered."

Dr. Julia Huxley, the *Oregon*'s medical officer, held a metal thermos in her left hand with two ceramic mugs looped by their handles over her index finger. She was all of five-foot-three and wore her dark hair in an unpretentious ponytail.

The brilliant doctor served a four-year posting as the chief medical officer at Naval Base San Diego before joining the Corporation. She specialized in combat surgery and ran the *Oregon*'s hospital-grade trauma unit and operating room.

Huxley set the mugs on top of what appeared to be a rusted fifty-gallon steel drum labeled *Grease*. It contained one of a dozen camou-flaged weapons scattered around the deck. In this case, it was an automated .50 caliber machine gun designed to repel boarders or fend off aerial attacks.

Huxley filled the mugs with steaming black coffee and handed one to Cabrillo.

"A little chilly this morning. You've been up here awhile."

Juan turned back to the rail as he took a satisfying sip. "Just the way I like it."

"The coffee or the weather?"

"Both."

They stood in silence for a moment, feeling the warming sun on their backs and the breeze, salty and brisk.

"'All I ask is a tall ship and a star to steer her by.' Do you know it?" Juan said, reciting a line from his favorite poem.

"I'm retired Navy, remember? Actually, I've got a better one."

"Let's hear it."

"All I ask is a fasting blood sample and a urine cup to get you by." Huxley grinned. "Tomorrow, my office, eight a.m. sharp."

"Seriously?"

"You're five months overdue on your annual physical, Chairman. Since our Libya ETA is a few days out, I thought this might be a good time to take care of it."

Like most men, Juan wasn't big on doctors, let alone physicals. He had enough residual aches and pains from injuries and wounds suffered in combat for a dozen lifetimes. He took all of it in stride—part of the cost of doing business. But a physical was just asking for bad news coming out of nowhere, a random reminder of his mortality, the end of a race he wasn't finished running.

"I'm fine."

"Of course you are. Let's just confirm that with an exam."

Juan took another sip of coffee. He didn't need her probing and prodding his nether regions to know how he felt. He did his own inventory every day, including wrestling with the phantom leg pain he suffered beneath his kneecap.

"I eat right, mostly, and abstain from known carcinogens . . . mostly. It's not like I'm going to change anything if one of your tests doesn't pan out the way you think it should."

Dr. Huxley's smiling face hardened. Her easygoing personality was for outside the surgical suite or exam room. But when "Hux" became "Dr. Huxley," she was as humorless as a bone saw.

Thanks to Juan's stubbornness, she hadn't been able to get him into the *Oregon*'s high-tech clinic, equipped for most medical procedures, routine and emergency. Since by default this morning's chat turned into an exam of sorts, her no-nonsense physician mode kicked in.

"Listen, mister. Unless I misread your file, you aren't licensed to issue a medical opinion about anything. And in my experience, anyone who self-diagnoses has a fool for a patient."

"Ouch."

"You owe it to yourself—but, more important, the crew of this ship—to be in top shape."

"I'm in great shape. I work out every day."

"Sorry, but burpees can't beat a case of colon cancer."

Just as he was about to concede defeat, skate shoes thundered on the steel steps behind them. He turned around.

"Murph. What brings you here?"

Mark Murphy stood tall and gangly. His wildly uncombed hair bustled in the breeze like a dandelion's seed head. His black T-shirt was emblazoned with the name of his favorite new band, Apunkalypse, along with the image of Leonardo da Vinci's *Vitruvian Man* standing not inside a circle but rather a strawberry-frosted donut with sprinkles.

Juan tolerated Murph's thirteen-year-old fashion sensibilities because the certified genius had been one of the world's premier weapons designers in private industry before Juan recruited him into the Corporation. Murph not only operated all the high-tech weapons systems on board but was constantly improving them and developing new ones as well.

"The electromagnetic pulse systems are installed and fully operational," Murph said in his now faded West Texas drawl. "You asked me to notify you when I was ready to start testing."

Juan nodded his approval. Murph had pulled everything into place in record time. Tactical weapons utilizing electromagnetic pulses—EMPs—were the cutting edge of weapons development, offensive and defensive. The power of the pulses to disrupt or destroy unprotected electronic devices—cell phones, computers, avionics, etc.—was well known in scientific and military circles. Naturally occurring events like solar flares produced EMPs. But they also could be generated artificially with devices like nuclear weapons. The American government proved the concept when it exploded a nuclear bomb high above the Pacific Ocean in its 1962 Starfish Prime experiment.

The nightmare scenario envisioned by U.S. strategic defense planners was an explosion of a nuclear warhead above the American heartland. The resulting EMP storm would likely result in a catastrophic American death toll because the country was utterly dependent on all things electronic in nearly every area of life—food, water, energy, communications, transportation, law enforcement and medicine.

Modern sea, land and air warfare tactical systems were equally vulnerable, making smaller tactical EMPs the newest war-fighting technology. Thanks to Murph's connections with DARPA, the Defense Advanced Research Projects Agency, and Overholt's influence within the intelligence community, Juan recently secured two such tactical EMP systems for real-world testing on the proviso he recorded those tests and supplied the data back to DARPA.

Heading to Libya, Juan wondered if DARPA might be getting more data than they'd counted on a lot sooner than they expected.

"When do you want to begin?" Juan asked.

"Now," Murph said.

Juan turned to Hux, hardly fighting back the grin spreading across his face.

"Sorry, doc. Duty calls."

He threw a muscular arm around Murph's neck and steered him toward the control room belowdecks. When Hux shouted, "I expect you in the clinic tomorrow, bright and early," Juan responded with a wave of his hand, leaving her to wonder if he were confirming their appointment or dismissing her suggestion.

21

Like every major seaport Juan had ever docked at, the air stank with a pungent mixture of noxious bunker fuel and rotting fish. Dockworkers in the distance shouted over the din of roaring engines and clanging steel.

Juan shielded his eyes from the bright noon sun with one hand as he stared at the PIG hanging in the air high above the dock. Max Hanley was working one of the *Oregon*'s cranes with the sweating intensity of a nearsighted eye surgeon.

Juan loved the PIG and didn't want it to drop. But he didn't love it as much as Max, who had designed the vehicle, a bigger, boxier version of the Humvee. Built around a Mercedes Unimog chassis, the powered investigator ground vehicle was a land-based version of the *Oregon*. Thanks to its modular design, articulated suspension and eight-hundred-horsepower turbodiesel engine, the oversize PIG was capable of many disguises, chock-full of weapons and built for both speed and distance.

Max hated the PIG moniker, but it stuck with the crew like old bubble gum stuck on the underside of a grade school desk.

The PIG was painted a faded green and white, the colors of the

Swedish Medical Missions, and bore the organization's logo as well. Bumpers were dented, panels rusted and mirrors cracked by Nixon's Magic Shop to give the vehicle a well-used appearance and to make it look as harmless as possible.

The *Oregon* bore the same color scheme, though not as weathered, with its new name—*Västra Floden*—etched on its bow and stern and a Liberian flag hanging limply on the jackstaff. Through the modern miracle of meta-material camouflage paint, an electrical charge applied to the ship's skin transformed the vessel's color scheme in the blink of an eye just hours ago.

The PIG touched down as gently as an autumn leaf on a still mountain lake, just inches from Juan's feet. Its shocks groaned beneath the weight of its load.

Juan flashed a big thumbs-up to Max in the crane's control room high above the deck even as he keyed his walkie-talkie. "The PIG has landed."

"I'll have the trailer down in a minute," Max said with an electronic crackle to his voice.

While a variety of weapons and small arms were carefully concealed on board the PIG, the bulk of its cargo consisted of antibiotics, surgical equipment and nutrient-dense MREs, meals ready to eat. Their destination was a refugee camp for women and children some twenty miles south of the small port where the *Oregon* was docked.

The civil war's temporary cease-fire had been allowing freer movement of emergency supplies. Unfortunately, it had also allowed for the freer movement of bandits, who pilfered most of the emergency restock. Now there were rumors the cease-fire had given way.

Hence the up-gunned armored PIG.

It had been several years since Juan and the PIG had been in Libya for an altogether different mission. Muammar Gaddafi was a tyrannical dictator, but at least the oil-rich country was relatively safe when he ruled it. Today's "liberated" Libya looked like the Wild West. Some feared it was on the verge of becoming a post-apocalyptic hellscape of war, slavery and death.

"*As-salaam 'alaykum*"—*peace be with you*—the customs official said. "Your papers?" he said in Arabic-accented English with an oily Gauloises cigarette dangling from his lower lip.

"*Wa 'alaykum as-salaam*"—*and peace be with you*—Juan replied. "*Ha hi 'awraquna*"—*here's our papers*—he added in faultless street Arabic.

The customs officer frowned at Juan with confusion; he wasn't used to seeing blond, Arabic-speaking men. He eyed the tall foreigner. With his full beard and close-cropped hair, Cabrillo looked like a modern Viking in a boonie hat and cargo shorts.

Juan handed over a thick leather folio with all the necessary documentation inside including the passports, visas, cargo manifest, destination and, most important of all, a five-hundred-euro note tucked away between two pages.

The customs official opened the folio and began thumbing through it, working the cigarette with his surly mouth, blinking furiously as the thick smoke of his Gauloise curled into his eyes.

Juan studied the man's face, stubbled with gray. He half wondered if the man could even read.

When the officer finally opened to the page with the big euro note, he pocketed it without breaking stride as he continued flipping through the rest of the documents.

Cabrillo knew the papers were in order—he had one of the best forgery departments on the planet working for him. But greedy customs officials, by definition, weren't reliable people. Just as he couldn't be trusted to do his job honestly, he couldn't be counted on to accept the standard bribe.

Just then, the two-wheeled trailer Max had promised lighted on the dock near the PIG, its cargo of MREs covered in a heavy tarp.

If the customs official were able to read, he would learn that the *Västra Floden*—Swedish for *West River*, a translation of *Oregon*—ported out of Stockholm but sailed under a Liberian flag and the man in charge of the cargo was Dr. Mattias Jansson. If he couldn't read, the official could at least see the photo of a bearded blond Jansson that perfectly matched the bearded face standing in front of him.

The official snapped the folio shut and handed it back to Juan, his dark eyes searching his face, then raking over the PIG and its trailer.

Juan saw the tumblers falling in the man's skull. He was clearly trying to decide if he should ask for another *baksheesh* from the wealthy Westerner.

Saying nothing, the official flicked his cigarette away and climbed into the back of the PIG. The plastic-wrapped pallets were stacked with boxes clearly marked as either pharmaceuticals or surgical supplies. The official ran his hand over the palletized payloads as if labeled in braille.

"It would be a shame for the children to not receive these," the man said in English from beneath the shaded interior.

"*Inshallah*," Juan replied, choking back his anger.

The Arabic word literally meant *God willing*. But the way Juan spat it out, it meant *Ain't happening*.

There was no way he was going to let this man shake down a charitable organization and, worse, raise the price of the bribe. That would only put future aid organizations in similar peril and force them to cough up much-needed cash just so this crook and his cronies could retire in Italy in a few years.

The customs official saw something cold and dangerous in the big man's blue eyes. He climbed back down with effort.

"Everything is in order. May Allah bless you on your journey through the desert for the cause of women and children," the official said as he yawned and turned away.

"That's what we're counting on, buddy," Juan whispered to himself as the customs officer pulled his handheld radio and climbed into his car.

Juan called the bridge on his walkie. "Time to saddle up. We're cleared to go."

22

The PIG's oversize tires roared on the thin ribbon of asphalt bisecting the desert. They'd passed a few concrete-block villages, in various states of ruin and repair, crowding the road in clusters along the way, and zipped around the odd donkey cart and camel herd limping along in the sweltering heat.

Max Hanley was behind the wheel. He insisted on driving today's mission. "How can I trust you hoodlums with this beauty if you insist on calling her a pig?"

Juan acceded to his friend's request. Max was the first man Juan hired when he conceived of the Corporation. He was a good man to have in a fight. Despite his age, he was fast with a pistol and even faster with his hard-knuckled fists and not shy about using either.

Juan rode shotgun—literally. A short-barreled, pump-action Mossberg was tucked beneath the dashboard in front of him. Murph, the weapons expert, rode in back next to Linc, the muscle, whose massive frame took up more than half the seat. His head was as shiny as a billiard ball.

Once they were long past the remnants of civilization, the GPS instructed them to turn off onto a dirt track, heading south. Juan thought they could've been riding the Rover on the surface of Mars. Islands of black rock floated in a sea of rust-colored sand. Cabrillo was glad of the vehicle's reliability. And even gladder for the air-conditioning.

Juan glanced at the backseat. Like any good operator, Linc was grabbing some shut-eye while the grabbing was good. Murph's head was jerking to a cacophony of heavy metal grinding in his earbuds as his fingers raced across a keyboard supported by a tray mounted to the back of Max's seat.

Juan pointed at his own ear and told Murph, "You'll go deaf with those things," but Murph just shrugged and mouthed, *I can't hear you.* Cabrillo rolled his eyes and shrugged. To each his own.

Juan reached beneath his feet and pulled out a thermos of cold water. He took a swallow and handed it to Max, who took a couple gulps.

"Another hour or so," Max said. "Good thing we don't need a gas station." They were out in the deep boonies.

Juan was hungry but he didn't want to tell Max to pull over so he could raid the Yeti cooler in the back. The *Oregon*'s youngest chef had whipped up a gourmand's version of MREs for the trip, a feast of grass-fed Angus roast beef sandwiches slathered in avocado mayo and Dijon mustard, a bag of freshly roasted, organic, sea salted macadamia nuts and cans of ice-cold pink grapefruit Perrier. The motto *Eat well, fight hard* was enshrined in brass letters over the entrance to the *Oregon*'s magnificent galley.

The quote was Juan's.

Cabrillo knew today's little adventure into the desert was a long shot, but it was his only play. When Overholt told him to go find the location of the Libyan meth pipeline, he was essentially asking for him to find the proverbial needle in a haystack. He had no idea why anybody actually would look for a needle in a haystack or why a needle would be there in the first place, but Juan knew that the only way to find one was to use a magnet—and he had one in Libya.

And her name was Oriel Swarbrick.

The Corporation made most of its cash in the mercenary trade, but early on Juan decided to invest in a variety of legitimate businesses all over the globe, from manufacturing to agriculture. None of the employees of these enterprises had any idea of the source of the parent company's funding or its purpose.

Because of these shrewd investments, the Corporation's retirement funds had swelled over the past decade. No one who worked for Juan long enough to be vested would ever want for money again for the rest of his or her life. Each crew member was free to cash in and walk away at any time as filthy rich one-percenters. But it told Juan a lot about the character of his patriotic crew that the vast majority of them stayed on, working long hours away from home and risking their lives in a cause they all believed in.

In the last few years, Juan also began investing excess funds in nonprofit organizations, including his favorite, Blue Ocean, working to restore and protect the world's aquatic environments. Despite his affectations of piratical larceny, he was raised to believe in the Golden Rule liberally salted with the idea of good karma.

The charitable groups he donated to had no idea who Juan was or the identity of the Corporation—let alone its mercenary mission. Through third-party sources, Juan kept track of their operations, budgets and requests as they arose, providing them with critical funding and supplies as needed, especially after a lucrative merc job. He considered this charitable giving as his "tithes and offerings" in gratitude to the Man Upstairs. Most of the bighearted crew chipped into the charitable fund as well.

Another one of the organizations the Corporation supported was Bila Houdoud—Arabic for *Without Borders*—a Libyan relief agency. Because of the civil war, it was in desperate need of antibiotics and surgical supplies. The camp they were heading toward was run by an old friend, Oriel Swarbrick.

Oriel was just the magnet Juan needed. She was probably the best-informed Western foreigner in Libya. Juan had served with the former British MI6 operative years ago in Nicaragua when he was still in the CIA. He knew she had quit the job a few years back after running ops in the Middle East. A mutual friend said she joined Bila Houdoud because she was trying to atone for her sins after two decades of bloody wet work while in service to the Crown.

He understood a little about exorcising personal demons. Her helping refugee women and children caught in the middle of a civil war was a whole lot better than hitting the bottle or eating a gun as too many of their colleagues had done over the years. Good works couldn't erase bad memories, but they made for much better ones.

At least it had for him.

As soon as Juan left his meeting with Meliha and Overholt in Istanbul, he returned to the *Oregon* and dashed off an email to Swarbrick promising the needed supplies and the planned date of arrival. His email was headed *Swedish Medical Missions* and was signed by Dr. Mattias Jansson. He needed the cover story in order to protect her and her organization.

The Swedish relief mission imprimatur also allowed him to deliver actual relief supplies, which he was thrilled to do. What the *Oregon* herself couldn't provide they supplemented with a stop in the Greek Port of Piraeus on the way to Libya. He didn't want to come in with the Tiltrotor because it would draw too much attention and it looked like a weapon of war. The PIG, however, fit the bill nicely because it appeared harmless. It didn't bother Juan that his PIG and crew were loaded for bear in the event things went sideways.

And suddenly, they did.

23

Just as they crested the rise of a small hill, they saw the gunmen blocking their way a hundred yards ahead, straddling three Ducati desert bikes. Each bike had a driver and a shooter cradling AK-47s.

Max hit the brakes and the PIG slowed to a shuddering stop. He turned toward Juan.

Cabrillo shifted in his seat. "Looks like our customs official called ahead to his friends."

"Now what?"

Just as the words left his mouth, a large-caliber rifle round crashed into the PIG's bulletproof windshield, scratching it slightly.

"Punch it," Juan told Max.

"Aye that."

Max stomped the throttle and the big, four-wheel-drive tires spun.

"What'd I miss?" Linc yawned as he sat up, taking up even more space in the back.

"Nothing yet," Juan said over his shoulder. "But it won't be long." Then to Murph he said, "Stay frosty, Wepps."

Wepps was Cabrillo's nickname for whoever commanded the *Oregon*'s array of weaponry.

"Aye, Chairman."

Before the PIG could get up to speed, the sand bikes cranked their throttles, fishtailing with their sudden acceleration. The gunmen raised their weapons as they neared and opened fire.

Some bullets crashed harmlessly against the windshield while others thudded against the armor-plated engine cowling. The PIG was nearly impervious to small-arms fire.

Max's boot was pushed against the floorboard as he hit the nitrous oxide booster, pushing the horsepower to nearly a thousand. The engineer grinned ear to ear. "Go, baby, go!"

The PIG and its pursuers closed quickly, the AKs blazing away.

"Chairman?" Murph asked, his fingers poised over his weapons keyboard.

"Not yet."

Juan wanted to keep the relief mission ruse alive as long as possible. If Murph failed to kill them all, word would get out that the PIG and its crew weren't what they appeared to be. Better to avoid a fight if at all possible.

Just seconds away from the PIG's ginormous front bumper, the Ducatis split to either side of the speeding truck, their guns still blazing away without effect.

Juan glanced into the big side mirror. The motorcycles were stopped in a cloud of dust and falling away fast as the PIG accelerated.

"Looks like they gave up," Juan said.

Linc shook his head. "They ruined my nap for nothing."

The Bila Houdoud refugee camp wasn't much to look at. Its chief virtue was that it enclosed a small *wadi* with a few date palms. The trees provided meager shade for the children playing outside and the women who were washing their clothes in the muddied water. The rest of the camp was a collection of plastic tents, portable toilets and barbed-wire fence.

Max pulled to a stop and killed the engine.

Two darkly hued Tuareg fighters in weathered desert camouflage stood in front of the gate, their AK-47s at low ready. Their faces and heads were hidden by *tagelmusts*—turbans dyed in the signature indigo blue of the Tuaregs, known in history as the blue people. Only their eyes showed.

Between them stood Oriel Swarbrick. Her plain, round face wore a friendly grin and a pistol hung on her hip. She stood five-seven, with graying red hair woven in a thick French braid unfazed by the rising wind. In her dusty pocket pants and shirt she looked like a stocky, middle-aged stevedore. And she was as tough as she looked. She didn't need the pistol. Juan remembered how she handled a couple of knife-wielding Nicaraguan gun smugglers back in the day with nothing more than an ax handle.

Juan exited the PIG flashing a wide grin. He put one of his big hands on his boonie hat to keep it from flying off his head.

"Dr. Mattias Jansson at your service," Juan said in his best faux Swedish accent. The wind was picking up, sand stinging his face.

Swarbrick's eyes widened like saucers.

"Juan Cabrillo, you old pirate!" she called out in Spanish. Her grin broke into a wide smile and a hearty laugh as she ran into his bear-hugging arms.

The two old friends embraced for a moment. It had been a lot of years since they'd seen each other. Juan glanced over at the armed Tuaregs. Even from there he could see their eyes smiling beneath their indigo turbans.

Cabrillo's crew stepped out of the PIG, leaving their weapons behind. Juan assured them that Swarbrick was a good friend and the Tuaregs merely her security.

Swarbrick stood back and took the measure of the man in front of her. "What brings you out here?"

"I'm with the Swedish Medical Missions Society."

"Nothing you did would ever surprise me, but something tells me that's not the entire truth."

"Well, technically, I'm not with the SMMS. But they asked me to deliver the shipment you requested. You are in a war zone after all."

"I don't care what your cover story is, I'm just thrilled to see you again. And the supplies you've brought. We're desperate for them."

"Pretty rough out here?"

"Between the bandits and the civil war, it gets a bit dicey. So long as we stay behind the wire and stay neutral in the conflict, we're relatively safe." She nodded at her two guards. "But I thank God every day for my band of Tuaregs, too. They keep an eye out for us." She glanced around Juan's broad shoulder. "Who are your friends?"

"They're good people, Ori. I'll introduce them to you as soon as we get unloaded."

Swarbrick turned around and issued a command in Tuareg to her guards. They both turned and headed for the gate to open it. Max took the hint and climbed back into the PIG. The others joined him.

"Seriously, Juan, why are you here?"

"Honestly, I saw your resupply request and I was glad to handle it. But I also have a favor to ask." He heard the PIG's big turbodiesel fire up.

"Anything. Name it."

"There's a major new smuggling network operating here and I have to find it. It's called the Pipeline. Or is connected to it somehow."

"What kind of network is it?"

"Huge amounts of fentanyl-laced meth are coming into Libya, destined for Europe. Tens of thousands of lives are at stake. We're just trying to find the source. Can you help me?"

Swarbrick glanced beyond the barbed wire. A couple little girls were laughing and squealing as the wind pushed their soccer ball around like an automated toy.

"You know, if either side knew a CIA agent had come out here—"

"I know. But I'm no longer with the Company."

"But you're working for somebody, aren't you?"

"Self-employed. But that's a story for another day." He nodded toward the girls. "And for what it's worth, the Pipeline is engaged in human trafficking."

Swarbrick's face darkened, betraying her hatred of the criminal scum that would do such a thing. "I quit the game ages ago. I don't know about any organization called the Pipeline."

"Have you heard anything? Rumors?"

The PIG pulled to a stop next to Juan. He signaled for Max to go on ahead.

"Rumors." Swarbrick sighed. "There are more rumors in Libya than sand dunes."

Juan and Oriel followed the truck as it rumbled toward the opened gate.

"What have you heard?"

She told him what little she knew.

It wasn't much.

"You know, dear boy, even if you find this meth supplier and take him out, another one will pop up in his place—and both of them will have government contacts protecting them. It's one giant game of Whac-A-Mole."

"I know. But it's what I do."

She patted him on the arm. "Just you and your friends be very careful."

"Same to you."

Juan informed the Tuareg guards about his encounter with the bandits earlier and warned them to watch for them. No doubt the armed thieves would figure out where their supplies ended up and it would draw them to the camp like flies to honey.

With the help of Swarbrick and her sharp-eyed guards, the *Oregon* crew quickly unloaded their relief supplies. They even found time to hand out the toys and candy they had brought for the kids. Murph found himself in the middle of the most disorganized soccer match he'd ever seen and loved every minute of it, laughing as much as the kids swarming all around him. Linc pulled an ammo box from the PIG's storage and gave it to the Tuaregs. It was loaded with a thousand rounds of AK munitions.

Juan and Oriel hugged good-bye and made promises they both knew they couldn't keep before he climbed into the PIG and headed back to the port.

They rode in silence across the expanse of desert, following the road that had led them to the camp. Lost in his memories of Nicaragua and Swarbrick, Juan wasn't paying attention when the PIG crested the next hill.

Max blurted out, "What the—"

But the thundering boom of the recoilless rifle blotted out his last word. Instead of three motorcycles blocking the road, there were now six bikes, each with two riders, along with a flatbed truck bearing a tubular anti-tank weapon that fired a large armor-piercing round.

The projectile glanced off Juan's door panel. Had the gunner aimed a forearm's length to the right, they'd all likely be dead.

"Wepps!" Juan shouted.

"On it." Murph's thin fingers danced across the weapons console as an electric motor powered an automatic grenade launcher through the roof.

Max's eyes were fixed on the men in the back of the truck loading another large shell. They were fast.

But Murph was faster.

The first thump of the grenade launcher came as the breech of the recoilless rifle was slammed shut. Too late.

The grenade struck the weapon directly and ignited the explosive shell inside the tube as three more followed right behind it. The truck and its occupants were killed instantly and the nearest motorcycle team knocked down in a hail of shrapnel.

The next six grenades rapid-fired like an Old West sheriff fanning his wheel gun. The targeting computer's aim was unerring, starting with the downed bike and its wounded riders struggling to stand. The high-explosive grenade cut them down like a scythe through dry grass.

The next four motorcycles were destroyed and their riders killed before they could crank their throttles. But the sixth motorcycle managed to speed away in a sandy rooster tail just as the last grenade hit the ground where the bike had stood seconds earlier.

"We can't leave any survivors to report us—or threaten the camp," Juan said.

Murph nodded. "Aye that." He laid down a fire pattern.

Four grenades later, the sixth team was blown to bits, the bike reduced to a flaming cartwheel that tumbled to a halt in the sand.

Max threw the PIG back into gear and sped away, careful to avoid the burning wreckage.

24.

Juan felt a little guilty about his encounter with Oriel Swarbrick. He had taken a chance with her security by coming out to see her, but it had been his only play. He was completely confident that he hadn't broken her cover or put the refugee camp at risk. And they did drop off much-needed supplies. Her heartfelt thanks for his generous donation to her cause was more rewarding than he had expected.

What she offered by way of intel wasn't quite as satisfying. The rumor Swarbrick had heard was that smugglers were using some kind of secret air base far out in the Fezzan in the southwestern region of Libya.

That wasn't much to go on, but that's all she could give and that's what Juan had shared with the members of his brain trust two days before. Now they were all sitting in the *Oregon*'s high-tech conference room.

Juan sat at the head of the long table. His eyes drifted to the memorial wall in the back of the room. In the Mexico pre-mission brief, Tom Reyes had sat right where Murph was sitting now.

He glanced back up to the big digital monitor on the near wall. It displayed a photograph of Libya taken from a satellite with the Fezzan region highlighted.

Eric Stone had downloaded the image and was working his laptop. Like his best friend Murph, Stoney was a brainiac. In addition to their respective helm and weapons station duties, the two of them were the *Oregon*'s undisputed IT experts. They had become fast friends when they were both in civilian weapons research and development.

Stone's official job was as the *Oregon*'s helmsman—a skill he acquired, ironically, only after leaving the Navy and joining the Corporation. As a squid, he hadn't served on fighting vessels. Rather, his active duty job was weapons R and D. The only crew member who could helm the *Oregon* better than Stoney was the Chairman himself.

"As we previously discussed, the Fezzan region is nearly two hundred thirteen thousand square miles of mostly desert," Eric Stone began. "Finding a rumored air base is approaching a Super Seigen's Magnum Opus level of difficulty."

"What language are you speaking?" Juan said.

"It's a really hard level in Super Mario Maker," Murph explained. "You know, the video game."

"Then say that. You know, for the old geezers." Juan shook his head. "And I'm hoping you've actually conquered the magnum whatever thingy, right, Stoney?"

"Of course."

Stone hit a key and nine markers appeared on the Libyan map.

"These are the known active military facilities scattered throughout Fezzan. We gathered these through a search of the CIA and DoD databases. We've been able to eliminate . . ."

Stone hit another key. Eight red X's blotted out eight targets.

"All but one of them."

"How did you eliminate them?" Juan said.

"Monitoring air and ground traffic on radar and optical from our own drones and hijacked National Reconnaissance Office satellite feeds," Murph said.

"And we monitored comms by focusing the Sniffer on keywords, possible code words, the whole shebang," Stone said. "Besides, since the Afghan war, heroin trafficking has been a huge problem, even on NATO facilities. There are active DEA and Interpol intel operations on each of those Libyan bases. We scoured their databases and nothing like this Mexican meth has popped up in their reports."

Juan leaned forward, hopeful, and pointed at the last remaining base on-screen. "What about that one?"

Murph nodded toward Gomez Adams, sitting in the corner, wearing his flight suit, a battered straw Stetson cowboy hat and two days' growth of beard. He looked beat.

"It was a Russian-backed facility. I took the AW out for a visual. But when I got there, it was wrecked."

"So much for the truce," Juan said. If they were headed inland, they would be walking into the middle of a hot war.

Stone hit another key. The last base x'd out in red.

"So we've got *bupkis*," Stone said.

"An old Slavic word for *goat droppings*, as in *nothing of value*. Zero," Murph added.

"It's actually Yiddish, derivative of the Slavic. But yeah, I got that," Juan said.

"It wasn't all a waste," Gomez said. "I got painted by radar half a dozen times and had two SAM batteries lock on me—probably just warning shots, but I wasn't going to hang around to find out. I've marked all those locations so we can avoid surface-to-air missiles in the future."

Juan turned toward Stone. "And here's the part where you tell me how you solved our Mario/Magnum problem?" He said it in a way that wasn't a question.

Soft-eyed Eric Stone nodded. "Yes, sir." He clicked another key on his laptop. "I got to thinking about it. Swarbrick said it was a secret air base. But the ones we saw weren't all that secret, were they? So I started digging around and found this."

The photo of an old Libya map appeared on the wall monitor. The words were in Italian. Libya had been invaded and colonized by Italy in 1911 until they were defeated by Allied forces in 1943.

"This is a 1937 Italian military map displaying all their facilities in Libya." Stone clicked another key. The screenshot was a magnified portion of the map. "And here is the location of their only air base in Fezzan."

Juan pointed at the screen. "That wasn't on your earlier map—the nine bases you ID'd before."

"No, sir. Because it's inactive and has been since the war."

"Have you confirmed this with satellite imagery?"

"Not exactly." Stone pulled up a photo from the NRO's database, photoshopped to fit the scale of the Italian military map next to it. "As you can see, it doesn't appear as if there's anything going on there."

"But if you look closely," Murph said as he stood, pointing at the map, "we think it's very possible that there could be camouflage tarps and other means to hide activity."

"Tire tracks? Movement?"

"We don't have a live feed over that exact position. I've found a series of photos shot over days, but they're inconclusive. There's a lot of wind out there. And if they're trying to hide, they're probably conducting their operations at night. And even covering their tracks, if they're serious about it."

"There's one more thing," Murph said. "I had the Cray computer run a flight traffic analysis over that area for the last week. No radar tracks in the vicinity. But Cray found this."

He pulled up a recorded IFF, identification friend or foe, dated the day before. It showed an aircraft flying toward the suspected Italian air base—and then disappearing.

"What happened?"

"Unclear. Most likely, the aircraft dropped below any radar track long before its approach but kept broadcasting its IFF. Someone on board figured out that that was a mistake and shut it off. The aircraft reappeared on radar several hours later and resumed its IFF broadcast on its way to Tripoli, its destination of record."

"What did Libyan air traffic control have to say about all of that?"

"According to their records, the aircraft suffered a temporary transponder malfunction." Commercial aircraft, like shipping, were required by law to broadcast their IFF signal to help avoid collisions or accidental shoot-downs by nervous military pilots, especially in areas of active hostilities like Libya.

Juan grinned. "And that's how you found the plane after it landed in Tripoli." Cabrillo knew if they could find the pilot, they might discover both the source and destination of the meth.

"I checked it out. Unfortunately, the IFF data they were pumping out was all bogus. I have no idea where they are, where they really came from or what their true identity is."

Murph shrugged. "I hate to argue from the negative, but I think that kind of behavior strongly indicates that was our meth delivery."

"I have to agree," Stone said. "The fact the disappearing plane vanished just before it reached our ghost air base is too strong of a coincidence."

"And right now, it's the only lead we have." Juan pointed at the screen. "If that plane dropped off meth yesterday, there's a good chance it's getting moved out soon."

Juan turned to Gomez. "Are you up for another flight to that position?"

The pilot grinned. "Already did the preflight check. I'm ready when you are."

"Get all the photos you can. Not just of the base but of the entire area—full spectral range."

"Then I'll need a geek to ride shotgun with me," Gomez said. "Might be a vomit comet if I've got to dodge any missiles."

Stone raised his hand. "As a qualified geek and certified non-puking member of the American Coaster Enthusiasts, I volunteer."

Three hours later, the AW landed on the *Oregon*'s stern. The landing pad was marked by a white H with a white circle around it. Technically, it was the hangar elevator platform.

Juan scrambled to the Tiltrotor in a crouch, its whining engines cycling down as the props slowed. He climbed into the cabin, clutching a tablet.

"You guys did great," Cabrillo said. "Murph's breaking down all the data you sent. Any problems?"

Gomez pulled the cans off his ears and onto his neck and flipped switches to complete the shutdown. The blades slid to a halt.

"Bumpy ride. Thermal effect plus lots of wind on the ground." He grinned and threw a thumbs-up to Stone in the back, sweaty and ashen-faced, unplugging his equipment.

"Yeah, bumpy," Stone confirmed as he unbuckled his harness. "We were corkscrewing through the air like the Wild Eagle coaster at Dollywood."

"A few radar locks on the way in and out. Didn't want to take any chances." Gomez drew big circles in the air with his finger representing his aerial maneuvers. "But we're all good."

"Judging by what you sent, it looks like we found our secret base," Juan said.

Stone pointed at the photo Juan had pulled up on his tablet. "Could be a tarmac—there—covered in sand. Tire tracks definitely would be swept away in the wind we felt. I think those are buildings—maybe a hangar, a warehouse. The others I'd guess were barracks. Possibly a maintenance shed. For all I know, they're all abandoned. But there are definitely some kind of structures down there."

"No sign of people?" Juan asked. Warning alarms blared as the hangar elevator began to lower with the aircraft and the three men standing next to it.

"If I were trying to hide, I'd keep my people indoors, especially in this heat."

Juan looked at Gomez. "You're a pilot. Do you think it's an active air base?"

"It's definitely a base. At least fifty-fifty chance it's operational."

Juan nodded. "The only way to know for sure is to put boots on the ground."

"If it's active, they'll have radar and anti-aircraft weapons, not to mention guards with guns," Stone said.

"It's flat terrain for a hundred fifty miles in all directions around that place," Gomez said. "I'd hate to be the idiot trying to fly into that wood chipper."

"Did you catch the weather report?" Stone asked. He handed his tablet to Juan with the weather radar track. The color finally was returning to his face, but a shadow swept across it as the hangar elevator pad descended below the main deck. Juan smelled the sweet oily scent of hydraulic fluid as the giant electric motors whined under the strain of their load.

"Looks like a big sandstorm coming in hard," Gomez said. "Sixty-mile-an-hour winds. Won't be possible to fly in that mess, or land, for at least twenty-four hours."

The sunlight overhead disappeared as another hangar pad took the place of the first one. The elevator shaft was lit by bright LEDs.

"At least the storm will keep the tangos from flying that meth out," Stone offered hopefully.

"Maybe they won't fly it out," Juan said. "They might drive it out."

"In a storm like that?"

"Hope is a lousy plan."

The elevator lurched to a creaking halt in the cavernous hangar deck. Aircraft maintenance techs came running up with a fuel hose and diagnostic instruments for inspection. Gomez clapped one of them on the back as they scooted past him and into the cabin.

"That storm is a godsend," Stone said. "Gives us another day for mission prep, evaluation and further analysis. If we get lucky, we might even be able to get an NRO satellite retasked over the area for a better look."

Juan smiled mischievously. "Agreed."

Stone smiled back, suddenly uncertain what Cabrillo was agreeing with. The Chairman wasn't known for getting excited about mission delays.

Juan threw an arm around his neck.

"When God sends you lemons, Stoney, it's time to make vodka tonics."

25

Juan marveled at the Libyan snowstorm swirling in front of his eyes.

At least, that's what the howling sandstorm looked like through his helmet's white phosphor night vision screen.

And he couldn't have been happier.

The old Italian air base would have been impossible to approach by air or land in clear weather without being spotted visually or on radar. But the clouds of high-velocity sand neutralized nearly all forms of detection, and in a storm like this, personnel would be hunkered down inside buildings and not standing watch outside.

Best of all, nobody would expect an incursion during weather as severe as this.

Thanks to Gomez's last-minute surveillance run in the Tiltrotor, Juan and his three-man team had a usable topographical map—and a lot of other data that just might come in handy. But the same moaning storm sandblasting his visor now prevented the Tiltrotor from depositing them close to the base.

No problem, Juan told his team as he laid out his plan.

The Tiltrotor had airlifted the *Oregon*'s newest light desert assault vehicle and dropped them off thirty-five miles northwest of the facility.

They were just beyond the storm's reach and within safety parameters for the AW's delicate turboshaft engines.

Unlike the boxy PIG—a heavily armored cargo truck—Max's latest brainchild stood low to the ground like a sharp-nosed dune buggy. Hanley had pieced it together with the help of one of the Corporation's senior armorers and former CIA warfighter, Bill McDonald, a man with extensive long-range desert patrol experience in Iraq and Saudi Arabia. Max called it the DIG, for desert insertion ground vehicle. But as usual, the team came up with its own acronym—DING—just to annoy Max, who hated the idea of a single scratch or dent marring one of his precious mechanical creations.

The DING was essentially a gunned-up sand rail. But unlike other desert patrol vehicles currently deployed by armed forces around the world, the four-wheel-drive DING carried a few advantages, including its three powerful electric motors. Not only was it fast—zero to sixty in 2.9 seconds—it had a towing capacity of over fourteen thousand pounds.

Best of all, its three electric motors were nearly silent even when running at full speed and generating maximum torque on its high-traction Mickey Thompson Baja Boss all-terrain tires.

Built around the Tesla Cybertruck platform, the DING could travel over five hundred miles on a single electrical charge and a further one hundred miles with its onboard emergency backup battery charger.

It carried a few other surprises as well.

The low-profile DING was perfect for this mission—fast, powerful and quiet. The Tiltrotor had dropped the lightweight vehicle just at the edge of an ancient dry riverbed that ran four feet below the desert floor. Even if radar or infrared sensors were active, the DING would be hard to spot.

To minimize their footprint further, they came in at three a.m. with just three operators on the mission.

Linc wedged his big, muscular frame into the driver's seat and buckled the harness. The steering wheel looked like a child's toy version in his big hands.

Raven climbed into the back, sitting beneath the automated pintle-mounted M60 machine gun. The weapon could be controlled remotely through any of their augmented-reality helmets and even by Gomez in the Tiltrotor or Murph in the *Oregon*'s op center.

Juan rode shotgun, his left knee bumping against a scabbard concealing a semi-auto Benelli M4 tactical scattergun. In his leg holster, he wore his favorite pistol, a high-capacity FN—a Five-seveN—and strapped to his tactical vest was a P90 submachine gun that used the same armor-piercing ammo. Both weapons were suppressed but in the noise of the storm it was hardly necessary.

The all-terrain DING raced along the uneven riverbed, jerking and bouncing the team against their harnesses, the infinitesimal whine of its electric motors swept away by the shrieking wind. They were coming from the barren, uninhabited northwest; an attack from that direction would be completely unexpected even if the weather were good. The base itself was quite remote, but there was one unpaved road that ran southeast past the base toward a small, abandoned village twenty miles away; another road ran northeast to the distant coast. It was a perfect place to hide a drug-running operation.

The plan was simple but not easy. They would infiltrate the base using the stealthy DING under the cover of both night and the sandstorm and grab a sample of the meth. Then they would exfil undetected to where Gomez and the Tiltrotor would be waiting to evacuate the DING and the team back to the *Oregon*.

It was a good plan, Juan told himself, as the low, uneven shadows of the old Italian air base loomed in his phosphor vision. But Mike Tyson's unforgettable voice rang in his head:

Everyone has a plan until they get punched in the mouth.

"Here," Juan said. They were on the sand-covered tarmac one hundred yards west of what appeared to be a barracks in Gomez's photos.

Linc lifted his size-eighteen boot off the throttle and punched the brake. The DING skidded to a halt.

The team only had a few hours to prep for the mission. Normally, Juan preferred to do actual physical mock-ups, but their information wasn't solid enough to build any. The special operators on the *Oregon* trained constantly for all kinds of contingencies. Juan was confident that those long hours of prep, combined with all their previous mission experience, was enough to carry out this small, clandestine operation.

As soon as Raven leaped out onto the concrete tarmac, Juan punched a switch on the DING's console, juicing the motor powering the machine gun's automated pintle. He then tapped the on-screen aiming reticle at the barracks. The gun raised up and swiveled toward its target with an electric whir. He whispered "Armed" into his molar mic but didn't need to; Linc and Raven could see everything he was doing on their helmet viz screens.

Anyone coming out of that barracks would be immediately targeted and cut down by the machine gun. Thanks to the ID chips planted in their helmets, the automated targeting program wouldn't allow the machine gun to aim at Juan or his team in the event they came into its line of fire. It was a handy feature, especially if they were in close-range contact with the enemy.

Juan crawled out of the DING and tapped his visor, downloading one of Gomez's digital surveillance maps onto the small view windows on all their screens. He tagged the first building's image and gave the order to follow him in.

26

Juan led the way, crouching low, heading southeast. The wind was at their backs, blinding anyone who might appear in front of them with stinging sand.

They crossed the tarmac and passed a squat, one-and-a-half-story building. Given its location, Juan figured it served as the air traffic control tower even though it was covered by a huge camouflage tarp.

They ran farther across another, shorter tarmac—no doubt the service runway for aircraft preparing to take off or heading for the hangar. There were still no signs of human activity, but Juan knew someone was there. Gomez had picked up a couple body heat signatures on his last IR pass several hours earlier.

Juan's first waypoint was just beyond the service runway, where a perimeter fence should be located. Aerial photos showed no sign of one, which made sense. A conventional fence would be hard to conceal and would therefore reveal the presence of an active installation. The best defense for the base was the fact no one knew it was there. Its second line of defense was the remote and unforgiving desert itself. The third was whatever troops and weapons were on base.

Juan assumed a laser-fencing device was there but would have been made non-operational in a sandstorm because it would be constantly triggered. His assumption proved correct as he pointed to the inactive laser transmitter just inches from the toe of his boot.

Just then, one of Linc's big fingers tapped Juan on the shoulder.

"Chairman, check out your three o'clock."

Juan turned in the direction Linc was pointing. He tapped the magnification toggle on his visor and the image zoomed three times closer. It was a square cage in the middle of a wide-open area between buildings, swinging and twisting in the wind. The charred remains of a human being lay crumpled on the floor of the cage, the stumps of its arms upturned as if in prayer.

"Poor guy," Juan whispered. He couldn't imagine a worse way to go.

"That's an ISIS play," Linc said. "Those loonies don't mess around."

Linc was right. Burning people alive was just one of the many gruesome acts the infamous terror organization was known for. In recent years, ISIS fighters had been hiring themselves out as mercenaries to carry out their twisted vision of holy war. They were known to be working for Turkish forces in Libya.

"At least we know the type of people we're dealing with," Juan said, gripping his submachine gun tighter.

Juan dashed for the nearest building. It was covered by a thick camouflage material held fast against the storm by steel cables, juddering in the high wind. He touched the fabric. Just as he suspected. The new Israeli camouflage known as Kit 300 made everything beneath it virtually invisible to thermal or optical detection.

Judging by the building's height and width, photo analysis determined it was likely the hangar. A pair of metal doors clanged and rattled in the wind. There was enough of a gap between them for Juan to shoot his rifle light through and take a look-see just in case it was something else.

"I see a pair of drones. They both have funky triangular box tail rudders. No markings. Turkish design, I think. Missile racks, but not loaded," he said. "Spare parts, machine tools. Yeah, it's a hangar."

"All clear," Linc said. He not only scanned the area with his eyes but also checked it with the DING's onboard targeting camera. There was no motion from the barracks.

"Should we check those birds out?" Raven asked.

"Not in the mission profile. But we'll let Overholt know about them. I'm sure somebody will want to pay a visit," Juan said.

He pulled up his digital map and put a target marker on two nearby buildings just south of the hangar and dispatched Linc and Raven to investigate them. He chose a third building for himself, the farthest away.

"Head on the swivel. Let's move."

The three of them dashed off. Even before he reached his assigned building, Juan could smell the stench of diesel fuel and gasoline. By the time he reached the shuttered doors, Raven was calling in from her location.

"Looks like I found the machine shop." Her helmet cam display confirmed it, the interior lit up by her rifle light.

Linc reported in next. "I'm standing in front of the motor pool. Two six-by-six transports, two technicals inside." His camera image focused on the latter, two Nissan 4×4 pickups with fat sand tires and machine guns mounted in back.

Juan peered into his building and called in what he saw: "Fuel depot."

His camera displayed several diesel and gasoline pumps. The fuel tanks must have been beneath the cement floor. Quite a reconstruction project, Juan thought, and all of it carried out entirely undetected. The Turks were good engineers. They had used those skills to rebuild much of the Muslim parts of the former Yugoslavia after their devastating civil wars in the nineties.

There were only two large buildings left to explore. They were still nearly three hours away from dawn, but every second they were on the ground they risked exposure. Time wasn't their friend. Juan put a digital marker on the larger of the two buildings, assuming it was a warehouse, and told Raven and Linc to meet him on the west side of it.

Juan dashed toward the building, camouflaged the same way as all the others. The rolling hangar door faced the tarmac and clanged on its rollers in the wind.

Raven snapped the padlock open with her bolt cutters. Juan gently lifted the door just high enough for the three of them to scoot under, then carefully lowered it back down, the gusts beating on it like a pair of fists.

Once inside, they popped on their rifle lights. They split up and scanned the cavernous space, searching for the meth and any guards that might be inside.

Their gunstocks welded to their cheeks, they worked their way around rows of stacked pallets of steel drums, cardboard and wooden boxes and even bottled water.

"Goldilocks don't see no bears," Linc said.

"Just keep looking for the porridge," Juan said.

"Chairman, over here," Raven said.

Juan checked her location on the viz screen, then scrambled over to her. At her feet was a long wooden packing case, its lid having been carefully pried off by Raven's combat knife.

Inside were rows of scoped automatic rifles with slings attached and their barrels slicked with Cosmoline.

"AKs," Raven said.

Linc stepped up. "And I just found pallets of ammo in the back." It was 7.62×39.

Raven nodded. "AK ammo."

"Grab one of those, Rave. We'll try to source it when we get back to the ship."

"Aye, Chairman."

Raven set her rifle down, slung one of the crated AKs across her back, secured the packing case and retrieved her weapon.

"Good find. But the clock's ticking. We'll give it five more minutes to locate that meth, then we're out."

"Aye."

"If we find the meth, don't forget to pull on your heavy gloves before you handle it, it's pure poison." His team were pros, but a safety reminder never hurt.

They each turned silently on their toes to head off in a different direction, the timer on their viz screens counting down.

Juan turned a corner and found a pallet in a far corner wrapped in a waterproof tarp. He pulled his razor-sharp "tiger claw" Karambit knife out of its sheath and carefully slit the tarp open at the top, trying to hide the cut.

Bingo!

Juan pulled the heavy rubber gloves from his pouch and put them on, then lifted one of the heavy bricks of meth from the top of the pile. A blue diamond was printed on the plastic wrapper.

"Just found the Diamante Azul," Juan said. He rolled the brick over in his hands. It alone was worth a small fortune. The entire pallet was some dirtbag's hedge fund, most likely Herrera's.

Raven and Linc, silent as cats, appeared out of the darkness next to him.

"That's a lot of crank," Raven said.

Linc grunted. "I wonder how many ruined lives and dead are stacked on this pallet."

"We should destroy it," Raven said.

"I wish we could," Juan said, "but we're under orders. No one can know we've been here. More important, we need to track where this stuff is going. So let's get to it."

Raven opened up a supply bag as Juan pulled out a thin metal tube and extracted a sample of meth from the brick. She held out a small plastic vial in her gloved hands. Juan deposited the poison in it and she capped it.

While Raven and Juan collected the sample, Linc attached a new kind of tracking device onto several of the other bricks. They looked like clear plastic Band-Aids, nearly invisible, especially when fixed to the bottom of a brick. Ideally, he'd put one on each of them, but there was neither the time nor enough trackers to do it. At least they'd know where some of these wound up. Something was better than nothing.

Raven opened up a safety bag and Juan dropped the metal tube in it along with the meth sample. She then offered him a strip of clear adhesive tape on her fingertip and he resealed the brick—it looked like it hadn't been touched at all. Finally, he replaced the brick in its original location.

"Done?" Juan asked.

"Done," Linc said.

Juan now took a roll of black tape from Raven's hand and resealed the tarp. Unless somebody was looking for it, he doubted anyone would notice the repair.

"We're out of here," Juan said.

"Roger that," Raven said.

They turned to leave, but something froze them in place.

A cough.

27

The distant, echoing cough shot Juan through with adrenaline, putting his senses on high alert.

The audio on all three helmets had picked up the sound and triangulated its approximate location.

"Kill your lights, add thermal to your night vision and follow me," Juan whispered into his molar mic.

Their helmets had multiple sensors, including the U.S. Army's latest white phosphor and thermal combination. The resulting image of a person looked almost like a scene from the movie *Tron*—white outlining black silhouettes. Juan was still getting used to the video game effect, but in the darkened warehouse it was the best they could do without revealing their own positions with their rifle lights.

Juan's gun was at high ready as he charged forward, the other two spreading out behind him. They ran a cover-and-move pattern, leapfrogging between pallets, until they reached the far end of the warehouse where the sound came from.

Juan's heart sank. He saw another cage like the one outside with a body lying on the bottom.

But the white outline of the form inside moved slightly. Breathing maybe.

Whoever was inside the cage was alive.

"Clear?" Juan whispered in his comms.

"Clear."

"Clear."

"Cover me."

Juan dashed for the cage. The body inside was facing the wall of the warehouse, its back to them, with one arm cuffed to a bar of the cage. It was hard to tell in the dark, but judging by the shape and small size of the body and the length of the hair, it was a woman.

Juan touched the cage's door, but it didn't open. He fished around in his utility bag and pulled out a mini metal vapor torch—the MVT. Each pressurized fuel cartridge held precisely graded aluminum and copper particles along with copper oxide. The resulting flame leaped over a mile a second at nearly five thousand degrees Fahrenheit.

He fired up the ultra-hot flashlight-sized unit and melted through the latch in seconds. He yanked the door open and crawled inside. He rolled the body over. In the dark, he could still see the bruises on her face. He sighed heavily into his mic.

"Problem?" Linc asked.

"It's Meliha."

Meliha Öztürk stirred restlessly as Juan loaded another fuel cartridge in the torch. He fired up the unit and cut through the handcuff locked around the cage bar. He held her arm so it wouldn't fall, but the sudden muscle relief woke her.

She startled at the sight of a man in a full-face visored helmet leaning over her. When she started to scream, Juan clapped a gloved hand over her mouth, then flipped the visor up.

"Meliha, it's me. Juan Cabrillo."

She could barely see, but she recognized the voice and the name. Juan covered her mouth until she nodded in recognition. He removed his hand.

For a nanosecond, Juan thought about his requirement of leaving no footprint. Rescuing Meliha might compromise it, yet sometimes the man—or in this case, the woman—became the mission. While her captors might assume she escaped on her own, torch marks on the door killed that possibility.

"Juan, how did you find me?"

Good question. And he had a million of his own for her. But this wasn't the time for a coffee klatch.

"Let's talk later. Right now, we need to get you out of here."

Meliha sat up, rubbing the wrist that had been handcuffed. "Don't worry about me. It's the others you need to take care of."

"The others? What others?"

28

Juan knelt by the door and worked his lockpicks. He was trying to break into the building nearest the eastern gate. The road running northeast to the coast stood two hundred yards beyond the camp.

The countdown clock now showed they had been inside the base perimeter for eighteen minutes—about three minutes longer than Cabrillo had planned. He couldn't escape the feeling they were on borrowed time, but the mission parameters had changed. The clock would just have to keep on ticking.

The lock clicked open and Juan pushed inside, Raven and Meliha close behind him, careful to keep silent. Meliha insisted on going with them. While she'd been roughed up pretty bad, Raven didn't see any signs of a concussion or internal bleeding after a quick med check in the warehouse. She gave Meliha the okay to join them.

Linc kept watch by the door. He checked the DING's fire control camera on his viz screen. Still no sign of tangos on the other side of the camp where it was stationed.

"Did you find the meth?" Meliha whispered.

"Yes. And I got a sample."

"Did you destroy the shipment?"

"I'm under orders to leave it alone. I've put trackers on it so Overholt can follow the trail."

Meliha stopped short. "Do you always blindly obey orders?"

"Only when I know they're right." He gave her a look. "Less talk, more walk."

She crept a few feet forward.

"There," Meliha said, pointing to the middle of the room. A dim lightbulb high up in the rafters barely illumined the space.

A dozen people lay cramped and restless in a large cage.

Before Juan could say, "Follow me," Meliha bolted in that direction keeping low, even more worried than Juan that they might be caught at any time. Juan admired her spunk. He also fumed inwardly at the man who had beaten her. He couldn't wait to give him a taste of his own medicine.

Meliha reached the cage first and knelt, Juan, on her heels, beside her. The dozen people all were women. She whispered to the nearest one. Raven came up behind Meliha and Juan as the woman awoke. Frightened, she almost started to scream when she saw the otherworldly helmeted monsters with guns kneeling by her cage.

Meliha instantly quieted her with a sharp admonishment in a language Juan guessed was Romanian.

"Who are these women?" Juan asked.

"They are Pipeline girls, traded for cash, guns, drugs. Some were kidnapped, others paid to get smuggled into Western Europe to start a new life."

"Let me guess. Their new life will be nothing more than forced labor, cleaning houses or working in factories and slaughterhouses."

"Or worse. Unless we can get them out of here."

Juan's temper flared. This was nothing more than modern-day slavery. There was no way he was leaving them behind.

The other girls instantly stirred awake and began chattering excitedly in a couple other languages. Meliha shushed them each in their native tongue. They were in the same physical condition as Meliha or worse. Even in the dark, Juan could tell that some of them, despite their unwashed hair and bruised faces, were attractive young women. Two of them looked like teenagers.

Raven and Linc passed their canteens through the bars and the women drank greedily, sharing as best they could. Meliha switched languages a couple times and gave brief answers to their anguished questions.

A dozen pair of anxious eyes settled on Juan. He turned toward Meliha.

"Tell them we're getting them out now."

Meliha smiled as she wiped away the hair matted on her forehead. "I already did."

"There's not enough room in the DING for all of them," Raven said.

"No worries." Juan loaded a fresh cartridge into the vapor torch to cut open the cage lock. "There's an Uber just around the corner."

Linc led the way back to the motor pool, his suppressed MP5 locked against his shoulder, with Raven tracking right behind him. The women followed her in a ragged single file, shielding their eyes from the stinging sand. Some limped, some needed assistance from the others. Raven had given them all a quick once-over. Some of them needed immediate medical attention that she couldn't provide.

Meliha and Juan took up the rear, herding the stragglers along. According to Juan's visor clock, they were twenty-three minutes into the mission. His spine tingled with every step—they were pushing their luck beyond any reasonable limit, but there was no turning back now.

They crossed the open space where the twisting cage and its burnt corpse still rocked in the wind. Meliha froze, her eyes locking onto the gruesome sight, as the other women trudged on.

"You knew him?"

"My guide, Ishmael. The two of us were captured by ISIS mercenaries just outside Wahat Albahr."

"The village you talked about back in Istanbul. You were searching for evidence of a massacre."

"Exactly. They murdered Ishmael yesterday. Bayur told me it would be my turn when the sun rose this morning."

"That ain't gonna happen," Juan said, laying a gloved hand on her shoulder. "Who's this Bayur character?"

"His name is Cedvet Bayur, a Turkish national. He's the regional commander."

"Turkish military?"

"Former. He's a contractor now. And one of the Gray Wolves I told you about. A criminal organization with ties to the national government."

Juan made a quick calculation. "If we find this Bayur character, that would prove your father was telling the truth about Turkish forces slaughtering civilians in Libya."

"Yes, it would."

"And maybe get him out of prison for telling the truth."

"Exactly."

It also occurred to Cabrillo that snatching Cedvet Bayur could be the key that would unlock the mystery of the Pipeline.

"If Bayur is here, let's grab him."

Meliha shook her head. "I overheard one of the guards say he left the base."

"Where do you think he went?"

"He must have gone back to Wahat Albahr in order to destroy any evidence that remained."

"Where is this village?"

"On the coast, approximately one hundred seventy-five miles northeast of here."

It was easily within the DING's battery range. If Juan and his team left immediately, they would arrive around dawn.

Meliha added, "That's where we need to go next."

"Sure, as soon as we get you all back to the *Oregon* and have the doctor check you out."

Meliha started to speak but held her tongue. She turned and ran to catch up with the others now gathered in a bunch on the long wall of the next building.

Linc was careful to use the buildings as cover but not waste time. He had the same countdown clock on his visor that Juan had. And he had the same concerns. But the motor pool was just across the way. In a few minutes, they'd be out of there and heading back to the rendezvous point with Gomez and the Tiltrotor.

The imposing African American sprinted for the motor pool's sliding steel doors with Raven staying put, covering his six, her eyes sweeping the area.

Despite the wind and her visor, she thought she smelled ammonia and some other familiar chemical. It suddenly hit her. She glanced over to her right.

A latrine.

Just as Linc reached the motor pool's doors, a uniformed guard pushed open the nearby door to the latrine, zipping up his fly as he exited, shirttails flapping. The man caught sight of a huge figure—Linc—pulling open one of the rolling doors. The guard opened his mouth to shout out an alarm but his warning was torn from his throat by the subsonic bullet fired by Raven's silenced pistol. His corpse dropped into the whipping dust.

Some of the terrified women quailed at the sight of Raven's pistol and the killing they had just witnessed, even though he had been one of their tormentors. Meliha quieted them with a few commanding words and the calming touch of her own strong hands.

"They good?" Juan asked.

"They're fine," Raven said. "Let's go."

Linc dragged the corpse into the motor pool and hid it under a tarp as everyone else dashed into the garage. Raven shut the rolling door behind them and flipped on a light switch. The *Oregon* team pulled up their visors so the women could see their faces. The smell of grease, gasoline and rubber tires hung in the air.

Juan turned toward the closest vehicle, one of the medium, six-wheel-drive 6×6 military cargo trucks Raven had found earlier. All the women would fit into it.

Juan turned to Meliha. "Tell them to get in the back of that truck. And fast. That guard will be reported as missing any minute. We're driving out of here now and taking them to safety."

Meliha told them what Juan said, but the women stayed frozen in place. Even when Meliha's expression darkened and she barked at them, they still refused to move. She asked why.

One of the women, a thin blonde, turned to Juan. She spoke in a thick East European accent. He saw the defiance in her pretty gray eyes.

"We not get in truck with men with guns."

Unconsciously, Juan lowered the P90 machine gun to his side. "We have to get you out of here."

"No men with guns."

Raven stepped close to the blonde. "You don't have a problem with me driving the truck, do you?"

The blonde looked her up and down. "No. We trust you."

Raven turned to Juan. "That okay with you, Chairman?"

Not really, Juan said to himself. But it wasn't like he was going to cuff these women and toss them in the back like a sack of potatoes.

"You ever handle one of these things? It's a manual transmission."

"My uncle owned a trucking company. I drove bigger rigs than this for him while I was still in high school."

"Then the gig is yours. You have the Tiltrotor's coordinates in your visor map. We're on the south side of the base right now. I want you to break south directly behind us for a hundred yards, then swing around west from the direction we came from—circle way out, past the tarmac, and head for the riverbed we came down. This storm won't let up for another two hours. With the distance, dark and sand, you should have enough cover to get to Gomez. Clear?"

"Clear."

"Let's saddle up." Juan turned to Meliha. "Tell the others to get in the back and to keep quiet no matter what happens."

"And you'll follow us?"

"No. It might be a wild-goose chase, but I'm heading to Wahat Albahr to find this Bayur character."

Meliha frowned, then turned and gave the order. Linc pulled open the tarp covering the back of the truck and the women began climbing in.

Juan told Meliha, "I want you to ride in the front with Raven to translate. She'll protect you."

"I should go with you to Wahat Albahr."

"That's not a good idea. You've already been through a lot. And I can't guarantee your safety if you come with me."

"I'm fine, really. And Raven can't guarantee my safety either. Besides, I know where the village is and what Cedvet Bayur looks like. I can help you identify him."

Juan looked her hard in her clear green eyes. If he had any talent at all, it was the ability to quickly assess the character of a person as well as their value to a given mission. Besides, Overholt had ordered him to assist her any way he could. Getting her father out of jail fit that parameter.

"Okay, you can ride with us. But you must obey my orders without question. All our lives depend on it."

"Agreed."

Meliha smiled her thanks, then guided the gray-eyed blonde into the front of the truck with Raven so she could translate as needed.

Juan had Linc and Raven disable the two pickup trucks on the other side of the garage. He didn't want anyone chasing Raven and her human cargo down with those murderous machine guns.

Juan popped the hood on the other 6×6 truck and yanked a fistful of spark plug wires out, then tossed them in a barrel of dirty oil. He spoke with Gomez on his comms, explaining the new plan and telling him to expect a full complement of passengers. Almost too many.

"I don't know if I brought enough peanuts and Bloody Mary mix," Gomez said, "but we'll make it work somehow."

"And call Hux for me, tell her what to expect and to get the clinic ready."

"Roger that."

Like many of his best plans, this new one was made on the fly.

But he was still expecting to get punched in the mouth.

29

Raven wasn't kidding when she said she knew how to handle the truck. Moments later, under the cover of darkness and muffled by the howling wind, she slammed the 6×6 into first gear. She headed south, beyond the air base's perimeter, to begin the wide-sweeping circuitous route west that Juan had plotted for her to avoid detection.

The big rig disappeared from Juan's visual just minutes after she cleared the base, the roar of its diesel engine bested by the wind. She would be back on the riverbed and well on her way to Gomez shortly if everything went according to plan. She wouldn't have any problems with the desert terrain on those big, knobby tires powered by six-wheel drive.

Aboard the DING, they'd be racing through the desert on the northeast road to the coast and would make much better time though they had farther to go. With any luck, they'd catch Bayur with his pants down and grab him.

Linc contacted the DING through his automated helmet controls and directed it to their position. The three of them piled in. Linc hopped into the driver's seat and Juan put Meliha in the shotgun position. He pulled out a pair of goggles stored in a cubbyhole and handed them to her. She pulled them on.

Juan would take the seat beneath the automated M60 machine gun, but before he did, he unlatched his body armor vest.

"What are you doing?" Meliha asked.

He motioned for her to lift her arms. "You're wearing this."

"I'm not a soldier."

"You don the armor or you walk to the coast. Your choice."

Even in the dark and with the wind whipping her hair across her face, he could see her eyes narrow with resentment. She was clearly not used to being told what to do by anybody, but her common sense took over and she agreed with a curt nod.

The heavy body armor—a pocketed vest that held removable, bullet-proof ceramic plates—was far too large for her. The shoulder harnesses hunched up past her ears as she sat in the seat. But it provided her with some additional protection and that was all that mattered to Juan.

"Time to roll," Linc said as he press-checked his pistol.

"Not just yet."

Juan dashed off into the swirling void.

Juan's eyes burned with the stench of gasoline as he doused the six-foot-tall pallet of meth bricks with a twenty-liter jerrycan he snagged from the fuel depot.

He hoped Overholt would understand why he was destroying the meth. Juan couldn't stop thinking about the death and destruction the pallet of murderous chemicals represented. Besides, his team's presence at the air base would soon be discovered. And once Bayur or whoever was running the operation found that out, the first thing they'd do is inspect the pallet of meth bricks, their most valuable cargo. There was no doubt in Juan's mind they'd figure out it had been compromised. They would soon discover the trackers and discard them. Trying to uncover the Pipeline through the bricks was now a dead end. The meth would wind up in the bodies of too many dead and dying Europeans, mostly young people.

He couldn't allow that to happen.

Juan shook out the last drops of gasoline onto the pallet, then tossed the empty jerrycan on top. This corner of the warehouse was only lit by the LED flashlight clipped to the pocket of his black tactical shirt. Juan lifted up his helmet visor, pulled out his favorite Zippo lighter from a pants pocket and a half-length of a Cuban cigar he'd been hanging on to and lit it. He took a few deep drags on the stogie to clear the fumes in his sinuses and got it glowing.

Juan's head snapped around at the crash of the warehouse's rolling door flying up and the shouts of two guards charging in.

The overhead lights popped on.

Juan took a last puff to fire up the cigar red-hot before tossing it on the run like a Peyton Manning fadeaway pass. It landed perfectly atop the pallet. The gas-soaked stack of chemicals instantly whooshed in a ball of flame. He felt the searing heat from the exploding fire against the back of his shirt as he sped along the far wall, his short, bullpup submachine gun grasped firmly in his hand.

The first guard rounded a corner and charged into view. Juan raised his P90 and fired on a dead run, stitching a line of high-velocity bullets from the man's chest to his jaw that tossed him against a pallet of steel drums with a ringing thud.

Juan leaped over his corpse and turned the corner, crashing into the second guard—a mountain of a man and hard as rock—tumbling the two of them onto the cement floor. The bearded gunman's AK dropped from his hands and skidded away just out of reach. He rolled over to grab it. Still on the ground, Juan raised his submachine gun, still on its sling, and ripped off a dozen rounds into his side, silencing the big man.

Juan scrambled to his feet and dashed for the open door. He turned the first corner of the building and crouched down, his eyes scanning for more targets but there were none.

The sudden ear-shattering blare of a klaxon's alarm told him it wouldn't be long.

Juan bolted for the next corner of the building, shouting to Linc into his molar mic, "Take off! Take off!"

As he turned the corner, he nearly crashed into the DING as it slid to a stop inches away.

"I will, soon as you climb in," Linc shouted over the klaxon blaring overhead.

"I should've known you'd show up," Cabrillo said as he leaped into the backseat. Self-sacrificing loyalty was a hallmark of his crew.

The flames burst through the warehouse roof like a volcano erupting.

"I always figured you for a juvenile delinquent," Linc said as he pounded the throttle. The all-electric vehicle accelerated instantly, throwing up sand and slamming Meliha against her seat.

More voices shouted in the distance as camp lights snapped on while the roaring fire mushrooming above the warehouse lit up the night sky.

An ISIS fighter ran around the side of the next building, shocked to see a vehicle racing in his direction just yards away. He raised his rifle to fire. But before he could get off a shot, Linc swerved toward him, smashing the front bumper into his uniformed torso with a sickening crunch that tossed the body aside.

"Floor it."

"Aye that." Linc grinned. "Hold on tight."

Juan was glad they had disabled the two pickups back in the motor pool garage. Meliha had already given Linc the coordinates for the village and he had input them into the DING's GPS map display. Their travel path was delineated in blue. Once past the perimeter of the air base, they'd head for the coastal road and ride safely away.

The sand rail charged for the road ahead. Two hundred yards beyond the perimeter, they escaped the warehouse fire now roaring behind them.

"Home free," Juan said as they sped into the night.

30

W here's the road?" Linc asked. They were two hundred yards past the camp yet the terrain had hardly changed. The DING ran dark for concealment. They were better served by their night vision devices as the wind picked up speed.

"We're on it, according to Gomez's photo map."

The all-terrain tires churned through the soft road sand. Though they were driving slower than they had anticipated, they were still making good progress.

A half dozen hot green tracer flashes shot past the DING and disappeared into the pitch-black gloom ahead of them.

"What the heck was that?" Juan said as he punched the rear camera's button.

Two distant shadows trailed far behind them, their machine guns spitting more fluorescent tracer ammo.

"Is that who I think it is?" Linc said.

Juan studied the camera image. "Two technicals hot on our tail."

"I thought we killed those trucks back in the warehouse," Linc said. He mashed the throttle and the DING leaped ahead.

"Unless they have a helluva mechanic, they must've had two more."

The pickups fell behind but kept plowing ahead, their headlights barely slashing through the torrent of sand.

Thunk!

A heavy round slammed into one of the DING's Kevlar armor plates.

"Them boys sure can shoot," Linc said.

"So can DING."

Juan engaged the auto-targeting software. The two patrol vehicles hardly registered on-screen, their images smeared by the blinding storm. But the glowing green tracer rounds lancing out of their machine guns gave Juan a general location. He slid a targeting reticle over to one of the shadows and the M60 machine gun behind him spun around on its electric pintle. Juan hit the fire button and waited for the gun to open up, but the targeting reticle couldn't lock on to anything because of the poor image quality and the pickups' radical twists and turns.

More rounds thudded into the DING.

Linc fought the wheel. "Losing speed!"

"Give her more juice."

"I'm flooring it now."

Juan leaned out of the vehicle. The right side appeared undamaged. But a quick glance out of the left side—with hot tracer rounds zipping past his skull—showed him that the two left tires had been hit. Lucky for them, they were run flats. The outer soft rubber treads were shredded and picking up sand while the hard inner tires kept them moving forward. The DING carried four spares, but they couldn't just pull over and swap them out.

Juan unbuckled himself and climbed up to the machine gun mount. He was totally exposed yet had no regrets about giving his body armor to Meliha.

The DING wasn't a heavily armored fighting vehicle; it was built for speed and stealth. Right now, it was losing speed fast. And they'd already lost their stealth. Standing up in the DING, with two ISIS merc machine guns firing at him, made him as vulnerable as a naked sumo wrestler in a spear-catching contest.

Juan engaged the manual controls as he seized the M60's grip and wedged the stock into his shoulder. The weapon was already racked and ready to fire. The trucks were closing the distance, bouncing behind them through the storm.

Juan pulled the trigger and let off a short burst. While he couldn't get a good visual on the tangos, he used their green tracer flashes for a target reference—and his own red tracer rounds to correct his shots as he ripped off three more bursts.

All misses.

"They're catching up," Juan said into his molar mic between the staccato roar of two more short bursts.

"I can't give you what I ain't got. Time to get defensive."

"Copy that."

Juan fought to keep his balance as Linc whipped the steering wheel back and forth in his hands to minimize their target profile.

Juan struggled to aim his weapon as the DING bounced and bucked like a frenzied bull, its tires slewing on the road. He white-knuckled the grip of the rear-mounted M60 machine gun and ripped another short burst into the swirling vortex of the storm, but the red tracers vanished into the gloom behind him.

Missed again.

Despite his helmet's viz screen, Juan could barely see the two pickups chasing them in the moonless predawn. Only the stream of their fiery green machine gun tracers slashing through the sand-choked air gave him any idea where they were. The DING's two shot-out run flats meant the ISIS *pistoleros* running them down had better shooting skills than he did or maybe just better luck.

Or both.

Either way, they were doomed.

Juan was running out of bullets. And time. With the two thumping flats slowing them down, the technicals were closing in fast despite the DING's powerful, whisper-quiet electric motors. More green flashes sparked behind them. Heavy-jacketed rounds thudded against the DING's Kevlar front armor panels.

Juan whipped around to check on Meliha, who was hunkered down in his oversize body armor. She forced a brave smile for him and flashed two thumbs-up despite her obvious terror.

"Thank God she's okay," Juan whispered to himself as more tracers zooped past his helmet.

"Could really use some help, Chairman," Linc said. His deep voice vibrated inside Juan's skull over the molar mic. "Those guys are ruining the paint job."

"Coming right up."

Juan spun back around, pulling himself forward by the machine gun's grip and welding his cheek to the bouncing stock. It was now or never.

He laid the EOTech's red holographic "donut of death" reticle on the nearest square shadow of pickup truck closing in fast and mashed the trigger.

Nothing.

Juan reracked the weapon to eject the bad shell and fired again.

Nothing.

"Gun's jammed," Juan said, fighting to keep his balance.

"So much for Plan B. I know you got a Plan C."

Juan dropped down into the bucking rear seat and strapped in.

"You know I do. But you're not gonna like it."

"I never do. But the alternative is worse."

"Out there—your two o'clock." He pointed into the darkness to the desert beyond the road.

"But Gomez—"

"A minefield. I know."

One of Juan Cabrillo's invaluable skills was improvisation under extreme duress. Like a grandmaster chess player, his brain instantly calculated every conceivable move and countermove to the game's final conclusion, always finding a way to win despite impossible odds.

Juan had studied the Lidar images Gomez Adams recorded in premission recon flight the day before. An old Italian minefield from World War II lay buried just yards beyond the road.

Juan punched the virtual toggle on the side of his visor. A map popped up, filling half the screen with a digital map and the feed from the DING's forward-facing, ground-penetrating radar. The same image appeared on Linc's visor.

"That's your plan?"

"We're ridin' the Dragon, baby."

"No. You're riding, I'm driving. Hold on."

Last fall, Juan and Linc had raced their Harleys down the treacherous eleven-mile stretch of blood-soaked Tennessee asphalt known as the Tail of the Dragon, infamous for maiming and killing reckless bikers.

Linc held his line of attack as long as he could before he felt an invisible reticle square up on the back of his helmet. The intuition tingling his spine had saved him more than once and he wasn't about to doubt it now.

He twisted the wheel hard right and stomped on the accelerator. All three of them were thrown against their harnesses and just as suddenly slammed back into their seats as the DING lunged over the embankment at the side of the road.

The front tires dug into the softer sand four feet below, but the instant deceleration launched them into their harnesses again like they'd been shot out of a cannon and straight into a net.

Juan glanced over at Meliha and saw that she was buckled in tight, still in the fight.

Brave woman, he thought.

"You see it?" Juan said. The first red dot of a buried land mine popped up on their Lidar screens. Green tracers cracked overhead.

"Easy-peasy," Linc said.

The DING slowed further as Linc slalomed around the first three mines lurking beneath the surface.

Driving into the minefield was a long shot. Juan was certain the ISIS mercs wouldn't follow if they knew about it.

And only an idiot would willingly drive there.

But Juan didn't see any other options.

He spun around. The headlights of the first technical dropped and bounced off the road hard and fast behind them.

"Here they come."

"Is there a Plan D?" Linc asked, racking the wheel back and forth.

"O ye of little faith."

The mines were laid out haphazardly, with enough room to maneuver between them, but more were appearing on the screen, closer and denser with each passing second. Juan zoomed out on the image. They had at least two klicks of field left to navigate.

An explosion roared behind them, the light and sound both muted by the moaning sandstorm. Juan whipped around in time to see the flaming pickup cartwheel end over end until it hit another land mine that shattered the remainder of the burning wreckage.

"One down," Juan said.

He watched the other one leap from the road, its headlights slicing through the swirling dust.

He grinned beneath his visor. "And one to go."

Green tracers pocked the terrain next to them.

"They've got guts, I'll give them that," Linc said.

"Guts I can spill into the dirt," Juan said, "it's their speed that worries me."

"Copy that."

"You better push it. There's a *wadi* beyond here. We can take cover there."

"Aye, Chairman." Linc punched the throttle. The DING lunged ahead.

Juan heard the hesitation in his voice. Fast through a minefield was a big ask.

But a 7.62×39mm bullet to the brain pan was worse.

Cabrillo's eyes fixed on the red mine dot colliding with the front end of their vehicle.

"Chairman!"

Juan's vision wiped away in a blinding white light.

He felt his body lift into the angry sky, high above a graveyard of sand.

31

Corkscrewing over a desert floor crowded with land mines, all Juan could do was brace himself for impact—and his imminent demise.

Strangely, he felt no fear. As time seemed to slow, he knew he had no regrets. He had lived his life full on and on his own terms. His death would be no different.

The DING crashed on its side with a bone-crunching thud that jerked Juan hard against his harness. His own grunt roared in his helmet. The vehicle rolled over two more times, the soft, heavy sand slowing them down with each bounce. The DING finally came to a standstill on its passenger's side. The three of them hung suspended in stunned silence.

"Where's the boom?" Linc asked.

"Everywhere but here," Juan said as he pulled his combat knife to cut himself loose. He figured the reason why they hadn't been blasted to kingdom come was that the explosion must have thrown them clear of the minefield. Equally miraculous, the DING stayed planted where it landed instead of caroming back into the field, its two left wheels still slowly spinning in the air.

"Thank the good Lord for that one," Linc said.

"With a little help from Max."

While the DING was lightweight and built for speed, Max had still managed to engineer it with a stout titanium undercarriage against land mines and other hazards.

Juan sliced his harness as he grabbed the overhead bar supporting the machine gun. He eased himself to the ground, staying as close to the DING as he could. It took Linc a few more seconds to extricate his much larger frame from his precarious position.

Juan yanked open his visor and knelt down next to Meliha. The right side of her armor-plated upper body was pressed against the sand.

"You hurt?"

"I'm fine. Please help get me out of this . . . contraption."

A heavy burst sledgehammered the DING's undercarriage. Juan instinctively covered her up, but they were perfectly protected—for now.

Linc stood next to Juan, an infrared monocular to his eye.

"Three hundred yards back. Still up on the road."

"Not as anxious to meet their maker, I guess."

"Always happy to oblige 'em if they change their minds," Linc said.

The howling wind couldn't hide the thundering roar of the distant machine gun as it opened up again. Linc ducked just as more rounds spanged against the titanium.

"As soon as they figure out they can't light us up with that machine gun, they'll try to come around to take us out—or at least confirm the kill." Juan pulled his pistol from its holster and held it out to Meliha.

"Do you know how to shoot one of these?"

Meliha snatched the pistol from his hand and yanked back the slide. A bullet ejected from the chamber. She grabbed it in midair with one hand, then hit the mag release button with her thumb, dumped the mag, pressed the loosed bullet back into the mag and reracked the weapon to put the bullet back in the chamber. The little demonstration took all of two seconds.

"Your father?"

"An expert marksman. He trained me well."

"You don't want to let those guys take you back."

"Trust me, they won't."

Juan nodded grimly. They'd have to get through him and Linc first before it got to that point.

"Just stay put—for now."

Juan stood and Linc handed him the infrared monocular. Three hundred yards away, the remains of the other truck still burned, the guttering flames slammed and tossed by the storm.

"The headlights are moving," Linc said. "Too bad our M60 is dead."

"When a door closes, find the window."

Juan handed the glass to Linc and climbed back up into the DING. He opened up a hatch and snagged a twenty-four-inch-long tube and stepped back down into the sand.

"Now you're talkin'," Linc said, admiring the weapon.

"I'll need you to draw fire for me. Just don't get shot when you do it."

"I'm a Black man in black tactical gear in the middle of the night. I figure my chances of not being seen are a skosh better than yours." Linc nodded at the tube—an M72 LAW rocket launcher. "You should let me take the shot."

"Rank hath its privileges."

Juan knelt down next to Meliha and flipped his visor back up. "Stay down and as close to the DING as you can. We'll be out of this jam in a minute."

Meliha smiled, making her big green eyes behind her goggles even bigger. "I believe you."

Juan smiled back yet wasn't sure he believed it himself. He pulled his visor back down. "On my mark."

"Aye, Chairman."

Linc climbed up into the DING, keeping the lowest profile his frame could manage, and laid the gun barrel on the door's saddle.

"Two hundred yards out. They've stopped," Linc whispered. "That's a long reach for your little toy."

About the maximum range, Juan reminded himself.

First used during the Vietnam era, the tubular M72 LAW rocket launcher was a light anti-tank weapon still deployed on battlefields around the world. It was cheap, simple to use and deadly effective against even the thickest armor.

Juan pulled the rear cotter pin, yanked back the inner tube and extended the weapon to its full thirty-six-inch length, arming it. The iron sights popped up automatically. In the dark, the crude sights would have been useless without his enhanced vision. The problem wasn't just the distance but the fierce wind the 66mm rocket would have to travel against. Hitting his target would be like sinking a hundred-foot putt on a bad-breaking green.

At night.

In a hurricane.

He'd just have to take his best shot and hope for the best. Juan put the tube on his shoulder.

"Do it."

Linc opened up with his 9mm machine gun. The lighter bullets struggled to reach all the way out to the pickup and the gusts tossed them around like darts in a wind tunnel. Even for a supremely skilled sniper like Linc, it was a nearly impossible target. But the goal wasn't to hit the truck—it was to get their attention.

He did.

The Nissan's machine gun swung around and opened up in a blur of tracer green.

That was Juan's signal to step out from behind the DING, fully exposing himself to fatal gunfire. His head snapped backward and he shouted, "Clear for fire!" out of habit, though he knew Meliha wasn't in the path of the rocket's exhaust. He laid the laddered front reticle on his aiming point high and angled according to the wind direction, whispered a prayer and squeezed the trigger atop the tube.

A giant plume of flame and exhaust whooshed behind him. The fiery projectile streaked across the sky in a wobbling arc, swooping up and over like a Frisbee on a long toss.

Bull's-eye! The Nissan erupted in a ball of flame.

Linc laughed like a braying donkey. "Are you kidding me? That was the greatest shot of all time."

"*Drive for show, putt for dough.* Let's get the DING righted, change those tires and get out of here before their friends show up."

"Aye that, Chairman."

Juan, Linc and Meliha easily shouldered the lightweight desert vehicle back onto all fours. It only took the two operators three minutes to swap out the tires, thanks to the specially designed quick-release wheel hubs like the ones used on Formula One race cars.

A quick scan with the DING's forward-looking Lidar pointed out a clear path back to the coastal road. Linc stomped the accelerator.

They'd still arrive around the rising of the morning sun, the promise of a new day.

But Juan couldn't help but wonder if that fatal Mike Tyson punch in the mouth was still waiting for them just over the horizon.

32

The sound cut through him like a knife.

Cedvet Bayur lay tangled in his bedsheets when his emergency cell phone rang. He leaped out of bed, shot through with adrenaline, before his brain was even engaged.

He stood on uncertain feet, disoriented in the dark; the thick curtains covering his penthouse windows blocked the predawn glow just beginning to light up the coast. In a flash, he cleared his mind and grabbed the phone on the second ring.

"What is it?" Bayur barked. His cottonmouth voice croaked, utterly dry from a night of whiskey and cigarettes. Bayur stormed to the refrigerator to grab a bottle of cold water.

"Sir, there's been an attack."

"An attack? How? What happened to the storm?"

"It's not clear, sir. The storm only slackened off a few minutes ago."

"When did this happen?"

"Two hours ago."

"Why am I just now hearing about this?"

"I've been conducting damage assessments, searches of the compound and the area, putting out the fires."

"In other words, you were afraid to call me."

"No, sir."

Bayur knew that was a lie. The man should have been afraid. He was only trying to make amends before he called. So far, he'd failed.

Bayur put the phone on speaker. "Details. All of them."

"Seven of our men killed, six vehicles destroyed or disabled, including two of our Nissans in a minefield."

"Minefield? What minefield?"

Bayur snapped off the lid to his bottle of water and gulped down a long, cold draught that soothed his parched throat.

"Apparently, there is a minefield just off the coastal road we were unaware of. Perhaps it was laid by the Germans or Italians during the war. We're uncertain."

"And what were they doing in the minefield to begin with?"

"Two of our patrol vehicles followed the assaulters out into it. Both were destroyed by mines."

"And the assaulters?"

There was a pause on the other end.

"Escaped."

Bayur cursed. He was as angry with himself as with his number two for the failure. He had trained them all. In a thousand years, he never would have guessed the Libyan opposition would have staged an attack at night in the middle of a storm.

Or did they?

"How many were there?"

"Unknown. To the best of our knowledge, a single desert patrol vehicle carrying three or at most four passengers."

Bayur drained the last of the water and tossed the bottle, fighting off the tinge of panic creeping into his gut. It would have required tremendous skill to carry out an attack in the middle of a storm of that magnitude. It also meant the enemy had found them, scouted them, formulated a plan and carried it out under conditions that he himself would have avoided at all costs.

A lot of the Russian mercs were former Spetsnaz operators and a few of them were working for the opposition. But something wasn't adding up. A Russian attack wouldn't have left a few dead. They would have burned the base to the ground and slaughtered every last one of his ISIS mercenaries.

"What aren't you telling me?" Bayur demanded.

There was another long pause on the end of the line.

Finally, "The meth shipment. It's been destroyed."

The tinge of panic exploded into a full-blown electrical storm that nearly shut down Bayur's whole nervous system.

"What? How?"

"Burned up."

Bayur cursed violently.

His Pipeline masters would have him killed for this failure.

Worse, his family's name would be sullied and his father put at risk.

Bayur's discipline returned. He'd survived and prevailed over countless ambushes and attacks by superior forces by keeping a cool head under fire. This was no different.

"Hold." Bayur muted his phone and marched over to the bed, snatching up his trousers.

Something wasn't adding up, Bayur decided. Why would the Russian mercenaries want to destroy millions of dollars' worth of drugs? Why not kill everybody and steal it? That was the Russian way of war.

If not the Russians, then who?

It could be anyone. If the destruction of the drugs was the objective, perhaps it was a law enforcement operation—or even a rival criminal gang. Whoever it was had resources and talent. His employer would need to know who was behind this attack. If he could find and capture them and extract all the necessary intelligence, he might win favor with his superiors. Whether or not they would spare Bayur's life was still in question. At the very least, his family's reputation might be salvaged.

Bayur unmuted his phone.

"What else are you withholding from me? Tell me everything or I will gouge out your eyes and leave you naked in the desert."

"Nothing else. Except that all the women are gone."

Bayur's hand nearly crushed the phone. He fought back the welling rage, calming himself.

"Then why do you say there was only one small vehicle? How could they have transported those thirteen slaves?"

"They stole one of our trucks."

"And that nosy journalist Öztürk? She's gone as well?"

"Yes, sir."

Another puzzle that didn't make any sense. Where would they have gone? And how would the truckful of women negotiate a minefield?

It couldn't.

Bayur pulled up the map of the area in his mind. If they didn't take the coastal road, where would they have gone?

Any direction except the coastal road if that's where the minefield was. They must still be in the area.

"You've searched for them?"

"Yes, sir. But with all our vehicles disabled or destroyed, we could only search the area by foot."

"Did anyone see the truck with the women?"

"No, sir."

"But they saw the attack vehicle?"

"Yes, sir. That's why the two patrol vehicles gave chase."

Interesting. That meant the truck didn't follow the same path as the assault vehicle.

"Where did you search?"

"All the way to the minefield in the north. Also west, east and south."

"Footprints? Tracks?"

"If there were any, the wind swept them away. As I said, it only began to die down just a few minutes ago."

"Can you launch the drones? Find out where that truck went?"

"Not yet. According to the pilots, the wind speed is still too high."

A thin sliver of sunlight peeked through the billowing curtains, kicked up by a sea breeze.

Bayur pulled on a shirt. Why didn't the assault vehicle escort the women in the truck—wherever it went? Either because it didn't need to or it had a different mission. Where would the assault vehicle be going to?

His mind turned back to that filthy journalist Meliha Öztürk. Her radical father had been a threat to the Gray Wolves until he was thrown into prison and silenced. No doubt his daughter had come snooping around the village on his behalf.

Cedvet Bayur had captured Meliha and her driver just outside Wahat Albahr. He thought burning her driver alive would have loosened her tongue regarding what she knew about the Pipeline or the Gray Wolves, but it hadn't. Nor had the prospect of her own immolation. Bayur had hoped that a long, sleepless night thinking about such a painful death would have broken her down. She was tough, for a woman, he'd give her that much.

Now he wished he'd just killed her outright. Instead, she'd escaped. Even with her limited knowledge of the Pipeline air base and the activities taking place there, she posed a threat to his superiors. And they would hold him accountable.

He shuddered at the thought.

He needed to recapture her. But where had she gone?

She probably told her rescuers to go to Wahat Albahr to gather evidence on her behalf. He knew her to be a determined woman. Most likely, she was traveling there with them.

If she uncovered the war crimes he'd committed there, the Gray Wolves would fall.

And so would he. In a most terrible fashion.

Bayur did a quick mental calculation. A fast-moving desert patrol vehicle could make good time. He looked at his watch. It would be arriving at the village within the hour.

Forget the other women, he decided. It was Öztürk and her mercenary saviors he had to find if he wanted to live.

He barked orders at his number two, then rang up the airport and ordered a civilian helicopter in his employ. He'd be arriving just as Öztürk and her mercenaries did. But he needed reinforcements. His best troops were deployed in a major operation near the Egyptian border. He needed to rely on the same local unit of ISIS mercenaries for backup. They had proven themselves before under his command during the assault on the same village and had the weapons needed to do the job.

He punched the private-elevator button to take him to the parking garage. A smile creased his face at the thought of Meliha Öztürk back in her cage, trembling with fear.

33

THE COASTAL VILLAGE OF WAHAT ALBAHR IN LIBYA

The DING crested a dune just as the first rays of dawn broke above the turquoise blue Mediterranean Sea. Far below were the remains of what had been a quaint little coastal fishing village.

Twenty years ago, this would have been a paradise. The kind of place a world-weary traveler would have dreamed to settle down in.

Now it was a post-apocalyptic nightmare.

"That's Wahat Albahr," Meliha pointed out, though it was unnecessary to do so. It was highlighted and named on the DING's GPS map screen.

"Quiet as a tomb down there," Linc said.

"It is a tomb." Juan lowered his binoculars. "Let's get down there."

"Aye."

A few minutes earlier, Juan had called the *Oregon* for a status update on the rescued women. Dr. Huxley told him that after a quick but thorough examination of each of them, she determined that none of the serious injuries that many of the women had suffered were life-threatening. Lack of sanitation and serious dehydration complicated things. And nearly all of them were traumatized by the experience and suffered severe emotional and mental distress as a result of their assaults. It was too much for the *Oregon*'s small clinic to handle.

"The good news is that Linda contacted Mr. Overholt. He made immediate arrangements for the women to be treated at the U.S. Naval Hospital in Naples."

"How long will it take the *Oregon* to get them there?"

"They're already on the way. Gomez is in the air now with them on the Tiltrotor. I didn't see any point in delaying treatment."

Juan was delighted with Hux and her team. And even more so with Overholt, who came through like a Spartan as usual. The only complication was Gomez. Cabrillo had planned to use the AW to egress the village with the DING. Now they were stranded.

As the desert patrol vehicle made its way toward the village, Juan sent an encrypted text to Linda Ross, the *Oregon*'s acting captain.

"We need to hitch a ride."

Linc followed the windswept road into the village, shaped like a T, slowing the electric motors to avoid the wrecked barbed-wire barricade that should have blocked their entry. As they entered the village square, where the two roads intersected, they saw more evidence of destruction.

There clearly had been a battle. Juan could make out the lines of defense. There were barricades that blocked the entrance on both ends of the road, trenches in the ground and sandbags on the roofs—all good positions for riflemen. The defenders should have been able to hold their ground.

But something had gone terribly wrong.

Swollen, fly-infested Libyan corpses lay scattered where they fell. Some were Arabs, others Tuaregs—a few blue *tagelmust*s stolen as war trophies.

The corpses that weren't completely stripped wore tattered makeshift rebel uniforms. Whoever won this battle took their guns and ammo for

spoils, along with grenades, bandoliers, fighting knives and even combat boots, judging by the bare feet.

The mud and concrete-block buildings were in various stages of ruin.
The least damaged were merely bullet-scarred. Many had holes punched
through them; several had been pulverized to dust by heavy ordnance.
Dried blood and tissue stained several of the walls.

Unless they had been attacked by overwhelmingly superior numbers,
they should have been able to put up a good fight. Instead, it had been a
one-sided massacre. Even bleating sheep in the slaughter pen would
have put up more of a fight than what Juan saw here.

"Over there," Juan pointed, heading for the left arm of the village T
and the last barricade.

Linc pulled to a stop next to a white man's corpse, his light skin
burned and blistered by the sun. Juan climbed out of the DING and
raised his helmet visor as he knelt next to the bullet-riddled body. He
recognized an exposed tattoo on his arm.

"VDV. Russian Airborne Forces," Juan said, breathing through his
mouth. "Spetsnaz."

"Russian military? Here?"

"More likely mercenaries," Meliha said. "Fighting for the Libyan
rebels."

"Those boys got game," Linc said. "Whoever punched their tickets
knew what they were doing."

"Cedvet Bayur is a very capable commander," Meliha said. "And he
has experience fighting Russians."

Juan pointed at the Russian corpse at his feet. "Is this enough evidence for you?"

Meliha shook her head. "These are all fighting-age males, not civilians. It won't help my father's case."

Juan stood and scanned the area. He saw a few more white Russian
bodies rotting in the sun. Birds were standing on them, picking away at
their remains.

"Silent as the grave" had a whole new meaning for Juan. Whatever romance the seaside village once held was ruined by the stench of rotting flesh and offal. He climbed back into the DING.

"Let's check out the other end of town."

A rifle crack echoed in the distance. A heavy slug slammed into Juan's door.

Linc punched the gas, throwing sand and grit. He threaded the vehicle between the two nearest buildings, blocking the shooter's line of sight.

Juan had seen the location of the shot posted on the DING's information screen. But with its sound locator wedged between two buildings, it wasn't possible to be precise. The post was just an educated guess.

A woman's voice cried out in the distance—just as another shot fired.

Juan shouted at Meliha, "Stay here!" as he and Linc grabbed their weapons, leaped out of the DING and raced toward the gunfire.

34.

According to the map on their helmet viz screens, the gunshots were coming from the graveyard. Juan and Linc raced to the first corner of the nearest building and stopped to check for more gunfire.

Meliha crashed into Juan's back with the sudden stop.

"I told you to stay in the vehicle."

"You are neither my husband nor my father. And remember, you're here to help me."

"I can only help you if you don't get your head blown off."

"So far, so good, wouldn't you say?"

"Just stay behind me—and do what I say. Got it?"

"Got it."

Another shot rang out. The sound reverberated on the crumbling concrete walls. The viz screen still located it in the graveyard.

Juan dashed out with the P90 in his fist and headed for the next wall. Meliha was right behind him and Linc took up the six.

Another shot rang out as a woman's voice shouted something in Arabic.

"She's commanding the demons to leave her village," Meliha loosely translated.

Juan answered in Arabic. *"Man yastatie 'an yalumaha?"*—*Who can blame her?*

Meliha smiled. "Yes, I forgot about your beggarly performance. Your accent is really quite good."

"My tuna casserole is even better."

Juan ducked his head around the corner. He was answered with a bullet that splintered concrete, stinging his face.

"Yeah, she's in the graveyard all right."

Juan and Linc made a quick plan. Juan then turned back to Meliha.

"I'm deadly serious. Don't move from here until I call you." Juan's voice hardened with command authority. "Understood?"

Meliha couldn't help but obey the order. "Understood."

"Good."

"Please don't hurt her."

"If she doesn't kill us first, we won't."

Juan nodded at Linc and the two of them sprinted away.

Juan dashed across to the next building, hoping to draw the woman's attention.

He did.

Another shot rang out. The bullet cracked into a mud brick wall several feet above his head. Juan ducked around the corner into a doorway across the way just as another round hit the dirt inches from where he had been standing.

"She might be crazy, but she can shoot," Juan said.

"Almost there," Linc said in his comms.

Juan ducked his head in and out of the doorway quickly. He saw a shrouded woman standing behind a tall, bleached headstone, a short, bolt-action rifle in her hands. She scanned the area looking for her target—Juan.

"She's a hundred yards back, just behind that headstone."

"I know. I saw her taking potshots at you." The former SEAL sniper chuckled. "She could teach me a thing or two. Hold tight."

"Roger that."

Juan stayed back in the shadows, waiting for Linc's signal.

"Ready."

"Here goes nothing."

The old woman tracked the buildings, seeking her target through the iron sights of her Carcano, a relic her father had stolen from an Italian soldier during the war many years ago. She was searching for the strangely helmeted demons she'd seen riding in the unusual car. She had almost shot one as he raced between the buildings.

Where had he gone?

Suddenly, a tall figure bolted out of a doorway down the street. She shouted curses at him as she aligned the sights with the middle of his back. He stumbled on a piece of concrete and crashed to the ground.

She both laughed and said a prayer before her finger squeezed the trigger.

A pair of strong arms wrapped around her like bands of steel and lifted her off her feet as she fired. The bullet flew high, missing its mark. She dropped the rifle in the sand.

The demon spoke behind his glass helmet, but she didn't understand him. She cursed and spat, kicked and screamed. She didn't speak his Devil tongue, but she heard the monster utter these words:

"Chairman, I've got me a live one."

The woman flailed and hissed in Linc's powerful grip as Juan and Meliha ran up.

"*Jinn! Jinn!*" the woman shouted, her mouth nearly toothless. *Demons! Demons!*

Her crazed, bloodshot eyes flared with fear while she again spat at them, raging.

"Pull off your helmets. You're scaring her," Meliha commanded. Juan complied, but Linc didn't dare let go.

Meliha laid a calming hand on the old lady, telling her they weren't demons but instead friends.

Linc felt the sinewy little figure slump in his arms, then begin to shake as she sobbed with relief. He set her gently in Meliha's waiting arms as Juan snatched up her rifle. He glanced around. There was a freshly dug grave and next to it an old trenching shovel. Lying beside the grave was a swollen corpse, its shirtless brown skin puckered with bullet holes and bayonet wounds. The young man's wispy beard and thin hair ruffled in the breeze.

"Look at her hands," Meliha said, holding one up. The leathered claw was bloody and blistered.

The old woman whispered into Meliha's neck. She translated as the woman spoke.

"She says she's been digging graves for the last ten days, but she is too old and too weak to bury them all. As a Muslim, it was her sacred duty to try."

Linc and Juan exchanged a look. As near as they could tell, the wiry little woman had dragged the bodies from the village by hand.

Juan surveyed the cemetery. At least two dozen graves appeared to be freshly dug. Scrap wood headstones were emblazoned with the names of the dead in crudely written Arabic script. According to Islamic practice, a body should be buried as quickly as possible, ideally in less than twenty-four hours.

The old lady began sobbing again as she spoke. Meliha translated.

"Many of them she had known since they were small boys. They were from this village."

"I don't like being exposed out here," Linc said. "No telling who might have an eye on us."

"Copy that." As Juan picked up the old woman's rifle, he asked her, *"Hal hanak 'ayu makan yumkinuna aldhahab 'iilayh?"*—Is there somewhere safe we can go?

The woman eyed him suspiciously, then nodded. She straightened up but leaned heavily on Meliha.

"Come with me."

* * *

After the old woman finally calmed down, Juan, Linc and Meliha made their way to the three-story, concrete-block house located on the village's main and only thoroughfare. Her name was Fadah. She had invited them in, away from the prying eyes of the *jinn* that had slaughtered her village.

Back in her modest second-floor kitchen, she fell into the habit of many poor people around the world—sacrificial hospitality to strangers. Juan set her rifle in the corner.

She apologized profusely that all she had to serve was mint tea without sugar, but they assured her they were grateful. She boiled the water on a solar-powered heating coil, a gift from the Gaddafi regime. The utilities had been knocked out.

While the water boiled, Juan sent Linc up to the roof for overwatch. He let Meliha interrogate the woman, knowing that she was desperate to gather the evidence she needed to free her father from his Turkish prison.

"Where are the others from the village?" Meliha asked. "The women and children? The old ones?"

"We were told by our militia to leave because a big attack was coming and so everyone left."

"But not you?"

"My husband and children are all buried here. Where else would I go? They would have no one to speak to them except strangers and *jinn* if I left."

"And the battle . . . You were here when it happened, yes?"

The old woman nodded. "I was in my house. Here, in this room, when it all happened."

"If it is not too painful, can you tell me what you saw? Who was fighting?"

"Our boys were behind the wire and on the roofs and everywhere else with their guns and trucks. They were being led by foreign officers. Infidels."

Meliha and Juan looked at each other. That explained the Russian bodies outside.

"And then the shooting started?"

"No. That's when the voice came into my head."

"You mean you heard a loudspeaker."

"No!" The old woman tapped her forehead with her tawny fingers. "In here. I heard the voice in here, inside my own skull."

"What voice?"

The old woman's eyes widened.

"The voice of God!"

35

"Did you really think God was talking to you?" Meliha asked as kindly as she could. She suspected the woman had been driven insane by the stress of living through a long civil war and by grief.

"No, of course not. It was the voice of Satan pretending to be God."

Now Meliha was certain she was crazy.

"And what did the voice say?"

"The Devil told everyone to drop their weapons and surrender or they would be struck blind by the Angel of the Lord. I had no gun, I was no fighter. But the voice was so loud in my head it scared me, so I hid under my bed." Fadah pointed at a small alcove with a sheer cloth door. A primitive cot with clean though badly frayed bedding could be seen just inside.

"Then what happened?"

"A few moments passed. I'm not sure how many. I was so frightened. But then I heard the boys shouting and screaming, so I ran to the window and saw them in the street. They were clawing at their eyes, as if they had been struck blind, just as the Devil had promised. That's when the guns started firing and the slaughter began."

The woman jumped up and ran over to the kitchen sink cabinet. She flung open one of the double doors and pointed inside. It was large enough for a child—or a skinny old woman scared out of her mind—to crawl into.

"I hid in here, afraid to move at all, while the killing was happening. All I could do was pray and cry. And then through the crack between the almost closed doors I saw them come into the room. They all had machine guns. I was so afraid they would see me. Especially the Turk."

"Who?"

"The Turk."

Meliha sat forward. "How do you know he was a Turk?"

"The accent, it's like yours. You are Turkish, yes?"

Meliha nodded. "Yes."

"I had seen him before, in the market a month ago, with other foreigners. They had no guns then. I thought perhaps they were tourists."

Meliha didn't dare hope yet had to ask, "Do you know his name?"

"No, but I recognized him from that day in the market. He had a scar on his face shaped like a hand." She splayed the fingers of her left hand against her cheek to illustrate. "As if the hand of Satan had touched him and melted his skin."

Meliha turned to Juan and spoke in English. "That describes Bayur perfectly."

Juan nodded at the frail woman standing in front of them.

"And she's the witness who will save your father."

Meliha nodded, her eyes glistening with tears.

Juan understood her emotions. She'd just won a hard victory that nearly cost her her life.

"We need to get Fadah to my ship before this Bayur character comes back to get her."

"Lower," Cedvet Bayur said into his comms.

He was sitting in the seat next to the helicopter pilot. They were flying into the early-morning sun and he was having a hard time seeing.

"Yes, sir." The pilot nudged the collective and the helicopter dove.

Bayur pulled the binoculars to his eyes.

There!

He leaned forward. There was a desert patrol vehicle parked just outside one of the three-story houses below—just like the vehicle described to him by his number two.

A driver, a gunner, perhaps a third passenger, Bayur thought to himself, judging by the vehicle's design. It could be another mercenary. Or someone else.

"It's that witch Öztürk," he whispered in his comms.

"Sir?"

"Nothing." Bayur gestured with his finger. "Take us up high, and circle around. We don't want any surprises."

"Yes, sir."

The pilot prayed the Turk commander didn't hear the relief in his voice. The thin-skinned civilian helicopter wouldn't survive a short burst of machine gun fire, let alone an anti-aircraft missile. He assumed both were likely hidden somewhere down there and aimed in his direction.

The chopper climbed as it turned, its nose pointing toward the nearby coast. Bayur lifted his binoculars again. His fighters and their weapons were already in position.

He saw a large cargo ship, rusted and nearly wrecked, steaming toward the bay. A stain of blackened smoke pouring from its single, rear-mounted stack fouled the pristine air.

Odd, he thought. What's a cargo ship doing here?

"One more circuit," he ordered the pilot.

The pilot swallowed his terror.

"Yes, sir."

Juan tilted his ear toward the ceiling. Distant rotor blades pounded the air, coming closer.

"We have company," Linc reported into his comms. "A civilian helicopter, by the sound of it."

"Bayur?" Meliha asked.

"No telling." Juan shrugged it off, wanting to keep things calm. "Probably just a crew heading out to an oil rig."

But inwardly, he knew.

Who else would it be?

Bayur adjusted the focus ring on his binoculars.

The image sharpened as a large Black man in tactical gear came into view on the roof far below.

"Americans," Bayur said, thumbing his mic.

"Sir?" the pilot asked.

Bayur ignored him as he issued orders to his militia commander.

"Commence operations."

"Chairman, we have tangos," Linc said into his molar mic.

"Copy that. What do you see?"

Fadah's face knitted suspiciously. "Who is he talking to?"

"His friend, the man who ran up to the roof." Meliha touched her jaw. "Through a radio you cannot see."

The old woman frowned, half doubting her.

"I count one armed pickup with eight, maybe ten soldiers," Linc reported. "Another vehicle—a truck with some kind of dish on top—hauling ten more troops, maybe more. A column of dust in the distance, can't quite make it out. I don't have a clear line of sight."

"*Oregon*. You copy that?" Cabrillo asked.

"Copy," Linda Ross said. "Putting eyes on you in thirty seconds."

Juan heard a deep, resonating voice thundering inside his head, powerful and compelling, and louder than his comms.

"Throw down your weapons and surrender to God!"

Because Juan used bone conduction in his comms, the voices resonating in his skull didn't shock him, but Meliha's eyes widened with terror.

The message was repeated in English—and then Arabic.

Fadah snatched up her rusty bolt-action rifle from the corner and charged toward the window facing the street.

Meliha grabbed for her, but the spry old woman slipped past.

"Devils!" Fadah cried out as she raced toward the window.

"Chairman, there's a tango drone heading your way," Murph said.

Fadah skidded to a stop at the window, raising her ancient rifle. Just as she found a target in her iron sights, a gunshot cracked and her head was thrown back.

The bullet killing her plowed into the painted cement wall just behind Meliha, her mouth opening in a silent scream.

"Sniper!" Juan shouted as he dashed over to Meliha, pulling her down with him just as another shot tore a chunk out of the wall. The God voice thundered louder in his skull, a mantra of doom.

Juan glanced at the old woman's corpse. All the datapoints came together, an instantaneous calculation deep within his subconscious mind.

Fadah's Devil voice was a drone.

"Shoot down that drone, Wepps. Linc, drop and cover your eyes."

Juan covered Meliha's body with his, burying her head in his chest.

"Close your eyes—now!" he told her even as he shut his own.

A moment later, Juan heard the familiar roar of a streaking anti-aircraft missile and the sudden, violent explosion high above them.

"Drone down," Murph said inside Juan's head.

But Juan knew it was too late.

Linc's scream echoed in his comms.

36

Juan leaped to his feet, lifting Meliha up by her shoulders.

He dragged her up the stairs to the roof, the God voice still roaring in his skull and hers, he was certain, judging by her tormented expression.

They reached the top of the stairs and knelt near the low perimeter wall that made the roof an open-air courtyard. Juan glanced up and saw the finger of dispersing missile exhaust high above them. It trailed all the way from the *Oregon* out in the bay up to the point of impact a thousand feet overhead. A puff of white smoke and fluttering debris from the drone marked the strike's location.

"Good shooting, Wepps," Juan said. He caught sight of the *Oregon*'s formidable bow wake as it raced toward shore.

The helicopter rotor blades hammering the air roared in volume; obviously ground forces had been spotted. Juan quickly glanced over the low wall. He saw another truck racing toward the village and more fighters running for cover and moving toward his position.

"More tangos coming in hot, Linda."

"We've got the pedal to the metal."

Fixated on the noise below, Meliha stood up to see the advancing troops. She was totally exposed.

"Get down!"

Juan grabbed Meliha and yanked her down just in time. Bullets stitched across the wall just where she had stood.

"Stay down!"

Meliha nodded, half in shock.

Juan scrambled over to Linc, lying fetal on the ground, his helmet torn away from his head, his hands covering his eyes.

"Wepps, take out that chopper," Cabrillo commanded.

"Aye, Chairman. Missile away."

The helicopter's motor revved as it turned away, the beating rotors changing their tune. The chopper had seen its drone get hammered to dust and decided to get out of there.

No sooner had Cabrillo given the command to down the helicopter than another streak of fire and smoke raced from the *Oregon* toward the sky just beyond Juan's range of vision. A crack erupted in the distance.

"Chopper down."

"Good shooting, Wepps. Stay alert and wait for my command."

"Roger that, Chairman. Be advised, more ground units are closing on your position."

"Linc. Whereya hit?"

"Not hit—blind!"

Juan pulled Linc's hands away from his face. The giant man's eyes blinked furiously yet Juan couldn't see any damage.

The whoosh of an anti-aircraft missile roared on the far side of the village. It streaked into the sky at supersonic speed until it erupted.

"Our drone is down, Chairman. Repeat, our drone is down. We have no eyes on you."

"Linda, Linc's down. We could really use that ride."

"One minute out. Sit tight."

Juan turned toward Meliha. "We've got to get him down to the DING and get out of here."

Meliha nodded. "I'll help you."

She rose to a low crouch and began to run toward Linc just as a thunderous boom echoed in the air.

Juan felt a concussion thump against his chest as a fireball exploded on the north side of the building.

He peeked over the roof's low wall. The shattered DING was burning furiously.

A bearded fighter with an empty RPG tube stood in the back of a pickup racing toward Cabrillo's building. The smoke from its motor still hung in the air.

Juan mashed the trigger on his machine gun and sprayed the vehicle, shattering the windshield, killing the driver. The truck swerved and hit a wall, smashing to a stop. The machine gunner was nearly thrown clear, but he regained his balance and opened up, hammering the roofline, shattering bricks and tiles just below where Juan stood. He ducked back down.

"Wepps, I need a guided mortar. On my mark."

"Aye, Chairman."

Juan hit the targeting reticle on his helmet, pulled it off and held it up over the wall, hoping like heck he was pointing it at the Toyota below.

"Target acquired," Murph said.

As Juan began to pull his helmet back it was struck by a burst of machine gun fire, knocking it out of his hands and shattering it.

The technical kept pounding the roof with his machine gun, keeping Juan and Meliha crouching low. Despite the God voice still thundering in his head, Juan heard the high-pitched screech of worn brakes slamming to a stop and moments later men's voices shouting as they raced up the stairs.

Juan turned on his heels and pulled a grenade from his vest and tossed it down the stairs. It clanged as it tumbled on the steps and then it cracked. Men's screams echoed up from below. Juan tossed another one, then sprayed the stairwell with gunfire, cutting off the screams.

A low moan came from the sky.

Juan's eyes tracked the wobbling mortar, plummeting almost directly toward them. His guts tightened.

It would be close.

In a flash, the speeding mortar disappeared below the roofline followed by a thundering explosion, throwing shrapnel and shaking the building.

Juan glanced back up over the side of the roof. The remains of the pickup were scattered for a hundred yards, along with pieces of the men inside. He dropped back down.

"Bull's-eye, Wepps!"

"There's more where that came from," Murph said.

"ETA thirty seconds," Ross said.

"And not a second too soon." Cabrillo glanced back over at Meliha, cradling Linc's head in her lap. The God voice was morphing into a thundering migraine. He had to get it stopped.

"Murph, you got a visual on a comms vehicle with some kind of dish on it?"

"Aye that, sir."

"Waste it now. It's breaking my skull."

More bullets crashed into the bricks below.

"Sending liquid love that way now. Kashtan online."

Juan visualized the round housing on the *Oregon*'s forward mast lowering, revealing the Kashtan's rotary twin cannons spinning up. Together, they spat out 30mm explosive tungsten-tipped shells at the rate of ten thousand rounds a minute like a laser beam of lead.

Sure enough, a moment later Cabrillo heard the short, violent burst of automated gunfire, like sheet metal being torn apart. A two-second blast sent over three hundred rounds downrange when only one was needed.

Before the Kashtan's gunfire's echo faded, the God voice cut off in Juan's head. He'd never felt so much relief.

"Tango wasted," Murph said.

"Copy that."

Juan dashed over to the south side of the roof, his mind clearing. He looked up and saw fighters stationed on two other roofs, pointing not at him but at the bay.

"Assault team launched," Linda Ross said. "Hux is on standby. Tell Linc room service is on the way."

Juan started to breathe a sigh of relief but the sudden roar of a diesel engine robbed him of the moment.

Black exhaust plumed on the far side of the nearest building. Juan ran along the western edge of the roof to see what it was.

His heart sank.

A T-72 tank clanked to a halt, using the corner of the building as partial cover. Juan doubted the *Oregon* could see its profile or the 125mm barrel pointed directly at his ship less than two hundred yards offshore.

The ship's giant waterline garage door was flung wide open. The assault team boats burst off the Teflon ramp—four machine-gun-mounted Jet Skis and two RHIBs packed with heavily armed operators. They splashed into the sea, streaking toward the beach, rooster-tailing water behind them.

"Wepps. There's a tank thirty yards due west of me and taking aim at you—"

"I see him—"

Too late.

The tank cannon roared.

37

No!" Cabrillo shouted as if that could magically shield the *Oregon* from the armor-piercing shell.

It didn't.

The erupting tank barrel radiated a single shock wave, tossing sand and dust a hundred yards beyond the cannon's mouth and pulsing through Juan like a maser. The recoil rocked the old Russian tank.

The speeding projectile roiled the air in its wake as it plunged into the open mouth of *Oregon*'s boat garage.

Cabrillo whispered a prayer, fearing the worst, that his crew was about to be wounded or killed.

His only consolation was the *Oregon*'s avenging electromagnetic railgun. Its automated black barrel had already risen above the bow deck and fired just as the T-72 unleashed its fury.

The railgun threw a non-explosive, twenty-three-pound tungsten rod at nearly eight thousand feet per second. It lanced the armored tank hull like a bayonet through a sheet of tin foil. The speeding tungsten round turned the tank's steel into an imploding hand grenade, liquefying the crew with atomized metal. The T-72's ammo compartment erupted, blowing the tank turret sky-high and tossing it five hundred yards away.

The resulting explosion sent more shock waves across the blue water over which Eddie Seng, MacD, Raven and the rest of the assault team now fearlessly raced.

With both Kashtan twin-barreled guns blazing overhead for cover, the *Oregon*'s assault team hit the beach unharmed and charged ahead, weapons up and ready for anything.

A final suicide attack by the remaining ISIS mercs was repulsed in a hail of gunfire, cutting down the last of the crazed killers. They were all dead before they hit the ground or bled out into the sand soon after.

A GAZ Tigr "Humvee"—stolen from the Russian mercs in the previous village massacre—made a furious getaway back up the coastal road. Two thousand yards away from the village, they thought they had escaped with their lives, but Murph fired a perfectly aimed railgun round that shredded the vehicle and the men inside it.

The battle was over.

"Idiots."

Cedvet Bayur lowered his binoculars. His men should have stayed clear of the road. Now the GAZ Tigr was a pile of twisted steel rendered useless for his escape.

The Turk hunkered down lower on the lip of the dune some thousand yards south of the village and two hundred yards away from the downed helicopter, the dead pilot still strapped in his harness. The man was a coward, no doubt, but an excellent aviator. Because of his split-second maneuvers, only the tail rotor had been hit by the missile. While the hard landing broke Bayur's arm, it snapped the hapless pilot's neck. After extricating himself from the safety harness one-handed, Bayur dashed for cover behind the dune, his only defense a Turkish-manufactured TP9 pistol.

Bayur watched three assaulters come looking for the downed helicopter. They found only the dead pilot in the wreckage. Fortunately for Bayur, they didn't bother searching just beyond the dune where he was hiding. Bayur decided that if attacked, he would empty most of the fifteen-round magazine on his enemies, saving the last bullet in the chamber for himself.

Ignoring the ache in his broken arm, Bayur raised his binoculars to his eyes again. He had witnessed the total destruction of the militia force and its ISIS cadre, including the T-72 tank. At least it had gotten off one shot before being destroyed by the mystery ship in the bay.

He cursed himself for not trusting his instincts earlier. He'd seen the derelict cargo ship heading toward the village but assumed it was harmless. Now that he had witnessed its incredible destructive power, he knew it wasn't what it appeared to be.

He twisted the binocular's focus knob until he could read the name on the green and white hull, rusted and badly patched.

"*Västra Floden*," Bayur read aloud in order to help him remember it. He saw a limp Liberian flag on the jackstaff.

It was all a ruse, he told himself. Despite the Swedish name, it had to be an American vessel. The Libyan rebels had the help of Russian mercenaries, but the Russians didn't have this kind of technology. So why were the Americans involved here? They had expressed no military or political support for the rebels. In fact, NATO supported the Tripoli government.

What was its mission?

A small team in a desert patrol vehicle had been responsible for the destruction of the Pipeline meth. But now he had witnessed a complex, highly technical military operation.

Bayur swung his glass over to the beachhead. The Black man he had seen on the roof was being helped into one of the RHIBs. The Turk smiled. Even from here, he could tell the American was blind.

Bayur's *schadenfreude* was ruined when Meliha Öztürk suddenly came into view. She was being helped into the last RHIB by a tall blond man dressed in tactical gear. Bayur couldn't hear a word the man was saying but he recognized him as a fellow commander due to his physical bearing and presence.

That man was the one responsible for his bitter defeat.

The RHIB sped away under the thrust of its large outboard motors, its journey covered by two armed Jet Skis that surveyed the wrecked village one last time before racing away. The other watercraft had already departed. The RHIB entered into the cavernous waterline door on the side of the boat and the others followed it in. Soon they would load up and depart.

Everything in Bayur told him to flee for his life. But it wasn't the American mercenaries he most feared, it was their commander.

Bayur had enough gold and Bitcoin stashed away that he could disappear somewhere in South America and live out his days in comfort. But he was always a soldier, first and foremost. And as a soldier, it was his duty to report to his superiors even if that report detailed only his personal failings over the past six hours.

Bayur's jaw tightened at the thought of calling in, but there was no other option. Coming clean might be a way to at least preserve his father's reputation. With his mind focused on his imminent demise, he nearly missed the sudden change in the ship's hull.

He pulled the binoculars away, blinking furiously and rubbing his eyes. He couldn't have seen what he just saw. He raised the glass again.

No, he wasn't imagining things nor was he insane.

The faded green and white paint scheme was now black and red, equally rusted and patched. He focused on the bow again and read the name out loud.

"*Vesturá.*"

As the boat garage door began to close, Bayur pulled out his encrypted satellite phone and punched the number for his immediate commander in the Gray Wolves organization.

A curt voice answered. Bayur gave him a brief yet accurate recounting of recent events, including the attack on his camp, the destruction of the meth shipment, the rescue of Meliha Öztürk and the annihilation of the militia at Wahat Albahr. He hesitated before providing the improbable description of the incredible mystery ship, its vast array of weaponry and its ability to change its appearance just moments before it raced away at mind-boggling speed.

The man on the other end of the line remained entirely composed throughout the report. Bayur knew that everything he had chronicled threatened his commander's life and career as much as his own. He asked for Bayur's recommendation on how to proceed.

"At all costs, we must capture that traitor Öztürk and, without a doubt, we must destroy the *Vesturá* and all her crew."

Bayur's commander agreed coolly, promising to accomplish both, and killed the call.

Bayur took that as a good sign.

But the fact his commander offered no assistance to him while wounded and stranded in the desert told him his life and service were now forfeited.

Cedvet Bayur stood on uncertain legs, cradling his broken arm. As he trudged toward the distant village, he set upon a plan to redeem himself.

38

Juan paced the carpeted floor in Dr. Huxley's office still in his sweat-stained tactical uniform, his hands clasped behind his back. The meth sample they'd seized was being analyzed in the *Oregon*'s lab as was the AK-47 that Raven had brought from the base. Both items could help provide the location of the next stop in the Pipeline. But right now, Linc's condition was the only thing he cared about. The first thing he did when they got back to the *Oregon* was get Linc to the clinic, after which he decided to camp out in Hux's office until he got word.

Meliha was sitting in a leather chair, fighting fatigue, also worried about Linc. She was exhausted, emotionally and physically, still suffering the effects of her brutal captivity but refusing to leave Juan's side.

"Why does everyone call you the Chairman? Are you like Chairman Mao?" She was trying to make him smile.

It worked. A little.

"Not exactly. I run my outfit like a company, not a military organization. So the executives all have corporate titles."

"Interesting. What is Linc's title?"

"He's in operations. He does it all, but his primary expertise is as a sniper."

"He is a very brave man. He will be brave through this as well, I'm certain."

"No doubt. I just hate that it's all because of me."

"You can't blame yourself. It was Bayur who blinded him, not you."

"But Linc was under my command."

"And because of you, he's still alive." Meliha smiled warmly. "You are a good Chairman, Juan Cabrillo. And a good man."

"Thanks."

Meliha saw Juan's growing concern for his friend. She wanted to take his mind off Linc for a moment.

"Your ship is most unusual. Would it be possible for you to take me on a tour of her?"

Juan nodded. "Sure. After I take care of a few things." Juan sniffed the air and his face soured. "Including a splash of Old Spice behind my ears."

"I can't wait to see it all." Meliha examined her filthy fingernails, crusted with dried blood and sand, then dragged her fingers through her matted hair anyway. "I must look frightful."

"I wouldn't say that."

The door yanked open and Huxley appeared, still wearing her scrubs.

"Doc?"

Huxley crossed over to her desk and fell into her chair. She'd been going at it, hammer and tongs, for the last several hours. She sighed.

"Your hunch was spot-on. I spoke with Murph and Stoney. They both agree that Linc was probably hit with what they called a dazzler weapon mounted on that drone they shot down."

Juan was familiar with the technology. Militaries all over the world were deploying non-lethal devices like low-powered lasers to both warn and temporarily hinder opposition forces. Civilian ships even used them against pirates. Back in the nineties, the Chinese had developed a dazzler that could permanently blind someone up to three miles out. It was ultimately banned under international law, but there was no doubt they had been employed. Gun control only affected the law-abiding, not the criminals.

"So what's the verdict?" Juan asked.

"I'm afraid he's stone-cold blind."

"Permanently?"

"There's no telling. I checked his eyes as thoroughly as I could."

Huxley's medical facility had the latest ophthalmology equipment for treating combat eye injuries as well as providing regular optical examinations for the crew. Though a highly skilled combat surgeon, Hux wasn't a board-certified ophthalmologist.

"As near as I can tell, there aren't any obvious signs of physical damage to the iris, retina, lens, cornea or, most important, the optic nerve in either eye."

"That's good."

"It is. But it also doesn't explain why he can't see. A good friend of mine is the head of the Wilmer Eye Institute at Johns Hopkins, the best in the world. I'll make the arrangements to get him there ASAP."

"Whatever he needs, he gets."

"That goes without saying."

"Can I see him?"

"Linc was pretty shook up. He's sedated. Right now, what he needs is sleep."

The doctor's tired gaze fell on Meliha. Hux thought she looked like she'd been through the wringer herself. She wondered if she had been with the battered women Gomez had brought to the *Oregon* earlier.

Huxley began to stand up. "I'm sorry, I should have introduced myself—"

Meliha bolted out of her chair. "No, please sit."

Juan smacked his forehead. "I'm sorry. I forgot to introduce you. Dr. Huxley, this is Meliha Öztürk. She's an independent journalist and human rights activist and also a mutual friend of Langston Overholt. Meliha, this is Dr. Julia Huxley, the *Oregon*'s chief medical officer."

The two women smiled and shook hands.

"Any friend of Langston's is a friend of mine," Huxley said.

"It's an amazing ship. And from what I've seen, a most impressive crew."

"Hux, if you don't mind, I'd like you to check Meliha out. Raven gave her a once-over, but she's not a physician."

"No, I'm fine," Meliha insisted. "Perhaps a shower and a little rest."

Huxley shot a glance at Juan: What's her story?

"You've been through a lot," Juan said. "You need to be examined by my doctor. She's the best there is."

Meliha shrugged. "I'm fine. Really. I'd rather just rest right now."

"It will only take a few minutes," Hux offered. "Nothing terribly invasive, I promise."

"If you want to stay on the hunt for Bayur and the Pipeline, I need Hux to verify you're good to go—or to fix you up so you can be," Juan said. "And I can't let you endanger my crew."

"What do you mean?"

"I have GPS trackers implanted in all my people in case they're lost or captured and we need to find them. I need to be sure this Bayur joker hasn't planted one on you. If he has, we need to remove it."

"Oh, I hadn't thought of that."

"That's okay. You're new to my side of the business. And I know you're dog-tired because I am too and it's hard to think straight. But here's the deal. If you want in on the action, I suggest you go with Dr. Huxley."

Huxley slipped her arm through Meliha's and coaxed her out of the door with a smile. Hux shot Juan a furtive glance and a wink. She then whispered to Meliha, "And when we're done, we'll find you some new clothes, too."

39

Eddie Seng and the other assaulters were securing their gear in the locker room when Cabrillo appeared in the doorway. Eddie, the team lead, had already called in the after action report—no one from the assault team had been injured, wounded or killed in the attack on the village. But Juan wanted to stop by to check up on them anyway before he hit the rack. His people were always his first concern.

"Thanks for the backup," Juan said. He was greeted by a roomful of nodding heads and smiles.

"What's the word on Linc?" Raven asked.

"Nothing's changed. He's sedated and getting rest. Dr. Huxley is making arrangements to get advanced eye care for him back in the States."

"When can we see him?" one of the operators asked.

"Check with the doc on that." Juan turned to MacD. "No problems, I take it?"

"It was a turkey shoot," MacD said. The big ex-Ranger ripped the Velcro straps to loosen his armored vest. "The only problem I had was that I ran out of targets too fast."

"That helicopter Murph shot down . . . Was there a corpse inside with a hand-shaped burn scar on his face?"

"Not that I saw."

Juan turned toward the rest of the room. "Anybody see anything?"

Heads shook.

"We found the pilot. No scar that I remember," Eddie said. "We did a quick sweep to make sure we weren't going to be ambushed on the way out. There could have been a body out there somewhere we missed. Didn't know he was a person of interest."

"No worries. Just curious." Juan had assumed Cedvet Bayur was on that chopper directing the operation. He was obviously mistaken.

"How're you holding up?" MacD asked.

Juan smiled, stifling a yawn. "Never better." He turned to Eddie. "Let me know when your mission debrief is. I'd like to sit in on it."

"You got it."

Juan tapped the doorway on the way out. Turning back, he spoke to the entire team. "Great job today. Crack a beer for me."

"They're already frostin' on ice," MacD said. "We'll save you a couple three."

MacD's thousand-watt smile dimmed slightly when he saw the Chairman step away with a slight limp.

Juan stood on the edge of the moon pool with Max Hanley by his side. Sparks were falling down from the scaffolding high up on the starboard bulkhead like dying fireflies. The work crews were repairing a couple damaged longitudinal stringers and welding steel sheet to the inner wall. A similar sheet was being attached on the outer bulkhead as some other minor repairs were being attended to.

The crude-looking patches would perfectly fit the *Oregon*'s "rust bucket" aesthetic. That was fine with Juan. She wasn't some Silicon Valley billionaire's pristine vanity yacht parked in a luxury port and visited by her owner only once a year for a family vacation and Instagram photos. The *Oregon* was a fighting ship and, like any fighter, she bore her hard-won battle scars with pride.

"How bad is it?" Juan asked.

"We got lucky," Max said over the whine of industrial saws and pounding of sledgehammers. "That tank only got off one shot before Murph took it out."

The *Oregon*'s chief engineer turned around and gestured toward the closed boat garage door. "That armor-piercing round came straight through that open door and slammed into the far starboard bulkhead. It punched a ragged hole yea big"—Hanley made a rough semicircle with his hands—"and shot through to the other side. It was on a flat trajectory, so it didn't rise and penetrate higher up."

Juan breathed a sigh of relief. The crew was stationed on the higher decks along with vital components like the ship's brain, the Cray supercomputer.

"No serious structural damage?"

Hanley shook his nearly bald head. "Nothing that affects her safety."

"Thank God for that."

"I already have. And I'll tell you what. If you had asked that tank gunner to hit the least damaging spot on the bulkhead, he couldn't have picked a more perfect target."

"How much longer to effect repairs?" Juan had ordered the *Oregon* out into international waters. Since they had no destination planned, he wanted to shut the ship down to maximize the safety of the repair crews.

"You know me, I like things neat and tidy. Everything that needs to be repaired or replaced will be completed by this time tomorrow, especially if Linda can keep things nice and quiet for a few hours."

"Thanks, Max. Keep me posted."

"Will do."

Juan turned to leave, grateful for his old friend's steady hand and engineering skill. They had gotten lucky all right, at least on this. But he knew that sometimes you made your own luck.

* * *

"It looks like I'm on the set of *The Andromeda Strain*," Juan said.

The technicians stationed on the other side of the large pane of glass were outfitted in hazmat gear with face shields. Brightly lit and on the chilly side, the entire lab facility felt like a computer chip maker's clean room.

Dr. Eric Littleton glanced up from his notebook. He was in charge of the *Oregon*'s biophysical laboratory. The white-coated scientist was a former arms inspector for the United Nations specializing in the identification of biological, chemical and nuclear weapons. He began his career searching for Iraqi weapons of mass destruction and ended it with the Iranian nuclear fiasco. As a scientist, he could no longer stomach the politics of weapons inspection. He was more than thrilled when Juan Cabrillo invited him into the Corporation.

It was an unfortunate reality that Cabrillo needed to hire someone like Littleton and fund his onboard laboratory. The complexity and lethality of weapons and contraband now being fielded by America's adversaries was expanding exponentially. A biophysical science division was needed to keep up with it all.

The lab had proven to be a surprisingly lucrative revenue stream for the Corporation especially in its contract work for foreign governments. In addition to weapons and contraband, the lab could also identify pollution and contamination sources to national and international environmental and regulatory agencies. It was highly technical work that allowed the *Oregon* to expand its reach into environmental and health security.

"I love that movie," Littleton said, setting down his pad. He nodded at the techs behind the glass. "That fentanyl-meth sample you gave me is dangerous as all get-out. We have to take every precaution with it, not just for the techs' safety but whole crew's." Littleton sighed. "Hard to believe that human beings willingly jam that lethal garbage into their bodies for recreation."

"How long before you get your results?"

Littleton pointed toward his techs.

"The first step is gas chromatography. That's where we'll separate out the components into a mixture. Once we do that, then we'll use mass spectrometry to calculate the molecular weight of those components. That will tell us precisely what's in that mess and how it's organized atomically."

"And that gives us the molecular fingerprints we can use to compare with the Diamante Azul profile Overholt sent us."

"Precisely."

"How long?"

"Eight hours max. Maybe sooner."

"Let me know as soon as you have the results. I need to get that information to Overholt ASAP."

Littleton nodded. "Consider it done."

40

Juan smiled as he sniffed the sweet tang of Hoppe's No. 9 bore-cleaning solvent that hung in the air.

The *Oregon*'s armory was neither the largest nor best-decorated department on the ship, but it was one of Juan's favorites. Located on the lowest deck, along with the machine shop, engine room and moon pool, the armory was where nearly all the small arms and ammunition on board the *Oregon* were stored. The only notable exception being Cabrillo's personal collection of machine guns, rifles and pistols. He kept those in a nineteenth-century railroad safe in his office that also accommodated hundreds of thousands of dollars' worth of foreign currency, gold and diamonds needed for payments during their operations.

As an avid gun enthusiast, Juan found any excuse he could to come down to this part of the ship, including almost daily practice at the soundproofed gun range next door. But he wasn't here for recreation.

Still exhausted from the mission and worried sick about Linc, Cabrillo wanted to follow up on the AK-47 Raven had secured at the air base before finally hitting the rack. Finding the origin of those guns might provide the next link in the Pipeline chain.

Mike Lavin, the *Oregon*'s chief armorer, stood at his workbench in a leather apron with a pair of magnified jeweler's glasses perched on his forehead. Raven's AK was completely disassembled and its parts neatly laid out and cleaned of Cosmoline.

"Whatchu got for me, Mikey?" Juan asked.

Lavin smiled. He held up a chunk of metal suspended between his thumb and index finger.

"The front trunnion," Cabrillo said. "The very soul of an AK."

"You'll notice that it's forged steel, not stamped." Lavin shook it in his hand to demonstrate its heft. "And it's high quality. Look here."

Lavin set the trunnion down, grabbed the swing arm and pulled the table magnifying glass close to Juan. The armorer pointed at a mark on the trunnion with his index finger with its missing tip.

"See that number? The twenty-one with the double circles around it?"

"Sure."

"That's the mark of the NITI factory in Kazanlak."

"Bulgaria?"

"Yup. First-rate stuff in the AK world. Mostly military contracts."

The Bulgaria connection surprised Juan. He assumed Albania would be their next stop in the Pipeline chain. In recent years, the former communist country had become the Colombia of Europe—a narco-state. When their big money couldn't buy off politicians or rivals, the notorious Albanian mafias resorted to violence. They had expanded their reach all over Europe, the Middle East and even into Latin America.

"So not Albanian?"

Lavin's magnified eyes blinked mischievously.

"The Albanians make cheap Chinese AK knockoffs—Type 56s, they call 'em. Stamped trunnions, not forged. No, if you want a truly battle-worthy weapon, you want something like the Bulgarian beauty here."

"Then we're looking for a Bulgarian criminal enterprise."

"Not so fast. I happen to know that the Albanian mafia loves Bulgarian AKs."

"And how would you happen to know that piece of arcane trivia?"

"Interpol put out a bulletin on it last year. The Albanian Nishani clan owns the gunrunning business in that part of the world."

Juan clapped Lavin on the shoulder. That was just the kind of lead he was looking for. He would confirm this finding with Meliha when he saw her next.

"Nice work, Mike."

"That's why you pay me the big bucks."

"And you earn every penny."

Cabrillo heard a click in his head. He still hadn't removed his molar mic comms. He hit the wireless remote talk button.

"Cabrillo."

Lavin nodded, acknowledging that Juan was on his comms. He went back to examining the Bulgarian AK as Juan made his way to the elevator.

"Just wanted to update you on Meliha," Huxley said. "I gave her a shot of antibiotics and a prescription of Cipro. She's been exposed to some nasty bugs lately."

"Injuries?"

"Bruised, a few scratches. X-rays show no broken bones or internal injuries. I offered to do a gynecological exam, but she assured me she hadn't been sexually assaulted."

"And you believe her? She comes from a very traditional culture."

"My strong intuition is that she's telling the truth."

"Thank God she dodged the bullet. Where is she now?"

"I took her to my cabin for a hot shower and then put her to bed in my guest bedroom. Out like a light, poor thing. Needs to sleep."

"That's kind of you to open up your place to her."

"Happy to do it. She's delightful. And she's got grit. Maybe you can fill me in on her details tomorrow." Huxley yawned heavily into her phone. "Sorry about that. I think I need to get some shut-eye myself."

"A shower and rack time sounds pretty good to me right now, too. Thanks for taking care of her. Tracking device?"

"She's good to go."

"Get some rest, Hux. You've earned it."

"You too, Chairman. I have my physician's assistant keeping a close eye on Linc. As soon as he wakes up, I'll let you know. I've already made arrangements with Gomez to fly him to the Navy Hospital in Naples and from there to Baltimore."

"Copy that."

Linc would be in good hands. Juan ended the call just before he cut loose with his own hippo-sized yawn.

A hot shower and a long nap was just what the doctor ordered, wasn't it?

Juan sat on the teakwood bench inside the huge green marble tile shower in his private quarters. The steaming hot water beat the fatigue out of his body with each pounding pulse from its eight multi-head jets.

The innumerable scars that raked across his body reddened with the heat. Each was a kind of GPS marker for every battle won and lost over the years, none more so than the swollen, blistering stump at the end of a leg blasted away by a Chinese Navy gunboat years ago. His combat prosthetic leg was stashed in the corner of the shower near the soap dispenser. It was too much trouble to hop in on one leg, so he didn't remove it until after he got the water going.

But take it off he did. The throbbing pain on the end of his stump wasn't the phantom kind that woke him in the dead of night, robbing him of sleep. This was real pain and he needed some temporary relief. He'd showered on one leg many times before, holding the assist bar like he was at the barre, but right now he was too dang tired to mess with it. The bench was a welcome relief.

He inhaled deep lungfuls of shower steam, letting the heat work its magic inside and out. He felt the nervous energy drain away, the knotted muscles loosen up and the dried salty crust on his skin wash away and swirl down the drain. He finally began to relax.

Cabrillo closed his eyes and felt the tiny drops of spray splashing his face like the tiny fingertips of an exuberant masseuse. His shoulders slumped as he leaned back against the cool tile. Taking a nap right here wasn't the worst idea in the world. He felt himself begin to slip away . . .

Until the blaring alarm slapped him awake.

Battle stations!

41

Cabrillo charged into the operations center, limping on his combat prosthetic, wearing a pair of gym shorts and a damp Caltech T-shirt that clung to his chest, his hair still dripping from the shower.

"Chairman has the conn," Linda Ross shouted. She knew Cabrillo had every confidence in her as his number three, but in combat he always took command.

Always.

She stepped aside with a nod as Juan fell into the "Kirk Chair." The op center's tiered semicircles of touchscreen workstations, sleek modern finishes and cool-blue LED lighting looked like the bridge of TV's fabled starship *Enterprise*. And thanks to Otis, the crew's name for the ship's automated control system, anyone could run the entire ship single-handedly—from the engine room to the weapons stations—while seated in the Kirk Chair.

Juan glowered at the close-up image of a frigate steaming toward them on the giant three-hundred-sixty-degree, high-definition wraparound display. The bulkhead-sized monitors gave the illusion they were all standing on the *Oregon*'s faux bridge high above decks. The only thing missing was a salt-tinged breeze and the warmth of the sun on their skin.

Ross nodded toward the frigate. "She was running parallel to our course until two minutes ago. As soon as she turned, I called battle stations."

"Good call."

Cabrillo scanned the automated stats window flashing red on the big monitor. The computer automatically identified the ship from its extensive database including its armaments and capabilities.

The Turkish Navy ship *Kızıl* was ten thousand yards out and coming on fast, her knife-edged bow splitting the water at her maximum speed of twenty-eight knots. The frigate deployed a nasty automated 76mm deck gun, eight Harpoon anti-ship missiles and a slew of torpedoes. Though little over half the size of the *Oregon*, the *Kızıl* was perfectly capable of blowing Juan's ship out of the water, and, by all appearances, that seemed to be its intention.

How the Turkish gunboat identified them was a question for another day. Right now, he was worried about the Turk's next move.

Cabrillo's memory quickly flashed back to the Libyan gunboat that unleashed its fury on the *Oregon* several years before, the two vessels trading blows toe-to-toe like ancient, three-masted ships of the line swapping broadsides. It had been a horrifically damaging and near-fatal encounter he preferred not to repeat. He doubted the Turkish warship barreling down on him would give him much of an option.

Just then, Dr. Huxley stepped into the op center with Meliha. Both women bore concern on their faces.

"Not a great time for a tour," Juan said.

"She wanted to know what was going on," Huxley said. "And so do I."

Meliha's eyes widened like saucers as they fixed on the giant wall monitor. Juan couldn't tell if she was overwhelmed by the high-tech operations center or the image of the Turkish gunboat running them down like a snarling hyena.

Hali Kasim, sitting at the comms station, turned toward Juan. "Incoming message from the *Kızıl*, sir."

"Put it on speaker."

"Merchant vessel *Vesturá*, this is Captain Köybaşı of the TCG *Kızıl*. You are ordered to heave to and prepare for boarding inspection."

Cabrillo couldn't believe the gall of this man. He had stolen a page from Juan's own playbook. This was setting up like that fishing trawler fiasco off the coast of Suriname.

"Captain Köybaşı, this is the captain of the *Vesturá*. We are in international waters and we are an Iranian-flagged vessel. You have no authority over my ship and no right to insist on a boarding inspection."

"You will heave to immediately and be boarded or we will open fire."

"That would be a big mistake, Captain Köybaşı. For what reason do you wish to inspect my vessel?"

"You are holding a Turkish national citizen, Meliha Öztürk, as a hostage against her will."

Meliha and Juan exchanged a quick glance. Neither said a word nor needed to. The determination on Juan's face said it all.

That ain't gonna happen.

"Ms. Öztürk is not being held hostage. She is being offered safe and free passage to a destination of her choosing."

"Then allow us to board you and verify her safety and condition."

"I'm not being held against my will!" Meliha shouted.

"Then tell the captain to allow us to board and verify your safety."

"That's not possible, Captain Köybaşı," Juan said, "not even if you say pretty please with sugar on top."

Köybaşı ignored the insult. "You will allow us to board your vessel immediately and escort Ms. Öztürk back to her family in Turkey or you will suffer the consequences."

A warning light flashed on Murph's console.

"Chairman. One of his Harpoons just radar-locked us."

Linda Ross shot Juan a look. Just one of those American-built anti-ship missiles could send the *Oregon* and its entire crew to the bottom.

"Engage automated defenses," Juan said.

"Aye."

Modern surface warfare happened at supersonic speeds, far too fast for human reactions. By putting the Kashtan targeting systems under computer control, its air defense missiles and rotary cannons could respond instantaneously to the Harpoon's threat.

A question flashed like a warning light in Juan's mind.

Was the Russian Kashtan's targeting computer smarter than the American Harpoon's?

They were about to find out.

Juan's eyes narrowed as he calculated. The *Kızıl* ran at full speed, all twenty-eight knots of it. His ship could do more than twice that.

Eric Stone, sitting at the helm station, read his mind. He turned around.

"We can outrun her, sir. And she'd never catch up."

"She doesn't have to. Those Harpoons scoot at around five hundred forty miles an hour. At this distance, they'd take us out in thirty-six seconds."

"Harpoon launch," Murph shouted as the launch warning alarm flashed on one of the bulkhead monitors.

Meliha gasped.

Red, yellow and green automated reticles appeared on the big screen, each color representing a different defensive system. They each picked up and tracked the surface-skimming missile as soon as it cleared its firing canister.

Eric Stone waited for Cabrillo's command. Surely he wants to put as much distance as quickly as possible between the incoming warhead and the *Oregon*, Stone thought. His hand hovered over the remotely controlled throttle.

"Helm, set a course for the *Kızıl*."

"Sir?"

"Straight at her. And right down her throat."

42

Stoney hit the helm's stick and throttle at the same time.

The *Oregon*'s rotating vector thrusters snapped around just as the pump-jets engaged.

The 590-foot *Oregon* turned on a dime and leaped forward like a sprinter out of the block achieving full speed in mere seconds. Everyone and everything not secured slammed against a bulkhead or crashed to the deck.

Just as an electric lightbulb received all its power when the switch was turned on, so, too, were the *Oregon*'s electric pump-jets. They were fully powered the instant the full-ahead signal was received—another huge advantage of the ship's revolutionary magnetohydrodynamic propulsion system. Running full out, the giant freighter's V-shaped monohull knifed through the dark blue water, stabilized by T-foils and fins.

With both ships charging at each other at full speed, the gap between them was closing at over one hundred miles an hour.

"Still confident in that new toy of yours, Wepps?" Juan asked Murph.

Murph swallowed hard. "Still in testing phase, sir."

"Can't think of a better test than this."

The weapons officer eyed the console in front of him. "Thirty seconds to impact."

The Harpoon looked like a shooting star racing toward them on the main screen and growing larger by the second.

"*Kızıl* still closing fast," Stone said.

"Noted." Cabrillo's eyes were fixed on the digital map on a side screen monitor tracking both ships, noting speed, distance and time until collision with the Turkish warship.

He was cutting it close.

Murph's earlier test demonstration of the new DARPA weapon when they were sailing for Libya was impressive. But they were just that—tests against a couple harmless target drones.

How would they fare against a real man-o'-war?

For the weapon to work, he needed to be within four nautical miles of the other vessel.

That was cutting it real close.

And the closer he got to the Turk, the more lethal the frigate's weapons became.

A half second later, one of the *Oregon*'s Kashtans suddenly loosed two of its missiles.

"Five-point-five seconds to impact," Murph said.

"I admire your precision," Juan said.

The two streaking missiles appeared high on the screen and raced toward the green square reticle narrowing on the Harpoon. Both missiles trailed white smoke from their roaring motors like skeins of fiery cotton.

The seconds ticked off like hours in Juan's adrenaline-soaked brain stem. The missiles exploded in succession a fraction of a second apart. Both twenty-pound warheads threw up fifteen-foot curtains of steel fragments. The Harpoon smashed into the first radius and was instantly destroyed.

The op center broke out in cheers.

"Splash one Harpoon," Ross said.

But the cheers died when two more Harpoons launched from the frigate.

"Wepps, have your toy ready. On my mark."

"Aye, Chairman."

The automated Kashtan loosed two more missiles at the incoming Harpoons. Nearly every eye was on the tracking monitor, hoping and praying to see two more splashes.

But Juan was focused on the *Kızıl*.

The first Kashtan missile erupted, taking out the first Harpoon, but the second Kashtan failed to explode and the Harpoon continued screaming toward the *Oregon*.

"Eighteen seconds to Harpoon impact."

"Hold steady. Wepps, ready the laser."

"Laser ready, Chairman."

The automated camera tracking the Harpoon zoomed in closer on the starry rocket. Everyone held their breath.

Six seconds later, the twin Kashtan 30mm rotary cannons opened up, throwing a wall of lead. The two six-barreled guns roared like jackhammers on sheet metal, reverberating all the way down to the op center.

The Harpoon shattered in a cloud of debris a mile from the *Oregon*.

Before more cheers could break out, Juan commanded, "Cannon now, Wepps."

Murph punched a button. High up on one of the four crane masts, the DARPA-designed microwave pulse cannon opened up. Unlike the Kashtans, it was practically noiseless, drawing all its power from the *Oregon*'s engines. In seconds, it flooded the *Kızıl* with a shower of electromagnetic pulses that fried every unprotected electrical circuit and computer chip on board the vessel.

"Wepps, now hit those comms antennas with the laser."

Murph calmly shifted to its controls. A push of the button burned up the antennas as the now dead frigate slowed in the water.

"Stoney, get us a one-eighty—and hit the smoke."

Stone grinned ear to ear. "Aye, Chairman."

Just like before, he slammed the helm stick and the *Oregon* pirouetted on its keel instantly. The ship creaked and groaned under the centrifugal force of the insanely sharp high-speed turn. Stone prayed his maneuvering hadn't turned the still-unrepaired damage belowdecks into something far worse.

As the *Oregon* showed her fantail to the angry Turk, she began belching out a trailing smoke cloud. It was laced with fine metal particles designed to blank any electromagnetic or optical surveillance equipment that might have escaped the EMP onslaught.

Juan's pinball wizard assault was designed to leave the *Kızıl* deaf, dumb and blind with a minimum of Turkish casualties. In his bones, he knew it had succeeded.

He sat back in the Kirk Chair and breathed a sigh of relief, confident his strategy would give him and his crew enough time and space to figure out where they were headed to next and what other dangers likely lay ahead. He glanced over to Meliha.

Her green eyes were fixed on him. A smile tugged on the corner of her mouth. She whispered a thank-you and followed Hux back to her cabin.

43

HOLY ISLAND

Standing barefoot on the cold stones of his monk's cell, Sokratis Katrakis gripped his encrypted cell phone in his weathered hand like it was a venomous snake. He both loathed and feared the device and used it only because of its utility. He loathed it because of his natural paranoia over government eavesdropping. He feared it because he was certain it was firing cancerous radiation into his brain when he held it to his head. He kept it at arm's length and only used it on speakerphone.

Right now, he would have preferred a case of stage IV brain cancer to the news he was hearing.

The monkish old man stroked his bushy white beard as the voice on the other end—a top Gray Wolf operative—reported the attack on the secret Libyan air base, the destruction of Herrera's meth shipment, the escape of the Turkish journalist and the failure of the Turkish frigate to recover her.

Despite his hatred of the Turks, he utilized high-placed contracts within the Gray Wolves to aid in distributing his smuggled wares. Business was business and Turkey was still a powerful gateway to both Europe and Asia.

Each word out of the Gray Wolf's mouth was another pump of the bellows firing a growing rage radiating in the old man's fierce green eyes.

"Why am I just now hearing about all this?" Katrakis asked.

"The *Kızıl* suffered a complete shutdown of its communications system several hours ago and only just now was able to repair itself."

"How is that possible?"

"The captain suspects some kind of EMP weapon of unknown origin."

"And this mystery ship? This *Vesturá*? Where is it now?"

"Unknown, sir."

"Any information on it? Is it American? British?"

"Unknown."

"The mercenaries who rescued the journalist—what about them?"

"Few in number, extremely capable, technologically advanced."

"You make them sound like little green men from Mars. Nationality?"

"A large African in tactical gear was seen. Most likely an African American. But whether he is American military or ex-military is unknown."

"He must be a mercenary," Katrakis said. He had sources inside the American intelligence community whose only purpose was to alert him to any American military action directed against him or the Pipeline.

"How much does Öztürk know about the Pipeline?"

"According to Bayur, very little."

"And you trust your man Bayur?"

"Until this fiasco, yes."

"Where is he now? I want to speak with him."

"He hasn't reported back since I last spoke with him. He is the one who identified the *Vesturá* and told us Öztürk was on board."

This was troubling news for the old Greek. His intelligence sources reported on Öztürk's recent work in Turkey and the Middle East, describing her as a "fearless and relentless" reporter and human rights advocate. Like her father, her political aim was to bring democracy to Turkey. And despite his organization's best efforts, she had eluded capture.

All that was worrisome. *For want of a nail the shoe was lost . . .*

"How does this affect our Pipeline operations?" the Gray Wolf asked.

"Maybe you should have asked yourself that question before you lost Öztürk."

"Sir, I—"

Katrakis killed the call, fighting the urge to hurl the phone against the nearest wall. Instead, he tossed it onto the paper-thin mattress on his cot.

The old Greek paced the icy floor, his feet slapping on the stones, raging over the swath of destruction wreaked upon his organization by this mercenary army and Öztürk. The question remained: how much more damage could they cause?

The destruction of the meth was a catastrophic financial loss but not an insurmountable one. Soon Hakobyan would die and his share of the profits would quickly make up the deficit. His decision to murder his old friend was already proving to be a good one.

There were more pressing problems at hand than money. He had to assume this Öztürk knew enough to worry his inferiors, otherwise why give chase? But if she knew enough to destroy the entire Pipeline organization, government authorities would be closing in already—and yet they weren't.

What bothered Katrakis most was the mercenary army assisting Öztürk. She couldn't afford that kind of firepower and expertise, so who was funding them? What was their agenda?

The old Greek sighed, exhaling through his long nose. Whatever Öztürk knew, it was only related to the Pipeline. She couldn't possibly know about the Kanyon project and right now that was his top priority. But the vast wealth he expected to garner from Kanyon would flow through the Pipeline.

He needed to find Öztürk.

Katrakis assumed she had learned something about the Pipeline because she had come to Libya, the source. If she learned anything more, it would lead her to one of the next nodes.

Katrakis picked up his phone and began making calls, beginning with the Albanians. He wanted to be sure that Öztürk and her capable friends would receive a warm welcome wherever they appeared. His only instruction was to capture the woman alive and to butcher the others, quietly if possible. He warned them of the danger they faced.

The Albanian laughed. "They should worry about us."

Katrakis made his other calls, with similar warnings to his Pipeline contacts, then finally hung up his phone. Despite his forewarnings and the bravado of his subordinates, he couldn't shake the feeling these mercenaries could prevail.

It occurred to him there was a way for him to take advantage of their strengths in a way that would also help him protect his family.

Katrakis also had the feeling that Öztürk was one step ahead of him. He needed to capture her or at the very least eliminate her. No easy feat with that mercenary army by her side.

The old man tugged on his beard.

Perhaps there was a way to get to her after all.

Katrakis' reverie was interrupted when his hairy ears picked up the distant beating of helicopter blades. He glanced at the hands on the old mantel clock standing on the primitive wooden shelf. It was almost time to leave for the shipyard, where his son Alexandros was waiting for him.

Before he could depart, he needed to finish securing the monastery and deal with the meddlesome abbot waiting for him patiently in the chapel for his weekly confession.

Katrakis chuckled. He would indeed make a full confession today and describe the murderous events about to unfold and how like Judas he would betray his dearest friend for the sake of thirty pieces of silver—and much, much more.

He smiled at the thought of watching the abbot's vapid, smiling face melt into a mask of horror.

The Greek's heart raced in anticipation of the events about to unfold. He marched to the cell's door full of joy.

Kanyon was now in full swing.

And there was nothing that could stop it.

44.

Though the *Oregon* was a fighting ship, one of its many perks was the five-star accommodations for the crew. This included a generous allowance given to each to furnish and decorate their individual quarters according to their personal taste. Juan considered it an important investment in his people; they spent many months away from home, family and friends. Cabrillo wanted them as happy and comfortable as possible to make up for the sacrifices they all were making.

In order to finish up the *Oregon*'s repairs, Juan had Stone drop anchor off the coast of Gavdos. At the southernmost point of Europe, the island had less than a hundred full-time residents and was not on the main shipping lanes. The *Oregon* had plotted a wide, sweeping circuitous route away from the *Kızıl* to avoid further detection. Hiding in Greek territorial waters gave them an additional measure of protection in case the Turks had somehow managed to track them.

With a couple hours to kill before an inspection tour with Max, Juan wanted to ask Murph some technical questions about what had happened inside his skull at Wahat Albahr. He headed down to Murph's cabin and was warmly welcomed in.

Murph wore a black T-shirt emblazoned with one of his favorite bands, Bad Avocado, with a rotten-fruit logo to match. He ushered Juan onto a replica of the bridge of the hovercraft *Nebuchadnezzar* from his favorite movie, *The Matrix*. The space they stood in was metallic and dimly lit with blue LEDs. Even the floor was a steel grate. The techno-grungy room was a perfect reproduction from the movie set except it was less cramped and Murph's technology was far more advanced than what the nineties production designers could have imagined. It was also littered with empty energy drink cans and beef jerky wrappers.

Juan counted no less than a dozen 4K monitors scattered around the room. The ones that weren't displaying the iconic plunging waterfalls of matrix programming language were loaded up with Murph's favorite online video games. When not on mission, he played several simultaneously, like a chess master schooling tables of amateurs in a public park.

With multiple PhDs under his belt, including one from MIT in his early twenties, Murph had the highest IQ on the ship. But for all his brilliance, he was stuck emotionally in his teenage years and often found himself a few rungs short on the ladder of social skills.

"To what do I owe the pleasure, Chairman?"

Juan went on to describe his experience of hearing God's voice in his head.

"What kind of tech is that?"

"They call it VSK, short for *voice-to-skull*. It's a psycho-electronic weapon. The U.S. military has employed variants of it in the war on terror."

"Effectively?"

"The bad guys in the turbans and flip-flops are pretty good with their AKs, but they're superstitious as all get-out. I messed around with the technology for a while when I was at DARPA. It was interesting work, but I prefer the high-impact kinetics to the mind control stuff."

"It looks like the Turks have acquired it. Or at least one of them has." He was referring to Cedvet Bayur.

Murph slid into a nearby command seat, a cyber-punk version of a dentist's chair, and scratched his wispy beard, thinking.

"I hadn't read anything about the Turks getting into the psych weapons. They might have bought it off the shelf from the Russians or the Chinese. Heck, maybe even us. But their weapons programs have been growing exponentially in the last few years. So I wouldn't be surprised if they developed it on their own."

"Any way to protect ourselves against it?"

"Generally speaking, I love the voices in my head."

Juan raised a quizzical eyebrow.

"I suppose that's some kind of a line from a punk rock song or movie you're referencing?"

Murph blushed. "Kinda both. Sorry about that."

"You were saying?"

"The best defense is to destroy the transmitter."

"Which you totally blew away with the Kashtan." That was Juan's way of telling Murph he forgave him for the bad joke.

Murph beamed.

"Yeah, I guess I did."

"Anything else you can tell me about dazzler technology?"

"It's part of what our military calls intermediate force technology—like the non-lethal stuff we're testing for DARPA. They're all variants of light emitters that either distract or blind the opposition temporarily." Murph's face fell. "At least that's the idea."

"You're worried about Linc."

"If he got hit by a strong enough laser—the kind the Chinese have used in the past—he's a goner."

"He's on his way to the best eye clinic on the planet."

"There's nothing anyone can do for a fried optic nerve."

"Any chance you can dig into that dazzler technology some more? Maybe find some answers that might help the doctors?"

Murph sat up. "Sure, anything for Linc."

"Not just Linc. If we run into another dazzler drone, our entire crew is at risk."

Murph's face darkened. "Then we'll just keep shooting 'em down. You can count on that."

Cabrillo nodded. Despite his lack of military experience, Murph had proven to be one heck of a combat crewman, especially on the weapons station.

"No doubt about it, Murph. No doubt at all."

45

Archytas Katrakis stood on the starboard bridgewing of his transport ship—formerly known as the *Mountain Star*—making its way north through the fabled canal. It was his favorite time of day. He sipped a hot American coffee thick with cream and loaded with sugar, savoring the chill of the early morning air on his face. His eyes studied the pink wash of the sunrise bathing the sand and the lone sentry in the distance, a rifle slung lazily from his shoulder.

The constant drumming of the big diesels far belowdecks drove his vessel forward. His was one of two dozen large commercial and naval ships in the northbound convoy, the only one allowed in each day beginning at six a.m.

It was also the only vessel carrying a hundred-megaton nuclear torpedo.

Or was it? He smiled at the macabre thought. He glanced around at the other cargo and containerships several hundred yards away. Who knew what each of them carried? Thankfully, the Suez Canal Authority didn't inspect transiting ships. And the likelihood of being boarded by an Egyptian customs agent was nil. His father's lucrative partnerships with Egyptian officials in arms smuggling over the years ensured his safety.

Still, Katrakis was anxious. He set his coffee down on the rail and lit a Marlboro cigarette and sucked in a lungful of the sweet tobacco. The big summit between the American and Turkish presidents in Istanbul was three days away. So far, everything had gone according to plan except for the near-disastrous encounter with the Indian frigate. Now that his ship was finally underway and making its way north toward the Mediterranean Sea, he could sense they were on the verge of victory. But the Suez Canal was not without its challenges, including its recent blockage by a grounded superfreighter. Katrakis wouldn't relax until they reached his final destination. And perhaps not even then. Delivering the Kanyon was just the beginning.

The summit was already big news in the region and heralded as a "significant historical event." He sipped more coffee, smiling to himself again. The news agencies had no idea how historic that meeting would be. When his father first proposed the Kanyon plan to him, Archytas recoiled at the horror of it. But as his father described the untold wealth and power the family would accrue from the destruction of Istanbul and its aftermath, he began to appreciate the sheer genius of the plot.

All that was moot, however, if his ship failed to arrive at its assigned station on time and release the Kanyon on its fateful mission. Katrakis checked his watch again.

So far, they were right on time.

46

Juan fussed with his freshly washed hair, looking in the bathroom mirror, his stomach rumbling with hunger. He was dressed casually but fashionably in a tight-fitting white cashmere Polo V-neck sweater, a pair of Tom Ford light gray linen pants and blue suede Berwick loafers. He barely heard the gentle knocking on his cabin door.

He opened it and Meliha was standing there. She wore a vintage sixties sheath dress that perfectly complemented her athletic build yet was nevertheless modest. Juan noticed it was the same color as her green eyes.

"You look amazing," Juan said. The compliment just slipped out of his mouth. He didn't mean to be so candid. He hoped he hadn't embarrassed her.

Meliha blushed. "Thank you."

"Won't you please come in?"

Meliha smiled as she stepped inside. She glanced down at her dress as Juan shut the door behind her.

"It really is quite lovely, isn't it? Dr. Huxley said Mr. Nixon made it for me. I'm surprised your ship has a dressmaker on board."

"Kevin Nixon was an award-winning special effects wizard in

Hollywood before he joined the Corporation. Now he runs his Magic Shop for us."

Meliha's eyes searched the large cabin. It was an Arabesque *mise en scène*, with vintage forties furnishings. Juan read her mind.

"Speaking of the Magic Shop, Kevin and his team designed this cabin for me after my favorite movie, *Casablanca*. What you're seeing here is the set from Rick's Café Américain."

Meliha affected her best Bogart voice. "'Of all the gin joints in all the towns in all the world, she walks into mine.'"

"You know it?"

"It is my father's favorite American movie." Her eyes swept the room. "It's quite an unusual décor for a warship."

"Conformity is no virtue in combat. More often than not, it's creativity that wins the day. So I encourage it whenever I can."

Meliha caught sight of an oil painting hanging on one of the faux stucco walls. The colors were starkly contrasted. A naked Cupid sported a pair of grayish brown feathery wings.

"Amor vincit omnia—love conquers all."

Juan was impressed. "You know your paintings, too."

Meliha crossed over to it and examined it in detail.

"It's one of Caravaggio's most interesting works. This is an excellent reproduction."

"It's not, actually."

"No, seriously, this is a wonderful copy."

"What I mean is, that is the original Caravaggio. An excellent copy is hanging in a Berlin museum."

"I don't understand. I saw this painting at the Gemäldegalerie a few years ago." Meliha's brow furrowed. "Is it stolen?"

"No, not at all. Art makes an excellent investment and we have one of the best dealers in the world who advises us on our purchases. Legitimate purchases."

"Why is a copy hanging in the Gemäldegalerie?"

"You'd have to ask them."

"Oh," was all Meliha could offer, impressed and stunned at the same time.

"Hungry?"

Meliha nodded. "Starving."

"I thought you might be. I took the liberty of ordering room service for both of us, if you don't mind."

"Not at all."

Juan pointed her toward the anteroom with its red leather chairs, matching tufted sofa and a vintage dining table.

She turned to him. "I hope you know this meal doesn't get you out of your promise to give me a tour of your ship."

"Of course not." Juan picked up the replica Bakelite phone and dialed a number. "We're ready for dinner when you are."

Juan pointed at the bar. "Something to drink?"

"Perhaps some water. I'm afraid what alcohol will do to my wits on an empty stomach."

"I understand." He poured her a sparkling Perrier water and then fixed himself a Buffalo Trace Kentucky bourbon, neat, and pointed her toward the sofa with his glass while he took one of the chairs.

Maurice, the *Oregon*'s chief steward, wheeled in the domed dinner service cart to the table. He wore his signature black suit and crisp white cotton shirt, with creases sharp enough to slice cheese. A thick mane of perfectly coiffed white hair bespoke his age, estimated to be in the eighties, though Juan could never find an official record. Forced into retirement from the Royal Navy because of his advanced years, he joined the *Oregon* and quickly became one of its most beloved members. He possessed a preternatural ability to glean information around the ship faster than an eavesdropping Amazon Echo.

Maurice lifted the silver dome, releasing an aromatic rush of rosemary, thyme and roasted lamb. He pulled out a corkscrew and began uncorking the wine.

"Dinner is served, Captain, M'lady. I present to you chef's signature rack of lamb, au gratin potatoes and fresh *haricot verts* served with a 2008 Chilean Clos Apalta, a Bordeaux blend. *Bon appétit.*"

"What's the latest scuttlebutt, Maurice?" Juan asked.

The dapper steward splashed a taste of the wine into Juan's glass.

As Cabrillo sampled it, Maurice said, "Mr. Lincoln is awake and in good spirits, and has eaten heartily. He is scheduled to depart on the Tiltrotor sometime later this evening."

"This Chilean is outstanding," Juan said.

"I selected it myself," Maurice said as he now filled both glasses. "Shall I serve you?"

"We'll take it from here," Juan said, waving him away with his hand.

"Very well, *mon capitaine.*" Maurice bowed to Meliha. "*Et mademoiselle.*"

The steward slipped away virtually unnoticed, shutting the cabin door silently behind him, as Juan began serving up the meal.

"He called you Captain and not Chairman."

"Maurice is old-school Royal Navy, so it's strictly Captain to him."

"You have an amazing ship and crew. Everyone has treated me so wonderfully. And the way you handled the attack at Wahat Albahr and the Turkish frigate was beyond impressive."

"My people are the best."

Meliha's attention turned toward the table. Her eyes feasted upon it.

"This food looks and smells absolutely delicious."

She took her first bite of lamb, rolling her eyes in ecstasy as the buttery-soft meat melted in her mouth.

Juan grinned. "I'm glad you like it."

He took his own bite of the succulent lamb. The chef had really outdone himself. They ate contentedly for a few moments until Meliha broke the silence.

"I've noticed quite a few women on your vessel."

"Nearly forty percent of my crew are women. Generally speaking, we only take on the most experienced and qualified people we can find. As time goes on, I expect that number to rise."

"And Mrs. Cabrillo? Does she serve on the *Oregon* as well?" Her eyes moved to the wedding ring on Juan's finger.

Juan's mood darkened. He set his fork down.

"Mrs. Cabrillo was killed by a drunk driver several years ago."

He didn't tell her that his wife was the drunk and that she had killed herself accidentally. He still blamed himself.

"I'm so very sorry for your loss." Meliha's face flushed. "I'm ashamed I even mentioned it."

"Don't be. Life happens. It was a long time ago. Please try the wine. It's outstanding."

Meliha took a sip. "Yes, it's truly wonderful."

They ate and drank in silence for a few moments, trying to regain their bearings.

Finally, Meliha said, "Given everything I've seen on your ship, your corporation must make a lot of money."

"Are you asking me on the record or off?"

"I'm sorry, I'm naturally curious. It's just a friendly question."

"Then yes, the business is a lucrative one. Unfortunately, we live in a world where our services are needed and we happen to be the best at what we do, so we charge a pretty penny. But we don't do it for the money, strictly speaking.

"My grandfather was a barber. He never had a lot of money yet he was one of the richest men I ever knew because it was people he cared about. He taught me to believe that the love of money is the root of all evil. Sure, what we make is a side benefit. And yes, we use it to make ourselves comfortable, to purchase the best possible equipment and to maintain our operations. But why we do what we do is out of love. Love of country. And love of life."

Meliha's eyes brightened with sudden understanding.

"*Amor vincit omnia—love conquers all*—literally."

Juan nodded. "Truth."

The two exchanged warm smiles and tucked into their meal, savoring the lamb and the wine. Juan hadn't felt this comfortable with a woman in some time.

It felt good.

While Juan hated to disturb the pleasant moment with business, he had a mission to accomplish.

"My people are convinced that the AK assault rifles we found in Libya are Bulgarian that are being distributed by the Albanians."

Meliha nodded, finishing up her last bite.

"That's right. The Bulgarians make some of the best guns around, but they wouldn't dare cross the Albanian mafia to move them."

"I'm glad you agree, because we've set course for Durrës."

"That's Nishani clan territory." She sat back. "It would make sense they were connected to the Pipeline. Still, it's rather a thin lead, don't you think?"

Juan's intercom buzzed. Hali Kasim's voice blared over the overhead speaker.

"Chairman, sorry to interrupt you. Dr. Huxley needs to speak with you. It's urgent."

"Thanks, Hali. I'll call her now." Kasim clicked off as Juan turned to Meliha. "Excuse me for a second."

"Of course."

Juan pulled his cell phone as he stepped away from the table. He noticed several missed calls.

"Hux, is there a problem?"

"I just got a call from a friend of mine at the Navy Hospital in Naples. She was treating one of the women we sent there, an Albanian. The patient just said through her translator that even though they were all blindfolded, she's certain they were caged somewhere in an Albanian forest."

"How can she know that?"

"She could smell the pine trees and she said she heard one of the men speaking her local dialect. But she can't say exactly where they were kept. I know it's not much to go on, but I thought you'd want to know about it immediately."

"It helps more than you know. Thanks for passing that along." He ended the call.

"Good news?" Meliha asked.

Juan told her what Hux had conveyed.

"Another thin thread," Meliha said. "But they add up to something, don't they?"

"They do indeed. Durrës is confirmed."

"What do you intend to do when we get there?"

"Gather evidence, collect intel and get out."

"The Albanians won't like it."

Juan sipped the last of his wine.

"Then I guess we're going to put a real hurt on their feelings."

47

SOCHI, RUSSIA

The large warehouse stood on the far outskirts of the Black Sea port. An idling refrigerated van marked "Sochi Botanicals" in Cyrillic letters was the only vehicle parked at one of its loading bays. Armed guards in civilian clothes patrolled the perimeter of the building. It was serving that evening as a temporary safe house for a clandestine meeting.

Inside, fifteen fighting-age Armenians, including three women, sat in the chilled air on packing crates surrounded by racks of fresh-cut flowers. They were part of the large Armenian diaspora that flourished in the former Olympic city known for the beauty of its beaches, forests and mountains. The President of Russia maintained an opulent summer residence not many kilometers away from where they sat, as did many of Russia's wealthiest oligarchs.

The young Armenians had been invited to the secret rendezvous because they were all known to be rabid nationalists who hated the Turks even more than they loved Armenia.

Their hard, angry faces were focused intently on the tall, hawkish man speaking to them who went by the name of Sargsyan, the Armenian equivalent of Smith or Jones. Handsome and charismatic, he was a known associate of David Hakobyan in whose name he was speaking tonight and whose reputation drew the group seated in front of him.

"I don't have to tell you that the Turks are responsible for the slaughter of our fathers and sons and brothers in Nagorno-Karabakh. I lost my only son there. And I know each one of you has lost a loved one. And some of you more than one."

Heads nodded grimly. A few swore under their breaths.

Sargsyan continued. "If we are to be honest with ourselves, the Turks produced better weapons than we had and deployed them more effectively against our valiant soldiers. But they deployed them in an illegal war of ethnic cleansing against our people and for that there can be no forgiveness." He pounded his fist into his palm for effect. "This must not stand!"

The eager Armenian nationalists all nodded in agreement.

"So what is to be done?" one of the women asked.

"Revenge, that is what is to be done," Sargsyan said. "Bloody, swift and sure."

"And how would we accomplish that?"

"Mr. Hakobyan has made arrangements for each of you to come with me on a mission that will strike terror in the Turkish heart for generations."

"When will this happen?" a man asked.

"It begins tonight, if you have the courage to join with me."

The young Armenians exchanged glances and whispers. Curious, the same woman spoke up again. "What is the plan?"

Sargsyan shook his head. "I can't divulge any plans until I have a committed team. Operational security requires it."

"How can we trust you?" another man asked.

"Because your heart is my heart, your grief is my grief, your hate is my hate."

"Very poetic," the young woman said. "But poetry never killed anybody."

"Then let me show you this."

Sargsyan yanked up a crowbar and approached a long packing crate marked "Flowerpots." He pried it open, tossed aside the lid and pulled out a shoulder-fired anti-aircraft missile launcher, brand-new and still bearing its Russian manufacturing tags.

Armenia had compulsory military service. Though only half of the men in the room had served in combat, all of them recognized the weapon. And most smiled.

So did Sargsyan. "I can't tell you at this moment what the precise nature of the operation is, but I can promise you that there are more of these involved. And there's still other weapons even more terrifying to our mortal enemy. But most of all, I promise you that when it is all over, an entire city will burn."

Sargsyan handed the missile launcher to the man seated closest to him and he took it enthusiastically. The woman next to him ran her hands over it like it was a precious jewel.

"We all know about the Turkish holocaust against our people and the recent war is just an extension of that vile act," Sargsyan continued. "The word *holocaust* means *destruction by fire*. If you want to see a true Turkish holocaust and get your revenge for the Armenian blood they have spilled over the centuries, you must come with me immediately."

"It sounds like a suicide mission," the woman said.

"The purpose of the mission is to kill Turks. As the mission leader, I have no intention of dying and I promise that you will not be committing suicide."

The young woman nodded her head, satisfied.

Sargsyan spread his arms wide like a loving father. "Who's with me?"

The woman stood quickly. All the others joined her.

Sargsyan smiled. "I'm so very proud of you. Follow me."

The fifteen Armenian fighters followed Sargsyan to the loading dock and piled into the waiting refrigerated van. He stuck his head in the door and told them to be quiet on the long journey ahead and pointed to a crate of thermoses full of hot sweet tea and black coffee. "To keep you warm," he said. The flower van was a necessary cover as they crossed borders, he explained. And he promised a bathroom stop within the next two hours.

"It's late. Get some sleep if you can."

He then shut the airtight door and locked it.

Sargsyan climbed into the passenger's seat and buckled up. "To the port," he told the driver.

The armed guards melted into the night as the van pulled away. Sargsyan checked his watch. He had made two twisted promises to those Armenian kids and he intended to keep them. He flipped a switch in the cab.

Within fifteen minutes, the young Armenian fighters would all be dead—but not from suicide. They would suffocate from the rapid removal of oxygen within their airtight compartment. Their bodies would remain perfectly preserved in the near-freezing temperature for the next step of the operation.

That would be the first promise he would keep.

And if everything went according to plan, they would indeed be part of the great Turkish holocaust, also as promised.

For a moment, he felt a pang of guilt for his betrayals.

He had no children, certainly no son who had died in the recent war. Like the kids in the back of the van, he also was of Armenian blood. And David Hakobyan had been a good source of income to him over the years.

But money was thicker than blood and Sokratis Katrakis paid in gold.

48

DURRËS, ALBANIA

The young Albanian Coast Guard officer was handsome by any standard, save for the acne scars that had left his cheeks pockmarked like the skin of a shriveled grapefruit.

It was only his third week on duty but he understood his job and that was to do whatever his commander told him to do. And his commander's job was to do whatever the Nishani mafia bosses told him to do.

Period.

In theory, he and his pilot on the small patrol boat were tasked with finding drugs and other contraband on board commercial vessels. The Port of Durrës had become a major distribution hub for narcotics and guns flooding into Europe.

Today his mission was to find a vessel named *Vesturá*, a worn-down, 590-foot-long bulk freighter flying an Iranian flag. It was described by the Nishani contact as green and white but, strangely, capable of rapid color changes—which made no sense at all. Stranger still, it was believed to be the operational base for a group of well-armed mercenaries who might be coming after the Nishani operation.

The Coast Guard man had been scanning the AIS receivers for a bulk freighter named *Vesturá*, but it hadn't shown up anywhere in the region.

However, a Liberian-flagged ship, the *Westfloss*, also 590 feet long, had approached the harbor and dropped anchor an hour earlier. According to its manifest, it was traveling from Spain to Greece with a load of agricultural products.

Even though it was late and his shift completed, he decided for the sake of his health—he was deadly allergic to gunshots and stabbings—he'd better check it out.

His patrol boat neared the ship, which dwarfed his vessel. Its rusted hull was painted a faded orange or perhaps it was just the rust that had taken over. The man's ears picked up the shrieking din of . . . pigs?

He was certain of it. His grandfather had raised pigs when he was a small boy. A slight shudder ran through him as he remembered the sound of them squealing and shrieking during the autumn slaughter.

He and the pilot, a gray-bearded old salt, exchanged a wary glance.

A pig boat.

A thick rivulet of green slime poured in a continuous stream out of one of the bilge pump valves and spilled into the blue Adriatic. The sickening smell was all too familiar. His hateful grandfather had made him muck out the pigpens one too many times.

"Glad I'm not climbing up into that garbage dump," the veteran sailor said. He grinned. "I'm just the pilot. You're the hero."

The officer was having second thoughts. A mercenary outfit wouldn't launch an assault from a pigpen. But his boss was anxious because his Nishani bosses were nervous and they bombarded him with constant requests for updates. Reporting back to them that there was nothing to report didn't alleviate the tension up or down the chain of command. At least by inspecting this particular ship, the young officer could tell his commander he searched a suspicious vessel and found nothing and perhaps keep on his good side. He would hate to lose this job. There were few employment opportunities these days other than working for one of the criminal syndicates, which the officer refused to do.

At least, not directly.

"Ahoy, down there," a voice crackled over the radio. "This is Captain Julio Diaz. Anything wrong?"

The officer picked up his mic.

"This is the Albanian Coast Guard. There's a chemical discharge coming from the port side of your vessel. I request permission to come aboard for an inspection."

"Chemical discharge?" The hearty voice laughed. "Is that what you call it? Permission granted. There's an access ladder on the stern. I'll lower it for you now. One of my men will escort you to the bridge."

"Thank you, Captain Diaz. I'm coming aboard immediately."

The captain's laugh burst over the radio speaker.

"I hope you brought your rubber boots."

The Albanian Coast Guard man was still reeling from shock as he boarded the *Westfloss*, deplored even more the fact he could barely read the faded letters on the rusting stern as he made the arduous climb up the unstable steel staircase.

What awaited him up top was even more worrisome as he was led to the bridge superstructure. Broken machinery, steel drums, discarded tools and even cigarette butts littered the deck. Chains were stretched across the places where railings had rusted away and moldy plywood was bolted onto bulkheads presumably where rust had eaten holes through the metal. It looked like a floating junkyard rather than a seaworthy vessel. But it was the increasing noise of the squealing hogs reverberating belowdecks that made him nauseous.

Standing now in the wheelhouse, he could barely see through the grimy windows, several of which were cracked. The linoleum floor was filthy and the windowsills littered with dead flies. In the enclosed space, the stench of stale cigarettes and pig effluvia was nearly overwhelming. An old video monitor was bolted to a corner of the ceiling, fed by a cable wrapped in curling duct tape. The monitor displayed four camera views belowdecks, all of them filled with masses of squealing pigs and the zombie-like workers tending them.

A voice startled the Albanian out of his stupor.

"Sorry to keep you waiting."

The officer turned around to see a disheveled fat man in yellow rubber overalls and black galoshes slathered in slime. He rubbed his hands with a filthy rag before he jutted out one of his meaty claws to shake.

The Albanian reluctantly took it.

"Captain Diaz?"

"*Sí*, one and the same."

The Albanian looked him over. The captain's sunburned face was framed by a graying beard and a drunkard's bulbous, veiny nose. His long, greasy white hair was pulled into a ponytail and thick glasses magnified the size of his bloodshot eyes.

"I need to see your cargo manifests as well as your shipping orders, Captain."

"*No hay problema*. I already have them here." Diaz stumbled over to the chart table and grabbed a worn leather folio. He shoved it into the Albanian's hands. "You will find my crew manifest and ship registration in there as well, *amigo*."

"Why have you dropped anchor in my harbor?" he asked as he began to flip through the documents.

"Engine problems. But I have the best engineer in all España working on it now. We will be getting underway by tomorrow morning at the latest."

"And why are you pumping hazardous chemicals into the bay?"

Diaz smiled, flashing tobacco-stained teeth. "It is all organic materials, I assure you. Very good for the fish."

The officer's eyes stung as he scanned the documents. He saw nothing irregular. He glanced back up at the monitor. On one of the screens, a pig flailed on a chain suspended above the deck as a crewman approached with a butcher's blade. The Albanian flinched and looked away.

"Ready for your tour belowdecks?" Diaz asked.

The Albanian slapped the folio against Diaz's broad chest.

"That won't be necessary. Be sure to get this garbage scow out of my harbor by seven a.m. tomorrow or I'll have your ship impounded." He cast a disgusted glance around the bridge. "Or scrapped."

Diaz bowed slightly like a gentleman dandy.

"Not a problem, I assure you."

"Well? What did you find?" the salty old pilot asked as he steered the patrol boat back toward the dock.

"I love the sea, but I'd rather kill myself than spend ten minutes of my life sailing on a ship like that."

The pilot chuckled, his hooded eyes squinting with glee.

The officer's face soured as he sniffed his shirt. He would wait until they docked before calling in the pig boat to his boss. He decided right then and there that if he ever inspected another vessel as filthy as the *Westfloss*, he'd quit the Coast Guard and emigrate to Ireland as a day laborer. He'd rather eat boiled cabbage with blistered hands than smell like a pigsty.

49

Eddie Seng was shoving another thirty-round mag into a pouch of his tactical vest when Juan marched into the gun room. The other team members were loading up their weapons, gear and ammo for the assault on the Albanian mafia compound.

It had been several hours since the Albanian Coast Guard man had boarded the ship and fled in disgust almost as quickly as he'd come. Once again, the Magic Shop had earned its moniker, producing the pig-harvesting videos, smelly effects and even plastic dead flies on the windowsills to create the necessary illusion.

"Change of plans," Juan said.

Everybody heard the edge in his voice and stopped what they were doing.

"Problem, Chairman?" Eddie asked. He and Juan had put together the assault plan and he had spent the last two hours prepping for the mission. The challenge was that the Albanian gangsters were no doubt alerted to a potential attack on their compound and were waiting for just this kind of operation. They would be gunned up and defending known territory, which gave them home field advantage.

"I just got off the horn with Overholt. We are under orders to minimize our footprint, which is spookspeak for *no guns, no killing.*"

"Not a problem so long as the Albanians are operating under the same rules," Raven said.

MacD held up his crossbow with a wide grin.

"Did Mr. Overholt prohibit frog-gigging these yahoos?"

"Trust me, I thought of you in particular," Juan said. "But we can't take any chances."

"Why the change of heart?" one of the junior operators asked.

"We're stepping onto European soil. A shoot-out in the EU's backyard would be bad optics for the U.S. government at the moment."

"And I take it the mission objective hasn't changed?"

"No. We're still looking for connections between what we found in Libya and anything related to the Pipeline—guns, drugs, people."

MacD ran his hand through his long blond hair.

"Did Mr. Overholt have any ideas about how we might accomplish that without getting murdered by these mob hitters?"

"No, but Murph does."

As if on cue, Murph stepped into the crowded room. All eyes turned to him.

"I'm all set up at the gun range."

Juan nodded at the rifles and pistols around the room.

"Everybody, secure your weapons and meet us there in five."

"Aye, Chairman," Eddie said.

Without a word, the team returned their secured weapons to their respective storage bins quickly and efficiently.

Juan waited for the last of them to clear the room before he snatched up a box of ammo for his favorite FN pistol and hid it under his tactical vest.

He was a good soldier and obeyed his orders whenever possible, but his people's safety came first.

The stars blazed like streetlamps in the cloudless mountain sky, chilling the early-morning darkness. The beefy Nishani gangster stood by the rough-hewn stones of the old hunting lodge, trying to escape the harsh breeze whispering in the trees. The wind made it even colder and it rattled the branches and shook the autumn leaves.

The gangster heard a sound like a man or a bear crunching in the forest. He shot his big flashlight into the trees but didn't see anything. It was only the wind, he thought, just like it had been a dozen times before. He didn't dare shoot his rifle blindly because his friends were roaming around out there on patrol.

They were all on edge. All the boss knew was that a band of mercenaries might be heading their way or down to the port. He had no idea how many there were or even who they were. Only that they had taken out a bunch of Turkish fighters—no small feat.

And there might be a woman with them.

The local port authorities were covering Durrës and the national police were helping protect their neighborhoods in Tirana. But out here in the mountains, it was only the mafia men from the local villages who stood guard. They were all good fighters and honorable, not like the young punks driving around Tirana in their big Humvees, blaring American rap music and flashing gold chains.

The tops of his ears burned from the cold. It occurred to him that nobody had called in for at least ten minutes. He squeezed the talk button on his walkie-talkie, but no one responded. He tried again. And a third time. He shouldered his rifle and pounded the radio in his hand, trying to make it work. Then he changed channels and called out again. Nothing.

A chill ran up his spine.

He unslung his AK-47 and moved away from the hunting lodge in a low crouch, his weapon up. His eyes watered from the cold, making it even harder to see in the dark. He suddenly felt dizzy and sick to his stomach yet he sped along the ancient rock wall anyway, certain he saw a shadow in the distance. But then the potbellied gangster doubled over and vomited. He dropped to his knees, just as his bowels released, and passed out in the dirt.

50

Juan held his FN (Five-seveN) pistol at eye level with the boss, a man named Doka, sitting in his banker's chair as Eddie Seng rifled through the Soviet-era file cabinets.

They were in Doka's office inside the hunting lodge, formerly the private preserve of Enver Hoxha, Albania's communist dictator, long since dead. Now owned by the Albanian mafia, its thick timber beams, rough-cut granite and vintage leather-upholstered furnishings were complemented by numerous animal trophies on the walls or posed on stands. Though hunting had been banned in the country for close to a decade to help replenish dozens of nearly extinct species, there was evidence of fresh kills all over the compound.

Another reason to take these jerks out, Juan thought.

The old Albanian was fixated on the rifle slung over Eddie's back. It looked like something out of a sci-fi movie. So did his augmented-reality helmet, its visor up.

"What kind of rifle is that?"

Juan couldn't tell him it was a DARPA-designed infrasonic weapon, another non-lethal device in their growing arsenal. That information was top secret.

"It's the latest Nerf gun," he joked. "Very effective."

"My men? All dead?"

Juan didn't answer. He wanted the crime boss to sweat. In fact, they were all alive and reeking to high heaven. One of the unfortunate side effects of the infrasonic disruption of their nervous systems was the loss of bladder and bowel control.

The unhygienic thugs were zip-tied like calves at a rodeo and stashed in the horse barn. The Albanians had been easy pickings in the dark thanks to Gomez, overhead in the AW, relaying live, infrared video of the compound to their augmented-reality helmets.

"Found some cages," MacD said in Juan's comms.

"Occupied?"

"Not lately. I found a pair of women's shoes left behind in here. And there's a sweet little dolly lying in the corner."

Juan's hand involuntarily squeezed his pistol grip tighter.

Doka's eyes widened liked turkey eggs. He couldn't hear the radio transmission booming in Juan's skull through bone induction. He threw his hands up.

"Money? How much do you want?"

Juan holstered his pistol before his anger got away from him. The old mafia boss slumped in his chair, relieved.

Raven stomped through the door, her cheeks red with the cold.

"Found this." She slapped a brick of meth marked with the Diamante Azul logo into Juan's gloved hand.

"Bravo!" The logo alone was likely proof enough it was Herrera's, but he'd have Dr. Littleton confirm it in his lab. Juan nodded to the AK slung over her back. "You check it?"

"Same factory stamp on the trunnion."

"Give Eddie a hand with the files so we can get out of here."

"Aye." Raven stepped over to the row of file cabinets and Eddie directed her to the one next to him.

"I could use a team like yours," the Albanian said. "Very professional. Name your price."

"Trust me, you couldn't afford us."

"Try me. My cousin is the head of our clan. Money is no problem."

Juan's eyes scanned the old man's desk. There was a photo of Doka standing on a brand spanking new, high-speed patrol boat—the kind used to smuggle contraband across the Adriatic to Western Europe.

"Quite the boat." Juan had seen it tied up at the pier on his way in. It indeed cut quite a line, even in the dark. In the photo, it was stunning. He pulled his phone and shot a picture of it.

"You like boats?"

"I like boats."

"She makes eighty kilometers an hour. I paid two million euros for her. She's yours if you let me live." Doka flashed an oily smile. "You can find her at the best slip, number one. The keys are even in the ignition."

"Maybe I'll just kill you and take it anyway."

That wiped the smile off the old man's face.

Juan turned around. "Eddie, we're burning daylight."

"I don't believe it." Seng was squatting in front of the lowest drawer. He pulled out an old-fashioned ledger and cracked it open.

Doka's jowly face darkened.

"I don't read Albanian," Eddie said, "but I can tell you it's in some sort of code. And there are lots of numbers."

"Bag it and let's get out of here. Call the rest of the team and we'll saddle up."

"I'll give you five million euros for that ledger," the Albanian said.

Juan cocked an eyebrow. "In gold?"

"Bitcoin. Even better."

"Bitcoin is a scam. Diamonds might work."

"That would take a while."

"Silver dollars? Mystic the Unicorn Beanie Babies? Pogs?"

The Albanian shook his head, confused. "A joke?"

Juan pointed at the ledger. "Yeah. And it's on you."

Doka lunged out of his chair with a roar, his gnarled hands clawing for Juan's throat and pistol at the same time. He moved fast for a fat old man, Juan thought.

Juan was neither.

Cabrillo threw a satisfying punch that clocked the gangster on the jaw and knocked his lights out, dropping him to the wooden floor in a heap. He zip-tied the man's hands and feet and then the team dashed out the door, heading back to the *Oregon*.

Juan ordered Hali Kasim to contact Interpol authorities and direct them to the hunting lodge to seize the contraband and arrest the mobsters; local law enforcement couldn't be trusted to do the job.

The morning's work put a serious dent in the Nishani organization and disrupted the Pipeline, even if only temporarily. Unfortunately, the criminal underworld, like nature, abhorred a vacuum and no doubt another gang would take its place in due course.

Juan checked his watch. There was just time enough before dawn. He called to Linda Ross over his molar mic as he also pulled out his phone. Max was in charge of the *Oregon* at the moment, but Ross would be on the bridge during an operation like this.

"Everything good on your end?" Linda asked.

"Mission accomplished, no casualties."

"Thank God for that."

Juan punched the send button on his phone. "I just sent you a photo of a boat I need you to check out. It's berthed in slip number one. I didn't see any guards when we passed through, but, just in case, take the *Gator*. We don't want to take any chances."

"What am I looking for?"

"It belongs to Doka. I have a hunch there's something on board worth finding."

"I'll bring Murph for muscle."

"Now you're scaring me."

"Anything else?"

"Don't take any unnecessary risks. If you can't get on and off undetected, get out of there. But if you do get a chance to look around, don't forget to scuttle it on your way out."

"Why scuttle?"

"Because I can picture the look on Doka's face when he finds out what happened to his precious boat."

51

Meliha was hit with the scent of salty sea when Linda Ross opened the hatch to one of the *Oregon*'s ballast tanks. Normally used along with the other tank to make the merchant vessel appear fully loaded when needed, it was now a two-lane, Olympic-length lap pool. The cavernous space shimmered with the light from the banks of LEDs reflecting off the water. The effect was enhanced by the fine Carrara marble tile lining the ballast's walls.

Ross, still wearing her submariner's uniform, led the way along the catwalk flanking the pool. A swimmer ducked beneath the water at the far end.

"What is this place?" Meliha asked.

Ross smiled. "The ballast pool is just one of several workout facilities scattered around the ship for the crew to use and enjoy. Nothing like a workout to burn off stress. And most of our people pride themselves on staying in top physical condition—especially that guy."

The swimmer emerged from beneath the water, his strong arms spread high and wide like an eagle's wings. A thrusting kick of his legs roiled the water behind him as his arms pulled through the seawater, raising his torso high above the surface, a picture-perfect execution of the butterfly stroke.

No crew member was more dedicated to the pool or pushing his physical limits than the man churning the waters in record time. Despite the weighted wrist bands, let alone missing part of one leg, Juan Cabrillo sped through the water effortlessly, his rhythm as steady as a locomotive engine.

Meliha couldn't help but admire the muscles of his shoulders and upper chest, rippling with each swing of his arms, digging into the water, and the flex of his abdominal muscles as his upper body rose for the next attack. She could hardly believe this was the same man she saw yesterday dressed like a fat Spanish drunkard, with a beard and in filthy overalls, playing the captain of a pig boat. Now he looked like a Poseidon, the Greek god of the sea.

Linda knew the look on Meliha's face. She felt the same way, watching her friend and commander speed along. Juan's athletic prowess and relentless discipline in the pool were undisputed—and the secret to his incredible physical abilities in the field.

It also made him a very attractive man.

The two women exchanged a knowing look.

Linda and Meliha stopped at the far end of the pool as Juan ducked beneath the water at the other end. He turned and sprang off the wall, reemerging a moment later and resuming his machinelike assault on the water, this time in a high-flying backstroke.

Despite his intense concentration, she knew he had seen them through his goggles. Max told her that Cabrillo had given orders for the assault team to hit the rack for a few hours before a debrief, but Juan decided to hit the water instead.

Finishing up his final lap, Juan tagged the pool wall and immediately checked his watch just as the alarm went off.

"Beat your time?" Linda asked.

Juan pulled his goggles off. "What's the point of living if you don't keep pushing?" He flashed an exhausted grin at the two women. "What did you find on that patrol boat?"

"Nothing we can use in a court of law. But I did happen to run across the manufacturing plate down in the engine room—*Katrakis Maritime*."

"Katrakis? Why is that name familiar?" Juan asked, still breathing heavily.

"The Katrakis family controls the largest private shipbuilding company in Europe," Meliha said. "And they're also one of the largest shipping and transportation firms in the region. The family has long been suspected of participating in organized crime."

"Pretty handy to have a shipping and transportation company at your beck and call if you're trying to smuggle contraband," Juan said. "You think they're connected to the Pipeline?"

Meliha nodded. "That would make sense. It's quite a coincidence that the Albanian mafia owns a Katrakis vessel. Perhaps we'll find even more connections in those files you recovered."

"But you just said the word. It might only be a coincidence," Ross said. "The Albanians probably drive Maseratis, too. That doesn't make Fiat a Pipeline co-conspirator."

"True," Meliha said. "The Katrakis family supposedly went clean after the death of the patriarch, Sokratis Katrakis, several years ago. But there are rumors that he never actually died, only went into hiding."

Juan lifted himself out of the pool and sat on the tiles, his one intact leg still dangling in the water.

"Only one way to find out. Where is Katrakis Maritime located?"

"I had to look it up. The shipyard is at the port on the island of Pharos in Greece," Ross said.

"Tell Max to set a course for Pharos immediately."

"Aye, Chairman."

"And join us in the debrief, please." Juan nodded at Meliha. "You, too, if you don't mind."

"I'd be honored."

The women turned to leave. Juan called after them, his voice echoing on the marble-lined walls.

"Linda, I forgot to ask. Did you manage to sink that gangster's boat?"

Ross smiled. "Yes, easy. She was designed for a quick scuttle. I opened up the seacocks and she sank like a rock. It's too bad, really. She was a beauty."

52

After a hearty breakfast of thick slab bacon, scrambled eggs and black Kenyan coffee in the ship's galley, Juan gathered with Meliha and his brain trust in the *Oregon*'s conference room.

Juan had spent an entire career as a CIA NOC—aka, a non-official cover, otherwise known as a spook—gathering intelligence all over the planet. While the *Oregon* was certainly built for combat, her primary mission was intelligence. Juan's appreciation for the art and science of said mission led him to recruit members from both military and intel organizations.

Linda Ross was the perfect example. In recent years, she had proven herself beyond capable as a ship's captain, yet she had spent a great deal of her Navy career as the intelligence officer on board Aegis-class cruisers. And Eddie Seng, his operations leader, had a storied career as a CIA deep cover intelligence operative.

In short, the *Oregon* was a boatload of spooks.

Juan needed information now more than ever. They were heading toward Pharos on the thinnest sliver of data in hopes of finding the next link in the Pipeline chain, but that was all they had. And when looking for clues, sometimes a hunch could be as solid as a spent bullet casing.

Still, Juan needed something more.

"Russ, you've been up all night while the rest of us were asleep. What did you find?"

Russ Kefauver was sitting next to Ross. He was a retired CIA forensic accountant who'd spent over twenty years searching through ink-smudged ledgers, floppy disks and hard drives unraveling the arcane finances of drug dealers, gunrunners and corrupt politicians. He'd broken cases from Singapore to Saint Petersburg. Despite years trapped in cramped offices and hunched over computer keyboards, he was remarkably fit. In his off-hours, he trained as a competitive powerlifter. His tailored shirt strained at the seams over his muscular frame.

"I had the chance to go over the materials Eddie pilfered from Doka's office. Interesting stuff. Especially this ledger. In my experience, these old ex-commie mobsters back in their heyday were almost always connected to their government security services. And the funny thing is, the commies were real cheapskates. They demanded their minions keep meticulous paper records. So what we found is that the mobsters kept that habit up even after the commies faded away, just the way they were trained. And that's what Eddie stumbled over."

"That ledger was all in code, according to Eddie. Did you break it?"

Kefauver grinned.

"Albania quit the Warsaw Pact, but the Soviets always maintained assets inside the country. I worked the Russian desk for eleven years, so I made a leap of faith and assumed Doka had been a KGB spy. Or at least an asset. And I knew that if he was, he would still be wedded to the old Soviet ciphers. I wrote a software program years ago that mimicked all their known codes and—voilà!—the secrets of the ledger began unfolding like a flower on a spring morning."

"Very poetic. So, what do you have?"

"Well, as I suggested, the secrets have only begun to reveal themselves. Right now, we have enough dirt on Doka and his underlings to keep them all in jail for five lifetimes.

"But what struck me was a really big bump of cash just a few weeks ago connected to a guy named David Hakobyan. I kept digging around and found his name all over the place going back several years."

"Hakobyan? I know that name."

Juan remembered a huge drug case from a decade ago. He had been a major player with a shadowy background. Hakobyan was implicated but never indicted due to lack of evidence, a hallmark of his career allegedly spanning decades. He retired from the drug trade soon after—or so everyone thought.

Could he be a link in the Pipeline as well? Juan wondered.

"I'm surprised an Armenian would work with the Turks."

"You're referring to the accusation of Armenian genocide by my people," Meliha said.

"Yes, I am." For the Armenian people, it was unforgivable, no less so than the Holocaust was to the Jews.

Meliha sat back in her chair.

"The genocide was a terrible tragedy. The aftermath of World War One unleashed chaos and brutality throughout the region. Terrible crimes committed on both sides. Every honest historian acknowledges that."

"You're right. Nobody has a monopoly on evil. In my experience, it's been fairly evenly distributed around the planet."

"But that doesn't excuse anything. My country must face the reality of its violent past if it is ever to move forward as a peaceful, democratic republic."

Juan nodded. Accepting responsibility for one's actions was a rare thing these days. His admiration for the young activist deepened even further.

"What about this Katrakis organization we're chasing down?" Eddie asked. "That's a Greek name. They're not exactly big fans of the Turks either."

"Don't miss the obvious," Ross said.

Eddie shrugged. "What's that?"

"Greed is thicker than blood. If Hakobyan and Katrakis are connected to the Pipeline, they're motivated by money, not fantasies of revenge."

Juan hoped she was right. Yet now wasn't the time to get philosophical. He turned to Eric Stone. The *Oregon*'s best helmsman was also a talented researcher.

"Stoney, you and Murph grab a couple of your people and see what you can find out about this Hakobyan fellow. Something tells me he didn't go for early retirement. And while you're at it, see if you can find any connection between him and the Katrakis organization."

Stone nodded. "We'll get right on it."

"I'll reach out to Lang about Hakobyan as well."

Cabrillo glanced around the table.

"We can't sit on our laurels, people. Eddie, let's pull up the Katrakis facility on the monitor and start putting together an operational plan. With any luck, we might be able to blow this filthy Pipeline sky-high and not get killed in the process."

"Luck, Chairman?"

"Like Eisenhower said, *Plans are worthless, but planning is everything*. So yeah, I'll take all the luck we can get because we're gonna need it."

As soon as the Pharos plans were laid out and orders issued for a training workup, Juan headed for his cabin to catch up on his paperwork and give Langston Overholt IV a chance to get to his office at Langley. The octogenarian was famous for his punctuality and early-morning regimen.

"Juan Cabrillo, my dear boy. What an amazing coincidence. I was just about to call you."

"Good news, I hope."

"That analysis your people did on the Libyan meth was first-rate. Your lab was right. The molecular signature matched up perfectly with the Herrera samples we have."

"My lab analyst is running the Albanian meth through its paces right now. But given the markings on the package, I'm confident it will also prove to be a Herrera batch of Diamante Azul."

"If so, that's two datapoints confirming Herrera as the drug source for the Pipeline."

"Then we need to go get him." Juan still had unfinished business with the parricidal drug lord. Justice for Tom Reyes was never far from his mind.

"Were it that easy. Víctor Herrera is even nastier and more dangerous than his murderous father. Nobody can get close to him. Everyone we've sent after him hasn't come back. He owns half of the Mexican national government. And his money has corrupted law enforcement and judges on both sides of the border. And anyone who isn't on his payroll is terrified to oppose him. I'm afraid that, at the moment, he's untouchable."

"Why don't we label these cartel leaders as terrorists and take them all out? In twenty years, the Taliban and al-Qaeda haven't killed as many Americans as the cartels kill in a single month with their filthy drugs."

"I quite agree. But I don't make policy, I only implement it."

"Then let me take a run at Herrera myself."

"A subject for another day. Right now, I need you focused on the mission at hand. Where, precisely, are you?"

"We're heading for the island of Pharos."

"What's the draw to those fabled Grecian isles besides the sunny weather?"

"An operation called Katrakis Maritime. There's a big shipyard there."

"I'm quite familiar with the name Sokratis Katrakis. He built the largest privately held shipbuilding company in Europe. He was long suspected of criminal behavior. But he's been dead for a while."

"We think the Katrakis organization might be the transportation source for Pipeline contraband."

"There's a certain kind of logic to that. Any proof?"

"That's why we're heading there—to find something we can use in court."

"I assume the Albanian mission led you in this direction. How did it go?"

Juan described the raid on the Albanian mob compound and the recovery of financial records, including the ledger that Kefauver deciphered.

"We've come across another old name you might remember. A fellow by the name of David Hakobyan."

"Hakobyan . . . Hakobyan . . . Ah, yes, I do remember him. He was suspected of being the moneyman behind a couple big drug syndicates years ago. A very clever man. We couldn't gather enough evidence against him to justify a simple arrest warrant, let alone an indictment. A conviction would have been impossible."

"How did he manage that trick?"

"Our sources said he had a perfect memory, which meant he never left a paper or electronic trail behind to tangle him up. Kept everything in his noggin. Without a mind reader, we hit a dead end. Hard to convict a man on a mere rumor of misbehavior. Good thing the Albanians are more forgetful."

"Any idea where Hakobyan is?"

"He emigrated from Armenia to Southern California in the sixties. He's been an American citizen for decades."

"Let me guess, he's in Glendale." A Californian himself, Juan knew that Glendale and its environs contained the world's largest concentration of Armenians outside Armenia.

"Correct. And he's never left the area. As I recall, he's something of a recluse these days. Hates traveling anywhere. I don't think he's even left the Golden State in all this time."

"Then it shouldn't be too much of an ask for you to arrange a twenty-four/seven surveillance on him until I get back stateside? If he's the moneyman behind the Pipeline, he could be the key to taking this whole thing down."

"I'll reach out to my friends at the FBI and make arrangements for it immediately."

"Thanks, Lang. I'll keep you posted."

"Stay safe, my boy. And Godspeed."

53

On combat patrols, Vice Admiral Sergei Volkov was as cold and merciless as the arctic ice that clogged the Barents Sea. The gruff submariner was a Hero of Russia and had assumed command of GUGI after the death of his predecessor from COVID-19. Broad-shouldered and prematurely white-haired—including his magnificent handlebar mustache—his staff called him the Polar Bear behind his back, as much for his personality as his looks. Subordinates only knew him as a hardened warrior and no-nonsense administrator, so it came as quite a surprise when he appeared in the office that morning beaming.

Perched in his tree trunk arms was a five-year-old little girl with golden ringlets and bright blue eyes. Stopping at each workstation, Volkov introduced his granddaughter, Anzhelika, announcing with button-busting pride that today was her birthday.

The little girl melted the hearts of everyone on duty, each making an exaggerated fuss over the angelic child. No matter that both she and her mother with her, the admiral's daughter-in-law, were civilians and not permitted in the top security facility. For the sake of the child's birthday, and their own careers, none dared challenge the infraction.

The little family made its way to the admiral's spacious private office, where a communications officer was putting the final touches on a portable microphone and speaker system. He just finished his final comms check as Volkov came through the door.

"Is everything in order, Lieutenant?'

"Yes, Admiral." He checked his watch. "The *Penza* will be in contact in two minutes."

"Excellent. You're dismissed. And shut the door behind you."

Before the lieutenant had quietly closed the door, Volkov took a seat in his tall executive chair and plopped his granddaughter on his knee, positioning the two of them in front of the microphone on his desk. His only son was the captain of the stealthy *Penza*, the Russian Federation's newest and most advanced submarine that carried a complement of conventional weapons and a single nuclear Kanyon drone torpedo. While the *Penza* was under strict orders to maintain radio silence for operational security, the admiral and his son had made a special off-the-record arrangement for him to surface today in order to greet his daughter on her birthday.

In all her short five years, her submariner father had always been with her on her birthday—until today. But her doting grandfather had insisted that "rank hath its privileges" and ordered his son to surface at a specified time for a short radio conversation with their beloved Anzhelika.

A vintage maritime windup clock ticked away on the wall, its minute hand hovering above fourteen, the second hand sweeping past thirty. Volkov whispered in the girl's ear, "How would you like a nice surprise for your birthday?"

She smiled as she fiddled around with the submariner's badge pinned to his chest. "Yes, I should like that very much. What is it?"

"Would you like to talk to Daddy today?"

The girl frowned, puzzled.

"But Mama said he is far away at sea and won't be home for a long, long time."

The admiral's eyes crinkled with glee as he pointed at the microphone.

"Yes, that is true, my heart, but you can talk to him with this micro-phone in just a moment."

"Like a phone?"

"Yes, my beauty, exactly like that."

She beamed with joy. "That would be the best."

The old man's heart nearly burst with pride as he reached for the call button. The communications officer had already set the assigned radio frequency. It was his responsibility to raise the *Penza*, then patch his son through to the his office for an intimate family moment.

The admiral's one concession to operational security was to limit the encrypted transmission to just thirty seconds. No doubt the American NSA would pick up the transmission. It was highly unlikely their com-puter algorithms would be able to make any sense of cryptographically scrambled birthday wishes. Even if they did, the *Penza* would quickly slip beneath the waves and disappear into the ocean depths to resume its secret mission far from the prying eyes of American spy satellites.

Volkov watched the second hand sweep toward zero, the designated time for the call. The lieutenant should be patching him in . . . now.

Nothing.

The admiral frowned. The second hand sped along like a torpedo, heading for six o'clock much faster than he cared for. He twisted the volume knob to maximum in case the transmission was faint, but all they heard was the crackle of static.

The door burst open and Captain Karatsev, the head of the commu-nications division, dashed in. His anxious face silently broadcast a mes-sage that he dared not speak.

"Captain?" Volkov asked. "What is the status of the call?"

"Sir? I . . . Technical difficulties, sir. I'm terribly sorry." He saw the child smiling beatifically at him. "Terribly sorry. For the inconvenience."

The admiral shot a withering glance at the captain.

What are you saying?

"Try again."

"We have tried several times, sir."

"Did you do an equipment check?"

"Yes, sir. All is in order on our—" The nervous officer caught himself. "Perhaps it is the atmospheric conditions that are blocking our communication." His eyes pled with the admiral to not ask any further questions.

"Understood."

Volkov watched his daughter-in-law stiffen with anxiety. She was the devoted wife of a career naval officer and nobody's fool. He offered her a reassuring smile.

"We'll make arrangements for another call later today," he said to her. "Not a problem."

Miraculously, his confident tone reassured the woman and her face visibly relaxed.

Volkov had learned long ago that truth seldom makes a man—or woman—braver.

To Anzhelika he said, "How about we get a special birthday breakfast for the special birthday girl? Would you like that?"

She nodded vigorously, shaking her curls.

The admiral laughed. Even the heartsick captain managed a smile.

"Then we shall get some breakfast."

"But what about Daddy? I want to talk to him."

"Later, my angel. Later."

"Are you certain everything is all right?" the daughter-in-law asked.

Volkov stood, still holding the girl. Now was not the time to tell the woman that her husband likely was sleeping in a watery grave along with the rest of his valiant crew. He kissed his granddaughter and shut his eyes, dreading the moment he would tell her what happened to her father. He didn't know if he was brave enough to do it. He would wait for the captain's report, yet in his heart of hearts he already knew his son was lost.

Volkov whispered in the girl's ear, "The cook will make you something very special just for you if you ask him."

"Oh yes, please! And then we can talk to Daddy."

Volkov kissed her again, fighting back his tears. "Yes, my angel."

Volkov handed the girl to her mother. "I'll be right behind you." He nodded toward the door.

She took the girl in her arms. "We'll be just outside."

As soon as she stepped past the captain, Volkov shut the door.

"What the hell is going on?"

"Sir, we've tried everything. Our systems are perfectly functional."

Volkov tugged on his big mustache, an old habit, thinking. There was no way in God's earth his son would have missed this call. Something had happened to the *Penza*. But what?

"Keep trying. And text me every thirty minutes on your progress until I return."

"Yes, sir."

"One more thing, Karatsev. Call Pavlichenko at the ministry of defense. He owes me a favor. I want a satellite retasked over the location where the *Penza* should be stationed. Perhaps we can get eyes on her."

The captain nodded.

"I will contact him immediately." He laid a hand on Volkov's shoulder. "I'm sorry, sir."

Volkov shrugged off the captain's hand. He wasn't ready to accept condolences from his subordinate. His eyes narrowed—a silent order to leave the room.

Karatsev did.

The admiral took a deep breath and composed himself. He knew the captain's efforts would all prove futile. But it was his duty to his granddaughter to give her the best possible day. Perhaps the memory of a wonderful birthday would soften the bitter ashes she would taste on this day the rest of her life.

And then it struck him like a hammerblow.

The Kanyon torpedo was missing, too.

54

Mark Murphy and Eric Stone presented their research on the Katrakis facility on Pharos to Juan and his team so they could prepare an assault plan.

What Murph and Stoney found was that Katrakis Maritime handled a wide variety of service contracts for commercial and military clients. But in the last decade, their shipbuilding operations had invested heavily in the construction of LGN—liquefied natural gas—tankers and support vessels.

The facility was enormous, larger than several football fields. Katrakis Maritime was currently engaged in multiple ship repair and construction projects simultaneously. Their conclusion was that if there was smuggled contraband on the property, it would take weeks to inspect every ship's hold, sealed container, warehouse locker and storage unit to find it.

Juan had been listening attentively, sipping coffee.

"I'm not convinced that they would actually keep contraband there."

"Why not?" Max asked. "It's a big place and it would be easy to hide stuff in."

"It's a big but also a legit shipyard with too many unauthorized eyeballs looking around."

"I agree, Chairman," Murph said. "If I were running their operation, I'd keep that stuff on the transport ships and make them handle their own security. If you start warehousing multiple shipments of people, guns and drugs, you're dealing with lots of traffic in and out and you're raising the number of possibilities for escape, theft or accidental discovery. Better to disperse your risk rather than concentrate it."

"So this place is a bust?" Max asked.

Juan shook his head. "Far from it. What we're really trying to find out is whether the Katrakis organization is facilitating the Pipeline. If they are, they'd most likely be doing it through their shipping operations, but they're probably greasing the skids with cash."

"If the Albanians are any indicator, that means we're looking for financial records and invoices, names and addresses," Stone said.

"Sounds like something you'd find in the main office," Juan said.

Murph smiled. "That's what we thought, too."

"We can't go in there with guns blazing," Max said. "Overholt's white-shoe friends in Foggy Bottom won't like it."

Juan drummed his fingers on the table, thinking.

In all his years of undercover work, Juan found that hiding in plain sight was the easiest cover. Nobody expects the happy customer coming in through the front door with a big smile on his face to actually be a thief casing the joint.

And that's just what Juan and Max were planning to do.

In order to get access to the main office, the job had to be large enough to interest the shipyard financially, but not so large they couldn't get to it immediately. At the same time, they didn't want any Katrakis people crawling around inside the guts of the world's most advanced intelligence-gathering ship.

"All we need to do is order an expensive part that needs to be loaded by crane onto the *Oregon*," Juan said.

Max nodded. "Sure. We just have to make sure they have it in stock."

"Not a problem." Stone had already hacked into the shipyard's computer mainframe. His fingers danced across his computer keyboard until he pulled up their inventory lists and posted it on the big screen monitor.

"What fits the bill?" Juan asked.

"Item number seven forty-nine ought to do it," Max said. "Stoney, print me a copy of that so I can pull the serial number off it."

"Roger that."

"Do we actually need one of those?" Juan asked.

Max shrugged. "No. But they don't know that."

Since Max was the *Oregon*'s chief engineer, he was the logical choice to contact Katrakis Maritime. But before he could make the call, the team needed to concoct a new history for themselves. The *Oregon* would now be named the *Cronenweth*, based out of Houston, sailing under the Panamanian flag. They would begin transmitting a newly generated AIS profile for all the world—and the shipyard—to see. According to its new falsified records, the *Cronenweth* would be carrying a load of heavy machinery bound for Bulgaria.

The art department got to work immediately printing new cargo manifests, crew rosters, licenses, insurance, customs paperwork and the like. It was a big job, but they had become quite proficient over the years, utilizing custom-built software, templates and databases of official forms, seals, and watermarks to create bulletproof forgeries.

And thanks to a single electrical charge from a computer keystroke, the *Oregon*'s special meta-material camouflage paint would instantly change to a new black and white color scheme.

An hour later, after the *Cronenweth* transformation had been completed and its new identity broadcast to the world, Max called the shipyard by satellite phone and reported he was experiencing propulsion difficulties. He supplied the shipyard with a serial number for the part they needed and inquired about its availability.

Was one available?

Amazingly, it was.

55

His top-floor corner suite with its wide windows provided Dr. Artem Petrosian with an unobstructed view of Olenya Bay. In the arcane algorithms of bureaucratic office politics, he supposed that was an acknowledgment of his status and unique skill set. In truth, it was a pathetic reflection of his true value to the Russian state and perhaps even to world history.

This morning, his view was completely obscured by a heavy fog that made him feel as if he were trapped beneath a translucent gray lid. This sensation caused sweat to bead on his forehead. Unconsciously, he changed his breathing pattern, a response he learned while in psychotherapy. Earlier in his life he had been treated with psychotropics to alleviate his acute claustrophobia. He considered his condition rather ironic, given the fact that he was employed in submarine warfare, the most claustrophobic of all military services.

Fortunately, he didn't actually serve on those nuclear-powered coffins. Dr. Petrosian was the chief software programmer for the artificial intelligence computer on board Russia's most advanced submarine, the *Penza*, and its related systems, including the Kanyon drone torpedo. He had spent the last twenty years of his life staring at computer screens, composing lines of code that were revolutionizing modern warfare.

An ethnic Armenian, Petrosian was born in Leningrad, the son of a Soviet naval officer. With his Van Dyke goatee and round steel-rimmed glasses, he looked very much like a graying Trotsky. Completely devoted to his career, he had neither the time nor inclination for a wife or children. He couldn't suffer fools, refused to participate in office social engagements and wasted no time on such petty pastimes as sports or even movies. His only vice was astronomy, observing the mechanical movements of distant stars in blissful solitude.

Despite his anti-social failings, he was promoted rapidly solely on the basis of his raw talent and work output. An admiring supervisor once characterized him in a fitness report as "unerringly rational and coldly efficient as his lines of code," a compliment Petrosian relished.

Not a man of emotion, the computer scientist no longer craved the approval of his lessers. Instead, he decided that he deserved to be properly compensated for his work, something the Russian government would never do. In fact, no government would. And the idea of becoming an entrepreneur or selling his services in the private sector like a common workman was beneath him.

Hence, his deal with David Hakobyan.

Petrosian held no particular hatred of the Turkish people, though he had no pity for them either. History was history. They had committed crimes against his people for which they had never answered and now they would. Destroying Istanbul wasn't an act of vengeance, it was simple, binary mathematics: what is tabulated on one side of the equation must be equally tabulated on the other side. The Hebrew God said it best: *An eye for an eye, tooth for a tooth, hand for a hand, foot for a foot.*

But all that really mattered to Petrosian was the chance to become rich and to demonstrate his superiority over his inferior employers by turning their own superweapon against them. Hakobyan was the perfect conduit to accomplish both.

Sitting now in front of his oversize computer monitor in a plush leather executive chair, he caught sight of the oafish buffoon who ran his division, laughing and joking with the pretty girls out on the floor. Petrosian only could begin to imagine the astonished look on his face when the truth of his treachery was finally revealed. Sadly, he never would. He would be far from this place and Russia would be embroiled in a world war that it likely wouldn't survive. And even if it did, this particular facility was high on NATO's conventional and nuclear targeting lists.

Petrosian had no reason to be nervous, everything was being executed according to his carefully laid plans. The *Penza* crew had been dead for days now and the Kanyon drone secured for transportation through the Suez Canal. Six months ago, he had applied for an extended astronomy vacation in the remote Andes beginning the day before the destruction of Istanbul—his absence and inaccessibility would be well accounted for when all hell broke loose. By then, he would be on his way to blissful anonymity in Thailand, living off Hakobyan's millions.

He was lost in thought when one of his junior programmers burst into the room.

"Dr. Petrosian! Have you heard?"

Petrosian awoke from his reverie. He swiveled around in his chair, thoroughly annoyed.

"Heard what?" Petrosian glanced over the programmer's shoulder. There was a great deal of urgent hustle and bustle occurring out on the floor, people snatching up phones, pounding keyboards and dashing to and fro.

"The *Penza*—she's lost!"

Petrosian felt a twinge of panic pinch his spine. He suppressed the urge to shudder. He swiveled around.

"What do you mean lost?"

"Admiral Volkov attempted to raise her on comms this morning, but she didn't answer."

"Of course she didn't answer. She's ordered to maintain radio silence for another thirty-five days."

The programmer shook his head as if speaking to a dim-witted child.

"You don't understand." He lowered his voice to a conspiratorial whisper. "The admiral made a secret arrangement with Captain Volkov—"

"His son," Petrosian interrupted. *What has the old fool done?*

"Yes. The two of them made an unofficial arrangement for the *Penza* to surface today so that Captain Volkov could wish his daughter, Admiral Volkov's granddaughter, a happy birthday."

"Madness!" Even Petrosian was startled by the tone of his own voice.

The junior programmer blanched, fearful they'd been overheard. He thought it wise to cover his tracks in case they had.

"It's the gesture of a loving grandfather. Who can blame him?"

"That transmission could have identified the *Penza* and its location. The whole point of the exercise is to surprise our enemies with its stealth, not blast birthday greetings from the middle of the Indian Ocean."

The programmer held up a cautionary hand, urging Petrosian to lower his voice.

Petrosian calmed himself. *All was not lost. Yet.*

"The failure to report in is easily explained," Petrosian said. "The *Penza* must have an equipment failure. Engine, communications—something."

The programmer shook his head. "Standard operating procedure in the event of a major systems failure is to surface and effect repairs. We've had satellites retasked over the area. The *Penza* has not surfaced anywhere along its predetermined course."

"Has the admiral considered defection?"

The Russian Navy feared a *Hunt for Red October* catastrophe almost as much as a nuclear first strike. If Volkov hadn't considered that scenario, Petrosian thought, perhaps he would now with this suggestion. *Anything to throw off suspicion.*

"Admiral Volkov already dismissed that possibility and declared the submarine and its crew lost."

Petrosian sat back in his chair. He covered his face with his pale white hands, shut his eyes tight and took long, deep breaths between his cupped fingers.

The junior programmer stepped away to leave the senior software engineer alone, assuming he was overwhelmed with grief over the lost *Penza* crew.

In fact, Petrosian was fighting back an attack of severe claustrophobia. The world was closing over him like a casket lid.

Several deep breaths later, Petrosian's fractured mind began to clear. His plan was still flawless; it was that idiot Volkov who ruined the time line. Hakobyan's money was still in his account, the *Penza* was safely entombed beneath the sea and the Kanyon well on its way to its fateful destination. There were only two questions that concerned him now.

How could he escape suspicion?

And more important, how could he avoid imprisonment, torture and death at the hands of the FSB?

The prudent course of action would be to remain in his job until his planned vacation departure date so as not to draw attention to himself. But there were risks associated with that strategy.

The FSB was quite efficient these days. No doubt a team of their ruthless investigators was already being dispatched. They would immediately begin questioning everyone in the building and would start with the top floor. Petrosian would be among the first interviewed.

Petrosian didn't fear a polygraph, he'd defeated them many times before. What he did fear was the unknown. Volkov's selfish action would not only result in his own demise but possibly draw Petrosian into the swirling vortex of suspicion.

And then there was Hakobyan. Petrosian had no doubt that the gangster intended to kill him after the Istanbul attack. How else had he managed to avoid arrest and imprisonment all these years unless he eliminated potential witnesses to his crimes? Petrosian had left a few digital bread crumbs behind to fool Hakobyan's assassins and lead them on a fruitless chase to Costa Rica.

But now? Surely the spidery gangster had access to information inside the Russian intelligence community. If he found out that the *Penza* was already listed as missing and presumed lost, Hakobyan would dispatch a hitman to take him out immediately in order to cover his tracks.

Yes, that made Hakobyan another wild card. Both he and Volkov had thrown sand into the gears of his finely tuned machine. There really was no other logical choice in the matter now.

He would work diligently for the rest of the shift, offer condolences to the grieving staff on his way out the door and return home, where he would initiate his emergency backup plan.

Barring any other unforeseen developments, he would arrive in Finland before midnight a free man.

56

PHAROS

The island was another sparkling jewel in the heart of the Aegean Sea straddling ancient trade and ferry routes. Many of its smaller blue and whitewashed houses along the coastline were straight out of a tourism brochure. But the stately buildings climbing up the city's treeless slope above the port reflected the island's historic Roman, Venetian and even Moorish influences. The oldest structure stood at the highest point on Pharos, a crumbling stone lighthouse dating back to the Greco-Persian wars that gave the island its name.

The *Cronenweth* dropped anchor in the bright blue waters near the crowded Katrakis shipyard. A berth wouldn't be available until the next morning.

That was perfect, as far as Juan was concerned.

To simulate a conventional engine all stop—the *Oregon*'s high-tech power plant ran on electricity, not bunker fuel—Cabrillo ordered the smudge generators shut down, cutting off the oily black cloud of fabricated exhaust belching from its decoy smokestack.

Minutes later, Juan and Max climbed into a rickety, twenty-foot motor launch hanging by ropes from a davit. They both wore grease-stained overalls and their fingernails were caked with engine grime. A couple deckhands lowered them by pulleys into the water. They tied off at the nearest Katrakis Maritime pier and made the long climb up the well-worn stairs.

At the top, they were greeted by a smiling, middle-aged Greek sitting in an electric golf cart festooned with the Katrakis Maritime logo. He wore a pair of pristine blue and white safety overalls with the same logo on the chest, an unsullied blue hard hat and a gold Rolex fixed to his thick, hairy wrist. He looked like a man who could handle himself in a fight, Juan noted, even if his fingers were manicured.

"Captain Deckard?"

"Guilty as charged," Juan said, pushing his Texas accent as far as he dared. They shook hands. Juan pointed at Max. "My engineer, Roy Batty."

"Mr. Batty, it's a pleasure."

"Same here." They shook. "Are you the fella I spoke to on the phone?"

"As Captain Deckard says, guilty as charged. My name is Stefanos Katrakis, at your service."

Cabrillo whistled, pointing at the giant facility. "And you run this entire operation? Mighty impressive."

"My brother Alexandros is CEO of Katrakis Maritime, but I'm the shipyard's general manager." He pointed to the two empty seats behind him with a salesman's smile. "And sometimes the chauffeur."

"That's mighty generous of you to take the time personally to help out a couple grease monkeys like us."

"Every customer is our most important customer, no matter how big or small."

"Well, you're a lifesaver 'cuz my *plantar fasciitis* is killing me these days and it pains me to walk," Juan said as he and Max climbed into their seats. The cart's shocks groaned under their combined weight. The Greek handed them two safety helmets and they pulled them on.

"Hold on, gentlemen."

Katrakis stomped the pedal and the three men raced along toward the main office. Juan knew it was some distance away. He had reviewed an aerial photograph of the entire campus again just before departing the *Oregon*.

They sped along through the vast shipyard, bustling with activity. Several vessels of varying size being repaired were tied up at berths while even more facilities and equipment were utilized in actual ship construction.

The sound of heavy machinery, banging hammers and rivet guns echoed across the concrete and off the big warehouses, assembly rooms and repair shops. All the noise made it hard to talk with Katrakis, which was fine by Juan and Max. The two were taking in everything as they drove, particularly the security measures. The yard appeared to be surrounded on the land side by high walls topped with razor wire. Pretty standard stuff, primarily to keep the surrounding city at bay, particularly its petty thieves.

The parts of the facility that were open to the sea were under camera surveillance. Juan counted just six unarmed security guards, dressed in bright orange jumpsuits, patrolling the huge perimeter in golf carts. He'd seen tighter security at a Boca Raton celebrity pickleball tournament. It confirmed his suspicion that expensive contraband wasn't being stored here.

Giant cranes dominated the skyline, none larger than the three gantry cranes straddling the three largest dry docks, which they were now passing by. The middle dock was empty, but the other two were occupied by giant LNG tankers, fully outfitted, freshly painted and nearing final completion.

Their most distinguishing feature was the five white domes rising one hundred twenty feet above their decks. These were the giant tanks that stored the liquid gas, each shaped like a round Christmas tree ornament and capped much the same way. The tanks were half above the deck, half below. A network of yellow pipes connected the tanks to their respective caps, where the filling and discharge portals were located. The rest of the ship—from the aft bridge to the forward crow's nest—was connected by green catwalks, perilously high in the air, that ran atop the tanks.

Juan thought it strange the middle dock was empty. There was clearly evidence that a ship had been there. Apparently, another LNG tanker had already been completed and launched at the expense of the other two now just getting finished up.

In the distance, Juan caught sight of a helipad and a familiar shape parked on the tarmac. He leaned close to Katrakis so he could hear him.

"Say, what kinda crazy airplane is that?"

"That is an AgustaWestland 609. It belongs to my brother Alexandros. If he were here, he would show it to you. It is his pride and joy."

"I never saw anything like it."

Katrakis took his hands off the steering wheel and drove with his knees.

"They call it a Tiltrotor because the wings turn like this"—he turned his freed hands upward—"converting it from an airplane to a helicopter and back, depending on the flight and landing conditions."

"Looks like something out of science fiction."

"There are only a handful of them in operation at the moment. My brother received one of the first."

"Wish I could have me one of those."

"It only takes several million euros and three years on a waiting list to get one."

Katrakis retook the wheel in his hands as Juan leaned back in his seat.

They finally arrived at the company office building, a modest, three-story concrete-block affair. Katrakis led them past the chain-smoking secretary into his wide office in the back. He pointed them toward two chairs facing his steel desk, cluttered with trays stacked with work orders and invoices, along with a laptop computer.

Juan watched a crane lift a giant slab of steel through the window behind Katrakis' head.

"Gentlemen, can I get you some water? Hot tea?"

"Nah, we're good," Juan said.

Katrakis picked up a pack of cigarettes and held them out to the Americans.

"Smoke?"

"No thanks," Juan said. He caught sight of a floor safe against the other wall behind the Greek.

If Katrakis had any useful information, it would be on the laptop, in the safe and possibly both.

Targets acquired.

Max leaned forward and snagged a cigarette out of the pack with his thick fingers. "Don't mind if I do."

He stuck the cancer stick in his mouth as Katrakis fired up his Dunhill lighter.

Max puffed contentedly. *"Efcaristó." Thank you.* It was about all the Greek he knew except for a couple choice swear words. One of his ex-wives was the foulmouthed daughter of a sponge fisherman in Tarpon Springs, Florida.

"Parakaló," Katrakis said as he lit his own. *You're welcome.*

Juan leaned forward. "Were you able to find that bearing we called you about?"

"Yes, of course. I had it pulled from our warehouse this morning. Will you need help installing it?"

"Roy here is aces with wrenches. But we'll need to pull into one of your berths so we can crane it on board."

"Of course. Number seven berth is available to you at ten a.m. tomorrow."

"That works just fine. My boys would like to get a little R and R here on your beautiful island."

"I'll give you a list of the best restaurants and bars in town. Hotels, too, if you are so inclined."

"I'd appreciate that."

"Tell me about that bearing. Any idea why it went out?"

Max shifted uncomfortably in his chair. "Bearings wear out."

"Especially if you don't maintain them," Juan said. He turned to Katrakis. "He does better with machines after they get broke."

"I understand," Katrakis said, sensing an opportunity. Poorly maintained ships required expensive repairs. And judging by the condition of theirs, he stood to make a lot of money off the lazy Americans.

"Tell me, Roy, how has your ship been handling lately? Less power? More vibration?"

Max shrugged. "Yeah, of course. That's what happens when a propeller shaft bearing goes."

Katrakis nodded sympathetically. "Yes, of course. Unless you have a shaft misalignment. Misalignment can explain the loss of power and increase in vibration. It can also be what caused your bearing to wear out prematurely."

Max reddened with embarrassment.

"I guess I never thought of that."

Juan almost smiled. With acting skills like this, Max should have been recruited for undercover work years ago.

Juan leaned forward. "Shaft misalignment? It's not exactly a lube-'n'-tune, is it?"

Stephanos shrugged. "To be done properly, it will take time and the kind of engineering expertise we have at our facility. Shaft realignment is a very difficult repair and something we specialize in."

Just like it says on your website, Juan thought.

"You're talking about dry-docking," Max said.

"Of course. Fortunately, we have extensive dry-docking capacity to accommodate you."

"I noticed on the way over here one of your dry docks was empty."

"We just launched a brand-new ship a few days ago."

"LNG tanker?"

Katrakis frowned. "Yes, as a matter of fact. How did you know?"

"I saw the other two. Those LNGs are high-tech. That means you fellas really know what you're doing here. I'm impressed."

Katrakis relaxed. "As a matter of fact, we do. We're the finest full-service manufacturing and repair facility in all of Europe."

"How long will it take?"

"That depends on a number of factors, but I assure you we understand that time is money. That's why we run our facility twenty-four hours a day. We'll take care of you as quickly as possible."

"Glad to hear it."

The twenty-four-hour schedule, that is.

"We're already behind schedule on our run to Antalya. How about we stop in for an inspection on the way back to Piraeus?"

"Let me check our schedule to see when we can fit you in."

Katrakis sat forward, punched in his laptop's four-character password and opened up his calendar. He asked, offhandedly, "Will you be paying through a bank transfer or do you want to open an account with us?"

"We're a cash-only operation, Mr. Katrakis," Juan said. "Maybe there's a discount?"

Katrakis shrugged. "I'm sure we can work something out. But I should warn you, a shaft realignment is an expensive proposition."

"Not a problem. We carry lots of cash."

That brought a wide, oily grin to the Greek's face. That kind of repair would cost thousands of dollars.

"We have a dry dock coming available on the third of next month. Will that fit your schedule?"

"Off the top of my head, I'm pretty sure it does. Go ahead and pencil us in," Juan said. "I'll confirm once we get back to the ship."

"We'll require a twenty percent deposit to reserve the dock." He named the amount.

Juan tried not to fall out of his chair. Not all pirates were on ships.

"I'll bring my checkbook tomorrow when we pick up the bearing."

"That will be fine."

Katrakis stepped over to a cabinet and pulled the doors open. He returned with three clean shot glasses and a bottle of ouzo. He began pouring, not bothering to ask if the Americans wanted to drink.

Juan and Max gladly obliged him.

Twice.

57

After Juan and Max downed their ouzos, Max excused himself to go to the restroom and get a visual on the rest of the office before the two of them returned to the *Oregon*.

While they had been visiting with Stefanos Katrakis, Eddie deployed *Oregon*'s long-range optical telescopes to check for additional security measures around the shipyard and Hali Kasim monitored the facility's cell phone and radio traffic. It seemed that security at Katrakis Maritime was as lax as it appeared and apparently Max and Juan hadn't set off any alarms during their visit. It was hard to believe the Pipeline would move millions of dollars' worth of contraband items and people through a facility with such poor security precautions.

Juan began to wonder if they were chasing their tail on this one. The manufacturing plate on the Albanian patrol boat only indicated that Katrakis Maritime built it. And maybe that was the only connection the Katrakis organization had to the Albanian mafia.

Then again, the Pharos yard was the only clue they had.

It was possible it wasn't a trans-shipment point in the Pipeline.

But the fact this might only be a shipbuilding and repair yard didn't mean the Katrakis organization itself wasn't connected to the Pipeline somewhere else.

A midnight visit to Katrakis' office was still the best bet even if it was a long shot.

Stefanos Katrakis hadn't lied. His shipyard was a twenty-four-hour-a-day operation.

In the early-morning darkness, cutting torches showered down sparks like fireworks from high scaffolding. Rattling forklifts trundled back and forth across the yard and the gigantic cranes groaned beneath their massive loads. All that noise and commotion was an excellent cover.

Cabrillo decided to keep the team as small as possible—just him and Eddie Seng. It was an easy job and the fewer people on the ground, the less likely they'd be discovered.

Juan and Eddie slipped onto the lowest platform beneath a far pier, pulled off their dive gear and stashed it out of the way. From Eddie's dry bag they pulled out Katrakis Maritime–logoed work overalls, safety helmets and boots that Nixon's Magic Shop had put together. Nixon made sure the outfits were properly begrimed and threadbare and even included a couple dog-eared company badges to heighten the illusion of authenticity.

Juan opened the other dry bag and pulled out a small plastic toolbox with a hastily crafted logo sticker slapped on it to make it look official.

The two former CIA field operatives were ready to go.

"Easy-peasy," Juan said into his molar mic, thinking about his friend Linc. It was something the big man said every time he stood on the knife-edge of an impossible situation. He wished the ex-SEAL were with him now. The last report they got from Johns Hopkins was that he was flirting with the nurses—a good sign.

Eddie nodded, catching the reference. "I miss him, too. Let's go."

Juan flashed him a thumbs-up and Eddie bolted up the stairs, Juan right behind him.

* * *

Juan and Eddie crossed the yard with relative ease, just two workmen busy about their tasks like everybody else. They kept to the shadows as well as their distance from the other workers, careful to avoid any suspicious behavior.

They arrived at the office without incident and Juan's set of picks easily defeated the simple door lock. They moved inside, keeping the lights off but using a red flashlight to navigate. The front office reeked of cigarettes.

They didn't worry about the office security cameras. Max's bathroom visit had revealed the digital recording device for the security system next to the printer in a back room. Eddie had packed a handheld magnet to wipe it. If Katrakis ever bothered to review the drive, the missing data would most likely be written off as a hard drive malfunction.

Katrakis hadn't even bothered locking his private office. His desk was in the same condition as when Juan last saw it and the safe door was still shut.

Eddie dashed over to the desk and tapped the laptop's keyboard. The monitor lit up instantly. Luckily, the computer was still powered up, which saved him precious time. He opened up a small, waterproof bag full of gadgets and pulled out a thumb-drive-sized device loaded with NSA hacking tools that could connect to any computer. He inserted it into the Thunderbolt port, the fastest on the laptop.

"I'll do the magnetic wipe while the hacker gets to work, then I'll get after the file cabinet," Eddie said to Juan on his way out the door.

Juan knelt by the safe. He had already opened his plastic case and pulled out a contraption that Murph called his safecracking robot. His genius weapons designer had slapped it together in a few hours by downloading open-source Arduino software—who knew there was an online safecracking community?—and scrounging spare parts like servos and motherboards from the IT department.

Murph had demoed his robot on Juan's old railroad safe. He had explained that it was a "brute force" application, meaning the robot tried every possible number combination until it found the right one.

"But the number of permutations can be astronomical," he'd explained, "so I've downloaded an algorithm that reduces the possibilities to a probable range. Instead of taking days to try every combo, it usually finds it within two hours."

Juan hadn't understood the math yet he'd appreciated the brilliance of the concept. The mechanism attached magnetically to the door of Juan's railroad safe while an adjustable chuck was fitted around its dial. The robot cracked the code in under two minutes and the lock clicked open.

"Does it work like that every time?" he'd asked.

"More than sixty-two percent of the time on the old analog combination locking mechanisms. It won't work at all on the newer digital stuff."

Juan couldn't provide Murph with the make or model of the safe in Katrakis' office, but he was confident it was an oldie—no computer backup or electronics. Just a Bakelite spin dial and a handle to open it with.

Juan now attached the robot to Katrakis' safe and powered it up as Eddie dashed back into the room.

"I killed the power to the drive and wiped it. We're clear."

"Outstanding."

The robot spun the dial back and forth, the servos clicking and whining with each rotation.

"Feels like we're robbing a bank," Eddie said as he pulled his picks to crack the file cabinet lock.

"Butch Cassidy and the Arduino Kid somehow doesn't have the same ring to it."

Eddie deftly cracked the file cabinet lock and started pulling out drawers.

"I'm looking for numbers because my Greek isn't so hot." The Chinese American operative began sifting through folders.

"Gentlemen, you've got tangos approaching," Hali Kasim said over their comms.

"How much time do we have?"

Max answered. "I'd say sixty seconds if you move your keisters now." He was in command of the *Oregon* tonight.

Juan turned to the safe. The robot was still spinning the dial. He made a decision.

"Find anything?" Juan asked Eddie as he powered off the robot.

Eddie slammed the file drawer shut. "Nothing, but I hardly got through any of it. We need to move."

Juan snatched up the safecracking robot and shoved it into its case while Eddie pulled the hacking thumb drive out of the laptop's port and pocketed it.

Juan shoved the robot case into Eddie's hands.

"You vamoose. I'll cover you."

"But—"

"Just follow the plan."

Eddie nodded and dashed out of the office, heading for the back of the building, as Juan lit up a cigarette from Katrakis' desk and headed for the front door. It crashed open with a bang as two muscled operators pushed through, the flashlights on their short automatic weapons pointed at his face, blinding him. A third man came in behind the first two and hit the overhead lights.

Juan blew out a cloud of smoke just as Stefanos Katrakis stepped inside. The Greek was simultaneously surprised and angry.

Juan shrugged as he took another drag. "Just thought I'd take you up on that offer of a smoke."

He stubbed the cigarette out in the secretary's crowded ashtray just before the two guards manhandled him to the ground.

58

Juan sat in a steel chair, his hands zip-tied in his lap, his ankles zip-tied to the chair.

Stefanos Katrakis paced back and forth in front of him in the tiny cell located in the basement of the office building. Judging by the heavy cologne clogging the air and his red-rimmed eyes, Juan guessed the Greek had been entertaining a lady friend when he got the call about the break-in. He barely had time to pull on sweatpants and a T-shirt before getting there. A glittering diamond ring graced one of his pinkie fingers.

The Greek's goons had frisked Juan and yanked his molar mic's wireless radio out of his pocket along with the neck loop. It only took the ugliest one about a second to figure out there was a mouthpiece attached to one of Juan's upper molars. Juan pushed the mic off with his tongue and spat it out on the floor before the man's long dirty fingers started rooting around in his mouth.

"I'll ask you one more time. What is your real name and why are you here? And don't give me that 'Decker' *skubala*."

Juan wasn't sure if Katrakis caught the *Blade Runner* movie reference or not.

"Decker's the name, what can I tell ya?"

"Where's your ID to prove it?"

"In my cabin on board the *Cronenweth*."

"We searched for your ship. It's gone and no longer broadcasting an AIS signal. What happened, Captain?"

"They must have left without me. Roy is kinda forgetful."

Whap!

The Greek's backhand smarted something fierce, especially with that diamond ring on his pinkie. Juan tasted blood in the corner of his mouth.

"Well, that wasn't very nice. I think I just might take my business elsewhere."

Whap!

The second slap was full-handed. He hit Juan so hard, the chair tipped back, nearly toppling him over. His watering eyes saw stars. Anger shot through him like adrenaline, but he checked his emotion.

"No ship's captain wears a molar mic."

"You'd be surprised."

"There's a rumor that a freighter is being used as cover for a mercenary operation. Is that what you are? A mercenary?"

"You've got me confused with someone else."

"What did you come here to steal?"

"Like I said, I just wanted a cigarette."

Whap!

"Call the police, Katrakis. Better yet, call my embassy. I've got rights."

"Who hired you? FSB? BND? DGSE?"

"I'm not sure. Can I buy a vowel?"

Katrakis threw another backhand. Juan rolled with it, lessening the blow, but the sharp ring caught the corner of his eye.

Katrakis rubbed his injured hand. "There's no police for you. No embassy. No rights." He leaned in close. Juan could smell the cigarettes and ouzo on his breath.

"The only thing coming to you, my friend, is hell."

* * *

Katrakis slammed the cell door behind him and it locked electronically. Juan was left alone, a single LED in the ceiling glaring down at him.

The room was surprisingly clean, though small, and more like a holding tank than an actual jail cell. Given the electronic locks, cameras and LED light, it must have been a high-tech affair.

Juan could have kicked himself for falling for the ruse of the unsecured office and facility. It made sense, the more he thought about it. If you make the place look like Fort Knox, there's got to be gold behind the fence.

Earlier, he lamented the loss of his molar mic, but now he thought it likely Katrakis had some kind of jamming technology in this room for just that reason.

Though Katrakis' goons had taken his watch, Juan guessed about an hour had passed since his capture. He hadn't heard any gunfire when he was getting cuffed, so he assumed Eddie got away. And the fact that Katrakis hadn't questioned him about Eddie was a good sign, too.

If Eddie reported back in, the plan would engage any minute now.

As if on cue, the single light in the ceiling blacked out and the electronic door locks clicked open.

Time to get to work.

The plan called for the *Oregon* to close in and open up with its microwave pulse cannon and shower the shipyard with an EMP storm if Juan hadn't reported back to them on the hour. Now Juan sat immobilized by zip ties in the pitch-black.

Not a problem.

Juan raised his closed hands to his face as if in prayer, then snapped them down toward his lap, breaking the zip tie like an old rubber band. His hands free, he unzipped the leg of his overalls. He opened up the hidden compartment in his combat leg, pulled out a pair of night vision goggles and powered them up, then pulled out the serrated Benchmade

Griptilian knife and flicked it open. He also removed another device from the compartment and shoved it into his front pocket.

Just in case.

Entombed in the basement without any light, his night vision goggles were only able to work because of an attached infrared illuminator. That gave him a real advantage. Instead of stumbling around like a blind drunk, Juan could move like a cat.

All his equipment had been protected from the EMP shower because he was belowground. So, too, were the cell's light and door lock, but their power source had been aboveground and knocked out by Murph's cannon.

After cutting his legs free from the zip ties, he slipped quietly out of the room. A few feet away, one of his armed captors was blundering around with his pistol drawn, groping his way toward the cell door and calling on his dead radio to no effect.

Juan dodged for cover when the guard turned toward the sound of his footsteps. The guard opened fire with his pistol, blinding himself with the intense flash of exploding gunshots that missed Juan entirely. Cabrillo charged at him in the confusion and clocked him hard against his square jaw, dropping him to the floor in a heap. Juan snagged his weapon, disabled it and tossed the mag.

Thanks to the new DARPA-derived special lens coatings on Juan's goggles, he was protected from the sudden blinding flashes, but the sound had pierced his eardrums like hot pokers. Next time, he'd stash some electronic noise-canceling earbuds in his leg.

The rush of heavy boots racing downstairs to the basement announced the arrival of another guard.

Juan stepped behind the closed stairwell and waited for the brave gunman who burst blindly through the door.

A sharp crack to the guard's temple with the butt of Juan's knife put him down. He grabbed the man's short-barreled carbine off the floor and bolted up the stairs.

59

Juan emerged from the stairwell gun up, rounding the corner low and ready to cut loose with a hail of bullets, a stealthy exfil no longer an option.

But the room was clear.

It was also dark, though a sliver of moonlight through the cigarette-smoke-grimed windows was enough to light up his night vision goggles like a movie screen.

The entire facility was in a blackout, but so was the surrounding village facing the *Oregon*. Unfortunately, that meant a lot of blown transformers, microwave ovens and car computers—at least on this side of the island. Thankfully, the island's hospital was on the other side of the mountain and its emergency backup power sources protected. With a little elbow grease, the entire island's electrical supply would be fully restored within twenty-four hours.

Juan made his way outside, hugging the walls, keeping to the shadows. The shipyard was blanketed in near darkness. When its operations had shut down, it had become a flurry of activity as workers rescued co-workers from scaffoldings and other precarious positions. Crashing metal, angry curses, whistles and commands rang in the air. Flashlights began popping on as they were dug out of old toolboxes and lockers that had protected them from the EMP wave. The place was starting to light up and that wasn't good for Juan's chances of escape. In the distance, he saw the shadowy movements of trained operators heading in his direction.

Anything powered by solid-state electronics was dead. But older vehicles from the pre-computer era continued to function including a giant industrial forklift rumbling across his line of sight. The driver in the open cab was bent over his wheel, straining to see up ahead, his dim headlights barely throwing any light. He was creeping along about two miles an hour to avoid hitting anyone or anything in the dark.

Cinching the carbine tightly across his torso, Juan dashed toward the forklift. He planted one boot on a metal step, grabbed the overhead guard like a chin-up bar and swung feetfirst into the cab like a battering ram, knocking the driver out of his seat and onto the pavement with a thud.

Juan's body fell into the chair as he grabbed the steering wheel for support. He killed the feeble headlights. He could see much farther and better with his night vision goggles.

Glancing down to make sure the man wasn't terribly injured in the fall and well out of harm's way, Juan stomped on the accelerator. The big machine took off, its front dual pneumatic tires burning rubber. Juan spun the steering wheel toward the piers just as machine gun fire flashed. Bullets ripped into the forklift's counterweight as he sped away. He was grateful the old fork didn't have any kind of speed controls or governors. Its diesel engine roared as he gained speed—thirty miles an hour and climbing.

More bullets pinged against the forklift. Juan glanced back. He saw another fork behind him, even larger and faster, chasing him down. Its lights were off. Somehow, the driver and shooter had managed to secure night vision goggles unaffected by the EMP storm.

Juan mashed the accelerator. He was still some distance from the pier. With night vision, he had no trouble seeing the confused workers stumbling around in the dark—but they couldn't see him. He had to drive around them to avoid killing them, moving so fast that sometimes his wheels came off the pavement.

A sudden cry and a sickening thud spun Juan's head around just in time to see the pursuing forklift crashing over a hapless worker, the driver unconcerned with the carnage caused by the pursuit.

Juan steered his machine toward the pier where he and Eddie had emerged earlier and stored their gear. Bullets sparked on the forklift's mast right in front of his eyes. A steel-jacketed fragment stung his face, but the wound was little more than a scratch. He hunched over the wheel, twisting and turning it to dodge men and obstacles in his path.

The forklift lurched violently when metal clanged behind him. He glanced over his shoulder and saw that one of the forks on the pursuing forklift had crashed into the vertical support just inches from his skull. Juan turned the wheel again and so did the driver behind him. Instinctively, Juan ducked as the long fork swung over his head, trying to decapitate him. It missed, crashing into the vertical support on his left.

A voice shouted in Greek. Juan didn't speak the lingo yet he understood the tone. A quick glance backward proved him right. The second operator had climbed up onto one of his forks and was holding on to the load carriage and shouting for his driver to get closer—no doubt so he could jump onto Juan's vehicle and grab him. Or worse.

Juan loosened his gun sling with his right hand as he turned the steering wheel with his left to keep the pursuing driver guessing about his next turn. With the rifle loosened, Juan twisted it underneath his armpit by the grip. When he sensed the rifle barrel was pointing in the right direction, he fired.

The burst of bullets didn't hit anyone—they weren't supposed to—but the string of flashing lights out of the gun barrel blinded both goggled men behind him just as he had hoped.

The driver, letting go of the wheel, grabbed at his ruined eyes. His front tire caught the edge of a sheet of steel, which torqued the steering mechanism. The top-heavy forklift toppled over with a metallic crash, tossing the gunman headfirst onto the pavement and crushing the driver beneath its cab.

Juan jammed the accelerator to the steel deck as his wheels hit the final pier. The machine raced across the planking, rattling the boards like a drumroll. He reached into his front pocket and popped the device—a miniature emergency air tank—into his mouth.

Juan felt the forklift fall away beneath him as he went airborne over the end of the pier toward the sea below. He kicked away as hard as he could to escape the cab before the machine hit the water with a thundering crash.

He almost made it.

What Cabrillo hadn't counted on was the right front tire dropping off the pier before the left. This caused the machine to rotate clockwise in its free fall toward the sea—the same direction Juan was leaping. The two objects of unequal mass nevertheless hit the water at the exact same time, but the cab's guard dropped over Juan, trapping him inside. The much heavier forklift sank immediately, threatening to drag Cabrillo down with it. But the Chairman kicked hard against the frame and cleared it as he stripped off his now useless night vision goggles. He clawed his way down into the dark, inhaling deeply from his mini-tank as the plunging forklift disappeared into the abyss.

Machine gun bullets churned the water above, the slugs arrowing past him in all directions. He dug harder. Several deep inhalations later, the mini-tank was spent. Juan cast it aside.

Nearly blind in the murky dark, Juan swam deeper and deeper. Turning back to the surface was a death sentence. A high-revving boat engine circled angrily above him now.

His burning lungs told him he was out of time. He stopped swimming to save the last molecules of oxygen in his blood. The hammer pounding inside his skull narrowed his eyes, not that he could see anything. A flickering light blurred in the distant gloom, but Cabrillo couldn't make any sense of it as his mind dimmed.

All he could do now was trust the plan—and the tracking implant embedded in his thigh.

About to pass out, he clamped his jaw tighter, willing his mouth shut against the involuntary sucking spasm that would soon follow and drown him. Suddenly, a strong hand slipped beneath Juan's chin and lifted it. With his last remaining reserve of energy, Juan clawed it away, but another hand pushed his flailing arms aside. His head was now locked in the crook of an arm and a soft rubber mouthpiece rubbed against Cabrillo's lips. He opened his mouth just enough to blow out the stale air burning his lungs, then took the mouthpiece between his teeth. He drank down the first full breath of oxygen from the Spare Air pony bottle. Nothing had ever felt so good in his life. His heart raced. A breath later, he felt the strong arms relax, then spin him gently around.

MacD's smile beamed inside the bright lights of his dive helmet. He unleashed the Velcro straps that held an extra pair of fins as Juan pulled off his boots and socks. Moments later, the two of them swam for the *Gator* mini-sub waiting just a hundred yards away.

60

THE AEGEAN SEA

Archytas Katrakis stood on the catwalk above the big diesel engine driving his vessel with the Kanyon torpedo still safely secured.

The engineers below wore ear protection to block the high-pitched thrumming, loud enough that they had to shout to one another. But the noise didn't bother him. The engine room was squared away like the rest of his ship. Despite the grease, oil and bunker fuel necessarily spilled, splashed and dripped over the course of operation and maintenance, its green-painted steel deck was clean enough to eat off. Belying his casual appearance and friendly demeanor, Archytas ran a tight ship the way his father had taught him. And God help the crewman who didn't rise to his standards.

A yellow light beacon flashed as the dead man's alarm sounded, shrill enough to overcome the deafening engine room noise. The specialized ringtone told him it was a call from the bridge and it was meant for him.

Something was wrong.

He bounded up two flights of steel stairs and into the soundproof engine control room and grabbed the nearest phone. His executive officer picked up.

"What's the problem?" Katrakis asked.

"We just received an encrypted communiqué from Alexandros. The Russians have reported the *Penza* lost at sea and have initiated a search-and-rescue operation."

Katrakis swore. This put everything at risk. They were still a day out from their target destination. So long as the *Penza* was invisible, so was he. No one was supposed to know the whereabouts of the Russian submarine and its nuclear arsenal, let alone that it was missing. A search for the *Penza* eventually could lead to him and his vessel as efforts were expanded. How quickly was anyone's guess, but it definitely posed a risk.

"Anything else?"

"The Russian security services report Petrosian has disappeared—"

Katrakis cut him off with a string of blistering expletives. Didn't that idiot Armenian understand that running would only make the dogs chase him faster?

But now was not the time to lose control. He calmed himself.

"Go on."

"Petrosian has disappeared and they're searching for him. Alexandros says the Americans are alerted as well."

Katrakis fought the urge to cuss again. If the Americans got involved, it would be a whole new game. But neither the Russians nor the Americans had enough time to figure out what had actually transpired or what the Kanyon would be used for until they saw the destruction of Istanbul on live television.

Unless some other unforeseen event opened a door.

If the Americans were now involved, the Turks would be notified. That would put the Turkish Navy patrolling the Bosporus on high alert and that could prove his undoing.

"Anything else?"

"Alexandros orders you to continue the mission as planned, proceeding to the final waypoint on schedule. He says that he will provide a diversion that will clear our area of operations so that the Kanyon delivery can proceed."

"Excellent. Destroy any records of this transmission and notify me immediately of any new communications."

"Understood, Captain."

Katrakis hung up the phone. Once again, his genius half brother had thought of everything. Why had he even bothered to worry in the first place? The discovery of the lost *Penza* was merely an inconvenience calling for extra precautions that Alexandros had already taken.

And from what he understood, if the Russians ever found the *Penza*, they would discover it was now wreckage scattered across the ocean floor. It would take them many weeks, if ever, to prove that the Kanyon had been stolen. By then, the world would be at war.

At least, that was the scheme Petrosian had presented. Katrakis wondered if the Armenian coward had somehow ruined that plan as well. He pushed the thought away. Even if true, he trusted his brother's brilliance to thwart any attempt to stop their mission.

His confidence restored, Katrakis headed for the galley.

61

Juan sat on the cold stainless steel examination table as Dr. Huxley cleaned out the scrape the bullet had left on his face with an anti-bacterial swab. It stung like a burrowing wasp, but he didn't care. He was still fuming over the fact he had nearly gotten killed and had nothing to show for it.

Eddie's hacker thumb drive had successfully broken into Stefanos Katrakis' computer. The good news was that the device was designed to bypass the laptop's hard drive and make its way to the shipyard's fire-walled cloud where the most important files would be stored. The bad news was that Eddie barely had time to download much of anything. All of it was encrypted and his IT people hadn't been able to crack any of it.

The whole point of the Pharos mission was to gather evidence against the Pipeline, but all he had managed to acquire was a beating, a couple nasty cuts and this wound.

"Another ten millimeters and you could've lost an eye. But then again, that diamond ring nearly took out the other one."

Juan touched the butterfly Band-Aid on the corner of his eye. The wound didn't need any stitches, but Hux wanted to protect the freshly cleaned scrape just the same.

She frowned at him like a scolding mother. "You need to learn to play nice with other people."

"I try, doc, I try."

Someone knocked on the exam room door and then opened it without waiting for permission to enter.

"Excuse me?" Hux said as Eric Stone burst into the room, tablet in hand.

"Sorry, Dr. Huxley. It's urgent."

"Stoney, you look like you're running late for the prom," Juan said. "Good thing I had my skivvies pulled up. Whaddya got?"

Stone beamed.

"You mentioned in your report an AW609 like ours parked at the shipyard. That seemed highly unusual to me."

"Yeah, me too. There aren't more than four of those babies right now in the civilian market."

"Which helped my investigation." Eric opened up his tablet and showed what it displayed to Juan. "It was easy to locate the aircraft registration numbers. One of them is owned by Katrakis Maritime. And the CEO—Alexandros Katrakis—has a commercial pilot's license. I doubt he flies the AW, but it's the kind of prestige aircraft a rich guy like him would buy for himself."

"Good catch. But you didn't rush in here to tell me that."

"All of that info was what I needed to hack into the Eurocontrol air traffic database and track the AW's flight history over the last year."

Juan grinned broadly. "And you found its IFF signal."

"Not exactly. It's off-line at the moment—but only just recently. Check this out."

Eric hit the tablet's play button. It showed a radar screen tracking of the history of the Greek's AW flight patterns. Twenty-three of twenty-nine total flights from Pharos went to one location. Eric zoomed in on it.

"That's a place called Holy Island, off the coast of Greece."

Juan examined the image. It was another long shot but worth following.

Juan slid off the table. He clapped Eric on the shoulder.

"Good work. I guess we got something useful out of that wild-goose chase after all. Or at least, you did. Set in a course for Holy Island."

"Already did. Just waiting for your orders to comply."

Juan nodded. "So ordered."

Meliha lay on top of her bed in Hux's guest suite catching up on some much-needed rest. The air was cool and the throbbing engines far below became the beat to a gentle lullaby. She was far more tired and sore than she had let on to Juan or Dr. Huxley; the last few days had taken a deep emotional and physical toll.

The Holy Island lead was a good one, but she couldn't imagine a monastery as a staging ground for drug-running and human trafficking. It would be interesting to see what connection, if any, the holy monks had to such unholy activities. She needed to collect her notes about everything that had happened between Istanbul and there. She had promised Juan Cabrillo the utmost discretion when it came to his ship and people yet she was still a journalist and there was a story to be told. She couldn't wait to upload it to her Substack account, but until she knew the end of the story, she couldn't begin to structure it, let alone tell it.

Meliha's silenced cell phone vibrated on the nightstand. Her eyes popped open—she hadn't realized she'd fallen asleep. She sat up and opened her phone.

She almost screamed.

Meliha sat in the co-pilot's seat next to Gomez Adams, finishing up his systems check. The turbines were already spinning up and the noise in the cabin rose with each turn of the blades.

Juan knelt down next to her, helping her to strap in her harness. He had to raise his voice to match the rising decibels.

Incredibly, the Turkish government had released her father from his high-security prison in the city of Edirne. However, all they allowed him to do was text Meliha, asking her to meet him at a house close to the facility.

She tried calling him back, but he didn't answer. She immediately went to Juan with the news. He smelled something fishy and had his people chase it down. They managed to find her father's phone and it was very near to a cell tower in the city. After reaching out to a few contacts, Juan confirmed that Dr. Öztürk had indeed been released but placed under house arrest. There were no other details.

Meliha was beside herself. She desperately wanted to follow through on the Pipeline investigation yet she wanted to see her father even more.

"I feel terrible not coming with you to the island. I hope you understand."

"I'd do the same thing if I were in your shoes." Juan patted her on the hand. "Just stay safe, okay?"

"I know how to take care of myself."

"No doubt. But as soon as you get settled, you call me, okay?"

She nodded. "Of course. And call me when you find out something at Holy Island."

"It's a deal."

"Maybe when this is all over we can meet again in Istanbul?"

"You can count on it."

Gomez gave Juan the thumbs-up. He slapped Gomez on the shoulder as Meliha pulled on her oversized helmet. Gomez had checked the flight path. He had to steer clear of the no-fly zone declared by the Turkish authorities to accommodate the arrival of President Grainger and other NATO dignitaries, but the detour wasn't substantial. He'd be there and back to the *Oregon* within three hours, long before they arrived at Holy Island.

Juan stood on the deck and watched the AW lift into the sky, the downwash of the blades pulsating against his chest. While he hated to let her out of his sight, she needed to get to her father and he had a mission to accomplish. She had told him repeatedly she could take care of herself. Juan hoped she was right because now she was on her own.

62

Thirty-five thousand feet above the Ionian Sea, President Alyssa Grainger sat in the high-backed leather chair behind her desk in the "Flying Oval"—her office on board Air Force One. She was reviewing her notes for tomorrow's summit with President Toprak. The secretary of state, Eden Parks, along with her press secretary, Summer Jones, were both seated on the plush leather couch directly across from POTUS.

Air Force One was due to land in an hour and President Grainger would be greeted by President Toprak with red carpet protocol at the airport.

The event had all been negotiated in advance, designed for maximum exposure. A fifth-generation Montana rancher, Grainger was the epitome of a strong, hardworking daughter of the West. But she also understood television and social media as well as any of her younger staff.

Grainger campaigned on a policy of no new foreign wars—and, in particular, no more forever wars. Her critics mocked her lack of foreign policy experience despite her Spanish-language fluency. Her common sense rejected the logic of the so-called security experts. In her mind, shedding precious American blood and spending borrowed treasure on decades-long wars that could not be won was both impractical and immoral. The majority of American voters had agreed with her.

The summit with Toprak was designed to keep her campaign promise and prove the career diplomats all wrong. Her goal was to rope in the Turkish strongman through her personal brand of diplomacy to prevent a future regional conflict and preserve the NATO alliance.

Grainger's administration had pulled quite a few strings to gin up media interest in the summit. She even went so far as to push through anti-trust legislation aimed at the big media conglomerates and the tech companies—a not so subtle hint for them to play her game. It was Grainger's first opportunity to impress on a world stage.

In the end, the media moguls were glad to play along, promising twenty-four/seven coverage, beginning with the two presidents meeting on the airport tarmac.

Optics notwithstanding, Grainger was desperately concerned about Toprak's recent proxy wars in Yemen, Iraq, Syria and Libya. Most disconcerting was his provocation of the Russians, whose personnel and equipment had suffered humiliating defeats at the hands of Turkish forces, most recently in Nagorno-Karabakh. Russia's President Ivanov, a cunning and ruthless nationalist, had been playing up talk of war and retribution against "Russia's eternal enemy, the Ottoman Turk."

Grainger knew that if Ivanov attacked Turkey, NATO would be obliged to defend them and drag the United States into the conflict. With an economy only the size of Canada's, Russia wouldn't be able to sustain a protracted war and would have to resort to nuclear weapons almost immediately to defend itself. That was too high of a price for the United States to pay for Toprak to satisfy his dream of a revived Ottoman Empire.

The presidential summit with Toprak was timed to coincide with the annual NATO defense ministers' meeting in Istanbul. That was Grainger's idea as well. She and Parks had come up with a package of generous subsidies and crippling embargoes—carrot and stick—to nudge Toprak away from his adventurism and back into the NATO fold. And they were bypassing the senior foreign policy experts on Capitol Hill to do it.

"Some members of Congress won't like this," Parks warned as she rattled off the last details.

"Some members of Congress wear adult diapers. I'm not worried about them."

Behind the scenes, Grainger had initiated a secret presidential initiative to help bolster the struggling democracy movement inside Toprak's regime. Langston Overholt IV had been tapped to lead the effort.

A light knock on the door interrupted their discussions. A sharply dressed Asian woman, Dr. Yang, hardly older than an intern, stepped in. Her face broadcast the bad news she was about to share.

"Yes, Lois?" Grainger asked.

"Madame President, I'm sorry to interrupt, but there's been a development. President Toprak's chief of staff just notified us the President's arrival at the airport will be delayed a few hours."

"For what reason?" Parks asked.

"He said it was a matter of national urgency."

Grainger smiled. "Thanks for notifying us."

Taking the cue, Dr. Yang left, shutting the door behind her.

Grainger stiffened. "Now we have the world's press corps waiting at the airport for a live shot of our historic meeting on the tarmac and Toprak's a no-show."

"That makes him look bad, doesn't it?"

"Just the opposite. By refusing to meet me, he's turned me into just another American tourist arriving at the airport."

"Turning our own media strategy against us," the press secretary said.

Grainger nodded. "And sending a very powerful message to the Muslim world that he'll not be dictated to by an infidel American woman." She blew air through her perfect teeth. "Question is, what are we going to do about it?"

"We can stay in the air until he arrives," Parks said.

"Unless he has more time on his hands than we have fuel."

"We can land," the press secretary said, "and head straight to our embassy. You can make a grand entrance tomorrow."

"Still the same game. He arrives late to the summit and we're still standing around holding our britches," Grainger said.

Jones was new to the job and still trying to make a good impression on her boss.

"Maybe we can divert to Athens, claiming engine difficulties, and arrive tomorrow."

"You can't imagine the security challenges that would present to the Greek government, let alone our secret service detail," Parks said. "And it sends the message that our most important airplane isn't properly maintained."

They batted around several more ideas, but none of them solved the essential problem. There was no way to make Toprak cooperate.

The President frowned.

"The truth of the matter is, we can't do anything that offends Toprak or else he might walk away from the summit entirely. I think he wins this round. We'll go ahead and land on schedule. Eden, give the SecDef a call and get him over to the airport to meet us."

Parks snatched up her encrypted cell and began dialing as Grainger turned toward her press secretary.

"Summer, throw together a little speech. Make sure you spin it so that nobody notices the egg on my face."

"On it." Jones gathered up her notebook and headed for her cubicle at the back of the plane.

Grainger leaned back in her chair, folding her hands. A moment later, Parks hung up the phone.

"SecDef is in a meeting, but his chief of staff understands the situation and will be sure he's on the red carpet waiting for you when we arrive."

Grainger nodded her thanks. "While Toprak may have won the first round, the fight isn't over yet."

"Agreed." Parks stood to leave. "It's a childish insult on Toprak's part. Everybody will see that."

"It's not the way we wanted to kick this thing off."

"Well, at least you have tonight's state dinner to look forward to. The ambassador has quite a menu planned. I hope you're hungry."

"To tell you the truth, I'm half tempted to skip it. It's hard to work up an appetite when you've had to swallow a bellyful of crow."

63

He made the fatal mistake of checking his watch.

The FBI agent was just one hour into his twelve-hour surveillance shift. He yawned, fighting his fatigue. He never could get used to sleeping during the day, not that there was any chance of it with his wife and kids home sick. Even the dog had thrown up twice on the carpet.

He managed to grab a couple catnaps on the couch, but that was about it. He shaved and showered and headed out the door feeling guilty as crap for leaving his sick wife alone to nurse the kids.

Right now, he was running on fumes, a second energy drink and sheer force of will.

His boss, the special agent in charge (SAIC), got the high-priority order straight from the director to put stakeout teams on David Hakobyan. But she didn't have the manpower to do a full-court press. The best she could do was deploy two agents, each on a twelve-hour split.

And since he had less seniority, he got the overnight shift.

It could've been worse. He'd spent six years in undercover narcotics work with the Denver Police Deparment before getting hired by the

Bureau. He'd seen it all on the street. Keeping an eye on an elderly Armenian who went to bed at eight-thirty every night was a cakewalk.

Hard to believe the old fart ranked as a high-priority national security suspect. The SAIC's brief was just that: the old man was previously suspected of underworld activity decades ago but now, suddenly, his name had been associated with an unnamed international criminal syndicate.

"So why aren't we grabbing a search warrant and tearing this guy's place apart?" the agent had asked.

"No judge would grant us one. Hakobyan's connection to the syndicate is tenuous. Besides, I looked into his file. Hakobyan won two harassment lawsuits in the nineties, one against the Bureau and one against the DEA. We don't want to get within a country mile of this guy or his lawyers unless we have to."

"And what are we watching for?"

"The director said—and I quote—'Report any suspicious behavior or visitors.'"

"Sounds pretty vague."

The SAIC slid her phone across the desk.

"The director's number is on speed dial. Why don't you call him and tell him that yourself?"

The agent was only ten years into a twenty-year career, upside down on his mortgage and riding out a couple minor dings in his personnel record.

"Ours is not to reason why . . ." The agent slid the SAIC's phone back across her desk with a smile.

"Smart move."

Fighting his heavy eyelids, the agent ran over the notes from yesterday. The events listed were painfully dull. The bodyguard-chauffeur, now identified from his California driver's and concealed carry licenses as Gevorg Grigoryan—six-foot-five, three hundred pounds, sixty-seven years of age, no criminal record—arrived precisely at nine a.m. in a 1986 Mercedes Benz 240D registered to David Hakobyan.

An hour later, he drove Hakobyan to a nearby drugstore—the day before, it had been to an Armenian grocery. Upon return to the house, Hakobyan worked for an hour in the apricot orchard behind it. At precisely five p.m. Lurch—his partner's name for Grigoryan—departed for his home, also located in Glendale according to his licenses, in said Mercedes. Lights out at the Hakobyan residence at eight-thirty p.m.

No visitors had logged in in the last forty-eight hours, the agent noted.

Make that forty-nine, he corrected himself.

While both agents agreed it would have been worthwhile to put surveillance on Lurch, they simply didn't have the resources to do it. If Hakobyan was back in the drug game, Grigoryan would have been a likely mule and the car well worth searching.

The agent yawned again. He wasn't sure how an apricot farmer posed a national security threat. But orders were orders.

He pulled out his personal phone and opened up ESPN to catch the latest stats on his beloved Dodgers. After that, he'd clean out his email inbox and maybe start working his crossword puzzle app. He checked his watch again.

Only ten hours fifty-two minutes to go.

An hour later, a panel van, rusted and dented, pulled to a quiet stop behind Hakobyan's property. The green vehicle was identified as *Gonzalez Lawn Care*, with a phone number, as well as *Se Habla Español* and the promise of *Quality Work for Cheap!* Its faded logo was a smiling mustachioed *hombre* wearing a sombrero and pushing an old lawn mower that was belching smoke and throwing grass like a snowblower.

Lado Zazueta had taken note of the FBI surveillance team yesterday. The Herrera assassin was both surprised and amused the American *federales* had even bothered. Surprised because it suggested Hakobyan had somehow become careless, amused because the team itself was both inadequate and incompetent. If he had found that FBI *cabrón* in a car out front playing with his phone on any street in Latin America, he would have slit his throat, sending a message to his superiors written in blood.

Lucky for him, this was Glendale.

Instead of a blade, Zazueta used a child's radio-controlled car to deliver a canister of aerosolized fentanyl beneath the vehicle and release it. Within a minute, the agent was unconscious and would remain so for the next hour. First used by the Russians against Chechen terrorists as knockout gas, Herrera's assassin had improved the formula. Unlike the Russian concoction, his worked faster and didn't kill the intended target.

Zazueta checked his phone. He'd planted a wireless camera in a neighbor's yard that kept an eye on the FBI vehicle. If the agent somehow managed to awake and exit, it would sound the alarm in the hitman's phone instantly.

He turned around and gave the back of the van one last glance. It was loaded with gardening tools and equipment, though not a lawn mower. Gevorg Grigoryan's bloated corpse hidden beneath a tarp had taken up too much room. Zazueta wasn't concerned. What cop ever pulled over a lawn care van?

The killer exited the vehicle dressed in his Gonzalez Lawn Care overalls with a backpack slung over his shoulder. He needed to work fast but also with precision. A fortune was riding on tonight's assignment.

His fortune.

64.

Zazueta tossed a quick glance through the darkened kitchen window. Hakobyan's place was quiet as a tomb.

His one concern had been the Armenian's filthy little dog, JoJo. Even in its pitiful condition, it might bark—the only anti-burglary device Zazueta had detected in his multiple visits to Hakobyan's house.

The assassin picked the door lock without scratching it and eased the door open. He stepped carefully onto the linoleum floor, shutting the door behind him as quietly as possible.

He felt the cold steel press against his temple just as the kitchen lights popped on.

"Don't move."

Zazueta recognized Hakobyan's reedy voice. He could see the old Armenian in his peripheral vision, standing next to him in his robe and slippers. The dog, cradled in Hakobyan's left arm, chuffed and whined.

"I won't."

"You have one minute to explain yourself before I blow your brains out."

Zazueta heard the click of a revolver's advancing cylinder.

"I need less time than that. I came here to get you out. I couldn't call. The FBI has you under surveillance. I was sure your phone was tapped."

"Get me out of here? Why?"

"I just learned that there is an assassin heading your way. I came to warn you. We need to leave immediately."

"Nonsense."

Zazueta felt the barrel pull away, relieving the pressure on his skull. He took that as a good sign. He slowly turned around.

Hakobyan pocketed the pistol in his brown-checkered bathrobe yet kept a grip on it. His thin, gray hair was wildly disheveled and his large, owlish eyes blinked behind his thick glasses.

Still cradled in the other arm, the dog stared at Zazueta through its rheumy eyes, trembling like a leaf and coughing.

"What assassin? Who sent him? Surely not the FBI."

"My source says it's a Russian. I have all the details in my backpack, along with forged identity papers, travel documents and credit cards to get you and JoJo to safety. Gevorg, too, if we can reach him. May I show them to you?"

Hakobyan shrugged.

"It's all a waste of time. But if you insist." He waved a liver-spotted hand at the kitchen table as he reached for a chair and pulled it out.

"Trust me, what I'm about to show you will surprise you."

Hakobyan took his seat while Zazueta remained standing. The Armenian sniffed the air.

"I smell mint."

The assassin's fingers wrapped around the extension cord in his pocket.

"Yes, you do."

Hakobyan couldn't have weighed more than one hundred thirty pounds. It therefore wasn't difficult for Zazueta to suspend the old man's frail corpse by the noose hanging from a beam in his office. It was fashioned from the same extension cord he used to strangle him moments before.

The assassin worked quickly, using a red headlamp to illuminate the space while keeping an eye on his phone camera and the digital countdown clock. So far, the FBI agent hadn't stirred, but time was running out.

The last time he sat in this room, he took note of the old IBM Selectric typewriter Hakobyan used to type his grocery lists. He also happened to catch the fact they were all in Armenian.

That had given Zazueta an idea. He reached out to Sokratis Katrakis with his proposal and the Greek readily agreed to it, adding his own particular twist.

Zazueta was intimately familiar with the famous Selectric; his father had been chained to one for years. It was a unique, analog solution for fast, efficient typing in the pre-digital world. Instead of using long keys and a carriage like a conventional typewriter, the IBM used a round typeball element—sometimes called a golf ball—embedded with a typeface. When a key was tapped, the ball advanced and rotated to the correct position and struck the paper. One of the golf ball's many advantages was that it could be switched out rapidly for a large number of fonts—including those in a foreign language.

A trusted Katrakis courier had delivered a slightly used Armenian golf ball and a pre-typed suicide note with instructions that he was to replicate it as written on a sheet of paper from Hakobyan's supply. However, since it was impossible for Zazueta to secure the paper from the Armenian in advance, he purchased his own. He reproduced the note on one sheet and brought along two dozen more that he would swap out with Hakobyan's own supply.

The first thing Zazueta did was to move the typewriter from its position on the shelf with his gloved hands to the center of Hakobyan's meticulously clean desk. He plugged it in, careful to minimize his touching it in order not to smear any of Hakobyan's own fingerprints.

Zazueta then emptied his backpack. He pulled the used golf ball out of its case and stood next to Hakobyan's corpse, manipulating it in the old man's fingers to put his fingerprints on it. Zazueta needed to switch out golf balls so that the lettering on the suicide note and ball matched. The Selectric keyboard would already have Hakobyan's fingerprints all over it, along with the hair and skin cells that any decent crime scene investigator would extract from the machine for clues.

Likewise, Zazueta needed to put Hakobyan's fingerprints on the suicide note. This took some time and finesse. He had studied the placement of full and partial prints on typewriter paper. He had to consider how and where they would appear on a sheet of paper as it was removed from its ream and also how it was inserted and then removed from the typewriter's roller. Zazueta had typed the note himself, but only after acquiring a Selectric of his own and then downloading an Armenian keyboard diagram as a guide. After several attempts, he finally produced an error-free document.

In the midst of that task, he thought about having the letter translated to see what it actually said, fearing that Sokratis Katrakis perhaps would use the suicide note to throw suspicion on Zazueta or his boss. But a voice in his head dismissed his concerns. Why would Katrakis put his best and only meth supplier in harm's way and disrupt his Pipeline operations? While Zazueta knew that an old gangster like Katrakis couldn't be trusted, his greed and sense of self-preservation were guarantee enough.

Zazueta next swapped out his supply of paper for Hakobyan's, which was stacked neatly on the shelf next to the typewriter.

The only decision that remained for Zazueta was whether to put the finished note in the roller or to simply leave it on the desk beside the typewriter. Would investigators inspect the paper closely enough to see if it had gone through the roller twice? Was there such a thing as a roller imprint they could match against Hakobyan's roller and another machine? These were the kind of questions that had made Zazueta a successful assassin, neither jailed nor killed for lack of attention to such details.

In truth, Zazueta doubted Hakobyan's suicide would merit an intense investigation. Most detectives were overworked, with too many cases already, and others were just plain lazy. Their first observations and conclusions were usually their final ones unless some piece of compelling counterevidence indicated otherwise.

In the end, Zazueta opted to leave the suicide note on the desk rather than risk smudging Hakobyan's fingerprints on the roller. He often found in his profession that simplicity was its own genius.

Zazueta took a brief moment to survey the scene and admire his handiwork. It had required a measure of creativity he hadn't exercised in quite some time. He didn't care why Katrakis wanted Hakobyan killed, but now that it was done his organization would see its Pipeline profits double, if Katrakis were true to his word.

And if Katrakis had lied?

Zazueta would pay a visit to the Greek and settle accounts with him. The old man would endure suffering beyond his worst nightmares.

Completely satisfied, Zazueta left the house as expertly as he had entered it. He would retrieve his surveillance camera and the radio-controlled car he had used to gas the FBI agent, then head for the desert, where he would drop Grigoryan's corpse and Hakobyan's filthy little dog into an extra-large steel vat full of acid.

All in all, he was quite pleased with himself.

What he didn't realize was that because of a confusion of time zone changes and calendars, he had actually committed Hakobyan's murder twenty-four hours too soon.

65

HOLY ISLAND

Gomez Adams rendezvoused with the *Oregon* after dropping Meliha off at the airport outside Edirne, where she caught a cab and headed into town to meet with her father. Adams offered to go with her, but she demurred, reminding him that the *Oregon* needed him in its search for Alexandros Katrakis and the Pipeline.

As soon as Adams landed the AW Tiltrotor back on the *Oregon*, the ground crew immediately refueled its tanks and ran it through a quick safety and maintenance check. Moments later, Adams lifted off again, with Juan, Eddie, Raven and MacD, for a reconnaissance flight.

They made several high-altitude passes over the small island, which was being buffeted by unusually strong winds that had cleared away the otherwise perpetual fog. The intel brief on the remote monastery was limited. It had first been inhabited by Orthodox monks nearly eight hundred years before and had been continuously populated by the devout and hermits since then.

"No women, no liquor, no fun," MacD had said while making the sign of the cross in the team room earlier.

The AW's long-range camera gave Juan a clear view on the console monitor of the landscape far below. There wasn't much to see. The island was mostly rock-strewn, with large swaths of green pasture populated by herds of goats and sheep. They spotted several small stone huts and caves where, presumably, the hermits lived. The only people they saw were a procession of hooded monks threading their way single-file to the chapel at the edge of a rocky pasture in the center of the island. The monks gave no indication that they heard the AW's rotors pounding above their heads, though it was doubtful they could have missed it.

The island's most distinguishing feature was the craggy mountain peak at the far eastern end overlooking the blue Aegean. Incredibly, an ancient monastery was perched near its summit. It appeared to be a smaller, more primitive version of the one down below.

"Right there." Adams pointed at the outline of a grassy landing pad near the monastery. "That's where I'd put down. Flat, no rocks, highest point on the island, easy escape."

Juan had hoped to find Alexandros Katrakis' AW on the island since its IFF was still turned off. That just meant it was parked somewhere else.

But where?

"Take us down."

Juan and the team exited the Tiltrotor, with their MP5 machine guns at high ready, and convened at the heavy wooden front door. They would enter the chapel and clear it just like any terrorist hideout. But Juan reminded his crew that this was a sacred space. And, by the look of it, not occupied at the moment.

"Stay frosty—and try not to break anything," Juan said in his comms as MacD yanked the door open and Cabrillo led the way in.

"Clear!"

"Clear!"

"Clear!"

Juan stood in the center of the chapel dimly lit by high windows while Raven stood guard at another heavy door leading from the chapel to the rest of the monastery. MacD stayed close to the main entrance while Gomez stood watch from the AW's pilot's chair, a Glock 17 in hand, the turbines slowly rotating in case a rapid escape was in order.

The cold chapel smelled like burnt candlewicks and the sea. The large, candled chandelier had been extinguished, but their weapons were illumination enough for the cavernous space. The light on Juan's gun threw shadows behind the primitive furniture and sacred objects.

One of those objects caught Juan's attention. It was a small bronze figure of a woman seated on a throne pulled by two lions. It seemed strangely out of place yet he didn't know why. He didn't recognize it from his fleeting memories of his grandfather's Catholic Church and he wasn't at all familiar with the Greek Orthodox faith. For a second, he thought about pocketing the figure to check it out later but decided that stealing from a church wasn't the kind of bad juju he needed right now. So he left it alone, but snapped a photo using his headset.

Cabrillo called to Raven over his comms.

"Take the point."

"Aye, Chairman."

The team made their way through the rest of the monastery, room by room, cell by cell. It was obvious the facilities had been recently occupied, judging by the linens, silverware and other accommodations. But otherwise the place was clear of anything remotely approaching contraband. Nor was there any intel worth scooping up—no photographs, maps, files, electronics or thumb drives. Not even a scrap of litter.

"Chairman, we have company," Adams said over their comms.

"How many?" Juan asked as the three operators dashed for the front entrance.

Adams chuckled. "Just one scrawny monk. But I'll tell you what. He's a climber."

The monk stood ramrod straight despite the gusting wind buffeting his bushy beard and rough-sewn woolen robe. His clear blue eyes were as wild as the sea crashing on the rocks far below. He stared at Juan fearlessly despite the weapons surrounding him.

The monk wasn't scrawny as Gomez had described him but instead sinewy, his limbs steeled by years of ceaseless climbing and hard labor. He reminded Juan of a hickory walking stick that, when properly wielded, could bash a man's brains in despite its lack of heft.

"Do you speak English?" Juan asked.

"Well enough," the man said with a decidedly English accent. "My given name is Lazarus."

"Raised from the dead?" Juan said.

"From offshore banking, actually, in my previous life. Who are you?"

Juan ignored the question and instead jerked a thumb over his shoulder.

"The place is empty. Where is everybody?"

Lazarus shrugged. "I have no idea who is here or who is not here. This monastery is off-limits to the rest of us."

"By 'the rest of us,' do you mean the monks we saw down below?"

"Yes."

"But others lived up here?"

"Yes."

"Who?"

Lazarus shrugged again. "We're not permitted to know. The abbot alone came up here to meet with a troubled soul. In truth, a benefactor, I believe. After he came to live on our island, many things improved." He nodded at the Tiltrotor. "But that thing scares the sheep and dries up their milk."

"Could that benefactor's name have been Katrakis?"

"Perhaps my English has faltered a bit over the years. I thought I made myself clear. Nobody knows who lives up here except for the abbot."

"Can I meet with your abbot?"

"No, you cannot."

"And why is that?"

"We buried him this morning."

Lazarus marched over to the edge of the cliff just beyond the AW. Juan followed him. The wind nearly knocked him off-balance. He half expected to tumble over the side at any moment.

The monk pointed down to a rocky beach.

"We found him down there yesterday. A horrible fall."

"An accident?"

The wind whipped the monk's beard like a flag. "It is a dangerous place. It has happened before. Perhaps it was his time."

Lazarus stepped back over to the Tiltrotor.

"I was sent up here when we heard your airplane. We assumed you were with the benefactor. This is his aircraft, is it not?"

"No, it's not. It's ours."

Lazarus laid a calloused hand on the AW's slick metal skin.

"Strange. It is such an unusual aircraft."

"What can you tell me about the benefactor?"

Lazarus flashed a knowing smile, as if he were dealing with the village idiot.

"Yeah, I get it," Juan said. "You don't know anything. But weren't you just a little curious about what was going on up here?"

"I have my own wicked soul and three hundred sheep to tend. I do not have time for curiosity about strangers. Besides, the abbot told us not to inquire after the matter. I suspect you're a man who understands orders and how to obey them."

"Do you mind if we take another look around?" Raven asked as she stepped forward. Her thick black hair was braided and pulled back, revealing the exotic beauty of her face.

Lazarus started to speak but stopped. He stepped closer to Juan and whispered in his ear.

"She is a woman."

"Oh, yeah, brother. She's all that and then some."

The monk lowered his voice further. "She should not be here. It is against the order."

Juan wanted to crack a joke at his expense but held his tongue. He couldn't pretend to understand the monk's religious beliefs yet he respected the man's devotion to them. Allegiance was something Juan could relate to.

"As soon as we have another look around, we'll get out of your hair."

The monk stepped back, unwilling to look at Raven—or allow himself to.

"We have nothing worth stealing on the island. Take what you need from us. We have meat, milk and cheese in abundance."

"Thanks for the offer. We don't want to steal anything. We're here to stop an international criminal organization known as the Pipeline. Have you heard of it?"

The monk's face ashened. "Criminals? Here? On this island? Surely not."

"And you haven't heard of the Pipeline? Or Alexandros Katrakis? Or gunrunning or drugs?"

"No. I have no knowledge of any of that."

"Can you tell me what you do know?"

"That you are men of violence standing on an island devoted to the peace of God. I will pray for your souls."

"Do that," Juan said. "We probably need it."

Suspecting that another search of the abandoned monastery was a waste of time, Juan twirled his finger in the air and Adams spun up the turbines. Cabrillo climbed into the co-pilot's seat and the others into the cabin. Moments later, the AW lifted off with a deafening roar. Juan glanced down at Lazarus, battered by the prop wash yet standing tall, his defiant eyes locked with Juan's as the Tiltrotor turned and flew away.

The trip to Holy Island had been a total bust. Juan weighed his options. The best one seemed to reconnect with Meliha and get a chance to shake hands with her dad before planning the next move.

66

The small regional airport easily accommodated the thunderous Tiltrotor as it landed in helicopter mode. The unusual aircraft, along with the attractive woman that disembarked from it, drew locals' attention. All eyes were fixed on the AW as it roared away into the sky while Meliha slipped into a yellow *taksi* and sped away.

Her father's prison was located in a remote area north of the bustling city yet the address he had given her was in a neighborhood just on the outskirts. She called her father's number twice, but he didn't pick up. No doubt he had forgotten to charge his cell phone. While he was brilliant in so many ways, technology both annoyed and befuddled him.

She made polite conversation with the curious cabdriver, who had been as rapt as everyone else at the spectacle he had just witnessed at the airport, but she was careful to avoid providing him with any information. Most likely he wanted to know if she was a rich or important person and what kind of generous tip he might expect. But it was possible he was a Turkish intelligence agent or at least an informer—MİT had a vast domestic security operation and she was high on their list of persons of interest.

The cab pulled to a stop in front of a modest, two-story house at the end of a very private, quiet street. She slipped out of the vehicle and dropped a large wad of Turkish lira into the cabbie's hand. He thanked her profusely yet didn't pull away until Meliha dismissed him with a curt nod.

She climbed the short steps to the house, half expecting her father to burst through the front door to greet her. She rang the doorbell, but no one answered. She glanced through the parlor window and saw nothing; the lights were off, as was the television set. The house appeared unoccupied. She double-checked the address given to her on the phone. It was correct. Curiosity rather than fear swept over her, a habit cultivated in her journalism career. She knocked on the door with sufficient enough force that it actually swung open on its hinges.

She stepped in. The room smelled dank and reeked of stale cigarettes. She supposed it was a halfway house owned by the prison rather than an actual residence. That made sense since it was the prison that had just released her father.

"*Baba?* Are you here?"

Footsteps thudded across the ceiling. She smiled. Her father was a little deaf.

Meliha called out his name as she ran up the staircase. The footfalls were coming from behind the door at the end of the hall. She opened it.

Her father was bound and gagged in a chair in the center of the empty room. A short, thuggish man standing next to him was pointing a gun at his head. Another man in a cheap suit leaned against a wall, smoking a cigarette.

"Who are you?" Meliha demanded as she stormed toward her father to release him. When she came near, the gunman backhanded her, sending her crashing to the floor.

Her father raged behind his gag, the veins in his forehead nearly bursting.

The smoking man stepped over and knelt down next to Meliha, still half dazed from the blow.

"Mr. Katrakis would like to meet you."

67

THE SEA OF MARMARA, TURKEY

In all the world, Archytas Katrakis feared only his father and it was that fear that drove him to succeed in all tasks assigned to him, including this one, the most important of all.

From the moment he retrieved the Kanyon torpedo twelve days before until now, the wily Greek had felt the intense pressure of completing the mission. Somehow, he had managed to avoid both detection and capture, all the while sailing in some of the world's busiest sea lanes. The close encounter with the Indian frigate and a nasty storm in the eastern Mediterranean had threatened to thwart his father's plans, but in the end he had been able to bring the Kanyon to this final waypoint.

Katrakis had been standing on the bridge of his vessel when it passed by the city of Gallipoli, infamous for the bloody World War I defeat of Winston Churchill's campaign against Turkish forces.

Unlike Churchill, his father's plan would not fail.

The body of water known as the Dardanelles—which his father still referred to by its ancient Greek name, the Hellespont—held an even deeper historical significance. The narrow strait, which led from the Aegean Sea in the south to the Sea of Marmara to the north, was also a watery division separating Asia from Europe, the East from the West.

And it was at the Hellespont that the Persian tyrant Xerxes came to cross with his massive invasion army to destroy the Greeks, only to find his bridges destroyed by the gods. In his anger, proud Xerxes took a whip of chains and lashed the water three hundred times to punish the Hellespont. It was such hubris that had allowed Katrakis' ancient Greek kinsmen to defeat the Persian king and drive him back into Asia across the very same body of water.

It was that same arrogance that drove the modern Turks to humiliate his country, yet Katrakis was confident his actions that day would bring an even greater defeat to an even more dangerous tyrant. Perhaps Greece would rise to its former glory, Katrakis hoped, but he doubted it. All that really mattered was that his family would survive and, like a golden phoenix, rise from the smoldering ashes of war insanely rich.

All the pressure of the last twelve days and the desperate fear of failing his father melted away to sheer elation when Katrakis dropped anchor. He had carried the Kanyon through the Dardanelles, one of the most crowded, hazardous and dangerous waterways in the world. The chief engineer had performed all the necessary hardware and software diagnostics on the Kanyon before they had entered the Sea of Marmara and cleared it to go. His radarman confirmed that no Turkish naval vessels were within sight; both the water and weather conditions were perfect.

In theory, it would have been possible to program the Kanyon to travel from the Indian Ocean to Istanbul all on its own without need of intermediate transport. Because of its stealth design, obstacle-avoidance capabilities and AI-powered navigational software, the Kanyon would likely have eluded any detection or collision in transit. And yet despite Dr. Petrosian's utmost confidence in its systems, he was concerned there were too many unknown unknowns at play in the real world that might have delayed its arrival. It was therefore decided that transporting the torpedo via the unremarkable *Mountain Star* was the safest bet. As opposed to more efficient computers, human sailors were inferior navigators, but they were more adaptable to changing conditions, and millennia of experience sailing the treacherous seas made them relatively reliable.

Thirty minutes after the transport ship dropped anchor, its keel doors had been opened and the Kanyon lowered into position and cleared of its rigging by the divers.

"Engage the motor," Katrakis said to his chief engineer.

"Engaged. Kanyon away."

Katrakis set the timer on a large digital clock. The torpedo had traveled nearly four thousand nautical miles to this point. Now Kanyon was just nine hours away from its final destination, a preprogrammed waypoint coordinate at the mouth of the Bosporus directly opposite Hagia Sofia, the very soul of ancient Constantinople. Once the city's holiest Christian shrine, it was converted to a blasphemous mosque under Toprak.

The Kanyon would travel under its own power, keeping as close to the seabed as possible and at minimum speed to avoid detection. That put the explosion at precisely the right moment for maximum effect as presidents Grainger and Toprak, along with all thirty NATO ministers, were scheduled to meet in the most widely televised session of the entire conference.

Those nine hours also gave Katrakis and his crew ample time to make their escape from the blast effects and nuclear fallout that would destroy Istanbul in a wall of contaminated water.

Katrakis surveyed the faces of his smiling bridge crew. They had accomplished their mission and were proud of it. He fought the urge to congratulate them. There was still much to do, including retrieving his divers and securing the ship.

Now it was Kanyon's turn to shine.

68

Fresh out of Pipeline leads, Juan set the *Oregon* on a leisurely course back to Istanbul. With the NATO conference in full swing, he knew the shipping traffic near the port would be congested with security measures.

Cabrillo stood in the chow line in the *Oregon*'s galley, listening attentively to one of his engineers describing his ground-up restoration of a 1958 Harley-Davidson Duo-Glide.

Today's lunch offerings were Highland venison, veal meat loaf and wild salmon steaks, along with a half dozen succulent vegetable and potato side dishes. The aroma of venison and salmon made Juan's stomach growl and he eagerly anticipated grabbing a sample of each.

Eric Stone caught Juan's eye from the doorway. He had an urgent look on his face and a computer tablet in hand.

Reluctantly, Juan gave up his place in line and headed over to him.

"What's up, Eric?"

"Good news. The team was scanning some recent DEA surveillance footage and came across this."

"Wait. How did you get DEA surveillance tapes?"

"It takes too long to go through official channels, so we hacked their database."

Juan had trained his people that it was better to ask forgiveness than permission, especially when national security was at stake and time was of the essence.

"Go on."

Stone moved closer to Juan so he could see the tablet screen. He tapped the play button. A shaky telephoto video camera lens scanned a crowd at a graveside funeral.

"What am I looking at?"

"A funeral held in Yerevan, Armenia, several weeks ago. But watch . . . here." Stone tapped the screen and it froze. He drew a circle around a man's face with his fingertip. "That's David Hakobyan."

"In Armenia? Are you sure? Overholt said the man never traveled outside California."

"The DEA facial recognition database confirmed it. It was his nephew's funeral."

"Okay. That makes sense. Maybe. So why are you showing me this?"

Stone hit the play button again and froze it moments later. He drew another circle around a different man.

"That's Alexandros Katrakis, CEO of Katrakis Maritime."

Juan raised an eyebrow. "A coincidence?"

"Hardly." Stone pulled up a different video clip. "This was shot forty-two minutes later." The video showed Hakobyan greeting Katrakis and the two of them getting into the Greek's Mercedes limousine, then, after a quick cut, the limo driving away.

Juan took the tablet into his hands and replayed the videos while Eric talked.

"We've already connected the Pipeline to the Albanians. And we had links between both Katrakis and Hakobyan to the Albanians. Now this links the two of them together. I think that puts the Katrakis organization and Hakobyan squarely in the Pipeline equation."

Juan clapped Stone on his shoulder. "Good work, Eric. You and the team."

Eric beamed, held up one finger, then affected his best infomercial voice:

"But wait! There's more!"

He took the tablet back and pulled up yet another video. He scrubbed it forward and circled the head of another man before handing the tablet back to Juan.

Juan examined the face. He didn't recognize it. "No clue."

"His name is Dr. Artem Petrosian."

"Armenian?"

"Ethnic Armenian but a Russian national. The CIA flagged him because the Russian FSB just declared him a person of extreme interest. Apparently, he's gone missing."

"And that's important because . . ."

"Because he's the chief AI software programmer for Russia's Main Directorate of Deep-Sea Research."

"GUGI." Juan scratched his head, thinking. "Wait a minute. That's where the *Penza* is based, isn't it?"

Eric nodded. "Exactly. Its maiden voyage launched about four weeks ago out of Murmansk."

Juan snapped his fingers. "And the *Penza* is the mother ship for the Kanyon drone torpedo. That probably means he designed the software for that system, too."

"Without a doubt."

Juan was all too familiar with the doomsday torpedo. The ongoing debate in the military journals was whether the apocalyptic threat was real or just another example of Russian vaporware—a promised system that never actually materialized. Juan had survived all these years by assuming an opponent was more capable than his armchair critics supposed. In his mind, the Kanyon threat was absolutely real until proven otherwise.

"So if the FSB is searching for this Petrosian guy, it means they think he's still alive. It would be a real intelligence coup to grab him up. No wonder the CIA is interested in him. If he's defected, he hasn't come over to our side or the Company wouldn't have flagged him."

"Defection is one possibility. The other is that he's simply on the run."

"For what reason?"

"Sabotage. From the chatter that's out there, it looks like the *Penza* and its Kanyon torpedo have been lost."

Juan's heart sank at the thought of an entire submarine crew dying alone in the depths of the sea even if they were adversaries—especially if they perished at the hands of a traitor. Better for them, and U.S. intelligence, if the *Penza* crew were still alive.

"Maybe there's another possibility." Cabrillo's brain was running scenarios, some of them downright terrifying.

Stone's face was puzzled. "Like what?"

"Any idea where that sub disappeared?"

"From what I've read, the *Penza* managed to shake off our surveillance when it dove under the polar ice cap. We've had no idea where it's been since. But the National Reconnaissance Office just ID'd one of the Russian Navy's newest search-and-rescue ships in the Indian Ocean. That vessel carries a Bester-class deepwater vehicle. My guess is that the *Penza* was last located in that vicinity."

"Show me."

Eric pulled up the real-time satellite video of the *Igor Belousov* rescue ship anchored in the Indian Ocean. Juan studied it, trying to line up the puzzle pieces, his mind turning over the facts like spinning a Rubik's Cube.

"Tell me about the funeral. Did you study the tapes at all?"

"I read over the transcripts. There was a lot of the small talk you'd expect. 'Sorry for your loss' and all that."

"Anything else?"

"A lot of hate thrown at the Turks and the Azerbaijanis."

"By Hakobyan?"

"Yeah, for sure. His nephew was in the Armenian Army and had been killed in the Nagorno-Karabakh war earlier this year. I read up on it. Looks like Turkish drones played a decisive role in the fighting."

"What about the Hakobyan–Katrakis meeting? What did they talk about?"

"There wasn't any audio. The DEA suspects the Mercedes limo deployed a jammer."

"And Petrosian?"

"There's a brief moment when he and Hakobyan shake hands by the graveside. They only exchanged a few words from what I could see. But there was no mention of the meeting in the DEA notes and no transcript."

"That doesn't mean Petrosian didn't meet with Hakobyan another time while he was in Armenia. It just means the DEA didn't catch it."

"Agreed."

"There's a connection between Petrosian and Hakobyan."

"Besides the fact they're both ethnic Armenians?"

"Think about it. Petrosian is a military scientist and Hakobyan is a big-money arms smuggler."

"Yeah. That makes sense. They might be trying to sell the *Penza* to the highest bidder—the Chinese, the Iranians, even the North Koreans."

"Not the *Penza*."

"Why not?"

"The Russians are as patriotic as we are. The *Penza* crew wouldn't play along with a scheme like that. And stealing a submarine would be a huge undertaking even for a criminal organization like the Pipeline."

"Then the *Penza*'s crew is dead for sure."

"And Kanyon is the prize."

Eric nodded. "Stealing the Kanyon would definitely fit in the Pipeline wheelhouse. But why would Petrosian bring Hakobyan in on the deal? He could have just sold it to the highest bidder and cut out the middleman."

"Petrosian might be afraid to do the deal himself and wanted Hakobyan, as the broker, to take all the risk."

"Which means Hakobyan takes all the profit."

"But there is another possibility."

"Which is?"

"Hakobyan has no intention of selling it."

Eric suddenly understood.

"He wants to use it."

"We've got to find that torpedo pronto."

"Kinda hard to find just one stealth torpedo on a planet covered in water," Eric said. "Especially one driven by artificial intelligence."

"Is the Kanyon's AI system capable of navigating long distances underwater?"

"No question. The Russians have topo-mapped as much of the ocean floor as we have, especially in this part of the world."

Juan pointed at Stone's tablet. "Can I see that thing again?"

Eric handed it over.

Juan pulled up Eric's map of the Indian Ocean and the location of the Russian deepwater rescue vessel.

"The Kanyon is designed to destroy coastal cities by generating a tsunami with its nuclear payload. Lord knows, there are plenty of high-population targets along every coast."

"Since it hasn't already detonated it must still be en route," Eric said. "But where is it going?"

"That's the question. I'll take a wild guess and say that the *Penza* was sunk in the Indian Ocean because Hakobyan's target is within striking distance of that location. Otherwise, why not sink it somewhere else?"

"With its nuclear engine the Kanyon's striking range is anywhere in the world it wants to go."

"Technically true. But near every potential target city there are crowded shipping lanes, underwater pipelines and all kinds of unseen hazards."

"An AI navigation system is designed to avoid all that."

"Sure. But AI isn't perfect. If you only had just one shot to pull it off, would you trust AI navigation to traverse thousands of miles of heavily trafficked water?"

Eric shook his head. "No. Too risky."

"That's why I think Hakobyan is transporting the Kanyon by ship. And it also helps Kanyon avoid detection."

"We still have the same problem. How do we find a stealth torpedo hidden inside a single ship somewhere out on the crowded ocean?"

Juan looked at the tablet again.

"Didn't we recently receive a Navy intel report about a frigate in the Indian Ocean with radar problems?"

Eric's eyes widened with recognition.

"That's right. The Indian captain developed radar problems after encountering a civilian ship. He reported it to his commander as a possible radar-spoofing incident. It wasn't far from the *Penza* location."

"What was the name of the ship?"

"I can't recall. But the Indians said its AIS was shut off. Whatever name they gave was probably fabricated."

"I've got a feeling our mystery ship might be the Kanyon transporter," Juan said. "If this really is a Pipeline operation, the ship was probably built by the Katrakis shipyard. We should be able to make that connection."

"If that ship was spoofing radar and didn't broadcast an AIS signal, I'll have to snag some optical satellite feeds and track it visually in order to identify it."

"First confirm it was a vessel capable of carrying an eighty-foot-long torpedo. If it is, track it backward in time to its most recent port. You should be able to get a legit ID for it there. Call me the instant you find out something."

"Aye, Chairman."

"And hurry. I have a feeling we're just now stepping onto the field and it's already the fourth quarter."

69

Cabrillo's next best hope of finding the stealthy Kanyon was Hakobyan. He needed to know what Overholt had discovered about the old Armenian smuggler. Juan put in a call to his former CIA mentor but had to leave a message. He was no doubt inundated with the NATO conference and the upcoming presidential summit in Istanbul.

Juan grabbed a coffee and headed for his cabin. Just as he arrived, Overholt called him back on his cell phone. He put it on speaker.

"Juan, my dear boy, sorry for the delay."

"The *Penza* is missing."

"How in the world could you possibly know that? That intel is strictly need-to-know. Well, of course you'd know. But tell me how you know."

"The CIA flagged a guy named Petrosian—"

"The missing software engineer."

"We believe he's connected to Hakobyan. Any word on Hakobyan from your surveillance teams?"

"Only that he's diligent with his apricot pruning," Overholt said. "How is he connected to the *Penza*?"

"I don't have anything solid. But my gut is screaming that Hakobyan's the driving force behind it. Petrosian and Hakobyan met at the funeral in Yerevan for Hakobyan's nephew. The *Penza* disappeared after their meeting."

"That's awfully thin evidence."

"You said yourself Hakobyan hasn't left Glendale since the Nixon administration. Something awfully important must have drawn him to Yerevan."

"You said it was his nephew's funeral. That seems rather compelling."

"We did a little more checking," Juan said. "Hakobyan had a brother in the old country who died several years ago. Hakobyan sent flowers rather than show up. Same with his sister-in-law. Same with his own mother."

"I see your point. But then again, maybe he regretted failing his earlier family obligations and wanted to make amends."

"That's absolutely possible. But it's also possible that his visit to the funeral was just a cover for something else entirely."

"Pipeline business?" Overholt asked.

"Most likely. We also discovered that Alexandros Katrakis was at the funeral and we have visual evidence that Katrakis and Hakobyan did meet up."

"Katrakis? The plot thickens."

"Whether this was about the Pipeline or something bigger, I'm not sure."

"But you're leaning toward the latter."

"Petrosian seems to be connected to the *Penza*'s disappearance and he might be connected to Hakobyan," Juan said. "We've already linked Hakobyan to the Katrakis organization and we've linked both of them to the Pipeline. What does the Pipeline do? It smuggles contraband, including weapons."

"The *Penza* is over three hundred sixty feet long. I have a hard time believing they've stolen an entire submarine and its crew and are trying to sell it."

"That's why I think the Kanyon torpedo is the target."

Overholt sighed. "The Russian doomsday weapon. And the *Penza*?"

"Probably destroyed, along with its crew."

"So what's your working thesis?"

"Our best guess is that the Kanyon was stolen off the *Penza*, then taken on board a transport vessel."

"Why?" Overholt asked. "The Kanyon is an autonomous underwater vehicle with an inexhaustible fuel supply."

"But it's still vulnerable to crowded shipping lanes, unforeseen hazards, mechanical breakdown, and so on. It's safer to transport it by ship closer to its intended target before letting it swim on its own."

"Have you located a transport ship?"

"I have Eric Stone working on that now."

"Any idea of the target?"

"If Eric can find the transport ship, we should be able to figure out the target." Juan's cell phone flashed. Eric was calling. "Speaking of which . . . Lang, hold on a sec."

"Sure thing."

Juan looped Eric into the call with Overholt.

"Lang, Eric Stone is now on the line. Eric, what have you got for us?"

"I tracked the mystery vessel to her previous port like you suggested—Singapore, as it turns out. Both the AIS and the harbormaster's log confirmed her name as *Mountain Star*."

"That's marvelous, Eric," Overholt said. "Well done."

"Is she a Katrakis boat?" Juan asked.

"Her record of origin looks sketchy to me. No telling where it was originally built. But as to ownership, I set Russ Kefauver on the hunt and he came back with a shell company owned by David Hakobyan."

"Bingo!" Juan said.

"Maybe your connection isn't so thin after all," Overholt said.

"Where is the *Mountain Star* now?" Juan asked.

"According to its AIS transmission, it's heading for Barcelona at full speed."

"The western Med?" Overholt asked. "Italy, France, Spain, North Africa—the target could be anywhere."

"I don't think so," Stone said. "I accessed the National Reconnaissance

Office's satellite imagery database. Fortunately, they store records for quite a long time. I tracked *Mountain Star* over the last two weeks, from the Indian Ocean to its present location. It ultimately convoyed north through the Suez Canal, then through the Aegean and the Dardanelles until it reached the Sea of Marmara. And here is where it gets weird. They dropped anchor for approximately one hour, then left."

"At a port?" Overholt asked.

"No. Just beyond the mouth of the Dardanelles and out of the main shipping lane. As soon as it pulled up anchor, it did a big U-turn and shot out of there at a high rate of speed, which it is still maintaining. Chairman, I just sent you a link to the satellite map with the location marked."

"That ship is running like a scalded cat," Overholt said. "They want to get away from there as fast as possible."

"When did it drop anchor?" Juan asked as he pulled up the map on his laptop.

"Approximately nine hours ago."

Juan scanned Eric's map. It showed a digital line tracing the *Mountain Star*'s route just as he had described it. A ship icon was steaming in the southern Aegean. But it was the anchoring location in the Sea of Marmara that caught his eye.

"Lang, when is the joint NATO conference taking place?"

"Presidents Grainger and Toprak are scheduled to address the NATO ministers fifty-eight minutes from now."

"Istanbul has to be the target and that's their time line," Juan said.

"We're still not absolutely certain," Overholt said. "And even if we were, we can't evacuate a city of sixteen million people in fifty-eight minutes."

"No. But you can cancel the summit or at least get President Grainger out of there," Juan said.

"Based on a hunch?" Overholt asked. "The President wouldn't go for it. The optics of fleeing a terror threat in the middle of a defense conference would be terrible, especially if it didn't materialize. I suspect the NATO ministers would feel the same way. How far away are you from Istanbul?"

"Five miles off the coast. Do we have any assets in the area?"

"Nothing that we can get on such short notice."

"Not even the Turkish Navy?"

"Not available," Overholt said. "Local vessels have been diverted north to the Black Sea for an anti-submarine warfare exercise."

"Now? During the conference?" Eric asked.

"It seems the Russians are playing chicken. The Turks got word Ivanov intends to run one of their improved Kilo-class submarines through the Bosporus right past the defense ministers while they're in session."

"I can see why that makes the Turks nervous," Juan said. "NATO calls the improved Kilo a black hole because it's nearly impossible to locate. And they've run the Bosporus gauntlet before with impunity."

"The Russians want to embarrass NATO, and the Turks in particular, and Toprak is furious," Overholt said. "He's ordered his fleet to put up a screen to keep Ivanov's sub bottled up in the Black Sea and out of their territorial waters."

"So it's really up to us to stop the Kanyon," Juan said.

"Do you think the Kanyon is already in position or in transit?"

"No way to know. But Hakobyan does. That's why grabbing him is our best and probably only shot at finding it."

"I'm calling the FBI now. Chances are this is all just one ugly coincidence and we have nothing to fear."

"Always the optimist, Lang. Call me as soon as you hear about Hakobyan."

"Will do. And excellent work, Mr. Stone."

"Thank you, sir."

Overholt rang off.

"Eric, are you at your station in the op center?"

"Aye, sir."

"I want you to put up a map on the op center monitor. Lay down a track of Kanyon from the drop-off point where *Mountain Star* anchored straight to Istanbul. Have it loaded and the team briefed by the time I get there. We've got a torpedo to catch."

"Roger that."

70

GLENDALE

He heard a distant ringing that roused him from a dream. His eyes fluttered open.

Where am I?

He rubbed his eyes as he searched his memory.

The FBI agent cursed as he startled awake inside his car, his head throbbing and his mind clouded.

How long had he been asleep? He checked his watch. Four thirty-three a.m.

He picked up his Bureau cell phone. He'd missed three calls.

He swore again as he opened up his voice mail. His supervisor had called him three times. Each successive message was increasingly strident. But it was the words *national emergency* that blew away the last vestiges of fog clouding his brain. She was on her way.

He bolted out of the car and raced for Hakobyan's front door, praying he wasn't too late.

A warrantless search and seizure would likely end his career with the Bureau but so would sleeping on the job. He didn't give a crap about his employment status—his country was in danger and it was time to act.

The agent shouldered his way through the front door with a grunt, nearly busting it off its hinges. He dashed inside, pistol drawn, shouting Hakobyan's name and announcing he was with the FBI.

He searched the darkened house room by room, looking for the master where the old Armenian was most likely located. He found it. But the room, like the unmade bed, was empty.

He ran down the hall to a half-open door, his pistol at high ready. He pushed through the door and saw a shadow looming in the center of the room. He flicked the lights on.

David Hakobyan was hanging from a beam in the ceiling, his neck noosed in an extension cord. The agent didn't touch the body. He didn't have to. He could smell it. Dead as a doornail.

The agent's eyes swept the room. They fell on the desk where a typewriter stood with a single typed page beside it.

He approached the letter, careful not to touch it or anything that would contaminate the crime scene. He leaned in close and scanned the note.

He couldn't read a word of the unfamiliar script.

He pulled his phone and dialed his boss to tell her the bad news about Hakobyan—and to call someone who could read Armenian.

71

THE SEA OF MARMARA

Juan dashed into the *Oregon*'s op center where Eric, Murph, Max, Linda and the rest of the team had gathered at his request.

Cabrillo didn't waste any time as he took the Kirk Chair. Eric's map was already up on the main monitor. A red line had been drawn from the drop-off point to the city of Istanbul straddling both sides of the Bosporus, the narrow waterway that tied the Sea of Marmara to the Black Sea.

Just sixty-six nautical miles of water separated the two points.

"Murph, put fifty-six minutes on the countdown clock—and pull up a live image of Istanbul on the side monitor."

"Aye, Chairman." He did both. A live image of the ancient city with its towering minarets and skyscrapers shimmered on a large wall monitor along with a digital clock that counted in reverse.

Juan scanned the room. Every face was focused on him. He saw the concern in their eyes—and their determination. He still hoped the FBI could shake the intel out of Hakobyan, but he wasn't counting on it.

"We're assuming the joint conference with Grainger and Toprak is the Kanyon's target and it begins in fifty-six minutes. That's how long we have to find a way to stop it."

Cabrillo pointed at Murph. "Tell us about the Kanyon and what we're up against."

"The *Penza* carries a single Kanyon-2 drone torpedo. It's the best Russian stealth technology, making it nearly impossible to find, especially at low speed and at depth even with sonobuoys. It's also completely autonomous thanks to its artificial intelligence software. Length is eighty feet, diameter six and a half feet, estimated weight one hundred tons."

"Propulsion?" Ross asked.

"Pump-jet, driven by a fifteen-megawatt nuclear reactor. Max speed is over seventy knots and max operating depth estimated at three thousand feet."

"Last I read, it carries a two-megaton warhead, right?" Max asked.

"That's the previous generation. The *Penza*'s new Kanyon-2 is believed to carry a hundred-megaton warhead."

Max let out a long whistle. "Why in the world would they deploy such a large warhead?"

"The Kanyon is a doomsday weapon, designed to trigger a giant tsunami with a nuclear explosion. The resulting tidal wave would wipe out an entire coastline and contaminate it with Cobalt-60."

"Trigger a tsunami? Is that even possible?" Ross asked.

"The U.S. Navy thought so. They were working on a tsunami bomb at the end of World War Two but gave it up after the Japanese surrendered. Istanbul is particularly vulnerable."

"How so?" she asked.

Murph pointed at the monitor.

"It's the largest city in Europe, divided by the Bosporus Strait, a relatively narrow channel separating the city into two halves. Kanyon would create a wall of water thirty feet tall—in both directions. Millions would drown and millions more would get sick and likely die for miles around from the radioactive poisoning. And that's not taking into account the destruction of the city's infrastructure, electric power grid, gas lines, farmland—you name it."

Cabrillo punched a button on the Kirk Chair and pulled up a map of the region.

"Wepps, where would you place the Kanyon for an attack on Istanbul? I mean where exactly."

Murph hit the map with a laser pointer he kept on his keychain.

"Istanbul is mostly on the southern end of the peninsula right where the Sea of Marmara ends and the strait begins. You could put it just inside the mouth of the Bosporus and do the job and avoid the possibility of detection as you move farther up the narrower and heavily trafficked channel."

"Stoney, readjust your track line on the map to that new point."

"Aye." Eric's fingers danced across the keyboard. The distance between the drop-off point and the new target location decreased by three miles.

Juan felt the tension in the room escalate.

"How would you detonate it, Murph?"

"I would use some kind of digital terrain targeting system, like cruise missiles use, but designed for underwater topography. When it arrives at its predetermined location—boom!"

Cabrillo pointed at Eric's map. "We have to assume the Kanyon is taking the shortest route. The question is, where along that line is it?"

"At seventy knots, it could get there in a less than hour," Max said.

Juan shook his head. "At seventy knots, it would already have hit its target if it was launched nine hours ago. I think it's on a slow roll, timed to detonate at the opening ceremonies. That's when the presidents will mount the podium with all those NATO ministers standing behind them and all of it on live TV."

"If it's already been launched, that means the Kanyon's moving at around seven knots," Ross said.

Cabrillo nodded. "Agreed. And that puts Kanyon's estimated current position at less than eight miles from the target. No room for error."

"And we're assuming we have the right target location," Murph added. "They might want to detonate it farther out from shore."

"We can't plan for all contingencies," Juan said. "We're going with your first instinct. Pray you're right."

"Okay, we have the direction and speed. But how deep is it running? The Sea of Marmara isn't a kiddie pool," Max said.

"While the Sea of Marmara is deep, the Bosporus is relatively shallow," Murph said. "If we search within fifteen miles of Istanbul, we're averaging around two hundred feet."

"Then that's what we'll plan for," Juan said.

"So what's the plan?" Max asked.

"We can't torpedo it ourselves because we don't want to accidentally set the whole thing off. And we don't want to dump radioactive material into the water either."

"So how do we stop it?"

Cabrillo turned to Murphy. "I need you to find the Kanyon's schematics."

"How? I doubt the Russians have published them."

"Then improvise."

"How much time do I have?"

"None. Get moving."

"Aye, Chairman."

"Max, you have the conn."

"Aye."

"Linda, you and I are heading to the moon pool. I've got a crazy idea."

Ross grinned. "Do you ever have any other kind?"

She didn't wait for his answer and raced for the door. If she was needed in the pool, she knew what her assignment was.

Juan barked out the rest of his orders, a plan finalizing in his mind even as he spoke. Long ago he'd discovered that bold action produced its own genius.

He told Murph what he was looking for—and to call it down to him in the moon pool while he suited up.

The op center buzzed with activity as his people jumped into their assigned tasks.

Juan stole one last glance up to the live image of Istanbul. It would be a whole lot simpler if Hakobyan would just spill his guts and tell them where the Kanyon was lurking. He hoped Overholt could pull that off in the next ten minutes.

But hope wasn't a plan.

Juan checked the clock.

Forty-six minutes and counting.

He dashed out of the op center. There was hardly any time for his plan to work. And none for a backup.

72

Linda Ross was a great ship's captain. But where she really excelled was at the helm of the *Oregon*'s two submersibles.

The small and stealthy *Gator* was the racehorse, her "underwater Ferrari," capable of surface speeds up to fifty knots for quick insertion and egress of personnel.

But now she was piloting the sturdy and plodding *Nomad*, recently refitted and upgraded for serious underwater repair-and-recovery work. Shaped like a blunt-nosed Tic Tac, it featured three bow portholes and powerful xenon lamps to help maneuver its two articulating mechanical arms. Each arm featured NASA-grade gripper hands capable of handling both the most fragile seahorse or tearing sheet metal. All that industrial capability came at the cost of speed and right now her electric motors were maxed out at twelve knots.

And there was still no sight of the Kanyon.

She checked her screen and confirmed she was on the tracking line dead center that Eric had projected and that her depth gauge read two hundred feet, where the Kanyon was predicted to be operating. Istanbul was behind her and the Kanyon was supposed to be in front of her.

It wasn't.

If the eighty-foot torpedo was as stealthy as Murph said, they wouldn't be able to pick it up on either their active or passive sonar—and they also wouldn't know if they had missed it. The Kanyon's projected position and depth were all guesswork. Had the Kanyon already passed this point? Had it been running deeper than they had assumed or on a different vector?

Ross couldn't shake the feeling they had missed it.

Everything in her wanted to slam the helm joysticks to the max and turn the boat around just to make sure the Kanyon hadn't snuck past her.

Her fingers gripped the controllers.

"Chairman—"

"Hold steady," he said, cutting her off.

Was he reading her mind?

The confidence in his voice calmed her instantly.

Her hands relaxed as her heart slowed.

"Aye."

She took a deep, cleansing breath—and caught sight of a shadow forming in the darkness beyond.

There.

The round nose of a slow-moving torpedo appeared a hundred yards out and thirty feet deeper down.

"Got it."

"How close?" Juan asked in her comms.

"Close enough. Maneuvering into position now. Are you ready?"

"Ready."

Ross's fingers deftly adjusted the joysticks and throttle to execute a stationary one-hundred-eighty-degree turn so that the *Nomad* was now pointed at Istanbul, the same direction as Kanyon. She allowed the torpedo to pass some twenty feet beneath her in order to avoid its collision sensors located in the nose.

Incredibly, the Kanyon registered on her sonar display like a void rather than an object. Her instruments couldn't give her an exact speed of the drone, but she judged it to be right at the seven knots that Cabrillo had calculated.

So far, so good.

"You've got this," Juan said into her comms.

Juan laid out his plan back at the moon pool while he was still suiting up. Timing was critical. If Linda didn't complete her part of the mission, Juan couldn't complete his and Kanyon would find its target.

Just as the tail end of the Kanyon passed beneath her, Ross eased the vertical thrusters down so that *Nomad* was trailing directly behind and just slightly above it. She spied the object in her lowest bow porthole near her feet, quietly plodding ahead and maintaining its course, apparently unaware of *Nomad*'s proximity. Her maneuver had worked.

Now came the next phase.

Ross accelerated her speed to just over seven knots. She wanted to catch up to Kanyon but not run past it.

The countdown clock was ticking. Four minutes had passed since she last checked it. Twenty-eight minutes until doomsday. She inched closer and closer to the Kanyon, her speed a mere fraction over that of the torpedo's.

It was now or never.

She turned to Murph in the co-pilot's seat. "You're up, kiddo."

"Aye."

While Murph didn't come up with the plan to stop the Kanyon, he was the one who provided the calculations upon which the plan now entirely depended. He wanted in on the action in case he'd messed those numbers up. Besides, nobody on the *Oregon*'s crew could operate the mechanical arms as deftly as he could. Absolute precision was required.

The mechanical arms and hands were linked to controllers attached to Murph's arms and hands. The *Nomad*'s limbs would move as Murph moved, guided by the muscular and electrical impulses in his forearms and fingers.

He extended the arms to their maximum reach of six feet and opened the claws as the *Nomad* inched ever closer. His target was the cowling, a thin circle of steel at the rear of the torpedo designed to protect the pump-jet.

It wasn't hard for Ross to hold steady given the *Nomad*'s position just above the Kanyon's wake turbulence. She nudged the submarine forward until Murph's claws were fully extended and hovering in position.

Murph squeezed his fingers together and the pincers locked tightly onto the cowling's steel frame. Nothing short of a nuclear explosion would loosen their grip. For all intents and purposes, they were practically welded onto the cowling.

Murph smiled, satisfied. "Locked."

"Perfect," Ross said. "Here goes nothing."

She reversed her electric engine, dropping her speed—and the Kanyon's—to just three knots.

How long that would last was anybody's guess.

"Chairman, you're up."

"Aye that," Juan said in her comms.

She glanced at the countdown clock.

It was almost too late.

73

On my way."

Juan's full-face integrated dive mask included its own regulator so he could speak freely and its wireless, ultrasonic transceiver allowed him to communicate with crystal clear comms underwater down to six hundred feet.

He engaged the underwater sea scooter as he made his way out of the *Nomad*'s two-person airlock located in the belly of the submarine. He felt like an otter slipping through a hole in the ice and dropping into a slow-moving river.

Three knots wasn't much speed when walking on land but underwater it was like trying to swim against a tide of mayonnaise, especially with an air tank, scuba gear and the heavy rig on his gut. The small, battery-powered sea scooter—a mini-torpedo-shaped towing vehicle with handles—had a top speed of 4.5 knots underwater. That was just enough to pull him forward the ten feet or so he needed to reach his destination.

Juan aimed the sea scooter forward, but unlike the *Nomad* above him, he picked up the Kanyon's pump-jet wake. While the turbulence wasn't bad, it made it hard for him to keep a steady line and it seemed to be increasing.

"Kanyon is accelerating," Ross said in his comms. "Nearly four knots."

It wasn't unexpected. The Kanyon was programmed to arrive at a specified place and time utilizing AI to adjust course and speed to accomplish its mission. If it sensed that its speed had decreased, it would deploy more engine power to return to its pace.

Juan goosed the throttle on the sea scooter and it surged forward as he pumped his finned legs to assist. But his progress was minimal. He heard the *Nomad*'s propeller increasing revolutions, the thrum of its electric motor rising.

"Juan. *Nomad* is reaching its max output. Kanyon is accelerating and I can't stop it."

"Copy that." The Kanyon's turbulence increased, adding to Juan's struggle.

"Four-point-five knots and climbing."

Juan mashed the throttle to squeeze out every last volt of electricity from the scooter's small but powerful battery as he beat his fins furiously in the water at the same time. His heart rate soared and his legs were already starting to burn, but he was just inches away.

He felt like he was sprinting up a mountain of gravel. He was barely inching forward and at this rate both he and the sea scooter would be exhausted before it could climb onto the torpedo.

"Linda—"

"Emergency thrusters—now!"

Even as she said it, the whine of the *Nomad*'s straining engine pierced the water.

Juan reached out with one hand toward the steel cowling just millimeters away. He stretched his arm farther as he tried to keep the sea scooter stable with the other.

His gloved fingertips touched the cowling but couldn't quite attain purchase. He could feel the Kanyon pulling away.

The *Nomad*'s batteries couldn't compete with the drone's nuclear reactor. Ross didn't have enough power to slow it. There was no way Juan was going to catch the doomsday weapon, let alone stop its fateful mission.

"Watch yourself!" Ross said as the *Nomad* lurched to starboard and then to port and then back again.

That last twist slowed the Kanyon just enough to put the cowling within Juan's reach. The fingers of his right hand gripped the smooth steel as he let go of the sea scooter. Cabrillo held fast. He fluttered behind the massive torpedo like the tail of a kite until his left hand finally gripped the cowling.

"Incredible job," Murph said in his comms. "Almost there."

Juan was too exhausted to reply. If getting to this point was like running up a mountain of gravel, his next goal would be the equivalent of free-climbing the sheer face of El Capitan with a five-hundred-pound weight attached to his ankles.

"Five-point-eight knots," Ross said. "And climbing."

Juan's next goal was the top vertical fin at the forward end of the cowling, located at the twelve o'clock position. He would use that fin like a rung on a ladder to make his way forward a few more feet to where the geometry of the torpedo changed. Beyond the cowling and fins, the torpedo tapered down like an ice cream cone. The tip of the cone was where the pump-jet exhaust was located. But the mouth of the cone was the section he needed to reach, according to Murph's calculations.

Right now, those few feet seemed like a million miles.

Cabrillo took a deep breath and gathered his energy to make the next leg of his climb. He leaned forward as much as possible to reduce his profile and thus reduce the force of water blasting against him as the Kanyon picked up speed. *Nomad* did what it could to slow the monstrous contraption, but it was a losing battle. The only good news was that the Kanyon didn't just rocket forward, just steadily increased its power instead. Juan was beginning to hope that he might be able to see this thing through even if Kanyon returned to its original speed of seven knots.

Any faster than that and he didn't have a prayer.

*   *   *

Two exhausting minutes later, his arms burning with lactic acid and his entire torso aching with the effort, Juan's legs straddled the narrowest part of the tapered end of the torpedo and gripped it with all his strength. He thought he would feel at least the slightest vibration of the Kanyon's gearing mechanism between his thighs, but he was wrong. The Russian engineers had rigged everything for perfect acoustical silence.

Now he could finally get to work.

His upper body pressed against the rubber surface as he reached for the dive knife strapped to his leg. He brought the knife up and gripped its handle with both hands, then stabbed the razor-sharp drop point as far forward as he could.

According to Murph, the Kanyon's gearing system was located there. If he could destroy the gears, the pump-jet could no longer function. If properly designed, Murph insisted, the AI would detect the catastrophic malfunction and automatically shut down its nuclear reactor before it could overheat. The Kanyon would be dead in the water.

"Seven-point-three knots and climbing," Ross said. "Kanyon's trying to make up for lost time. And my battery's draining faster than a beer keg at a frat party."

The knife wavered in the rushing tide of water like a fishing line in a river. Juan tightened his grip around the handle and pulled the blade toward him. The weight of water flowing over him seemed to increase exponentially with each incremental advance in speed. He could hardly raise the knife and lift it forward for the next cut.

"Increase . . . reverse."

Totally gassed by his herculean efforts, Juan could only speak on the exhalation of his breath.

"I'll do what I can," Ross said. "Hold on."

"Not . . . much . . . choice."

Juan felt the Kanyon shudder gently between his legs. He assumed

CLIVE CUSSLER'S HELLBURNER   357

Linda was repeating her jerking maneuver, like a dog trying to wrestle a bone out of its owner's hand. It had worked before.

The Kanyon's four small directional fins began twisting in the water, causing the torpedo to buck and yaw.

Linda called into his comms. "The dang thing knows I'm attached and is trying to shake me off."

Juan's thighs squeezed even tighter as he dragged the knife vertically across the two parallel cuts, but he barely managed to keep the blade buried in the rubber. He'd finish it in just another few seconds.

The Kanyon had other ideas.

The entire body of the torpedo suddenly rotated back and forth on its axis in sharp little movements, like the agitator inside a washing machine. Juan lost the knife and watched it shoot perilously close past his mask—its sharpened point would have easily penetrated the glass if he hadn't moved his head at the last second.

He reached forward with his fingers and grabbed the far edge of the cut rubber and pulled with all his might. It felt like he was doing the world's slowest, hardest pull-up. He prayed that the rubber sonar coating would give way.

It did. Millimeter by millimeter, the rubber began peeling back like a banana skin. But it was taking every last ounce of Juan's remaining strength as he applied constant muscle-busting pressure, his grip weakening with every passing moment. He only needed a few more seconds to expose enough metallic surface to carry out the final task. He didn't know if he had enough gas left in his tank to pull it off. He dug into his deepest reserves and allowed himself the possibility it just might happen.

The Kanyon had another plan.

74.

The Kanyon spun on its axis, a complete three-sixty.

Cabrillo should have been thrown clear.

But his adrenaline-fueled legs squeezed even tighter against the torpedo's rotating hull and his ironfisted grip on the cut rubber coating kept him planted in place.

Despite the sudden surprise of the rapid spin, Juan heard the distinct metallic snap of the *Nomad*'s twin mechanical arms. The two vehicles separated instantly.

The single spin of the Kanyon had done its job. But the AI program had another trick up its sleeve. An explosive burst of speed sent it blasting forward.

Juan barely had enough time to duck his head against the rubber hull; a moment later, his neck would have snapped like the *Nomad*'s mechanical arms, killing him instantly.

Ross's voice crackled in his comms, then disappeared as he got beyond wireless range. The *Nomad* was being left far behind in Kanyon's wake and Juan was left alone to ride the speeding rocket to Hell.

Through sheer force of will, Juan held on with his left arm as he raised his upper torso just enough for his right arm to slip around and grip the limpet mine in its carrier attached to his belly.

The limpet originated just before World War II. It was a small mine designed to sink a ship by attaching it to the metallic hull below the waterline with powerful magnets. Juan possessed an updated, high-tech NATO version of the weapon.

The plan that Juan came up with put him below the waterline—way below—and the device he just detached from its rig had some of the most powerful magnets on earth. All he had to do was move the limpet less than twenty-four inches forward, attach it to the exposed metal surface and vamoose, letting the mine do its job.

But the impossible challenge he faced now was to get the mine from his torso to the exposed metal skin he had just laid bare. At the current speed, he didn't stand a chance. There was too much force of water pressing against him to move the heavy mine the short distance required.

His only chance was to hang on tight and wait.

If the AI software was true to form, it couldn't keep Kanyon running at this accelerated speed and stay on its time line. Juan was certain the burst of speed was designed to get the Kanyon clear of *Nomad*—no doubt the *Oregon*'s submarine was an "obstruction" the AI program had sensed. As soon as it detected it was clear of that obstruction, it would slow itself to get back on schedule.

Just as Juan had the thought, the Kanyon responded in kind. The torpedo slowed to less than five knots.

Though now it was moving slower, there was still a lot of force being exerted against him. The effort to place the mine still required all his energy. He lifted the limpet by its handle with both hands and placed the flat surface against the exposed metal. He pressed the button that activated the magnets and the mine snapped into place with a satisfying clang.

Cabrillo turned his head around. The *Nomad*'s severed claws still clung tightly to the cowling behind him. The sub itself surged toward him at full speed, its broken arms extended forward like a wounded penitent. He could barely make out Murph and Linda's backlit heads in their portholes far behind him.

He now had a decision to make. The limpet mine detonated by virtue of a timed fuse. By pressing a button, he could select either one minute or five. The latter time gave him the widest margin of safety. The concussive force of a nearby blast could kill him.

But five minutes was a long time, especially if their calculations were wrong. What if the self-destruct coordinates were less than five minutes away?

Juan's choice was clear. He couldn't risk the lives of sixteen million people in order to save his own.

He selected the sixty-second timer, hoping that the *Nomad* would be close enough for him to scramble into before the explosion. It would shield him from the blast—so long as they were far enough away. Otherwise, he'd be putting Murph's and Linda's lives at risk as well.

Juan let go of the limpet and relaxed his legs, letting the momentum of the multi-ton Kanyon begin to slip away beneath him. A wave of relief washed through him as his entire body relaxed from the superhuman efforts he had exerted over the last several minutes. He was utterly and completely drained, devoid of any capacity to even swim away. No matter, he thought. He'd let the Kanyon do the swimming for him.

The blackened shape of the long torpedo eased ahead and his body lifted. Of all the crazy missions he'd ever been on, this one was high on the list, yet he'd somehow managed to pull it off. His spirits soared—

Until his right leg jerked, roped against the Kanyon as it plowed ahead through the murky waters.

He had managed to kill the Kanyon all right. But now it looked as if he'd managed to kill himself as well.

75

Given the risk of the mission and the fact it was his own plan, Juan refused to let anyone else attempt to plant the limpet on the Kanyon. But Cabrillo wasn't interested in a suicide mission either. He had attached himself to a safety tether hooked on his back harness and connected to a spool in the *Nomad*'s airlock so they could reel him in in case of an emergency. It was a similar rig to the ones the astronauts used on their space walks and had seemed like a smart move at the time.

What no one had foreseen was the Kanyon's crazy Eskimo roll to clear away any obstructions. When the torpedo had rotated three hundred sixty degrees, it had inadvertently wrapped the tether line around the tapered part of the torpedo near the cowling, pinning Juan's leg beneath it. He hadn't felt it because it was pressing against his prosthetic leg—the one he used for combat dives.

Though physically exhausted, Juan's mind was still on point, allowing him to will away the fear that would have gripped most other people. Instead, he slipped his hand down to grab the dive knife secured to his leg and . . . remembered that he dropped it.

Maybe his mind wasn't so sharp after all, he thought, as he was pushed onto his back, unable to fight the current pummeling his exhausted frame.

"Sitrep!" Ross called through his comms, now back online. "What's wrong?"

"*Abuelo* always told me to carry a pocketknife," Juan said. "But I lost mine."

"We're close—hang on."

"I'd prefer not to, actually."

"Did you set the five-minute timer like I suggested?" Murph asked.

"Murphy's Law strikes again."

"Don't blame me. You better get out of there now."

"Roger that."

Juan reached down to a holster on his left leg and pulled out his TEC Torch, a breaching tool used by special operators. He carried one as part of his standard combat diving kit. It looked like a small baton but carried a huge wallop of thermal energy, generating a five-thousand-degree flame that lasted all of two seconds. That was more than enough time to burn through two inches of plate steel—or a thin safety cable.

Still on his back, he switched hands, gripping the torch as tightly as he could, determined not to let it fly away like the knife had before. He punched the arming switch with his gloved thumb and began to sit up so he could reach the cable to cut it with the flame.

But his strength had fled. He didn't have the muscular capacity to right himself in the surging water.

No matter, he told himself, as he rolled over and stretched out his right arm, his thumb hovering over the firing button. But try as he might, he couldn't reach the tip of the torch to the thin cable just inches away.

He could fire the torch and hope the flame was hot enough to reach that far and do the job. But he wasn't sure if the current somehow would affect it or unsteady his aim.

"I'm guessing you've got less than thirty seconds, Chairman," Murph said.

Juan stretched and strained, trying to calculate the impossible. He only had one shot at this because there was only one cartridge in the torch. It was a flip of the coin: do it now or later. He would live or die by his decision.

He made it.

Instead of aiming for the cable, Juan raised the torch to his calf and hit the firing button.

The torch erupted in a blinding light of flame like a welder's arc. Two seconds later, the torch died, its fuel spent.

And Juan was still attached.

Somehow, he hadn't cut cleanly through his artificial dive leg, a titanium prosthetic designed and weighted for underwater swimming. The neoprene around his calf was melted away, exposing the ruined limb beneath. The metal tubing was still intact, but barely.

Juan jerked and kicked his leg in every direction, trying to snap the last small connective tissue of titanium. He thrashed like a hooked fish until he heard a small metallic click and knew the last of the rod had finally given way. The torpedo continued on its journey, carrying away his finned foot and the rest of his ruined prosthetic.

Another surge of relief coursed through him as he watched the torpedo ease away. A new burst of adrenaline energized him. He began backstroking with his arms and frog-kicking with his legs to get some distance.

"We're coming up right behind you," Ross said.

"That was pretty slick," Murph added. "You were cutting it pretty close."

"Yeah, I guess I was—"

The limpet mine erupted.

76

"Ouch, doc It's kinda bright."

Juan squinted against the penlight shining in his eyes. He sat on the exam table in Dr. Huxley's darkened clinic.

"No sign of concussion." She clicked her penlight off, then snapped on the overhead lights. "You got lucky. Again."

"I got Linda Ross. Didn't need any luck."

The explosion had knocked Juan out cold. But Ross had been close enough to effect an immediate rescue of sorts. She scooped up Cabrillo's motionless body in the *Nomad*'s broken arms like Mary holding Jesus in Michelangelo's *Pietà* and carried him slowly to the surface so he wouldn't get the bends. She called ahead for medical assistance and by the time she cleared the moon pool, Huxley and her emergency responders were on the scene. Mostly, all Juan had needed was a tank of oxygen on the ride up the elevator to the clinic.

Juan climbed off the table. He was sore all over like he'd run three supermarathons in a row yet he felt no actual pain from any kind of damage. The ordeal underwater had been one of the most physically demanding of his life and proof once again of the value of remaining in peak physical condition between missions.

"I'd recommend you take some time off, but I know I'd be wasting my breath. I suppose this is as close as I'm going to get to the annual physical we've been talking about."

Juan smiled. "Maybe some other time."

"Congratulations, by the way. Hali piped Murphy's blow-by-blow description of the operation through the whole ship. I was on edge the entire time. For a moment there, I thought we lost you."

"Well, here I am."

"Seventeen minutes later and we wouldn't be here. Presidents Grainger and Toprak owe you their lives."

That explained the round of applause from the engineers he got when he fell into the stretcher next to the moon pool, Juan thought. He shrugged.

"We all do our jobs. If it wasn't for Linda and Murph, I couldn't have done mine."

"You did an amazing thing, Juan. I'm sure sixteen million Turks would tell you the same."

Huxley backed off. She knew Juan wasn't big into compliments. But he was her friend and she was proud of him.

But she was also his doctor.

"So, no headache? Ringing in the ears? Anything I need to know about?"

Juan glanced down at his body clothed only in a crinkly paper surgical gown. They had stripped off his scuba gear in search of wounds.

"To be honest, a couple aspirin and a change of clothes would be nice. Maybe a cup of coffee, too. Oh, yeah. And a leg." He lifted up his stump.

Hux smiled. "Coming right up."

She shut the door behind her as she left the exam room.

Juan laid back on the table to rest while he waited.

He was glad it had all worked out. But his work wasn't done yet. Ross told him on the way up the elevator that the Kanyon had been stopped in its tracks and, just like they'd hoped, had taken on water from the explosion and was sinking fast at the rear. It would soon settle on the bottom.

The question now was what to do with it.

He could talk to Max about bringing it on board through the moon pool or even towing it. But a waterlogged nuclear torpedo was nothing to fool around with. No telling what environmental damage they might inadvertently cause lifting and transporting it—not to mention the possibility of somehow setting the warhead off.

On the other hand, he couldn't just leave it there. He needed to pass the baton. But to whom?

Juan sat up and jumped off the end of the bed onto his one whole leg and hopped over to the phone on the wall.

"Hali, I need you to get out your Rolodex and make a call for me."

"Whose number am I looking for?"

"Dr. Richard Dellinger at Naval Sea Systems Command, Washington Naval Yard."

"I'll patch him through to the satellite phone when I connect."

"Thanks, Hali."

77

Thirty minutes later, Juan was back in the Kirk Chair with one hand wrapped around a steaming cup of fresh black coffee. He felt the nervous energy in the op center. Everybody wanted to come over and congratulate him for the Kanyon mission, but Max had warned them not to. It just wasn't his style.

More important, it was time to get back to work.

He had spoken with his old friend Dr. Dellinger by satellite phone—all off the record. Dellinger was the executive director of the command and himself a former U.S. Navy diver with SUPSALV—Ocean Engineering, Supervisor of Salvage and Diving—the Navy's division responsible for such operations. Cabrillo filled him in on Kanyon's location and disposition and asked him to coordinate his efforts with Overholt. He didn't need to tell Dellinger that absolute secrecy was required. The doctor promised to be in Istanbul with a reliable salvage master within the next eight hours to begin coordinating recovery efforts.

Juan then reached out to Overholt to give him an update. He had to leave a voice mail. He wasn't surprised. Presidents Grainger and Toprak were chairing the NATO conference at that very moment.

Right now, the *Oregon*'s mission was to sit tight and keep sea traffic away from the Kanyon. They were keeping an eye on the torpedo now resting like a dormant volcano on the seafloor by virtue of a pair of underwater surveillance drones.

Juan wondered how Meliha's reunion with her father was going. He thought about calling her but wanted to give them their space. He knew she would reach out to him when the time was right.

Hali turned in his chair at the comms station.

"Chairman, Mr. Overholt is calling for you."

"Pipe it over here, please." Juan pulled on his wireless headset.

"Aye."

Cabrillo tapped a button on the console.

"Lang, thanks for calling back."

"That's fantastic news you left, Juan. Well done. Congratulate the crew for me."

"Will do. How's the conference going?"

"You know how diplomacy works. It's a combination of fey ballroom dancing and ruthless cage fighting by people who are generally good at neither. But at least Toprak is still here. I was half expecting him not to show at all or to storm out on any pretense. All in all, I'd call that a raging success. And good news about Dr. Dellinger. That was a smart call on your part."

"I told him to call you first because you're the one who will be footing the bill. In the meantime, I'll just sit tight until his team arrives."

"Excellent."

"What did the FBI find out about Hakobyan?"

"That's one of the reasons why I've called. I was just handed the text to his suicide note."

"Suicide? When?"

"They're estimating within the last twelve hours. They only just discovered his body a few hours ago. I'll forward the entire transcript over to you shortly."

"I thought he was under twenty-four-hour surveillance."

"He was. But the FBI couldn't secure any warrants and there was only a two-man team to cover everything. Budget constraints, apparently."

"So they offered up a fig leaf instead of a trench coat. Figures. What did the note say?"

"They had to find an Armenian American FBI agent to translate it. I won't bother you with the whole thing. The key wording that caught my attention was this: *I knew as soon as I turned the television off, my life was complete. I refuse to die in prison. I die instead by my own hand with my eyes filled with the glorious vision of a city drowned and a city burned. Death to all Turks!*"

"That note doesn't make any sense," Juan said. "On a couple levels."

"Always the astute observer."

"None of this had happened yet he writes it in the past tense. Unless he's a time traveler from an alternate universe or he's a raving madman, something smells fishy."

"I agree. There's no doubt in my mind whatsoever that a sociopath intent on slaughtering millions would want to see his murderous handiwork. The conference has been the most widely televised and streamed international event since the last Olympics. No way he would have shuffled off to the great beyond before watching it in high-def. I would say he was murdered. Or what's the term? *Suicided*?"

"My money's on the Katrakis family. No honor among thieves and all that."

"I concur. We can get to the bottom of it later."

"What do you suppose Hakobyan meant by a city drowned and a city burned? Was he referring to one city being both?" Juan asked.

"That accurately describes the Kanyon bomb destroying Istanbul by tidal wave and nuclear blast."

"But he didn't say a city drowned and burned, he said a city drowned and a city burned. Two indefinite articles, two nouns," Juan said. "I'm afraid he's referring to two separate cities."

"I had the agent review her translation of that phrase twice. She insists the wording is exactly as translated. And now you know why I've called."

Juan did indeed. The gravity of the moment washed over him like a wave of molten lead.

"We have another city to save."

Juan didn't realize everyone else in the op center was listening in on his conversation until the team turned around in their chairs and faced him at those final words *another city to save*. The concern on their faces matched his own.

"Istanbul was clearly the target of the Kanyon. Any clue as to the other city?" Overholt asked. "The obvious guess would be Ankara, the national capital and the second-most-populous city in Turkey."

"It's not Ankara."

"Then where?"

"It's İzmir."

"Why do you say that?" Overholt asked.

"In my downtime, I read some background research my team put together on the Katrakis family. İzmir was formerly known as Smyrna when it was Greek territory. Alexandros' grandmother was born there. She barely escaped the city when it was destroyed by the Turks in 1922. The Turkish Army slaughtered the Greek civilian population in the streets and burned the city to the ground."

"Familial vengeance. The oldest kind. They're planning a bloody symmetry."

"That's what I'm thinking. İzmir is the 'city burned' along with everyone in it—all four and a half million souls."

"You know where. Do you know how?" Overholt asked.

"I've got an idea."

"Focus your attention on İzmir. I'll handle the Kanyon operation."

"I already gave Dr. Dellinger the Kanyon coordinates. We'll just pray that nobody stumbles across it before he gets here."

"Get cracking, son. No telling how much time is left on the clock, if any."

"Roger that."

Juan ended the call, pulled off his headset and stood.

"I know you all caught the gist of that call. Our job is only half finished. We don't know exactly what we're up against, but we know what's at stake."

Cabrillo turned to Eric Stone.

"Helm, set a course for İzmir, full speed ahead."

78

A live optical display of the entire region—from the Bosporus Strait to the Aegean Sea—showed on the op center's primary bulkhead monitor. A blue circle was the *Oregon* racing toward İzmir, which was circled in red.

Eric had laid the throttle wide open. To even casual observers, the image of a nearly six-hundred-foot-long cargo vessel racing along at almost sixty knots would have been startling. It couldn't be helped. While the last thing Juan ever wanted was for the *Oregon* to draw attention to itself, there was too much water to cross to reach İzmir and not enough time to do it.

"We know where he's going to strike," Max said, "but how is the Katrakis organization going to pull this off? Another Kanyon?"

"Or just a dirty bomb loaded in the back of an eighteen-wheeler," Murph said. "There's a gazillion ways to destroy an open city."

"No doubt about that," Juan said. "Yet I can't shake the feeling in my gut about something I saw back on Pharos. There was a brand-new LNG tanker missing from the dock and it had been recently launched."

"Whoa!" Max said. "Liquefied natural gas? That's nasty stuff. I read somewhere that one LNG tanker has the explosive power equivalent of fifty Hiroshima bombs."

"In theory," Linda said. "In reality, liquefied natural gas is very safe. It's transported at supercooled temperatures of minus two hundred sixty degrees and it's not even pressurized. I've seen videos of people drinking it. LNG only becomes combustible fuel after it's gasified by heat at a specially designed facility. But while it's in its cooled and liquid state, it's not dangerous at all."

Max shrugged. "So maybe Wepps is right after all. A dirty bomb or a stolen missile. We should be looking for something like that."

Juan picked up a phone and punched in Eddie Seng's number.

"Eddie, any progress on those cloud files your people were trying to crack?"

"As a matter of fact, our Cray supercomputer just broke through. I'm scanning the files right now. Mostly financials. Not much to see by way of drugs or guns, as near as I can tell. I've sent those over to Russ Kefauver to take a look."

"Katrakis Maritime is a working shipyard. Any schematics for the ships they're building?"

"Let me look."

Juan heard mouse clicks over the phone.

"Yeah, I found a whole file of them."

"Come over to the op center and we'll put them up on one of our monitors."

"Sending the files to the mainframe now. Be there in a minute."

A minute later, Eddie was standing in the op center with his laptop. The schematics file folder was open on the wall monitor and he was connected to it.

"Anything in particular you're looking for?"

"An LNG tanker," Juan said. "Brand-new. Remember the two that were at Pharos, nearly completed?"

"Sure do. Come to think of it, it looked like one had just launched."

"That's the one I'm looking for."

"Murph, lend me a hand, will you?" Eddie said. All the computer terminals in the op center had mainframe access to the same schematics folder.

"Eric, do you still have that link to the NRO satellites you accessed earlier?"

"I keep it on my desktop."

"Pull up the shipyard at Pharos. Find that missing tanker and track it. You'll have to go back several days. Probably not more than a couple weeks."

"Aye."

Juan dropped into the Kirk Chair as his team got to work. The cloak-and-dagger intelligence-gathering operations of the earlier generation—his own, he had to remind himself—had mostly given way to the furious clacking of computer keyboards and the steady hum of central processing units.

Minutes later, Murph and Eric called out almost simultaneously.

"Got it."

The blueprint-like schematic of an LNG tanker named *Cybele* appeared on a second wall monitor next to the live map. A recorded image of that same tanker departing Pharos was displayed on a third.

Eric pointed at the recorded live imagery.

"That was taken four days ago. I'll fast-forward to see where it's headed."

Eric scrubbed the video. The tanker rocketed west toward an island near the Port of Piraeus until it docked.

"It's an LNG transfer facility."

"A gas station," Max said. "She's getting a fill-up."

"Where does she head to next?" Juan asked.

Eric scrubbed forward.

"No . . . no . . . no . . . no . . . NO!" Murph jumped out of his seat, his face ashen.

All eyes turned to him.

"What's the problem?" Juan asked.

Murph pointed at the schematic page he pulled up on the second screen.

"That ship. It's not a tanker. It's a Hellburner!"

79

W hat in the Sam Hill is a Hellburner?" Max asked.

Before joining the Corporation, Murph had been one of the world's foremost weapons designers. That also made him a weapons design history buff.

"In the fifth century B.C., the Spartans built the first fireship and launched it against Athens during the Peloponnesian War. They packed a vessel with wood, set it alight and let the wind carry it into the Athenian line of battle to burn their ships. Fast-forward a thousand years to an Italian engineer named—"

"Can you hurry this up, please?" Juan asked.

"Sorry. Bottom line: the Italian packed a galleon with seven thousand pounds of gunpowder and destroyed a bunch of Spanish ships in a single blast. They called it a Hellburner. Biggest man-made explosion in human history up to that point."

Juan frowned. "But Linda said LNG wasn't dangerous."

"She's right."

Murph pointed at the schematics with his keychain laser pointer.

"So long as LNG is in a cold, liquid state, it's safe. But when it vaporizes, it's highly explosive. In 1944, one square mile of Cleveland was burned to the ground by an accidental LNG leak. A tanker this size is at least twenty times larger than that leak. The damage would be exponentially greater."

"Explain how this could happen."

Murph pointed out a series of automated discharge valves, pipes, switches and vents.

"If you get the right mix of LNG vapor and air, this stuff turns deadly. And that's what all these systems are designed to do: vent the LNG into the warmer air at just the right mixture, then set it on fire. Once the fire is lit, it will burn the vapor. The resulting flame follows it back into the tanks, where it then superheats and vaporizes the LNG rapidly—I mean, like, a matter of nanoseconds—causing an explosion and fireball."

"Like a fuel–air explosive," Max said.

"Same principle, for sure. The specs say that tanker is designed to carry thirty million gallons of LNG. Given that capacity, the *Cybele* could easily incinerate a city the size of İzmir in a fireball. But it gets worse."

"How?" Juan asked.

"I pulled up the stats on İzmir. Turns out one of Turkey's largest LNG facilities is located there. On any given day, up to four LNG tankers are docked there. If Katrakis has timed his attack properly, he might be able to detonate the entire facility—other tankers, storage units, active pipelines, the works. God only knows what would happen after that."

"Juan, take a look at this." Ross pulled up a different page of the schematics at her station and put it up on the monitor.

Cabrillo recognized the systems. He had designed the *Oregon* himself to be completely operated by Otis when needed. "That ship is entirely automated."

"There's crew quarters for only six people. But it could easily be run without anybody."

"Great. A Hellburner drone," Max said.

"You nailed it."

"Chairman, there's another problem," Murph said.

Juan faced him at his weapons station. "What else?"

"This ship is also armed with automated, containerized anti-ship and anti-aircraft missiles."

"Eric, can you visually confirm what Murph just found on the schematics?"

"Let me see what I can do."

Stone zoomed in on a still image of the *Cybele* still docked at the Greek LNG facility. He got close enough to see a man in a hard hat standing on the bridgewing. He started to move away to find the containerized weapons.

"Wait a sec, Eric. Can you identify him?" Cabrillo asked.

Stone instantly pulled up the Cray's facial recognition program and put the man's shadowed mug in a reticle. Eric tapped the scrubbing key, advancing the image one frame at a time, until the man looked up. That gave the Cray a clear facial image to capture. The name of a Chinese engineer employed by the facility popped on the screen.

Juan felt the collective disappointment in the room. They were all hoping to see the name Alexandros Katrakis.

"Hey, what's that?" Max asked. "On the fantail."

Eric backed the image out and then zoomed back in. The large, familiar shape was covered in canvas and tied down.

"I'll be dipped in chocolate and rolled in nuts," Max said. "That's an AW."

Juan nodded. It wasn't a photo of Alexandros Katrakis, but it was the next best thing. It was his AW that led them to Holy Island. The high-tech Tiltrotor was almost as unique as a fingerprint.

"That tanker is definitely our target," Juan said. "Now we just have to find it. Eric, fast-forward your video to the present time."

"Aye."

Everybody watched the giant tanker depart the LNG facility and head east, making a beeline to the Turkish coast. The image darkened with the passage of video time until the light had faded, nearly sunset—current time. The image became live.

The *Cybele* was charging toward İzmir.

The entire room fell silent like the air had been sucked out of it—because it had.

The *Oregon* was too far away to stop it.

80

Sokratis Katrakis knelt close to the young Armenian fighter and touched her face. Her refrigerated flesh was cool but pleasant beneath his fingertips.

"Such a waste," Alexandros Katrakis said, standing close by. "She was a pretty girl."

"Not a waste." The old Greek stood. "This death brings purpose to her meaningless life."

The Armenian woman was the last of the dead fighters placed in various compartments around the ship—all part of an elaborate effort to protect the Katrakis family. After the fiery destruction of the tanker, bits of Armenian DNA would be recovered in the water and on land. In addition, deepfake videos, photographs, a declaration of war and other planted evidence would be released to his trusted media sources. Offshore accounts and shell companies linked to Hakobyan would own or finance everything connected to the operation. Just as they had done with the *Mountain Star*.

All these subterfuges would help spread the lie that Hakobyan had paid for a band of Armenian terrorists to hijack his ship and use it on a suicide mission to destroy Smyrna. They would also help prove Katrakis Maritime innocent of any complicity in the holocaust.

Yes, Smyrna, he told himself again.

He would rather die than say the Turkish name, İzmir, for his mother's beloved city.

"Is everything ready?" Sokratis asked.

"All according to plan."

"Not all. But enough."

The ancient mariner had weathered many dangerous storms in his youth as a captain on the high seas. Ships sunk, cargoes ruined, lives lost. But none of that mattered so long as he survived.

Kanyon's failure was obvious. There should have been reports of Istanbul's mass destruction by now. Something went wrong. Had someone in his organization betrayed him? Not likely. Few outside his immediate family knew about it and blood was a sure bond. The others were tightly bound to him by insatiable greed and soul-crushing fear.

Hakobyan must have failed or betrayed him. The Mexicans either dropped the ball and botched his killing or double-crossed him by conniving with the Armenian. Fools! He could have promised them even more than Katrakis had offered.

No matter. Smyrna was still in play and he himself would see it through to the end.

81

Any doubt about the target was dispelled when Eric Stone posted a photograph on the video board. It depicted the sculpture of a woman seated on a throne atop a four-wheeled cart pulled by two lions. Juan glanced at the photo.

"That looks like the bronze statuette from the chapel on Holy Island," he said.

"I found it, based on the photo you sent me. This one's from a mosque in İzmir. It's Cybele, the patron goddess of Smyrna."

"The ancient Greek city now called İzmir," Juan said. "It can be no coincidence that our LNG tanker carries her name. The city has to be the target."

Despite the *Oregon*'s mad dash toward İzmir, the *Cybele* was still beyond their reach.

Cabrillo had long-range kinetic weapons to strike the LNG tanker, but he didn't dare risk using them for fear of blowing up the vessel. Even at seven miles from port there was the possibility of extraordinary destruction if something went sideways. He needed to disable the *Cybele* without setting it on fire—and fast.

Juan ran the calculations in his mind. Even at his high rate of speed, he was still fifteen minutes away from getting a visual on the *Cybele*.

His other concern was his own vessel. Surely the tanker's radar had picked up the *Oregon*'s large signature barreling toward its position. No telling when the *Cybele*'s automated fire control system would decide to light him up.

Cabrillo was all out of options.

Except one.

"Wepps, ready the D-CHAMP."

Murph grinned. He had a funny feeling the DARPA-modified cruise missile would be called upon. It was the last system that DARPA had asked the *Oregon* to test in real-world conditions. And as far as Murphy was concerned, it didn't get any more real than this.

Designed to knock out enemy electronic and computer networks, D-CHAMP was a cruise missile with a microwave-generated EMP cannon strapped to its protected underbelly. The EMP cannon blasted out high-voltage pulses of focused electricity and was targeted by a remote operator—in this case, Murph.

He scrambled over to the improvised D-CHAMP control station, flipped on the power switches, then wrapped his hands around the throttle and flight controls.

"System is armed and ready."

"Launch."

"Aye, Chairman. Putting it on-screen."

Murph punched a button and a live image of the D-CHAMP's containerized launcher appeared on another bulkhead monitor. The *Oregon*'s auto-adjusting digital camera compensated for the dark. He punched another button and the launcher cover popped off just before a white-hot flame washed out the camera's sensor. When the camera readjusted for the washout and a clear picture returned, all that appeared was a roiling cloud of white exhaust fogging the area.

The D-CHAMP was on its way.

Murph pulled up a digital tracking image on another screen. Every eye in the op center was glued to the monitor. At six hundred miles an hour, the cruise missile was far too slow to avoid the anti-aircraft missiles the *Cybele* deployed. The only chance Murph had to defend against them was to keep the D-CHAMP skimming as close to the water as possible to stay under the tanker's radar.

In fourteen seconds, they'd find out if it survived.

Moments later and miles away, Murph's steady hand flew the D-CHAMP cruise missile just inches above the Aegean, low enough to avoid the tanker's radar and barely high enough to avoid hitting the rolling chop.

The *Cybele* sailed on an easterly setting toward the Turkish coast. Murph put the D-CHAMP on a southerly course approximately a mile behind the ship's stern. Even if the missile was picked up by the *Cybele*'s radar, it wouldn't be on a collision course and likely not identified as a threat until it was too late.

A quarter mile from his target, Murph put the missile in a ninety-degree turn and made a run toward the ship, too close in for the anti-aircraft missiles to operate. He then lit up the onboard pulse cannon strapped to the cruise missile.

Murph bathed the *Cybele* in a shower of electromagnetic pulses. According to DARPA's specs, one blast should be enough to disable the vessel, but he planned on several since the pulse cannon had enough power for dozens of discharges.

He wanted that ship deader than dead.

ON BOARD THE *CYBELE*

Sokratis Katrakis stood near the windows on the darkened automated bridge over one hundred fifty feet above the sea, staring at Smyrna's bright city lights glowing on the distant shore. He reached for his beard to tug on it out of habit, but it was missing. When he left the monastery, he also abandoned his asceticism—including his uncut beard. Clean-shaven for the first time in years, he felt like a much younger man.

His son Alexandros stood at a nearby console, hanging up a phone.

"The crew has boarded the Tiltrotor," Alexandros said. "Ready to lift off when you are."

Sokratis exhaled deeply, satisfied to his very bones. He'd waited a lifetime for this night. Within the hour, Smyrna would be a roiling cauldron of funereal fire. The last place he wanted to be was on the ship when that happened. He and the others would hover high in the sky and safely away from the port when the first explosion happened, but they would enjoy the spectacle with a God's-eye view from the Tiltrotor.

"It's time," Sokratis said as he turned on his heel.

A monitor alarm sounded.

"What is it?" Sokratis asked as his son dashed over to another station. But in his heart, he knew. He had helped design the ship. The anti-aircraft radar had picked up a target.

The sudden, deafening roar of a cruise missile skimming far below their field of view confirmed it.

Before Alexandros reached the console, every piece of electronic equipment and all their lights shut down, leaving the two men swallowed up in darkness. The distant glow of Smyrna shimmered in the windows.

"All systems down!" Alexandros said.

"Engines?"

"Dead."

"EMP?"

"Most likely."

How? Who? It didn't matter. Sokratis fought the rage boiling up inside him. Now was not the time to lose control. There was still one last chance to finish the mission.

He gave his orders to Alexandros and headed for the engine room.

82

ON BOARD THE *CYBELE*

Sokratis Katrakis stood on the catwalk overlooking the pitch-black engine room, his vision illuminated by a chemical glow stick taken from the emergency supply locker. Normally he would have been wearing ear protection and using hand signals to communicate because of the deafening roar of the gas-fired main engines. Now all was silent as the grave.

He had begun his seafaring career in the belly of one of his father's tramp steamers, shoveling coal into the boilers until his young hands blistered and bled. Bathed in the heat of the boiler's flames, he had learned to love the miracle of maritime engines, powerful and sure. He was drawn to them like women and found solace in their beating hearts. To see his engines lifeless and still was like embracing a dead bride in a cold honeymoon bed.

The night had shocked him.

On the verge of complete victory, *Cybele* drove relentlessly toward the shores of Smyrna, the ancient city unaware of her impending doom.

But as soon as the lights snapped off and the electrical systems died, Katrakis knew they had been hit with an EMP strike. He swore his heart skipped a beat with the electrical surge. The ship was now bathed in utter darkness; the silver moon hardly shone through the cloud cover.

There was still a way to lash out at the hated Turks—but only if the goddess of vengeance favored him this night.

The tanker was still being carried forward by the momentum of its speed combined with the weight of its cargo. It wouldn't exhaust itself for another five miles.

Manually de-cocking the valves and flooding the warm steel decks with subzero LNG would vaporize the liquid enough to make it combustible. The conditions would have to be near perfect, but it was technically possible. The vapors could then be ignited from a distance and the ship destroyed.

But each passing moment slowed the vessel and eventually it would stop before it reached its intended target, impotent and helpless.

He needed to get the ship back under power. There was only one option.

Footfalls thundered behind him. Katrakis turned and saw the green glow of a chemical stick illuminating the stairwell before the shadow of his son Alexandros appeared. He ran over to his father, breathless.

"Six of the eight valves are opened. The remaining two won't take much longer."

"And the Tiltrotor?"

Despite being in the midst of catastrophe, Alexandros couldn't help but grin at his father's foresight. Over his own objections, his father had insisted on installing an expensive, military-grade EMP protection package on the cutting-edge of avionics for just such an emergency.

"The preflight checklist is complete. We're ready to leave when you are."

"Excellent. As soon as the remaining valves are opened, get your people loaded in. I'll be right behind you."

"Father—"

"I have one last thing to do."

"Then let me help you."

"Do as I say. Time is our enemy."

"But Father—"

The words caught in the younger man's throat. The green glow in his father's flaring eyes only heightened their terrifying aspect. Even there, in the bowels of the crippled tanker fated for destruction, Sokratis Katrakis was not a man to be crossed.

Katrakis laid a strong hand on his son's shoulder. Despite his age, his crushing grip was still hard as iron.

"My son, all my life I've waited for this moment of revenge. Nothing will prevent us from accomplishing it."

Sokratis had raised his family on the catechism of Turkish horrors inflicted on the innocent Greek civilians of Smyrna and how his mother had suffered violently at their hands so many years ago.

Alexandros nodded. Whatever needed to be done would be done.

"Understood."

83

ON BOARD THE *OREGON*

Juan Cabrillo stood on the *Oregon*'s faux bridge with a pair of high-powered binoculars. He kept his ship a respectable distance from the crippled *Cybele*. One of his observation drones flew high over the hulking shadow of the slow-moving tanker, its lights completely out. The boat was eerily silent, with no sign of life.

Juan didn't like what he could see—and what he couldn't see. The ship was shrouded in wispy fog that also trailed behind it. The *Cybele*'s shape could barely be made out. Only the forward momentum of the ship kept the bow clear.

"What are we looking at?" Cabrillo asked.

Linda Ross stood next to him, a pair of binos pressed to her eyes.

"My guess is that we're seeing LNG vapors. If the crew opened up the valves, the liquefied gas is hitting the decks and spilling over into the water—both of which are warmer than the LNG. As the ship slows further, that cloud will accumulate enough substance to become an explosive hazard."

"Then if we're going to sink it, now's the time," Max said as he lowered his binoculars.

A sudden whine of turbines throttling up shattered the silence. Like a bat geolocating its dinner, Juan's head turned toward the stern of the *Cybele*. The teeth-rattling roar of a pair of Pratt & Whitney engines erupted across the water as it climbed into the night sky.

"Chairman—tango aloft!" one of the radar techs shouted over his radio.

He needn't have bothered. Juan could easily make out the form of the AW Tiltrotor despite the fact its lights were off. Its only illumination was the dim glow of the cockpit instrument panel.

"That's gotta be Katrakis," Max said.

"Wepps, you got a bead on him?" Juan asked on his radio.

"Sure do."

"He's worth more alive to us than dead," Ross said. "No telling how much he knows. I say let him go and we track him."

"We let him go, we may never find him again," Max said. "Who knows what he'll be up to next."

The Tiltrotor rocketed through the low, thin cloud cover.

"Wepps—take him out!"

"Aye, Chairman."

The single anti-aircraft missile launched with an earsplitting roar out of its tube. Juan didn't need his binoculars to track the fiery trail. Seconds later, a fireball erupted behind the veil of clouds. He tracked the chunks of burning wreckage as it plunged toward the sea. Nobody could have survived that kind of destruction.

"Tango down."

"Wepps, ready the Kashtan. We've got to stop this thing without hitting the storage tanks and blowing us to kingdom come. I want you to take out the bow—carefully."

Max chuckled. "The Russian can opener. Nice."

"Kashtan coming online."

High above the decks, the cover to one of the Kashtans lowered with the whine of a hydraulic motor. Its twin rotary cannons spun up.

"Chairman, I just spotted two people on the *Cybele*," Gomez's voice crackled on the radio.

"Where?"

"On the bow—"

"Wepps—belay the Kashtan!"

"Aye. Powering down."

"Gomez, what are those people doing on the bow?"

"Can't quite make it out. Looks like they're tied up."

"Can you ID them?"

"Not at this distance."

"Drop your drone and get a closer visual."

"Aye."

"Hux, are you online?"

"Here, Chairman."

"Get me a fix on that GPS tracker you put in our friend."

"Give me a second . . . I'm pulling it up now."

Juan felt his pulse racing like a runaway train. He knew Hux's answer before she gave it.

"Got it . . . Oh, dear. She's on the *Cybele*!"

Meliha and her father were prisoners on board the Hellburner.

84.

Juan climbed into the *Oregon*'s AW wearing a silver fire-resistant jumpsuit. The rotors had already begun their slow spin up.

Eddie Seng, MacD and the rest of the Gundogs all volunteered to take his place or at least accompany him. There wasn't anybody else he'd rather go into a gunfight with, but there wasn't any opposition on the other side of the wire and Meliha was his responsibility. The LNG cloud was another animal altogether. He couldn't risk anyone else's life on an unknown like that. He ordered the *Oregon* to steer clear of it.

An oxygen mask hung around his neck and a bottle was strapped to his back. He carried a sling bag with two emergency oxygen masks for Meliha and her father.

"That suit should protect you against the freezing vapor," Dr. Huxley said. "But don't count on it for long. And whatever you do, get that oxygen mask on before you get close to the deck."

"And don't dawdle," Max added, shouting over the whining turbines. "That bucket of bolts is slowing down and the fog is accumulating."

Cabrillo attached the winching hook to his harness.

"And no cigars," Ross added. "At least, not until you get back."

"You're all a bunch of worrywarts. I'll be back in no time." He pointed at Murphy. "Wepps, you stay frosty on that railgun. Soon as I give the word, you cut loose."

Murph nodded, his mop of hair tornadoing around his head in the swirling air.

Cabrillo called into his molar mic. "Gomez, time to rock and roll."

The others knelt down as the rotors pitched and accelerated. The air from the beating blades pulsed against their bodies in crashing waves, nearly knocking them all down like bowling pins.

Juan threw a lazy salute at his team as the AW lifted off and tilted away into the dark.

Juan and Gomez had worked out the details for roping onto the deck before they took off. The biggest kinetic risk was the possibility the AW had accumulated enough excess static electricity to spark a fire in the vapor cloud. The *Oregon*'s ground crew routinely bled off the AW's static charge after each flight for just that reason and the Tiltrotor had discharge wicks. Still, it was a risk.

Fear of sparking an explosion was also the reason Juan knew he couldn't fire his holstered FN pistol while on board the tanker. He knew he wouldn't need it. The opposition had already been dispatched with one of Murph's anti-aircraft missiles. But he felt naked without it.

Even though a stiff breeze was no fun to fly in, Gomez really wanted one to dissipate the LNG fog that was thickening moment by moment as the tanker slowed. Juan gave him an idea for the next best thing.

Gomez did a flyover, low and slow, bow to stern, minimizing the throttle and maximizing the rotor pitch to generate as much downwash as possible and blasting the fog away like a leaf blower.

He circled back around, then hovered in position, keeping the rotor wash directly over Meliha and her father, who Juan could now clearly see were chained to the bow.

Cabrillo's blood boiled. That psychopath Katrakis had shackled them to a front-row seat for the planned holocaust of the Turkish city.

Juan kicked the descent line out of the door and fast-roped down.

Gomez hovered as closely to the deck as he could while maintaining a constant distance from the still-moving tanker.

Cabrillo's feet hit the deck with a splash of liquid methane. He charged over to the two huddled, shivering Turks, battered by the cyclonic winds of the Tiltrotor.

"Juan—I knew it was you," Meliha said. "How did you—"

"No time to talk. We've got to get the two of you off this boat before she blows."

"Mr. Cabrillo, we thank you!" Meliha's father shouted. "Please—I urge you. Take my daughter first."

"No worries, sir. A tandem rig is on its way. But first things first." Juan ripped his Velcro straps and unharnessed his bolt cutters. The long-handled blades snipped through the tempered steel lock hasps like scissors through a marshmallow.

Thanks to Gomez's rotor wash, the fog was staying clear of their little area, so Juan skipped pulling out their masks. At moments like this, his pilot's skill really shone through. Juan marveled at how Gomez could lower the weighted cable practically into his pocket and still keep his distance from the moving ship without crashing into it. It was like threading a needle in a hurricane.

Juan helped Meliha into her rig as her father pulled his on. Juan double-checked them both to make sure they were secure before signaling Gomez to winch them up.

Just as their feet lifted from the deck, the entire ship shuddered.

Linda Ross called over his comms.

"Chairman—the *Cybele*'s engines just fired up!"

85

"hairman, secure yourself to your ascent line and let's get out of here," Gomez called over his comms.

Juan tossed his bolt cutters aside and charged for the line. Just as he grabbed the carabiner to hook into his harness, Eric reported over his comms.

"Rising heat signature in the aft compartments—the engine room. Looks like a fire."

Juan pulled up the ship's schematics in his mind's eye. Like most LNG tankers, the primary fuel source for the engines was the off-gassing vapors from the fuel tanks themselves. Those had clearly been disabled by the D-CHAMP strike.

But this tanker also had an old-school auxiliary diesel engine, as analog and reliable as Grandpa's John Deere tractor. The ship was slowly gaining speed again.

Juan suddenly saw the murderous plan. Katrakis had set the engine room on fire as the ship charged for port, hoping the combination of LNG vapors and flames would collide at just the right moment and blow the tanker. Even if that didn't happen, there was still the very real chance of setting thirty million gallons of flammable liquid ablaze near an LNG off-loading facility crowded with other LNG tankers.

"Wepps, you on the line?"

"Aye."

"Chairman—the rope!" Gomez shouted.

Juan ignored him.

"Wepps, start cutting loose."

"But you're still on the ship."

"You have your orders. Do it!"

Murph paused momentarily. "Aye, Chairman."

"Gomez, clear away—now!"

"Aye." The Tiltrotor darted away, whisking Meliha and her father to the safety of the *Oregon*.

Murph had new orders. Rather than shoot off the bow with the Kashtan, Murph would use surgical precision to puncture the LNG tanks with the railgun far below the waterline. Supersonic tungsten rods had enough power to penetrate deep below the surface, allowing the escaping fuel to dissipate harmlessly into the Aegean and sink the vessel before it exploded.

But now the ship was back under its own power—and on fire.

Juan needed to get to that heat source. If he could stop that engine and kill the fire, the *Cybele* would finally be rendered harmless.

The first tungsten rod plowed into the forward tank. It threw water into the air like a wave crashing against a rock and shook the steel deck beneath Juan's boots.

That was his cue to run.

86

Juan ran full out along the length of the deck racing for the stern, his boots splashing in the fogging liquid methane.

Giant geysers of water erupted above the deck as he dashed past the domed tanks, each blast rattling the steel hull. He knew the ship wouldn't take on water until the tanks were emptied. The narrow tungsten rods weren't punching huge holes in them. No telling how long the ship would stay afloat.

Cabrillo slowed when he reached an aft ladder that led down to the engine room. He pulled out his tactical flashlight and raced down the steel rungs, the bright illumination his only hope of avoiding a collision with the bulkheads, crashing into doors or tripping over the landings. He skipped rungs to hurry his way down.

He knew he'd arrived in the deepest part of the ship when he flung open the last door and was hit with the roar of the giant auxiliary diesel engine and the sweet-acrid stench of burnt hydraulic fluid. He pulled on his oxygen mask and headed in.

As he arrived on the final landing, he felt the heat against the exposed part of his face and saw the first flames surging up on the far side of the engine. Battery-powered yellow fire alarm lights shot through dirty black smoke clouding overhead. The heat inside his silver, fire-resistant jumpsuit began to rise. He felt like a wiener, wrapped in tinfoil, tossed onto a campfire.

He had to kill the fire. But first he had to stop the engine.

The ship's steel hull rang like a distant hammerblow against a bell as another one of Murph's tungsten shells found its mark.

He dashed over to the far side of the racing diesel motor. The cut hydraulic fluid lines overhead poured onto the engine's hot metal surfaces, feeding the growing fire. The flames were hottest where the fluid hit the engine assembly—right where the engine's manual stop/start lever was located. Juan prepared to sacrifice his hand to the flames in order to pull it when through the choking smoke he caught sight of the lever itself. It had been sheared away.

Sabotaged.

There was no way to shut it down.

But he still needed to douse the flames before they overwhelmed the ship and ignited the LNG. He had to find the fire-suppression delivery system.

Down beneath the waterline and cocooned in steel, he doubted the engine room's electronic circuit boards had been fried by the D-CHAMP's EMP pulses. The emergency fire extinguishers should have released by now—they must have been disabled. Fortunately, he could still activate the pressurized system by hand.

Juan turned from the scalding heat. He spotted a row of red CO_2 tanks bolted to the far bulkhead. He ran over and punched their system's red emergency button—and nothing happened. He pounded it again several more times, but it was no use. His eyes scanned the row of tanks. Their manual bypass levers had been destroyed.

Juan swore.

The hull clanged again even louder when another one of Murph's tungsten bolts slammed through the ship's steel skin. Yet the Cybele was still holding to its steady, relentless course straight for İzmir, and so far there was nothing they could do to stop it.

Time for Plan D.

87

Juan spun the hatch's wheel and raced into the compartment behind the engine room where the mechanism for steering the ship was housed. He flashed his tac over the hydraulic rams, which turned the ship's rudder by electronic command from the bridge. Even though the controls were now disabled by the EMP strike, the rudder still maintained course. If Juan couldn't stop the *Cybele*, maybe he could move the rudder and turn the ship away from İzmir.

He continued scanning the compartment with his flashlight until the beam fell upon a brass wheel, waist-high, at the far end of the steering mechanism.

"There you are, my lovely," Juan whispered as he dashed over to the wheel. Its gearing was smooth and precise. Juan turned it to the one-hundred-eighty-degree mark on the rudder's indicator. In a matter of miles, that angle would turn the ship full circle. But before then, Murph's gunnery work should have taken its toll.

Juan wiped away the sweat stinging his eyes. In the short time he'd been in the compartment, the temperature had risen twenty degrees due to the growing fire in the engine room and smoke rolling in overhead like a black tide.

Cabrillo had just saved the city. He still had to save himself from a fiery end.

Juan dashed out of the steering compartment's hatch into a wall of heat. Raging flames engulfed the big diesel motor like a burnt offering to an angry sea god.

Cabrillo covered his face with his gloved hands to shield his eyes from the acrid incense of smoke choking the engine room. Another hit by one of Murph's tungsten rods rang the hull like a tolling bell at a funeral.

He made a run for the far bulkhead and the ladder that would take him topside. In the roar of the engine room, he barely heard the muted feral grunt behind him as a wrench thudded into his right shoulder. Stabbing pain shot down the length of his arm, now rendered useless.

Cabrillo whirled around low and ducked just as the red-handled pipe wrench swung above his head in a potentially skull-crushing blow, crashing against the pipes behind him.

Even with the man's nose and mouth obscured by the oxygen mask, Juan recognized the harsh green eyes and craggy, clean-shaven face of Sokratis Katrakis from his file photos. Despite his advanced age, the old Greek was stunningly agile and strong.

Unwilling to fire his gun up on deck for fear of igniting the methane fog, Juan felt no hesitation in the burning engine room using his weapon to stop Katrakis from killing him.

With his gun arm stunned, Juan reached across his torso with his good left one to the holster on his right hip. Normally, he could draw and fire his weapon on target in under a second. But the pistol grip was in the worst possible position for his left hand—in effect, it was upside down. In the few seconds he took to try to twist his wrist around so that his left could get a proper grip, Katrakis had raised the wrench high above his head with both hands like an ax.

Juan saw danger looming out the corner of his eye and sidestepped a blow that would have brained him. As he raised his gun to fire, the wrench smashed into it, delivering a glancing blow to Juan's fingers. The searing pain loosened his grip and the gun clattered to the deck.

Katrakis lifted the pipe wrench to his chest. But instead of chopping at Juan with it, he thrust it headfirst at him like a sword. The heavy steel jaws thudded into Cabrillo's sternum, but his bulletproof vest spared the bone from cracking. The impact snatched his breath away and knocked him on his heels. Cabrillo stumbled backward until he crashed into the bulkhead.

Katrakis charged again, raising the red-handled pipe wrench high over his head for a final killing blow.

His right arm useless and his left hand wounded, all Juan could do was lower one shoulder—and charge.

Cabrillo closed the distance faster than Katrakis could swing the wrench. The Greek's elbows crashed into Juan's broad back and the wrench hardly made contact. Juan's legs pumped like a sprinter's as he drove into the wiry Greek's torso. The weight and strength of the younger man against the smaller frame of the older man was no match. Juan crashed the man's spine against a support beam, causing him to drop the wrench.

With Katrakis still pinned to the beam on wobbly legs, Juan reared back to smash him with his left elbow, but the man threw a couple fast counterpunches with hard, gnarly fists that hammered against the side of Juan's face. His eyes watering and his ears ringing, Juan finished delivering his strike, swinging his elbow through the flurry of Katrakis' fists. The first swing missed its mark. Cabrillo swung again, putting all his weight behind it. His elbow found its mark, smashing into the Greek's throat and crushing his larynx.

Katrakis clutched at his neck, clawing for the air that wouldn't come, and staggered away. Juan chased after him, reaching around his waist with his good left arm to pull him down and finish him off before he could find another weapon.

Katrakis twisted around in Juan's tentative grip and clawed at Cabrillo's face, trying to gouge his eyes out with his long, iron-hard fingers. Juan headbutted the bridge of his nose with the force of a cattle-killing bolt gun. Blood exploded inside the old man's oxygen mask as he stumbled backward, his arms splayed wide to catch himself from falling.

Instead, he tumbled into the roaring flames devouring the engine. The Greek's methane-infused overalls combusted like a welder's torch.

Whatever screams Sokratis Katrakis could manage through his crushed throat were swallowed up in the melting plastic of his mask as he fell to the deck, writhing in the unquenchable fire.

Juan Cabrillo raced away from the hellish scene, cradling his busted shoulder with his bad hand. He left his gun behind. Even if he could find it, he couldn't pull the trigger anyway. What he really needed was to get out of the smoking inferno before he choked. Or worse.

He charged up the steps two at a time toward the deck far above for whatever fate awaited him there.

88

Juan reached the top of the engine room stairs, barely managing to pull the hatch open with his weakened left hand. He pushed his way through, the flickering firelight behind him illuminating the passageway. Grimacing with pain, he managed to pull his tactical flashlight from his pocket, then ran the length of the narrow corridor and headed up the next flight of steel-treaded stairs. Another railgun round slammed into the hull in the distance. The ship seemed to be listing slightly to port and down at the bow, but Juan couldn't be certain in the blacked-out, disorienting stairwell.

Juan ran up the steps, grateful he wasn't trying to swim his way to the upper decks. His upper torso battered and exhausted from the fight with Sokratis Katrakis, he wondered how he was going to finally get off the dying ship once he made it topside.

Just three more decks to go.

Cabrillo reached the top landing and worked the hatch's handle with his injured limbs. He pulled it open and pushed through. As he cleared the hatchway, he saw a crewman in his overalls racing toward him, a flashlight in his hand.

Both men saw each other at the same time. The crewman charged forward, his intention obvious.

Juan ran straight at him.

In the darting, handheld light, Juan caught a glimpse of the bearded face with its shockingly green eyes coming at him. He'd seen it before on the DEA video.

It was Alexandros Katrakis.

How?

He wasn't on the Tiltrotor after all.

There was no question in Juan's mind Katrakis was heading for the steering compartment. The *Cybele*'s turning after he'd adjusted the rudder had alerted the Greek shipbuilder that his vessel had veered off course from İzmir. If Katrakis wanted to put the *Cybele* back on course, he had to get past Juan—and that wasn't going to happen.

Three steps into his charge, Juan lowered his shoulder and collided with the Greek, bowling him over. Katrakis oofed when Juan crashed into him, but he absorbed the hit and wrapped a strong arm around Juan's neck to pull him down. They crashed to the deck with a thud. One flashlight died and the other skittered across the deck, spinning, flashing like a strobe.

Without the use of his hands, all Juan could do was yank and twist his upper torso to try to break the younger man's grip. Worse, he was dealing with a trained fighter. Cabrillo felt the Greek's powerful legs wrapping around his body and his hand grabbing his right wrist—the opening salvos to executing an arm-breaking Kimura, a move named for Masahiko Kimura after his defeat of a renowned Brazilian jiujitsu master.

Juan had trained in jiujitsu for years as well. But the two of them weren't rolling at the local dojo for bragging rights. The hatred in Katrakis' flashing eyes told Juan it was a fight to the death and the searing pain ripping through his already damaged right arm told Juan he was about to lose.

Juan felt Katrakis rolling on his hip beneath him. This would open Juan up and allow Katrakis to slip his other arm beneath Juan to create the unbreakable lock that would shatter his right arm. Juan countered with his own twisting move that was countered instantly by Katrakis. They coiled and grappled in the dark like snakes, the deck listing more steeply with each passing moment.

Juan was staying one step ahead of Katrakis' attack, but he was flagging; unable to use his left hand or his right arm, all Juan could do was avoid a fatal trap. But each effort required every ounce of his waning strength and he didn't have the power to neutralize the Greek, let alone break free. Distracted by a jolt of pain shooting through his shoulder, Juan couldn't stop Katrakis from spinning around in a move that put Juan on his back and his right arm in a lock between the Greek's powerful legs that could snap his elbow like a twig.

Juan only had one option.

His right leg was free. He turned on his hip just enough to shove his right heel between Katrakis' legs directly beneath the pelvic diaphragm. Juan felt the click of the trigger below the knee of his stump just before his artificial combat leg recoiled from the force of a twelve-gauge, double-aught buckshot shell fired from the emergency pistol in the leg.

The passageway echoed with the Greek's soul-shattering cry as nine steel pellets shredded his perineum. Katrakis loosed his grip and Juan rolled away from the man's quivering body as he gasped.

Juan didn't wait for the Greek's final act. He felt neither pity nor remorse. Alexandros Katrakis had intended to do far worse to millions. His fate was his own doing.

Cabrillo climbed to his unsteady feet, picked up his tactical flashlight and headed for the upper deck. With the LNG tanker on the verge of exploding, he couldn't risk bringing the *Oregon* in too close or even for the AW to attempt another rescue. His only hope was that the deck was clear and he could make his way to the free-fall lifeboat at the stern.

When he hit the first steel rung, he felt the last of his energy reserves draining away. It was going to be a long climb. He doubted he had enough gas left in the tank to climb the next flight of stairs let alone fight another death match. He prayed there weren't any more surprises waiting for him.

89

Juan plodded up the last steps until his feet finally hit the landing. Now that he had cleared the lower decks, he called over his molar mic for an update, but there was still no response. The signal was probably blocked because he was still entombed inside walls of steel.

Juan made his way to the hatch leading to the deck. Its porthole was partly lit orange. When he was close enough to see through the thick glass, he could feel the warmth radiating from the door.

The flickering light was in fact a raging wall of fire. Gauzy wisps of methane gas swirled past the portal.

The ship was going to blow at any minute.

The thundering rotors of the AW now hammered overhead. The swirling fog dissipated and the flames retreated, if only briefly.

Juan ripped the oxygen mask off his face and tossed the oxygen bottle back down the passageway behind him. No point in making himself a Roman candle. He glanced up through the porthole and saw the Tiltrotor hovering just twenty feet above the deck. Gomez was clearing the way for Juan using the AW's enormous rotor wash to keep the fire at bay and clear the vapors before enough mass could accumulate to fuel an explosion.

With the break in the fire, Juan pulled open the warm hatch, his hands nearly useless for anything but the reception of pain. He wrestled his way through and shouted into his mic.

"Gomez! Get that bird out of here!"

He waited for a response but got nothing.

His mic was dead.

The Tiltrotor slipped backward away from Juan, still parallel to his position. The AW's rear cabin door was open and MacD was standing in it. The aircraft yawed and jerked in the thermals created by the shipboard conflagration.

Juan glanced fore and aft. Flames leaped high into the night sky, trapping him where he stood. There was no way to get to the stern and the lifeboat. His only chance was the AW, but if it came any closer to the tanker, it could be destroyed by a surge of flames or the imminent explosion.

Juan saw MacD shouting something and pointing at his ears with both index fingers, confirming Cabrillo's comms problem. The roaring fire threw orange reflections across the Tiltrotor. Unable to communicate with his team only increased the risk to all their lives and the entire *Oregon* crew. Cabrillo assumed his unit had been damaged in his fights with the Greeks. But there was one other possibility.

Juan quickly ran his fingers over his chest, feeling for the connecting wire that linked the tactical neck loop to the relay box. It was fine. He then felt for the wire that connected to the radio. It was disconnected. He clumsily unzipped his protective suit and reconnected the wire. Sweat was pouring off him now.

"Comms back online," Juan said.

"Hold your position. I'm coming in with the cable," Gomez said. He fought to keep the AW in place.

"Belay that—and stay well back."

"You gotta get off that boat, boss!" MacD said.

"We're not leaving without you," Gomez said.

In the few short seconds Gomez had backed away, the roaring flames had charged ahead, coming perilously close to Juan's position. His face tingled with the heat, the LNG burning three times hotter than gasoline.

If Gomez didn't leave, all three of them could get killed.

Cabrillo sprinted for the railing twelve feet away. He glanced over the side. He could feel the heat prickling his back as the inferno raged behind him, but far below, the cold, dark Aegean Sea beckoned, free of flames.

Summoning every last bit of adrenaline in his body, Juan willed himself up onto the rail and leaped.

The familiar sensation of free-falling was heightened by his elation from escaping the fire. He knew he'd hit the water hard from this height, but he'd rather drown than burn alive—and both were preferable to the death of his friends in the AW, who wouldn't leave him on deck. If he survived the fall, he could swim out of harm's way and they could fish him out of the water.

Juan had crossed his arms over his chest as best he could and pointed his boot toes downward like an arrowhead to lessen the impact of crashing into the water. The rush of cool air against his face increased as he accelerated. The feeling was exhilarating.

But the sudden eruption of fire on the water broke the spell.

He was diving feetfirst into a roiling cauldron of flames.

Juan made himself as sleek and rigid as he could, willing his large frame into a spear now hurtling toward the ignited wall of water. He hoped his weight and velocity would plunge him deep enough below the surface that he'd have a fighting chance to survive.

Juan took a deep breath and braced himself for the pain to come, falling from such a great height. His legs tensed like steel bars—the combat leg had the advantage here. If his legs and arms splayed out when he hit, a lot could go wrong. Broken limbs, loss of consciousness, drowning. Or worst of all, he might stay afloat on the surface and burn alive.

Gomez was shouting Juan's name in his comms when the toes of his boots hit the water. His legs held firm, but it felt like he was crashing through a half inch of plywood. In the nanosecond that followed, the rest of his body followed into the sea—by some miracle, his arms remaining glued to his chest. Seawater rushed over his face like a gushing fire hydrant as his body arrowed deep into the gloom.

As he began to slow, Cabrillo glanced up, conscious that his comms had died yet thrilled to see that the orange flames were only dancing on the surface. But the air in his burning lungs was under heavy pressure now. He fought the urge to let it out.

When his body stopped its downward trajectory after some twenty feet, he began to swim away from his entry point but the familiar whine of a high-revving motor caught his attention. He turned in the direction of the fast-approaching noise above him. As he glanced up, he could hear—or was it feel?—the AW's rotors pounding the surface, creating a fire-free zone some forty feet across.

Juan kicked hard for the surface, leaving his mostly useless arms at his side. He saw the familiar wake of a Jet Ski turning circles in the fire-free zone. Cabrillo angled in that direction.

His head broke the surface just as the Jet Ski zipped past. He let out a huge blast of air from his burning lungs, then gulped in more. Drops of water slung by the AW's rotor wash stung his face. A daylight-bright xenon lamp flashed down from above and lit him up.

The ski turned on a dime and raced over. Eddie was on the throttle and Raven was braced in the rear with a rope. Eddie slowed for a second as Raven lassoed Juan with a rescue harness, then gunned the engine and sped away from the tanker and toward the *Oregon*, dragging Juan behind like a fishing lure. The AW tilted in the same direction, racing ahead.

"How you doing back there?" Raven asked in his comms. The waterproof molar mic only functioned above the surface of the water.

"Never better. Thanks for the ride."

Juan's eyes were fixed on the burning tanker receding behind him. He wondered how much longer it would burn before it sank.

He didn't have long to wait.

The ship erupted in a cloud of fire.

Fortunately, enough LNG had been drained away by Murph's rail-gun that the explosive force was limited to the ship itself, shattering its perforated hull. By the time Juan and the team reached the *Oregon*'s boat garage, the *Cybele* had slipped harmlessly beneath the waves in a haze of methane fog miles from the Turkish coast.

90

İZMIR

Cedvet Bayur steadied his breathing as he set the tip of his index finger against the hair trigger. A bead of sweat slid down the hand-shaped scar on his face.

Perched high on the hilltop far outside the city and hidden by a copse of trees, the Turkish Gray Wolves operative had a perfect line of sight toward the safe house far below. He had already adjusted his high-powered scope for range and wind and his suppressed semi-automatic rifle's magazine was filled with his own, hand-loaded bullets. With his broken left arm in a sling, it had taken him longer to set up the rifle, but now it was primed for the shot.

He had never missed a target before in conditions like these.

Or in this case, two targets.

Both that witch Meliha Öztürk and that meddling American operator were in his field of view, sitting at a table behind a large plate glass window, chatting and laughing and sipping wine.

They wouldn't be for long.

He hadn't seen either of them since the day of the helicopter crash in Libya yet his hate for the both of them had only grown. Limping wounded from the battlefield in utter defeat, he had sworn vengeance on Juan Cabrillo, who had bested him. The big American's death would wipe away the stain of defeat. He also needed to kill Öztürk before she could testify at his father's trial the following month.

Most important of all, his family's honor was at stake. Only blood would satisfy.

The Turk settled the crosshairs on the American first because he was a trained operator and would seek cover if a first shot splattered Öztürk's brains all over the tablecloth.

The woman would freeze in panic at the demise of her friend—lover, most likely—and that would make her an easy second target.

Bayur's heartbeat slowed until it was nearly imperceptible, matching his breath. He waited until the two coincided, then gently touched the trigger.

The rifle jumped slightly in his grip when it fired and a bullet hole appeared in the glass right at the American's head.

Nothing happened.

Cabrillo hadn't even flinched.

It wasn't possible.

Bayur fired again and still Cabrillo chatted away and laughed. Bayur turned the gun toward the woman and fired two rounds into her torso.

Nothing.

The blades of a helicopter roared up behind him. Bayur rolled over just in time to see six Turkish special forces operators fast-rope out of the aircraft. He raised his rifle to fire, but the pressure of a pistol barrel against his skull told him to stop.

"Drop the stick, friendo," Cabrillo said.

Bayur let the rifle fall from his grip, utterly confused. The big American had appeared out of nowhere, like a ghost.

Turkish operators thundered up to their position, their machine pistols pointed directly at Bayur.

The Gray Wolves operative turned and looked up at Cabrillo's smiling face at the other end of his barrel.

"I don't understand."

"Holographics." Juan pointed at the safe house window with his pistol. The laser-generated Juan and Meliha holograms were still chatting and laughing and sipping wine. "Once you fired your first shot, my people triangulated your position. We knew you were up here somewhere."

"The woman?"

"Safe at home with her father, no thanks to you."

The Turkish soldiers grabbed Bayur by the neck, hauled him roughly to his feet and marched him toward the hovering helicopter.

Juan watched the Turks harness up the Gray Wolf, satisfied he had kept his promise to Meliha to capture him. She was well aware of the grim fate awaiting him at the hands of his jailers, yet it wasn't vengeance she sought. She needed Bayur's testimony to fully clear her father's name and to hold Yusuf Toprak to the democratic reforms he had recently promised, starting with the military.

She was an impressive woman, Juan thought as he marched down the hill toward the safe house. He powered up his cell phone to give her the good news. When the screen finally came up, he saw a two-word text message from Eric Stone.

Found him.

He knew exactly what it meant.

Time to go.

91

THE GULF OF MEXICO
SIX DAYS LATER

Víctor Herrera's luxury yacht was anchored two miles off the coast of Veracruz. He sat on the stern deck at the portable control station perched on the teakwood table. Speed boats loaded with his ex-military gunmen patrolled a wide perimeter around his ship, underwater cameras kept a lookout for sub-surface threats and radar kept an eye on the sky. He was safer out here than in his compound.

Herrera's primary *sicario* and second-in-command, Lado Zazueta, hovered over his shoulder, staring at the computer screen. The young drone technician stood on the other side of the murderous cartel boss. The former engineering student had quit his studies at UNAM to become Herrera's full-time drone assassin and instructor, his father's gambling debts finally forgiven. He'd spent the past hour patiently teaching his boss how to operate the new Chinese drone. With Hakobyan dead, the Turkish supply had disappeared.

"The Chinese system is better anyway," he had assured his mercurial employer.

Herrera uploaded a photo into the targeting software. The Veracruz police captain, an incorruptible and fearless law enforcement officer, had put a dent into Herrera's Gulf operations, signing his own death warrant.

The cartel boss then pulled up the camera fixed to a rooftop across the street from the captain's headquarters. The live image showed Captain Valdez, through a large corner office window, working at his desk. An easy target.

Herrera was a quick learner. He pulled up a third window and double-tapped the captain's building on the map, instantly uploading the GPS coordinates to the drone's navigation system.

"That completes the target recognition package," the technician said. "The kamikaze drone software will now seek him out and destroy him."

"Two kilos of C-4 should do the job," Zazueta said. "If the blast doesn't kill him, that bulletproof glass will shred him like a plate of *carnitas*."

"Now what?" Herrera asked the technician.

The beardless young man pointed at the keyboard.

"You're ready to launch. Touch that engage key and the automated system will do the rest. Estimated flight time is seven minutes. We can watch on camera all the way to the kill."

Herrera chuckled at the image of the captain at his desk. He had no idea that death was minutes away.

"Say your prayers, *Capitán Cabrón*."

"*¿Listo?*" the tech asked.

"Ready."

Herrera punched the engage.

The drone's eight blades instantly fired up and lifted it from the deck. Captain Valdez's photo flashed in the targeting image.

The drone rocketed two hundred feet up vertically, then paused.

Herrera shot a quizzical look at his technician. Before the man could say a word, the drone plummeted toward the yacht.

ON BOARD THE *OREGON*

Juan Cabrillo sat in the Kirk Chair staring at two wall monitors.

The first monitor had a live feed from his reconnaissance UAV circling five thousand feet overhead.

The second monitor had a live feed from Herrera's drone hovering just a hundred feet over the cartel boss.

Each monitor was showing Herrera's yacht from a completely different perspective.

Events unfolded quickly.

The drone camera suddenly dove and crashed into Herrera's upturned, screaming face. The image died in the explosion.

Seconds later, the overhead shot showed the yacht erupting in a ball of fire. Herrera's patrol boats charged toward the flaming wreckage, but there were no survivors.

Murph had hacked into the Chinese system and switched out Captain Valdez's photo for Herrera's with a simple drag and drop with his mouse.

The Chinese drone accepted the new target and acquired Herrera instantly, overriding its GPS instructions to complete the mission. An excellent software feature resulting in a perfect kill.

Murph was right. The Chinese drones were good.

Max, Eddie, Raven and MacD had gathered on the bridge with the others to watch the unfolding scene.

"That's for Tom," Max said.

Juan nodded. "For Tom!"

Juan settled into his chair, taking in the sight of the burning yacht.

He knew killing Herrera wouldn't bring back Tom Reyes, but it settled the score. His friend had been killed by Herrera's drone. It was only fitting Herrera suffered the same fate.

Overholt wouldn't like it, but he'd understand. And ultimately be grateful.

"Chairman, I've got a video call coming in from Baltimore," Hali reported.

"Johns Hopkins?"

"Actually, I'm showing it's from a Harley-Davidson dealership on the Pulaski Highway."

The video screen burst with the larger-than-life image of Linc straddling a showroom motorcycle. Everyone gazed at the feed in disbelief.

"Linc!" Juan nearly shouted the name, surprised to see the ex–Navy SEAL dressed not in a hospital gown but leathers and boots.

"Chairman, the new Softails are in. Perfect bikes for that ride down the coast of Patagonia that you always talked about."

"You can see?"

Linc flashed a megawatt smile at the camera. "It was just a case of temporary blindness. All it took was a little rest and everything came right back. In fact, my vision is the best it's ever been. I hope I didn't lose my job?"

The crew on the bridge erupted in cheers for their comrade in arms.

Juan had to choke down his emotions and simply shook his head. He'd hoped that Linc might regain some of his vision but hadn't expected a full recovery. Nor Linc's return to the *Oregon*, which was the best gift of all.

"So what do you say?" Linc asked. "Do we have some time for a bike trip before the next assignment?"

"Without a doubt," Juan said, smiling with elation. "The road ahead is all ours."